Regret
and
everything
After

MARLA HOLT

This is a work of fiction. Similarities to real people, places, or events are entirely coincidental.

REGRET AND EVERYTHING AFTER

First edition. August 23, 2022.

ISBN: 978-1735926490

Written by Marla Holt.

Author's Note

Dear Reader,

Thank you for picking up a copy of *Regret and Everything After*. Before you begin, I wanted to let you know that this book does discuss sexual assault, sexual abuse from church leaders, Evangelical Christian cults, and one of the main characters does have a stalker. This sounds like a lot of trauma packed into one book, but as someone who grew up in conservative evangelical spaces, I feel like it is also, unfortunately, and accurate depiction of what it is like to live in and leave those circles. Please trust me to guide you through the characters' vulnerabilities and to that Happily Ever After. I guarantee, it's worth it.

———●———

-MARLA

Chapter One

The silver Prius had stopped following Samantha three and half miles ago, but her heart still hammered in her chest. Samantha never thought she'd find a silver Prius terrifying. But every time she saw one, her heart jumped up into her throat and she had trouble getting in a full breath around it.

She'd only had a mile to go before she made it to work whenThe silver car had pulled up behind her at a stoplight. She hadn't been able to make out the driver around the sun's glare on the windshield. So Samantha had had to hop back on the highway then loop back around just to make sure that the vehicle wasn't following her.

As far as she knew, Mason hadn't figured out where she was working now, and she wanted to keep it that way. Even if she was now twenty minutes late to a job that she hated.

The good thing about being a bartender was that it was relatively easy to find a new job when you needed one, but not all service industry jobs were created equal. Samantha had gotten her start at a chain restaurant then honed her skills in an upscale nightclub. Now she was working in a divey sports bar.

Samantha didn't have anything against sports bars. She just hadn't ever had much energy for sports, which made it difficult to connect with her customers.

She was kind of getting the idea of baseball—or at least enough to understand who played for the Royals—but even as she memorized the game schedule and brought home enough tips to pay her bills, she also felt all her specialty cocktail skills withering with every Bud Light she poured. She also hadn't really made friends with any of the other bartenders, so even when she jogged through the front doors, apologizing as she dashed behind the bar and through the office door to stow her things in her locker, she knew she wouldn't find any sympathy.

Samantha cringed as she tucked her purse and keys away. Brett, her manager, was behind the bar, which meant Shauna had left to pick her kid up from school already. So she had inconvenienced everyone.

Brett was the kind of bar manager that hid in the office or schmoozed with customers, drinking the bar's tap beer, rather than the kind who helped out behind the bar. With any luck, Brett would leave at five and not hang out at her bar all night, watching the games and generally making her uncomfortable.

It wasn't that she thought Brett meant to make her uncomfortable. He didn't pay any special attention to her when he stayed. It was more like he just didn't have anything else to do. But even one stray glance her way always put Samantha on edge. She knew what it was like to have a man she worked with show just a little too much interest.

Her relationship with Mason had started innocently enough with him sitting at her bar on his nights off, buying her shots when they worked together, paying for meals, changing her kegs.

But then she'd made the mistake of hooking up with him. Or, at least, *she'd* been hooking up. Apparently Mason had been falling in love, because when she'd passed on a repeat, Mason became incrementally more aggressive until he was everywhere she went. He'd trade shifts so he was always working with her, grocery shopped at the same time she did. He even showed up at the restaurant when she met another guy there for drinks.

Samantha had been so creeped out that she'd called the police, but they'd told her there was nothing they could do if he was just showing up in random places—there was no way they could prove intent to harm.

She'd been fuming when she'd hung up the phone, but her roommate, Charlotte, hadn't been surprised. "I told you they wouldn't do anything."

"Well, what am I supposed to do—sit around and wait for him to attack me?"

That was the night she and Charlotte had started looking for new jobs and a new apartment so they could put physical distance between themselves and Mason. Charlotte found a job first, snagging a position at a steakhouse. Samantha's search had taken longer though she'd been applying everywhere. But she wanted to be employed nowhere near the nightclub. Because if Mason was able to sniff her out around Solaria, working close by would make it that much easier for him to follow her elsewhere.

She hadn't been picky about where she'd applied, but there had been a couple of places where, when she'd shown up for her interview, she'd known she couldn't work there. This place had been one of them, but the day after her interview, Mason had cornered her in the break room at Solaria and forced his hand down her pants as she tried to fend him off.

He'd only stopped when Charlotte and one of the kitchen guys had come in together, and the giant grill cook had pulled Mason off her and shoved him into the bank of lockers.

Sam had quit Solaria on the spot and accepted the offer from the sports bar the next day. At least the camera footage had finally allowed Samantha to be granted a restraining order.

But she still worried that he'd been watching the day she and Charlotte had moved out of their old apartment to one on the Kansas side of the city. Maybe the Missouri River would protect her from him somehow.

Even with a new job, a new apartment, a new phone, and her brown hair bleached blonde, Samantha still felt exposed. Like she had no real protection. She could call the cops if he showed up, but what if she couldn't get to a phone? And what happened in nine months when the restraining order expired?

She didn't like to think about it.

As Samantha checked to make sure that the location tracking on her phone was off before she stowed it away for her shift, she noticed a missed call and voicemail from an unknown number, and the hairs on the back of her neck stood up. Surely it wasn't him, right? There was no way he'd have been able to get her new number. The only people who had it were Charlotte, her sister, Amanda, and the approximately thirty-seven restaurants she'd applied to in the last three weeks when she decided she really couldn't do the sports bar thing anymore.

Samantha wanted to listen to the voicemail, just in case, but she was late enough as it was.

Sure enough, as she tied her apron around her waist and emerged from the office, Brett frowned at her. "You're more than twenty minutes late."

"I know. I'm sorry. Traffic was bad."

"That's the third time in two weeks."

Samantha cringed. Each tardy appearance had been for the exact same reason as today. Well, today had been the first day a silver Prius had been directly behind her. All the other days, it had simply been nearby.

She knew she was being paranoid. The driver was probably some innocent parent on their way to pick their kids up from school or something and just happened to share part of their route with Samantha, but she couldn't pretend not to panic whenever she saw that car.

"I'm sorry. I didn't mean to be. I will leave earlier tomorrow, just in case." Maybe she'd miss the silver Prius if she did and save herself the adrenaline boost. The only problem was that she usually spent as long as she could at the public library looking for and applying to jobs, and she always took every last free moment she had looking for something better.

Because she had to believe that things would get better from here.

"Even so, I'm going to have to write you up."

Samantha's heart stuttered for another reason. She'd never been written up before. Not at school. Not at a job.

She wasn't even clear on what a write-up meant. Only that she wasn't fired—yet.

She nodded and swallowed around the knot in her throat. "I will do better. I promise."

Thankfully, Brett left her alone after he made her sign her write-up and took off at five. It was a Thursday night, so she was the only bartender on, and she only had a server until nine. That meant she'd basically have to clean the entire front half of the place herself before she left. Which also meant she'd have to convince one of the kitchen guys to stay late so she wouldn't be alone in the building as she finished closing. None of them liked to do it.

She usually had to end up buying them shots as a bribe. And the too-low balance in her bank account was not going to like that tonight.

Charlotte came in when she got off work at eleven. She was serving in an upscale steakhouse that closed at a reasonable hour and made her tons of cash tips. Samantha was a little bit jealous because she was barely scraping by, but all night she'd been fantasizing that the voicemail on her phone was from the upscale hotel in Lenexa, offering her the bar manager job she'd applied to without an interview.

"You're picking at your cuticles," Charlotte said as she sipped her whiskey. Samantha didn't even have the sweet vermouth here she needed to make a proper Manhattan.

Samantha tucked her hands into her apron pockets and didn't try to pretend she wasn't sparking with nerves. "There was a silver Prius behind me on the way to work."

"I am going to kill that fucking asshole."

"I couldn't see the driver."

"But you panicked all the same, didn't you?" The accusation in Charlotte's eyes stung, even if Samantha knew it wasn't directed at her.

"I was late for work."

"Because you had to drive around until you were sure the bastard wasn't following you."

Samantha sighed. "I don't even know that it was him. It could have been an environmentally conscious soccer mom."

Charlotte rolled her eyes and knocked back the rest of her whiskey. "Puh-*lease* stop making excuses for how deeply that man-child hurt you. You're messed up about it. That's not anything to be ashamed of. This shit is scary."

"But it's irrational to be afraid of a car."

"He. Is. Stalking. You. He tried to fucking rape you. It is not irrational to fear him."

"I got written up for being late today."

Charlotte shook the ice in her glass then plunked it down on the bar. "You need to tell them."

Samantha shook her head. She had mentioned her pending restraining order in an interview once, at the French restaurant where she'd desperately wanted to work. And they'd hired Hannah Barringer instead. They didn't flat-out say that it was because Samantha came with too much drama, but she'd been told that they'd gone with "the safer choice."

Whatever.

Samantha would find something, and eventually her stalker would get bored and move on. Hopefully, he'd realize that stalking was scary and creepy and he didn't want to be like that. That was a charitable thought, right? Wishing her stalker personal growth?

Anyway, she didn't want him to limit her life any more than he was already.

So she told Charlotte about the voicemail, because even though she was technically not allowed to be on her phone while she was on the clock, there were only three people in the bar, and only Charlotte was paying any attention to her.

"You haven't listened to it yet?"

"What if it's him?"

"What if it's a job interview for nine am tomorrow morning, and you're going to miss it because you're putting off listening to the damn voicemail out of fear?"

"I'd probably miss a job interview at nine in the morning anyway. I'd be asleep."

Charlotte rolled her eyes and pushed her glass to the end of the counter.

"If you don't go get your phone, I'm gonna do it myself."

Samantha replaced Charlotte's empty glass with another double whiskey then grumbled the whole way to her locker and back. She glared at her friend from behind the bar the entire time she waited for the voicemail to play.

But then the person who had called began to speak. He sounded friendly and professional, but there was an inherent likeableness to him, and she knew her glare had melted into hypnotized shock.

When it was over, she had to play it again.

"Hello, Samantha. This is Blake Fairchild. I'm calling about the bar manager position you applied for. I'd love to talk to you more in-depth about the position and tell you about my vision for what I want Garden and Gather to be, see if we're a good fit."

He went on to name the coffee shop where he was holding interviews and a time in early afternoon the next day.

Sam turned off her phone screen and set it on the bar in front of her.

"Why do you look like you've seen a ghost?" Charlotte asked.

"Because it was a call about a job. A potentially really good job. Finally."

"I told you," Charlotte said, and Sam did the only mature thing she could think of: She flipped her best friend the bird.

———————◉———————

"I'LL HAVE NONE OF THAT bartending nonsense in my house."

Blake's dad's voice entered the kitchen before his footsteps did. And when he *did* cross the threshold, he hauled himself to one of the chairs in the breakfast nook and heaved like he'd just sprinted a quarter mile instead of walking from the living room to the kitchen.

Blake tried not to worry, but his dad's breathing had only gotten worse since summer had come, and the lingering bronchitis excuse was wearing thin. But James Fairchild didn't go to the doctor unless—in his own words—he felt like he was dying.

His mother didn't sound concerned in the slightest as she said, "They're mocktails, Jim. Just juice and coconut milk."

His dad harrumphed in his chair, and Blake placed a little paper umbrella in the glass and balanced a skewered cherry on the rim. Then he handed the drink to his mother.

Ever since he'd started taking bartending classes, his mother had been requesting all the drinks she'd never had the opportunity to try in her youth. Partly because she'd gotten pregnant with him when she was only twenty, and partly because his father had been a different person back then and she'd never had the chance to play and party like most people in their early twenties. She'd basically been a mom to both Blake and his father, even though she was almost ten years younger than his dad.

But since she'd never partied, she'd never developed a taste for alcohol, and his dad had given up his vices almost twenty years ago and didn't allow alcohol in his house. Not that Blake would try to bring any in. His father was a lot easier to be around since he'd stopped drinking.

At least, he had been until Blake had left the church. That was something his father might never forgive him for.

And it was just another thing for which Blake would always harbor guilt. But at the same time, he couldn't apologize.

After his life in Topeka had collapsed in on itself, he'd needed time and space to get reoriented. To find his true center, learn how to trust himself again. And taking the vacant youth minister position at his father's church would have felt a lot more like a cage than a way to move forward.

That Blake was finding freedom and grounding in building a restaurant and learning all the parts he needed to run one had become an insurmountable wedge between them. Especially after he'd started bartending school.

Blake had never been a huge drinker. Beer every now and then, maybe a little more often than that the last couple of years he'd been in Topeka, when he'd discovered Paradox and craft beer and started dating one of the bartenders.

But in his father's eyes, drinking at all was a sin against the body and against God, and what Blake wanted to do with his restaurant was basically offering up a bacchanalian temple meant for worshipping the pleasures of the flesh. When really, all Blake wanted to do was create an intimate dining experience where it was safe to be free and honest and authentic. He wanted a place where his guests could gather over good food and indulge in a drink or two over dessert, because those were the kinds of things that created connections.

Blake had spent so much of the last few years feeling untethered that he was desperate to feel connected to anyone. Maybe if he created a place where he wanted to be, there might actually be a place where he felt like he belonged.

"Take a sip," his mother said as she took a seat next to his dad at the table. "It's like a tropical milkshake."

Blake sampled his own drink, and his mom was right. Without the rum, it was exactly like a tropical milkshake.

"It will go so well with the kabobs I'm making for dinner. Blake, can you be a dear and make up the *sofrito*?"

Blake cringed inwardly. He'd introduced his mom to the ingredient via his former best friend who was originally from Puerto Rico. Blake had spent so much time with Nicolas and his family when he'd lived in Topeka that he'd learned to expect *sofrito* to be the base of most recipes Nicolas prepared. And the one he brought to church potlucks to use as a condiment to enhance the taste of the otherwise flavorless food available.

Blake's mother had seen Nicolas use it to start his own mother's recipe for *arroz con pollo* for Asher's fifth birthday party, and she had been obsessed with it ever since. She mostly used it as a condiment, like he assumed she meant to do tonight.

She had placed all of the ingredients together in a bowl in her refrigerator, including the onion, cilantro, and sweet peppers she must have gone to the Latin American market to find, because the only other time Blake had seen them had been when he'd gone with Nicolas to East Topeka to find them in a store that Blake would never have dared venture into on his own.

Nicolas had spoken to the proprietor in Spanish and offered him a fist bump over the counter like they were old friends. Then he'd introduced Blake as a friend, and the proprietor, in English, had asked Nicolas if Blake had realized yet that Nicolas was a lousy cook. Nicolas had chuckled and agreed that he was.

Blake disagreed. He'd never learned to cook much of anything. He still lived off frozen food and takeout, so the way that Nicolas could toss meat and vegetables and spices into a pan and give Blake something to eat that tasted good, even if it didn't look like much, seemed like magic.

But Blake had barely spent two hours with Nicolas in the last two years, and it was all his fault. There were times, like now, when Blake missed that friendship so much his chest hurt. When that happened, he had to fight to remind himself that he deserved more than perpetual guilt and shame.

Yes, he'd screwed up, but everyone had healed and moved on. It was okay for him to do something that would make him happy. That's what Garden & Gather was supposed to be.

Sometimes it felt like a joke that he was opening a restaurant, since he didn't know much about food other than how to eat it. But as Blake had tried to explain to his father, the thing he missed most about church was the people. He missed being in the mix, being a part of something. And he knew it wouldn't be as simple as mingling amongst his guests at the restaurant—he would be busy dealing with farmers, distributors, plumbing problems. But there would be days where he would be at the bar, getting to know the regulars and joking with his employees.

At least, that's what he hoped.

"I don't like it," his dad said and dropped the mason jar mug his mom had purchased specifically for these drinks onto the table with a *thunk*. "Yvette, bring me one of those lemon fizzy things, will ya?"

His mother rolled her eyes and pulled a can of seltzer water out of the fridge with zero complaints, even though his dad was being an ass.

In Blake's opinion, his mother was entirely too patient. And his father was being immature.

"What don't you like about it?" Blake asked, turning from where he'd been coarse-chopping the ingredients for the *sofrito*.

"Too sweet."

Blake bit his lip as he dumped the peppers into the food processor. They hadn't even added any extra sugar to the drink. Just used the natural sweetness of the pineapple and coconut milk.

"I think it's perfect," his mother said as she scooped his dad's drink up off the table and took a sip. "And now I get two." She kissed the top of James's head, and he patted her hip fondly.

Blake turned away from the show of affection and switched on the food processor. Witnessing intimacy between anyone only underlined how much Blake had screwed up all his relationships. His friendship with Nicolas. His romance with Rachel. His chance at a family of his own.

When Blake finished the *sofrito* and joined his father at the table, his dad shot him a hard look that had been his default lately. "Your cousin's getting married next month."

Blake glanced at the invitation that was pinned to his mother's corkboard next to the refrigerator. "I saw."

"You're coming?"

"Of course. I'm happy for Faye and Rick."

"Only because it's not taking place at the church." His father grumbled, his head angled toward the windows, as if Blake didn't even deserve his direct criticsm.

This was the first family wedding there had been since Blake had left Grace Bible, but there had been other family events at the church that Blake had avoided. Baptisms, Christmas plays. "That's not why."

"So you can go to a special event wedding, but you can't make it to Sunday services to see your family weekly?" The can of seltzer water crinkled but didn't collapse under the weight of his dad's grip.

The fact that Blake couldn't confide in his father anymore hurt more than anything else. He'd once been his most trusted advisor. Blake had come to him with questions about everything from theology to doctrine to leadership advice. And now? Well, his dad was so preoccupied with how Blake wasn't physically involved in church anymore that he didn't understand why Blake needed time away to sort himself out.

"Showing up for Faye is important, and I'm working through the rest."

His father snorted. "It's been a year and a half. You screwed up. You ask for forgiveness. You commit to doing better, and you move on. Keep doing the work you were called to do."

Blake stirred his virgin colada with his straw while he watched his mother finishing up their dinner on the grill through the kitchen window to his left. It was fine if his dad didn't exactly approve of the restaurant venture. Blake had known he wouldn't from the start. He figured his dad would eventually have to accept that "restaurateur" was Blake's profession now, even if he was disappointed his son was no longer a member of the clergy.

But he couldn't just come right out and say, "I can't remember anymore if God called me to the ministry or if I went to seminary because that's what you wanted for me and I was too young to know the difference." That was the way to destroy his relationship with his father forever.

"I didn't just screw up. I ruined my life, destroyed my career, and brought everyone I cared about down with me."

His father scrubbed his hands over the stubble on his chin as if to say he'd lost patience with Blake's pity party. "And all of them have moved on. You make them sound happy, even. You're the only one that's miserable."

"I *am* moving on—that's what the restaurant is."

"Stop grousing, you two," his mother said as she breezed in through the back door. A platter of succulent smelling meat and the pleasant sweetness of grilled vegetables was balanced in one hand.

He and his father both looked down into their drinks until his mother sat between them and pinned Blake with hopefully mischievous eyes. "So tell me who you're bringing to your cousin's wedding."

Blake tried to hide his grimace by taking a sip of his drink. "I hadn't thought about it," he said out loud, but on the inside, he was groaning. He could never win with either of them.

Chapter Two

At first, Samantha had been proud of herself for showing up at the coffee shop early. *Early* wasn't exactly her thing. Just about the only thing she was on time for these days was church on Sunday morning, but she wanted this job. She just wished she didn't have the extra time to stress about the interview.

She'd had to comb through her computer to find the ad she'd replied to and the cover letter she'd written to remember what the heck Garden & Gather even was. It had definitely been one of those résumés she'd sent out and forgotten about because it was such a long shot. But Garden & Gather was a brand-new restaurant in a well-to-do neighborhood with a website that hadn't been live three weeks ago when she'd applied. She scanned it now as she waited, noting that the website somehow made the place look trendy but classic, high end yet approachable. The kind of restaurant that featured craft cocktails and craft beer.

Now she was so excited that she was bouncing in her seat. Because if she got this job, she would be running the bar that served those things. Running *her own* bar. Well, mostly. It would still be owned by the man across the coffee shop talking to Hannah Barringer. The man that was so gorgeous Samantha couldn't make herself look at him straight on.

Her palms itched, and she wiped them over the knees of her best dark skinny jeans, hoping they didn't leave a mark.

How embarrassing would that be? Sweat stains on her knees the first time he saw her. Maybe the table would cover it.

She didn't want him thinking about her knees or her sweat when she sat down. Sam wanted him to be thinking about how capable she was as a bartender with management experience and a genuine smile. And maybe he'd also think she was cute.

In a professional way.

Because she was a professional.

Her customers trusted her. They took her advice on what kind of drink to order, which beer would go best with their meal, and what kind of gin they should put in their martini if they were actually going to order a martini. Or at least they had, before she'd started at the divey sports bar.

God, Samantha wished she was making more martinis.

That's why she was here. She wanted to work in the kind of place that served drinks in a coupe instead of a shot glass. When she was twenty-two, serving up Bud Light bottles and Vegas Bombs had been fun, but she'd also been part of the shot-and-cheap-beer crowd. As she'd gotten older, learned more about alcohol, and became a better bartender, her palate had matured, and she wanted—no, needed—to level up her place of employment to match.

The restaurant Blake Fairchild was opening sounded like her dream come true.

His ad had read: "Up-and-coming intimate bistro seeking knowledgeable manager with restaurant and bar experience."

Up-and-coming intimate bistro, Samantha thought to herself with a smile.

She could picture it now. A small restaurant with low lighting, tasteful music, and candlelit tables for two. There would be a long mahogany bar with spotlights meant to make the liquor bottles shine, and she'd work at a sedate pace, having time to build a rapport with regulars every night of the week while she crafted classic cocktails with top-shelf spirits.

Sam sighed into the fantasy, her shoulders dropping away from her ears as she imagined how much more sleep she'd get working at a place that closed at eleven instead of two in the morning.

And good Lord—what else could she get done during the day when she wasn't sleeping until noon?

She might actually finish painting her bedroom. Maybe she'd finish the book that had been on her nightstand for more than a year or finish a blog post for a change. All she'd managed to do for months was post a handful of new recipes to Instagram based on popular TV shows.

There were so many possibilities that came along with this job.

That was what Samantha would focus on instead of how her potential new boss was so attractive that she'd burned her tongue on her coffee because she'd been staring at him and not paying attention to her piping hot Americano. He was possibly the most beautiful man she'd ever seen with carefully curated chocolate-brown hair and a short beard that defined his angular jaw. His sparkling brown eyes were so distracting even from a distance that Samantha was a little afraid that once they were actually looking at her, she might forget how to speak.

But right now, she'd forget that he was currently talking to Hannah. Freaking Hannah Barringer. The two of them had been competing for the same jobs since Samantha had started bartending. Samantha had beat out Hannah for the assistant manager job at Solaria but had lost the last job she'd applied to at that French restaurant to her because apparently Hannah didn't have a stalker. Fine. Hannah could have the job at Le Châteaubriand. It was Sam's turn to win.

She realized she was staring at Blake Fairchild again as he offered a small chuckle at something Hannah had said. And if she wasn't mistaken, he was about to notice and glance up at her. Sam's eyes bounced back down to her résumé so quickly her head spun a little.

Great. Now she was dizzy all because a cute guy had probably looked at her.

Her heart pounded in her chest. She felt like she was fourteen again, and that was so stupid. She could not mess this up.

If she had to go back to work at the sports bar tonight with no prospect of leaving soon, she might actually wither away from despair right then and there.

Get it together, lady, she chastised herself. *You are totally capable of landing this job. Stop thinking about how hot the boss is. You can't date anyone at work ever again—you already know that doesn't end well. And this is the* boss. *You never,* never *date the proprietor.* Even if the image of him hiking her up on her imaginary mahogany bar and kissing her neck while his fingers found their way inside her jeans was something her mind conjured up with very little convincing.

Stop it. He's way too old for you anyway. He's got to be, like, thirty-five. And you're twenty-five. That's . . .

She cocked her head to the side and made a tickmark on her napkin for each of the ten years in difference. Actually, that age difference didn't bother her at all. She quite liked the sound of dating someone who was a little older. A little more mature. More experienced. Willing to . . .

And now she was thinking about him on his knees, and that was just so, so inappropriate on so many levels. She rubbed her palms over her knees again. Maybe if her knees were sweaty when she approached his table—whenever he was finally done talking to Hannah—he would imagine her on *her* knees for him.

Good Lord—the twinge of pure want that spasmed through her at that fantasy had her squirming in her seat.

So inappropriate. Especially since Samantha had never actually done that with a guy. Well, kind of—the one and only time she'd tried had been embarrassing, as had most of her sexual encounters, which was why she avoided them most of the time.

Apparently, devastatingly handsome men made her lose her mind entirely.

Oh God. They were standing up, and Sam was next. And she knew she looked like a mess.

Deep breaths. That was the key. In through the nose, out through the mouth. *Good. Now close your mouth so you don't look like you're gaping.*

She smoothed her hair and tried to calm her heartbeat through her breathing, but she'd always been crap at yoga and all that metaphysical, spiritual stuff. Or any spiritual stuff, really. Given her background, that wasn't all that surprising, even if it didn't stop her from trying to figure out where she belonged. Charlotte had never stopped giving her a hard time for trying a new church every week, but Samantha couldn't shake the notion that maybe the way she'd grown up with all her strict rules and isolation had meant she'd missed out on the good things that happened in regular churches.

So far, she wasn't any closer to figuring out what those good things were.

Maybe she should try again. If that meant going to the same church twice or picking up yoga again, Samantha wasn't sure. Possibly both?

Neither one was going to help her now, but that didn't stop her from whispering *Please, baby Jesus, help a girl out, will ya?* when Blake Fairchild swiveled his gaze toward her, expectant curiosity in his eyes.

———◉———

HIS FIRST THOUGHT UPON seeing Samantha was that she was exactly the kind of girl he would have dated for show when he was still working at Grace Bible. Younger. A sweet-looking blonde who would be so flattered by his attention that she wouldn't think too hard about how detached he was while he fantasized about the brunette firecracker he'd rather be with.

Blake shut those thoughts down as quickly as he could. He didn't do that anymore.

He didn't do anything anymore when it came to women. Not for almost two years now. He didn't deserve any woman's attention, not after what he'd done. And honestly, dating someone else when a very specific brunette firecracker was still the fantasy at the forefront of his mind felt wrong.

She was getting married soon. And on one level, Blake was happy for her. She deserved that happiness.

But on another level, Blake was still chastising himself for messing up the best relationship he'd ever had.

He remained standing as his first interview of the day left and his second, Samantha Reynolds, approached.

She was nervous. He could see that from a mile away. He would have to put her at ease.

Blake settled his features into a soft smile. One that he knew from practice made him look more approachable. It was meant to say *I know I can be intimidating if you're shy, but hey, I don't bite. At least, not hard.*

She returned his smile with a sheepish one of her own even as she clutched her padfolio to her chest like it was what allowed her to breathe.

"Samantha?" he asked, offering his hand.

"Yes. It's nice to meet you, Mr. Fairchild."

"It's just Blake, please. I don't even think my dad goes by Mr. Fairchild. My science teacher grandfather scarred us all for life on that one."

Her head fell to one side as her brows crinkled.

What was he doing? Blake knew better than to talk about his family in front of strangers. All it did was make them uncomfortable.

"He wasn't a nice man," Blake offered by way of explanation as he gestured toward the chairs. "Let's sit and talk about the bistro. It's a far more pleasant topic than my grandfather."

Samantha's tentative smile returned as she nodded and followed his lead, taking the seat across from him.

He shuffled the stack of résumés in front of him so that hers was on top. "Tell me about why you want to work at the bistro."

Samantha's face changed as her smile turned from meek to brilliant. She transformed from the mouse he'd taken her for to a woman with a purpose. He was so distracted with the dazzling blue of her eyes that he didn't notice she'd knocked his coffee over with her padfolio until the cup hit his lap.

With a yelp, Blake leapt to his feet, an unfortunate dark stain spreading over his new gray trousers.

"Oh my God—I'm so sorry." Samantha jumped to her feet as well, yanking napkins from the dispenser in a wad as she did. She darted forward as if she were going to dab at the stain herself but pulled up short when her eyes took in where the majority of the spill had landed.

With a blush stealing over her cheekbones, she offered up the wad of napkins.

Blake took them, but there was no way he was going to dab at his crotch in public. He was just glad that what coffee had been left in his cup had cooled to room temperature. Instead, he wiped up the seat of his chair then blotted at where the coffee had soaked his stack of résumés and job descriptions.

"I have a spare copy of my résumé," she said, and he had a feeling her voice wasn't normally quite so high pitched.

He didn't necessarily need a copy of her résumé. Blake had basically memorized it. Hers had been the interview he'd been looking forward to the most. Though that was possibly because her original work experience was in the same small city where he'd gone to Bible college. And perhaps he was curious how she'd gone from a degree in English Education to a bar manager, because with her cardigan and sweet pink shirt, she looked a lot more like an English teacher than the last bartender he'd dated.

He reminded himself again that he wasn't thinking about Rachel today. His current venture had nothing to do with how much he missed her. It was more about how he needed to do something that was truly his, and when his mom had tried to get him to take over her bakery so she could retire, Blake hadn't been able to shake the idea of an intimate restaurant. The kind of place he would have taken a woman back when he was dating regularly, but also the kind of place where long-married couples would become regulars for their weekly date nights. The kind of place that would make top ten lists for their Sunday brunch and have a waiting list for Valentine's Day.

Maybe it was his penance for destroying so many relationships, but Blake wanted to do something that might atone for his sins, even if it was only in small ways and for other people.

And so far, the restaurant had kept him busy. Busier than he'd expected, actually—first, with the renovations, then with planning the menu and hiring a chef.

Now he needed someone to run the front end of the establishment. To basically show him how to be a restaurateur, because outside working in his mother's bakery as a teenager, Blake had zero experience. Every single person he'd interviewed had been more qualified for his job than he was. All he had to offer was his mother's investment and a little bit of money of his own.

"Thank you," Blake said and accepted the sheet of paper from Samantha as he motioned for her to sit back down at their table.

Once seated, he gave the résumé a perfunctory glance, but the woman still had nearly ten years of experience in the restaurant industry, though she must have started serving when she was sixteen if that was the case. Was that even legal?

He'd been taking classes, bartending and Safe Serve certification. He'd also been through training with the ABC about ID and liquor laws. He knew it was illegal for anyone under the age of eighteen to serve alcohol. Though it was possible she'd worked somewhere that didn't serve alcohol. Or she'd served it illegally.

But if she had, Blake couldn't hold that against her. She'd only been a minor. It would have been the people she'd worked for who were at fault.

Since the position description sheets were soaked with the last half of his flat white, he described the bistro and what he would expect of the person who was hired. She nodded along like she wasn't surprised by any of it, which was better than the last girl who had shown surprise that he wanted the bar manager to confer with the chef and design drinks to pair with the specials each month.

Blake didn't think that was a lot to ask. And he was happy to see that despite her nerves, Samantha seemed to agree. Then he wrapped up his vision for the bistro and asked, "Why do you want this position?"

A smile so wide and brilliant broke over Samantha's face it was like watching the sunrise break over the horizon. "It's my dream job."

And that was all Blake needed to know.

Chapter Three

"Knock, knock!" Blake's mom called from the back door as she let herself in. She did this every time she stopped by. The space used to be her bakery, but she'd signed the lease over to Blake late last year, and even though he'd never take his mother's key from her, she still liked to announce her presence.

"We're out here," Blake said, closing the binder he'd taken out to show Samantha once she arrived for her first shift. There wasn't technically a "we" here yet, but Blake was expecting his new manager any moment. The nervous anticipation fizzing in his chest meant he couldn't wait to share with her the work he'd done so far: the schedule of events he hoped to implement, the contracts he'd arranged with liquor suppliers.

And he couldn't wait to get her opinion about how the bar should be set up. Part of his research had been visiting restaurants similar to what he wanted to do with Garden & Gather. But he didn't have the practical experience of working a busy Friday night behind the bar—yet—and he wanted her to be able to build her dream bar.

That was why he was excited. It had nothing to do with how cute she was. Blake wasn't attracted to cute.

He liked dangerous women. Women he wasn't supposed to like. Women who got him into trouble. His adorable new bar manager—he watched as she chose that moment to let herself in the front door in her silky green blouse and torn jeans—reminded him so much of the last church girl that he'd dated that he *shouldn't* be attracted to her.

Blake had never been more bored in his life than when he'd tried dating Pete Schnacker's daughter. Heather wasn't to blame, of course—she was exactly who she'd been raised to be. An obedient, self-sacrificing young woman who had adopted all of Blake's opinions for herself because she'd never realized she had the agency to develop her own.

When he'd taken her out to dinner, she'd always ordered the cheapest, safest item on the menu as if she were afraid to spend his money. Blake had encouraged her to order what she liked, that money wasn't a worry when he invited her to dinner.

She'd started ordering whatever he ordered at dinner after that. At first, he'd taken that as a good sign, that she was willing to try new things and figure out what she liked on her own. But after he'd ordered the same entree from the same seafood restaurant three weeks in a row and she'd done the same—even though it was obvious that she wasn't a fan of fish—it was clear she was only doing what she thought would please him.

Blake didn't want her to please him. He'd honestly felt bad for her. Not just because he'd also been fighting his temptation for another woman at that point, but because when he'd broken off their relationship, she'd looked relieved. Like she couldn't make the decision that they weren't right for each other without his permission.

Heather had told him she thought he was probably a bit too wild for her and she wasn't sure how to make him happy.

He'd told her that it wasn't her job to make him happy, and she'd looked extremely confused. Blake had encouraged her to figure out what made *her* happy, and she'd just sat quietly, staring at him like he'd rocked her world. Or broken it. He'd never quite been sure.

She'd moved away not long after that, and Blake wished her nothing but the best because he'd definitely fucked up his life after that, going after what he thought would make him happy. He'd been wrong. He'd traded moments of ecstasy for years of turmoil.

But as Samantha grinned at him and flicked her eyes toward his mother in question, Blake thought that maybe why he liked Samantha—as an employee—was because she *did* know what she wanted. She was passionate about what she did but was ready to leave the world of nightclubs and dive bars behind in favor of something more intimate.

Like his restaurant.

He'd watched her eyes dance as she talked about the various restaurants she'd worked in and how she'd stayed at the nightclub so long mostly because the tips were so good, but that she'd left to look for something more. She was motivated by the opportunity to create a menu from scratch. That someday she dreamed of opening her own restaurant, but that working to build a new one was the next best thing.

He liked her ambition. Blake wished he'd found a passion for something other than church when he'd been that young. Something to please himself instead of doing what his dad wanted him to do.

His father still didn't approve of the idea of Blake opening a restaurant that served alcohol, but his mother, who had always been supportive of Blake—even in his darkest moments—had reminded her husband at dinner the other night that to stay competitive, serving alcohol was a sound business decision. She continued by pointing out that Blake's restaurant was the kind of place where people were meant to imbibe in sensible libations—glasses of wine or fancy cocktails—not the kind of place where people went to chug beer and take shots.

Blake blinked, realizing he'd been stuck in his head, a place he'd been finding himself ruminating in too often since his world had fallen apart. Correction, not since his world had fallen apart—since Blake had done everything he could to destroy his own equilibrium. Since he'd torn down the infrastructure of his entire life brick by betraying brick.

And maybe he didn't deserve to reclaim the friendships he'd destroyed, but he was tired of living in the rubble.

So Blake shone one of his brightest smiles at Samantha and held a hand out to his mother. "Samantha, this is Yvette, my mother. Mom, this is Samantha, Garden and Gather's new Bar and Front-of-House Manager."

In the few steps his mother took across the room to shake Samantha's hand, Blake saw the light of matchmaking spark in her eyes. She shot Blake a grin brighter than his own, and he knew exactly what she was thinking. But she'd be disappointed, of course.

Sweet or not, Samantha was his employee and far, far too young for him. She was barely twenty-five. He couldn't, in good conscience, date someone almost thirteen years his junior, especially not someone on his payroll. Blake may have made some questionable moral decisions in his day, but even he wasn't comfortable with that power dynamic.

"It's such a pleasure to meet you, darling," his mom said, pulling Samantha into the welcoming hug she gave everybody. "I can't wait to see what you make of this place. My son has a vision, but Lord knows he needs help making it a reality. Do you know he's never actually worked in a restaurant? I told him he needed to find a job and work as a waiter rather than just taking all of these hospitality classes and dating bartenders, but mothers only know so much, I suppose."

The tips of Blake's ears burned as Samantha raised questioning eyes to his. "I worked in your bakery," he reminded his mother.

She dismissed him with a wave of her hand. "I'm not saying I don't think you're capable—just that a little more practical experience would make opening this place less of a shock when the time comes. But it's a little too late now, I suppose."

Then his mother turned to Samantha. "I know you two have work to do, but I brought coffee and cupcakes—the same recipe I used when this place was mine. Sit down, have a treat, and tell me all about yourself."

She led his dazed-looking employee to the table in the corner away from the construction equipment that he'd been using as a makeshift desk.

She shifted his files and research to an empty chair and said, "Blake, be a dear and bring the cupcakes in from the car, will you?"

———◉———

BLAKE'S MOTHER WAS not what Samantha had expected. During her interview, Blake had mentioned that he was turning his mother's old bakery into a restaurant. Since Blake was in his thirties, Samantha had pictured a sweet, stout lady in her sixties with short, curly hair who wore too-big jeans and pink sweatshirts with kittens on them.

But she should have known that Blake didn't spring forth from the ether well-groomed and immaculately dressed. His mother looked just like him. Sharp, expressive features, eyes that sparkled, and a billion-watt smile. Her hair was still the same chocolate brown as her son's but accented with tasteful golden highlights, and she was almost as tall as he was in her designer heels and skinny jeans.

Samantha definitely was not cool enough for this family in her Target shoes and thrift store clothes. She resisted the urge to fold her feet under her chair to hide the scuffs that no doubt were on the inside heel of her boots.

The space, though still undergoing renovation, was also larger than Sam had imagined it would be. She'd always thought of bakeries as small, cozy affairs with two or three tables, but this was the perfect size for a café. There was room for just enough seating to keep them busy but not so much that they'd lose the intimate feel Blake had described in his explanation of the restaurant.

She especially liked where he'd torn out the standard floor-to-ceiling storefront windows around the door to the patio and added a greenhouse-style dome. Samantha could already picture it filled with ferns and herbs and strung with fairy lights. It would be the spot where couples would pose for selfies and snap photos of the sous-chef cutting fresh herbs for their entrées.

"It's impressive, what he's envisioning, isn't it?" Yvette asked, and Samantha realized she'd been ignoring the other woman in favor of daydreaming.

"I can't wait to see it finished."

"Or to get behind the bar?"

"Oh, definitely. I am so relieved to leave the dive bar life behind."

"That's where you're coming from?"

Samantha nodded, feeling her face heat. "I've worked in one sort of club or another since I was eighteen. First serving then bartending after I turned twenty-one. I moved to a sports bar a few months ago, but that was so I had less responsibility while I looked for my dream job."

It was only a partial lie. There was no way Samantha was bringing up Mason at this stage in the game and scaring these nice people off.

"Well, I can't say I know much about nightclubs, but I'm sure it's a hectic environment with such loud music."

Samantha offered a half smile. She couldn't argue about the music. She would have to remember not to shout at the customers over the bar once Garden & Gather was open.

"This is going to be a perfect fit for you. Blake was certainly excited after your interview. I haven't seen him so enthusiastic about anything in a long time. That was a refreshing change for me. These past couple of years have been difficult for him."

Samantha was tempted to ask *how so*, because to her eyes, Blake was almost more myth than man, a handsome man who dressed well and knew how to style his hair. Someone who had the means and the drive to open his own restaurant. Someone who seemed kind and was apparently a mama's boy, even well into his thirties.

If he weren't her boss, Samantha would definitely be developing a crush on him. But since he *was* her boss, she wouldn't. Plus, he was so much older than her. It wasn't improbable that he was getting over a heartbreaking first marriage or something, and that was as good a reminder as any that Blake was in an entirely different league when it came to love and relationships, so she was determined to squash any signs of budding attraction. Sam would keep everything strictly professional.

The back door opened and closed, and Yvette sat up straighter, asking "And did you grow up in the city?" like there had been another question on the subject.

So they were pretending they weren't talking about Blake? Got it.

"Um, no." Samantha shifted in her seat. The subject was dangerously close to the uncomfortable truth about how and why she'd even ended up in Kansas City to begin with. Her apartment was nowhere near this well-to-do suburb. And the run-down, too-crowded house in Southern Missouri she'd grown up in was probably the kind of house Yvette had never set foot in. "I grew up near Springfield. I moved here after college for work."

"That must be lonely with your family so far away."

Samantha nodded as Blake appeared with a tray of coffees in one hand and a plastic carrier full of cupcakes in the other. As far as Sam was concerned, a three-hour drive wasn't enough space between her and her family.

She didn't really want to tell this delightfully kind woman that she didn't speak to her parents, that she hadn't had contact with anyone but her sister in years. But she was saved from providing any more personal information by Yvette, who handed her a large black coffee and said, "Blake lived in Topeka for about twelve years, and I know it's barely more than an hour away, but it was too far for me. I love having him nearby again."

Blake set the container of cupcakes on the table, and his mother promptly handed him one. "And here I thought once you closed the bakery, you'd stop force-feeding me sugar," he said even as he discarded the wrapper.

"It's my love language." His mother winked at Samantha as she handed the younger woman one as well. It was vanilla with pink frosting piped in the shape of a rose with a little candy pearl at the center.

"This is beautiful."

"Thank you," Yvette said, taking a lavender one for herself. "I am actually starting to enjoy baking again. It's more fun to do when it's something I *want* to do versus something I *have* to do."

"Well, you're going to *have* to do it sometimes," Blake said just before he bit into his yellow rose.

"My cupcake recipe will be featured on the dessert menu," Yvette said, a catlike expression of satisfaction curling over her face from lips to eyebrows. "And I promised to make them myself for special events. But the point is, I'm not doing the same thing every day. I am free to do what I like in my dotage."

Samantha almost snorted her cupcake. Yvette Fairchild did not appear to be in her dotage. Sam was still having trouble reconciling that this woman was Blake's mother and not his sister or best friend. This was the woman who had raised him. And she was exactly the kind of woman Samantha wanted to claim as her best friend or sister. She couldn't imagine a world where she would be lucky enough to have a woman like this as a mother.

Grief weighed her heart down as she remembered everything she missed out on by disconnecting herself from her family. But it was quickly lifted with a swift reminder that any tender moment with her family was usually accompanied by twice as much abuse *and* by Blake saying, "I only hope my dotage includes regular spa days and yoga retreats."

Yvette swatted at Blake's arm, causing him to smash yellow frosting onto his nose. "Hush, you. I spent thirty-five years working on my feet six days a week. I deserve all the foot massages I can afford."

Blake swiped the frosting off his nose with the back of his hand. "Of course, you do. I'm just saying—it's not like you're confined to a rocking chair knitting afghans."

His mother's eyes brightened. "Oh! But I *did* sign up for a knitting class! Our first project is a baby blanket. I figure I'll save it for when you finally give me a grandchild. Or for when Faye has one, since she'll probably come first at this rate."

The tips of Blake's ears pinked just like they had earlier, but his face remained impassive as he said, "Just make sure you knit it in a gender-neutral color, and you'll be fine either way."

Yvette ignored him completely and turned to Sam. "Faye is my niece. She's twenty-five and getting married next month. This one hasn't been in a serious relationship in years." She cocked her head in her son's direction. "Though I suppose I am grateful I won't be knitting a black baby blanket. I loved the idea of Rachel, but my eyes just aren't what they used to be. I'd never be able to see what I was doing with black yarn."

Blake's cheeks flushed this time, and his ears were practically glowing red. Who the hell was Rachel? And why would she want a black baby blanket?

Blake's response was quick. "Oh, but you still could. I just found out that she and Nicolas are expecting. Maybe that *is* who you should knit your blanket for after all."

Yvette's grin faltered, slipping into a frown, and Blake swiped his coffee cup off the table. "If you'll excuse me, I need to check on something in the back before Emil gets in."

Samantha's brow furrowed. What had just happened there? Had Rachel and Blake been together once upon a time? Was she his ex-wife? Was she married to someone else now?

Yvette watched Blake stalk into the kitchen, her lips pursed. Then she turned to Samantha while worrying her wedding ring. "I always end up pushing him too far too fast. But it's been almost two years since he and Rachel split up. I guess it's still too soon for jokes."

Samantha could tell the older woman tried for a breezy smile, but her lips quickly collapsed back into a frown. She took that to mean that Rachel was definitely the ex-wife. Had she and Blake not been able to have children? Had Rachel not wanted children with Blake? Was that why her pregnancy with this other guy was such an insult? Sam couldn't shake the feeling that she'd unknowingly meandered into a minefield, and now the scuffed heel of her boot rested on a trigger.

"Anyway, I'm sorry to put you in the middle of all that. I just want to see him happy. He's my only baby, and no matter what it looks like from the outside"—she gestured to herself and then the space they sat in—"it hasn't been an easy road for us."

"I don't have any opinions," Samantha said just a little too quickly. Partly because she couldn't imagine being an only child, and partly because she didn't want to show exactly how keen she was to learn about Blake's past. "I'm just happy for the job and nothing but thankful to Blake for offering it to me. This job is exactly what I was looking for."

Yvette grasped the hand that Samantha had resting on the table. "I know, honey. And even though I just met you, I have a feeling you are exactly what this place needs. I shouldn't have brought up Rachel—I know better. I just want my son to be happy again, and that includes him accepting what he can't have anymore. He's never quite forgiven himself for how that relationship ended, and all I want is for him to realize that he was meant for more."

Tears pooled unbidden in Samantha's eyes. Not for whatever it was that Blake had suffered through, but because of what she would give if only her mother would show half as much concern for her as Blake's mother showed for him.

She swallowed back the lump in her throat and said more quietly than she meant to, "I've always wanted to learn how to knit. My grandmother used to, but she never taught me."

"Oh, you should come with me, and we can learn together. The classes are Saturday mornings. We can get coffee and donuts beforehand, and then I'll be guaranteed to know at least one person."

"I—" Samantha didn't know how to tell Yvette that she normally spent Saturday mornings in bed after closing down the bar, but she supposed she only had one more week of that, and she could always sleep when she got home since Garden & Gather wouldn't be open for a few more weeks. And it wouldn't necessarily be a bad idea to make friends with Blake's mother, since it looked like she was going to be more involved than Blake probably preferred.

"Don't forget about the donuts, dear. You can't say no to donuts."

Samantha allowed a smile to unfurl, a small, tentative, but happy one. "You're right, I can't. I'd love to go to knitting class with you."

Yvette clapped her hands. "Hooray! I am so excited. We are going to be such great friends, you and I."

The glow of acceptance burned in Sam's chest for approximately two-point-five seconds before she caught sight of Blake standing behind his mother, arms crossed, a frustrated frown dimming his otherwise brilliant features.

Well, crap.

Chapter Four

Samantha's first day hadn't gone at all how Blake had expected. In his mind, he'd pictured them behind the bar, laughing while developing cocktails and picking a discreet place for the cash register and iPads to live. But she'd been subdued and withdrawn the rest of the afternoon after his mother had left, and it was all his fault.

He'd known exactly what his mother was doing. It was what Yvette always did when there was a young, single woman within ten miles of him. She was working her clutches into Sam, and then she was going to gain the poor girl's trust and thrust her into Blake's path at every opportunity. Samantha would suddenly show up at family dinners, in the pew at church on Sunday morning—hell, she'd probably even show up at his cousin's wedding if he gave his mom enough time.

At least Samantha hadn't been at his parents' house when he'd shown up for dinner the night before. It had blessedly just been him, his mother, his father, and that damn empty place setting.

At some point, his father had started keeping an empty seat at the end of the table that was meant to be an open invitation for Jesus, God, the Holy Spirit, or all three at once to join them at the table. Even when Blake had been part of the church, he'd thought it was a little weird. Now it just seemed like it was a whole seat reserved for Blake's father's failed expectations of his son.

Blake would have rather found Samantha in that chair, even if she'd been fiddling with the golden cross she wore around her throat like she'd done throughout the entirety of her shift the day before.

But at least his mother hadn't gone that far with Samantha yet. Even if she had brought her up at dinner so his father could tell him he'd better "square this one away" before he lost her to someone else—again.

Blake had rolled his eyes and ignored his father's oblique reference to Rachel. James Fairchild clung to an inaccurate interpretation of what had driven his son away from Topeka, and Blake really didn't want to get into it.

His mother pretended she wasn't going to try to push Blake and Samantha to have more than a professional relationship by saying "Not for Blake, dear. I want her to be my friend. If I don't hang on to at least one friend in their twenties, how else will I keep up with all the new slang and the new social media platforms? I wonder if she can show me how to use TikTok."

Blake didn't believe Yvette for a second. He'd never once been interested in any of the girls his mother flung at him, and none of them had been his employees. He definitely wasn't going to start with his bar manager.

But Samantha had caught him allowing his frustration to show through his usually carefully controlled exterior. He didn't let his guard down often or allow others to see his true emotions—especially not when they'd just met—and this was why. Because now Samantha thought his frustration was with her and not his mother, so instead of the personable, excited new employee he'd wanted, he now had a somber, strictly professional one who only asked him about recycling bins and liquor distributors and how many bartenders he was looking to hire and at what pay. They'd gone over all the information he'd planned to but with none of the natural camaraderie he'd wished for.

Was it so much to hope for some measure of friendship from his employees?

Blake had been woefully low on friends these last couple of years. He'd had a built-in group of drinking buddies when he'd worked on the construction crew, but though Blake could be a chameleon, he still never liked to drink too much in a sea of men who guzzled down Miller Light like water. When he'd left that job in the new year, those friends had fallen away, and Blake was in a new kind of solitude he hadn't thought would still be a part of his life.

When he'd first left Topeka, he'd thought he'd have himself sorted out by now. That once he got away from all the temptation and the shame, he'd have settled into something fulfilling.

He'd expected to forgive himself by now. And he'd expected that once he'd forgiven himself, everything else he'd always wanted—the life he'd promised himself—would just sort of fall into place. The wife, the kids, the house, the job.

So far, the only promise he had was of a job that would likely keep him busy seven days a week and an apartment he didn't hate but one where he'd already lived a year longer than he'd planned.

Nothing had worked out the way he'd wanted so far, and he was done with feeling that he had zero control over his life. The one time he'd tried to take control had been a disaster. He'd made all the wrong decisions, and now he was paying the price.

So he just wouldn't think about it anymore.

It was fine if his mother wanted to make friends with his bar manager. It made no difference to him—he had better things to do. Like reconnaissance and research by once again dining alone at another highly rated bistro in the city. And reminding his mother not to smother his new employee and allow him to find his own girlfriend.

But even as he thought about it, he scrubbed his hands over his face. Good Lord—what would she tell Samantha about Rachel? She wouldn't have much to tell; his mother had never even met Rachel, but she'd wanted to. Badly.

If Blake let himself dwell too long, he'd be surly the rest of the night, so he tried to channel his old self. The self he'd been before he'd screwed everything up. He'd been popular, put together, and certain of his course in life.

Blake was none of those things now, but as he rolled up the sleeves of his new blue shirt and laced up his boots, he told himself he could pretend. He could put on a sport coat, go to a new restaurant, order a drink at the bar, smile at the hostess, and watch how they did everything. He could take notes. Eat at a table in the corner, watch how the night unfolded, and then do what he did every night and pretend that he was fine going home alone.

⸺⊙⸺

SAMANTHA WAS EIGHTY-five percent sure Blake hadn't seen her yet. He was sitting at the bar with his back to them, but it was so obvious he was scoping out the place that she was half-tempted to invite him to sit with her and Charlotte just to give him a better cover.

"Stop looking at him." Charlotte gripped Samantha's chin and wrenched her head around so that she wasn't craning her neck to spy on her boss.

"I'm sorry; I can't help it," Samantha said as she rubbed her palms over her jeans just like she'd been doing before the interview. "It makes me nervous that he's here."

"I'd be nervous, too, if I had to work with a man that looked like him and I had to keep my pants on all day."

"Shh!" Samantha clapped her hand over her friend's mouth. "What if he hears you?"

Charlotte batted Samantha's hand away. "Oh, I am more than certain that Mr. Sexy Pants knows how hot he is. One does not look like a supermodel in everyday life and just go around pretending they don't. What's his name again? We should call him over."

Samantha ducked as if to hide behind her martini glass. "Oh my God. I seriously can't take you out in public."

"What? We came out to celebrate your new job. He gave you said job. Why shouldn't he be invited?"

"Because yesterday was awkward, okay? First, I'm hanging out with his mom and working for him, then we just *happen* to show up at the same restaurant on a random Thursday night? He's going to think I'm stalking him."

"No one is going to think you're stalking them in Westport. They're just going to think you're hungry and have a taste for overpriced cocktails, which you were, and you do, so no harm, no foul."

Samantha was still hungry. Their entrees hadn't arrived yet, and she was kind of in that appetizer-or-cocktails-not-both place in her budget, even for a celebratory night out.

"Yes, well, my drink has been empty for ten minutes, and I don't see our server anywhere. You should probably go order us another round at the bar."

Charlotte's drink had not been empty for ten minutes. It had been five, and the only reason was because Charlotte didn't know how to not chug alcohol. Samantha had always suspected that Charlotte didn't actually like alcohol, she'd just had to drink to fit into her sorority in college so she'd figured out how to guzzle it. Even something that should be sipped, like the Hendrick's martinis they'd ordered.

Samantha chewed her lip and glanced down at her own drink. It was getting low, since she'd been using the gin to attempt to ease her hunger pangs. She'd only planned on buying one round of drinks and then switching to water, but when she peeked over her shoulder again, she could see Blake tapping something into his phone with a stylus. A fucking stylus.

"Come on, I know you want to," Charlotte teased.

She did want to. As annoying as Charlotte was being, Samantha didn't like how she'd left things with him yesterday. She wanted to apologize and tell him that she would cancel plans with his mom if it bothered him, even if she *was* secretly excited to learn how to knit. She liked being warm in the winter, and she looked hella cute in beanies. Sam could stock herself up on hats and scarves and be toasty year-round. But if it made things weird at work, she could totally find a different class. Or do it the old-fashioned way and find some YouTube videos or something.

"Would he come over here if he recognized you?"

Samantha wasn't sure how she knew the answer to that question, but it was unequivocally yes. Blake wouldn't pretend he hadn't seen her or didn't know her. He would come over immediately and probably offer to buy her a drink just because she was here.

God—it would be rude not to do the same thing, wouldn't it?

Charlotte's wicked smile made it clear she knew she'd gotten her way. But seriously? Sam knew exactly what her friend was thinking: that if she went and talked to Blake, they'd magically become best work friends and then lovers, and afterward he wouldn't just look like Prince Charming, he'd actually *be* Prince Charming. Like somehow his attention would magically fix all of the problems in her life.

But really, Samantha was only after the paycheck. A good job with better hours and even further away from *him* would go a long way to setting her on the right path.

The least she could do was be polite.

Samantha took a deep breath, finished her martini, and made her way to the bar. There was an empty seat next to Blake, but Samantha leaned her elbows on the counter next to it, keeping the stool between them so it wouldn't look like she was trying to creep on him on top of everything else.

Thank the Lord the bartender was there to take her order before she had a chance to turn to Blake, so he had already noticed her by the time she was done ordering.

Which made it seem like their meeting was more of a coincidence than the result of the full ten minutes it had taken her to calm her nerves and approach.

"Is a gin martini your drink?" he asked, the iridescent brightness back in his eyes, a curl of a smile playing over his lips.

"A dry martini is my drink. Which should always be made with gin unless the person asks for vodka. But if they do, you know you can never trust them."

His grin widened to reveal a dimple almost hidden by his beard, and his eyes nearly pinged they were shining so brightly. "Aha! I always knew bartenders judged you by the type of drink you ordered."

She eyed his half-empty beer glass. It was definitely a beer, but it was a bright pink color. "You like sours?" she asked with raised eyebrows.

He tapped a finger against the bar. "And IPAs. Whiskey, sometimes."

Samantha nodded. About what she expected.

"You're judging me now, aren't you?"

She shrugged, fighting her lips' desire to tilt into a flirty smile. "Maybe."

"And?"

"You're a guy. One who isn't afraid to try new things and is secure enough in his masculinity to drink a bright fuchsia beer in public." She shrugged again. "Could be worse."

Blake snorted out a muted laugh and raised his glass as the bartender set the new martinis down in front of her. She clinked one against his with the slightest tap so she didn't spill any of her favorite gin.

"So who are you here with?" he asked, scanning the restaurant behind them. The way his eyes surveyed the crowd made her wonder if he was hoping he could pick out her companion based on who looked most suited to her the same way she could tell a lot about a person based on the drink they ordered.

"My friend, Charlotte. We worked together for a while. Now she's my roommate."

Blake spotted Charlotte, who was not being discreet about staring at them, and nodded in her direction. Charlotte gave them a mischievous smile accompanied by a teasing finger wave.

"So not your girlfriend, then?"

Samantha snorted, imagining what her family back home would say if they thought she was in a relationship with a woman.

"And no boyfriend?"

Sam's heart started to thud against her ribs. His eyebrows were tilted upward with way more interest than he should be expressing for so, so many reasons.

"No boyfriend." She had to suppress a shudder. Samantha wasn't sure she was going to be in the market for a boyfriend anytime soon.

But then Sam's heart stopped for two entire beats when he said, "Damn."

What the fuck was that supposed to mean?

She stared at him, not sure if she should be offended or if he was hoping she had a boyfriend so he would have an easy excuse to curb his wild and undeniable attraction to her.

"Sorry," he said, and she decided his sheepish expression was her favorite. It was somehow more genuine, more honest than his smile. "It's just that my mom takes personal offense at the fact that I'm still single at my age and has been known to befriend younger women with at least partial intent to throw them at me. Maybe if you had a boyfriend, we could keep her from attempting that last part."

"Oh" was all Samantha could think to say. She'd had the impression that his mother had been genuinely trying to make her feel welcome. She'd thought that was the way Yvette greeted all new people in her life, but maybe she'd been mistaken? That would be disappointing. Samantha had already grown attached to the idea of picking up a new substitute mother figure.

Blake was still looking at her like he expected her to say more, so Samantha scrambled to collect her thoughts through her disappointment and confusion. "But we work together."

"Exactly," Blake said, tapping his knuckles on the bar in a short, sharp rap. "That would be awkward, wouldn't it?"

Samantha nodded, perhaps a little bit too enthusiastically. "Yeah, totally. It would be."

Blake raised one of his eyebrows at her, and the luminous amusement radiating from his eyes was enough to make her stomach flutter and her heart skip a beat. How was it possible for one person to be so beautiful?

Well, she'd seen his mother. She knew exactly how possible it was. She just didn't see it often.

"Good," he said, and some of the shine eased from his irises like he could adjust it with a dial. "You'll have to be on your guard. My mother can be devious."

Out of the corner of her eye, Samantha caught sight of the server dropping their food off at their table. "I should—"

"Go, eat." Blake motioned toward her table. "Enjoy your evening, Samantha."

It shouldn't have, but the sound of her name on his lips sent a shiver down her spine. She thought she'd suppressed it, but when Charlotte asked for the bill and their server told them their meal had been paid for by a gentleman at the bar, Samantha wondered if maybe, somehow, she'd had the same effect on him.

Chapter Five

S amantha contemplated skipping her knitting date with Blake's mother Saturday morning. She almost called and cancelled three times. But then she remembered the text from Blake, the one that read: *I gave my mom your number. I'm sorry. I know I'm weak. I can't tell her no.*

She'd told him that it was all right, thanked him for the warning, and that had been that. Well, outside a text confirming their appointment to go over applications on Monday and scheduling what would become their standing Tuesday morning department head meeting between Blake, Samantha, and Emil, the chef she had yet to meet.

Samantha didn't know why, but she kept pulling up that text message and rereading it. There was something about his relationship with his mother that felt special, and Samantha wished she could capture just a little bit of that for herself.

The last time she'd seen her own mother, the woman who gave birth to her told her that as far as she was concerned, Samantha no longer existed. So there was that.

Maybe that was why when Yvette called and asked if they could meet at a donut shop not far from the yarn store, Samantha'd responded that she would be delighted. It wasn't weird to want to borrow your boss's mother for yourself, was it? Just for a couple of hours?

Yvette was waiting for her when she arrived at the shop Samantha would have driven right past. It wasn't like the pretty shop near Solaria—the one done up in pink—at all. This was a tiny place in a shopping center with a dingy sign and cheap plastic booths. But there was a line out the door.

Thankfully, Yvette spotted Samantha through the window and waved her in, and the crowd gathered outside the front door parted to let her through as Sam dodged several narrowed eyes and angry glances as she passed.

"I got here early and snagged the last two bear claws." Yvette bounced on the toes of her red-bottomed heels and shoved a giant pastry in Samantha's face. "They are heaven in the form of fried dough. Trust me."

Samantha took the sweet from Yvette but couldn't take her eyes off her shoes. She didn't know what brand had the red bottoms, but she could bet those shoes cost as much as her half of the rent. Was it normal to wear couture heels to knitting class?

"Thanks." She spied the line that curved down the shopping center's sidewalk. "Do I have to get in line for coffee?"

Yvette squealed and clapped her hands, and Samantha decided that this woman had entirely too much energy in the morning. Though, as Yvette hoisted a full cup carrier into the air, Samantha realized Yvette was probably so jovial because she'd likely had a full night's sleep. Sam'd had only a short nap after closing the sports bar.

"I didn't know what your favorite was, so I got black coffee, coffee with cream, coffee with cream and sugar, and a mocha, just in case. I obviously already had my coffee and free refill while I was waiting for you. And three donuts, but I'm pretty sure the caffeine burned off the calories from the bear claw and the other two donuts I ate." She winked. "Don't tell my husband."

Samantha only then noticed the box of a dozen more donuts resting on the table next to the cup carrier Yvette had just set down beside it. She smiled as she took the empty seat across from Blake's mom. "Don't worry. What happens on girls-only time stays on girls-only time. And I'll take the one with cream, no sugar."

Yvette plucked a large cup from the paper holder and held it out, a huge grin on her face that must have been from a sugar high. Because even if she'd managed to slip a little whiskey into her coffee, it was still way too early in the morning to be sloshed. Besides, Sam had a feeling that wasn't how Yvette rolled.

Samantha took a long pull of the coffee. It was the perfect temperature: not so cold that the bitter aftertaste bled through, but just cool enough to guzzle. And with as little sleep as she'd gotten last night—combined with her nerves about her date with Blake's mom—Samantha might've just needed to drink every coffee in that carrier, even if the liquid was frigid by the time she got to it. Caffeine was caffeine.

But then she took a bite of her bear claw and collapsed against her seat as the sugar and butter melted over her tongue and the cinnamon sparked along her taste buds. "Oh my God." The words came out in a state of near ecstasy that might have embarrassed Samantha had she been less exhausted. "Okay, now I understand the line. That is amazing."

"Wait until you try the chocolate glazed. Pure ambrosia, that one."

Samantha took another bite of her bear claw and swallowed it down with a gulp of coffee. "I'm not sure anything can best what I just ate."

Yvette grinned as if to say "Just you wait" and opened the box to display an array of multi-colored donuts with icing that sparkled in the overhead lights like precious gems on display. "My plan is to bring these with us to class and make sure we're everyone's favorites from day one. What do you say?"

Samantha didn't think Yvette needed to worry about being likable, but the donuts wouldn't hurt. And sure enough, when they arrived at the yarn shop and placed the donuts in the middle of the table, everyone squealed. The teacher even grabbed one as she reminded everyone to wash their hands before they started shopping for the yarn they were going to use to make their blankets.

Samantha was not prepared for how expensive yarn could be. She'd assumed it was around five dollars a pound like the scratchy acrylic her grandmother had always used from the craft store back home. She had to admit that a baby blanket made out of that stuff wouldn't be very nice, but what did she know? She didn't have much experience with babies—or with knitting, for that matter.

But as she trailed Yvette through the store, she had a horrible sinking feeling that she could not afford this hobby. They were supposed to make a blanket that took three skeins of worsted-weight yarn, and almost every skein of yarn Yvette picked up to coo over was at least twenty dollars apiece. Samantha definitely did not have sixty dollars to spend on yarn. She barely had the forty dollars to cover the class.

"What do you think?" Yvette asked, holding up a brilliant emerald-green yarn with subtle variegation. "This is gender-neutral, right?"

"It's gorgeous."

"It makes me happy. Like a greenhouse strung in twinkle lights and gemstones." She nodded toward the stone-colored yarn in Samantha's hand. "Is that what you're getting?"

The yarn she held was mostly gray but had soft tones of tan and pink and a pastel blue color running throughout. It was gorgeous, but it was also the most expensive skein she'd looked at so far.

"Oh, no." Samantha placed the yarn back on top of the pile she'd plucked it from. "I think I need to check out the clearance section."

"Nonsense." Yvette plucked up three skeins of the yarn Samantha had been admiring. "I basically bullied you into this—the least I can do is foot the bill. Is that what you want?"

Samantha nodded but couldn't meet Yvette's eyes as she said, "I really can't accept—"

Yvette cut her off. "Go grab one of those chocolate-glazed donuts before the girl with the septum ring decides she wants it. And while you're at it, ask her where she got it done. I've been thinking I need one for myself."

Samantha spluttered out a laugh and glanced at the table where indeed there *was* a woman with a septum ring, probably around Blake's age, eyeing the last chocolate-glazed donut. The piercing looked good on her, but was Yvette serious about getting one of her own? By the time Samantha turned around to ask the older woman if she was, Yvette had already made her way to the checkout counter, credit card in hand.

She would let Yvette win this one, but someday soon, Samantha would make sure she paid her back.

CONSTRUCTION HAD FINALLY wrapped up enough for Blake to move into his office instead of spreading his work all over the tables out front. Everything was still covered in dust, but at least he could organize everything and hopefully, eventually, be able to pull up his receipts without covering himself in debris.

Today, he'd dressed in jeans and a t-shirt he didn't mind getting dirty, a plain gray one he'd picked up at a box store. He'd donated his extensive collection of Grace Bible ministry t-shirts last year. Wearing them was too much of a reminder of how royally he'd screwed all that up. The job. The example he was supposed to be. His relationship with Rachel—every time he saw one of those damn t-shirts, he remembered the way Rachel had worn them without asking after they'd spent the night together. Did she wear Nicolas's t-shirts now?

Probably.

Blake hadn't actually seen them in the same space since they'd gotten together, but he did follow Rachel's Instagram feed, and that was enough. Their existence was idyllic in her photographs. The two of them always smiling, their kids outside, their fixer-upper house slowly transforming into a cozy country cottage.

Every time he scrolled past one of her images, the same blast of regret struck his chest like a bolt of lightning. He'd nearly unfollowed her a million times just because the shock sometimes stole his breath. But Blake couldn't begrudge them their happiness, even if Nicolas was once again living the life Blake wanted. And once again making it look effortless.

Blake knew it wasn't effortless, that Nicolas had suffered. That Rachel had grieved. That they'd spent months apart before finding one another again. But still, seeing photographs from their wedding and knowing that he hadn't been invited hurt.

But Blake hadn't deserved to be there.

Torturing himself, Blake pulled out his phone and scrolled until he found the most recent posts from Rachel's feed. The wedding had been last weekend and had taken place outside near sunset, basking Rachel in the golden glow of the setting sun. She was radiant. Her dark hair was styled into long waves, a crown of roses so deep red they were almost black rested on her brow, and she held a matching bouquet in her hand. Someone had convinced her to wear a cream-colored dress. Its trailing sleeves and high waistline made her look like a fairy-tale princess. And Nicolas, his hand on the soft new roundness of her baby bump, grinned like he'd just been crowned king of the world.

The picture both zapped that jealous place in his chest and made him tear up at how happy he was for the people who had once been so important to him. And he wasn't sure how to reconcile the two feelings yet. He still wasn't sure if he wanted to be the one in the photo with Rachel instead of Nicolas or if he just wanted to find someone who made him as happy as they seemed to make each other.

Blake was wiping the tears from his eyes when his father strolled straight into his office. No knock. No apologies. No nothing.

He harrumphed at the sight of his son crying then stuck his hands in his pockets and strolled around the room like he was the county inspector looking for faults. "The place looks like it's coming together."

Blake certainly hoped so. They opened in three weeks, and he was terrified they wouldn't be ready.

He sniffed and wiped his eyes with his wrist. Blake couldn't hide his emotion from his father, but he also knew his father wouldn't ask him what was wrong. Strong emotions were meant to be kept private, something to be dealt with on his own, between him and God. Outwardly, the only acceptable emotions to display were strength and confidence. Steadfastness.

Vulnerability was weakness.

Blake had never felt more fragile than he had in these last two years. And part of him yearned to be able to confide in his father, to tell him that he was tired of performing, of trying to be who everyone else thought he should be. That maybe he *had* screwed up massively, that he'd estranged himself forever from the two people who had taught him how important honesty was, and he was finding it difficult to breathe under the crushing weight of the guilt.

But instead, he only shrugged and said, "Let's just hope all the deliveries arrive on time for opening day."

Blake didn't know how to tell his father that he was afraid to have an honest conversation with him because he couldn't disappoint James any more than he had already.

"Hope doesn't have much to do with it if you're not trusting it to God."

Blake held back his grimace and had to concentrate to unstick his tongue from the roof of his mouth. He didn't have words for comments like those anymore. All he felt was disapproval. Disappointment. And Blake knew his disillusionment with the church would only drive a deeper wedge between himself and his father.

He didn't want to end up like Kat, who hadn't spoken to her parents since she'd introduced them to Naomi, her girlfriend, last year. He desperately wished his parents could be like Naomi's parents, who had raised two queer daughters to be proud of themselves, to go after what they wanted both personally and professionally.

Not that Blake was anything but straight. But if he weren't, he had no doubt that his mother would continue trying to set him up with whomever she thought he might like, but Blake wasn't certain his father would ever speak to him again. Or that he and his mom wouldn't have to meet in secret. And that hypothetical abandonment bothered him more and more as time went on.

"Unless you're above praying now," his father said as he slipped *The Craft of the Cocktail* off the shelf behind Blake's desk. Blake had only just shelved it there, and he didn't appreciate the way his dad cavalierly flipped through the book then dropped it onto a pile of files on Blake's desk that he'd been trying to organize. "You're glorifying vice with all this."

Blake snorted an involuntary laugh as his gaze fell on the book his dad had uncovered by removing the one full of alcoholic beverages. That one was titled *Gluttony* and had a photo of a giant hamburger on the front. Oh, the irony.

"I'm creating jobs and building a community."

"Your mother's bakery did that."

"Yeah, well, mom's community isn't exactly my community."

His father cocked his head to the side as if he had too much to say and he couldn't decide what to say first. He went with "I think you're stuck on that bartender friend of yours, and that's what all of this is about. You're creating this for her."

Blake leaned back against the bookshelf behind him and crossed his arms. "Which bartender friend?" He knew who his dad meant, but Blake wanted him to say her name.

"That Rachel woman you were fornicating with a couple of years ago."

"You mean the woman I bought a ring for? The one I wanted to marry?"

His dad's lips disappeared into the beard that was the salt-and-pepper version of Blake's. "I didn't know you'd bought a ring." His voice softened like he hadn't entertained the idea that his son had ever been in a serious relationship—or even wanted one.

It was on the tip of Blake's tongue to say that his mother had known. He'd told her he wanted to propose even before he'd said anything to Nicolas and asked his friend to go ring shopping with him. But the fact that his mother hadn't confided in his father made him bite the words back. There had been a time when sharing that Yvette had kept something from James would have ended with him and his mother cowering in the closet while his father rampaged. And though his dad had been sober for years, Blake still hesitated to share too much.

His urge to protect his mother usually won out over everything else.

"Yeah, well, I screwed that one up anyway. But Garden and Gather isn't for Rachel. It's for me, Dad. Because I need to figure out where I belong."

His father shook his head, and Blake sighed. Regardless of how much his father had learned about his relationship with Rachel just now, the gates had closed. James hid behind a fortress of church-regimented ideals. Blake had nearly given up hope that his father would ever accept that Blake had left his former vocation.

"You belong in the ministry."

Blake uncrossed his arms and picked the book up off the pile of folders, placing it back on the shelf as he shored up his own defenses. He still felt like his father could home in on the way Blake's heart thudded in his chest, on the way he feared delving into this conversation with him. Because Blake wasn't even sure he believed in God anymore, let alone in his ability to lead others closer to Him.

"I am flattered that you want me to work with you. But I don't—"

"Helloooo, my darlings!" Blake's mother's voice rang out from the dining room. "We saw your cars outside, so we know you're both here."

Her voice grew closer with every word, and Blake could make out the sound of two sets of footsteps. His heart started thudding for a whole new reason. This morning had been the knitting date, which meant that those second set of footsteps likely belonged to—

Samantha followed his mother into the office, a blissful smile on her face which melted as she glanced between Blake and his father.

"There you are, dears. I brought treats." If his mother noticed the tension between her husband and son, she said nothing. She dropped a kiss on James's cheek as she passed and plopped a greasy sack Blake suspected was full of tortilla chips onto her son's desk. Then she planted a kiss on Blake's cheek as well before spinning in a circle in the middle of his office. "You've done so much with the place in the last few days. I'm really starting to see a restaurant."

"Thanks," he said at the same time his father asked, "And how was knitting class?"

Samantha shrunk into the far corner as if she wished she could disappear. Blake fought the instinct to go to her and pull her back into the conversation, to assure her that she wasn't intruding on a family moment.

"Brilliant," Yvette offered in response to James's question as she fished in her bag for something while crossing the room to her husband's side. "I mean, I am atrocious at it so far."

She pulled a wad of green yarn and wooden needles connected by a cord from her oversized Coach bag. "Luckily, Samantha is a natural. We're getting together again on Tuesday, and she's going to help me get started properly. She got further than anybody else in class. You should see her project."

Samantha's cheeks flushed pink, and Blake could tell she'd rather fade into the woodwork than have all the attention on her.

"Show them, dear," Yvette said, drawing her by the hand out of the corner. "No need to be shy around these two. They're perfectly harmless, I promise."

Blake's father met his eyes before his gaze flitted back to the women. The trepidation Blake saw there told him more about his father than his dad had ever said aloud. James Fairchild did not consider himself harmless. He considered himself a caged wolf, tame in the right circumstance but viscous as soon as the lock was released.

The idea saddened Blake, because there were times when he also viewed his father that way. Though it had been decades since either he or his mother had had any reason to feel that sort of fear, somewhere, deep down, Blake couldn't forget.

At Yvette's coaxing, Samantha pulled her knitting project out of her own bag. The yarn was a gray that looked so soft, Blake was tempted to run his fingers over the small stripe of ridged stitches Samantha had knit so far. "I only got about three rows in, but I did get the hang of the stitches pretty fast, even if I'm still slow at it."

"Compared to me, you're lightning fast," Yvette said. "Now what are you two up to?"

Blake met his father's gaze again, and both clearly decided not to divulge their topic of conversation—the same one it had been since Blake had turned down the youth minister position at his father's church a year and a half ago.

"Just unpacking the office," Blake said.

His father amended, "And I came to see if I could take him out to lunch. It appears you two have already eaten."

Yvette grinned. "There's this adorable little Mexican restaurant next door to the knitting shop. We went with a bunch of the girls from class for tacos afterward. But I can grab you both some takeout. I know the chips are only a snack for you two."

"I've eaten already," Blake lied. He hadn't had anything since his protein smoothie after his run this morning, but he'd had enough of his dad's judgment for one day.

"That's wonderful, because after my eventful morning, I am exhausted." Yvette affected a yawn and hooked her arm through her husband's. "Drive me home so I can nap? We can come back for my car later."

"Whatever you want," his dad said, unmistakable fondness for his wife in his eyes.

"Blake, be a dear and drive Samantha back to her car?" his mother asked then named her favorite donut shop. Blake nodded once, knowing resistance was useless.

When his parents had gone, Blake turned to Samantha with raised eyebrows. "See what I mean?"

Chapter Six

Samantha felt her cheeks flush even deeper than they were already. "You did warn me. I'm sorry. She really was lovely all morning, but I suppose I should have seen this coming when she wanted to come here."

"It's okay. She's sneaky." Blake shook his head and snatched his keys from the top of his desk. "I assume you need to get home."

She nodded. "I have my last shift at the sports bar tonight."

Blake grinned. "That's right. Then you're all mine." As soon as the words were out of his mouth, the tips of his ears burned bright red and he tripped over the foot of his desk. "I meant professionally. Not—"

"It's fine." Samantha wasn't sure they would ever get over this awkward sexual tension bubbling between them, but she did her best to brush his comment off. "I knew what you meant."

Blake led her out to his car, which was exactly what she expected it to be: a black sports car sort of thing. She wasn't knowledgeable enough about cars to know what it was, but it perfectly matched his manner of dress and the luxury she'd seen from his family so far.

They were quiet for the first few minutes of the drive, and the lack of discussion grated on her nerves. They should've had plenty to talk about, right? She had so many questions about the restaurant, and she was so excited to get well and truly started, but most of her questions would probably be answered in their meeting on Monday. And, well, she was a little bit stuck on how he'd been right about Yvette pushing them together.

"So that was your dad?" Samantha cringed. Lamest opener ever.

"Yeah. His name is James. Sorry I didn't introduce you. We were—"

"You were arguing?" Samantha guessed. James had been breathing too fast, and Blake's jaw had been clenched when they'd entered the office earlier.

Blake squirmed in his seat then reached to shift gears on his car as if trying to hide his discomfort. "We weren't arguing exactly. Things have been . . . tense . . . between us since I left the church."

Samantha felt a pulse deep inside her chest as she learned about this common ground between them. "What do you mean 'left the church'?"

"Oh." Blake twisted his left hand on the steering wheel for a second and squirmed again like he hadn't meant to give away that much information. "That's just what I used to do when I lived in Topeka. I was on staff at a big church there, doing everything from youth to children's ministries. I was on the outreach team when I left, working with the local colleges."

Samantha would not have guessed that. She'd assumed he'd worked in a more professional capacity, like at an advertising company or as an actuary or something.

"So, like, you were in charge of all the children's ministries? For boys and girls?"

Blake quirked an eyebrow at her as he drove, and she dragged the cross pendant on her necklace up and down the chain.

"Yeah."

She nodded then realized he must find her question odd, because he kept sneaking glances at her out of the corner of his eye. "It's just that, where I grew up, the girls were only ever taught by women, usually our moms. The boys would go with one of the dads for Sunday school. We all worshipped together as a group, but gender was more important than age group like I've seen at other churches."

Blake nodded as he drove. "What about non-binary people?"

Samantha shook her head. Male headship had been such an ingrained part of her childhood, she hadn't really encountered the idea of gender fluidity until she went to college. "Conformity was mandatory."

Blake nodded again. "But the women were allowed to teach?"

"I mean, we were all homeschooled, so it was our mom's main job to teach us. But on Sundays, our lessons were mainly concerned with biblical womanhood and preparing to serve our husbands."

She could see Blake nodding again out of the corner of her eye. "Sounds like you're from an even more conservative church than I am."

Samantha kept her focus out the window. She didn't think she could handle it if he pitied her after she let him into this private part of her past—it was why she rarely spoke about it. "I think of it as more of a cult these days."

"Wow. That bad?"

"My parents haven't spoken to me since I left for college against their wishes."

Samantha bit her lip, and her heart pounded when she saw Blake's beautiful features fold into a frown as he merged onto the highway. "But you went to a Bible college."

"Yes, but I had to leave home to go there."

"That's—"

"Ridiculous?"

"Yeah."

Samantha shrugged. "Maybe not. I mean, I did become everything my parents feared. An independent, unmarried woman of the world doing sinful things with my time and serving the Devil's drink for my job."

Blake groaned as he pulled up to a stoplight. He swiveled his head so he could look her in the eye, and Samantha couldn't fight the pull to face him. She was not prepared for how the thrill of his full attention trilled in her stomach.

"Sorry. It's just that one of the biggest things I always told my college students was that they couldn't do things just to please their parents: choosing majors, picking romantic partners, attending the right church. It was their life, and they had to make the decisions that they could live with—the rest was between them and God. You did what you needed to do, and that's commendable."

Samantha shrugged then crossed her arms in an attempt to hide how his approval had her fingers trembling. She wanted to tell him that she went to college because she was desperate to get out and because she was afraid that if she didn't leave, the same thing that happened to her sister would happen to her, but she wasn't ready to share that much about her past. Instead, she asked, "And is that what you believe now? That our personal decisions are between us and God?"

The light changed, and Blake sighed as he pulled into the intersection. "I think that sometimes we're a lot more honest with ourselves when we take God out of the equation. That it's most important to make decisions for yourself that you can live with. And to think about the consequences—the *real* consequences, not just the outcome you want."

Samantha wanted to ask if he was speaking from experience, if that was why he'd left the church and why she heard a tinge of regret in the tone of his voice, but that's when she saw it: a silver Prius turning right out of the intersection and taking the space behind them in traffic.

It couldn't have been Mason. No way could he have tracked her. She'd been all over the place with Yvette, and Mason would have no way of knowing she was in Blake's car at this very moment. Besides, he should be showing up at Solarium for the Saturday night shift right about now.

Blake's windows were tinted, so while Samantha would have normally kept her eyes straight forward and tried to ignore the silver car in her side mirror, she allowed herself to peek over her shoulder once, twice, knowing she wouldn't be seen by the other driver. But the car was too far behind them to make out the driver clearly.

"Hey, are you okay?"

"I'm fine." It was a lie. Sam's heart was pounding in her throat and threatening to block her breath. But she also couldn't help throwing a glance over her shoulder again. She decided the silhouette could be Mason's, and her heart thudded even harder.

"You look like you're going to pass out," Blake said. "Do I need to pull over?"

"No!" Samantha yelled, her voice cracking. "Keep going. If you can lose the car behind us, even better."

She watched his eyes track the car behind them through his rearview mirror. Then he nodded once. "Okay."

Blake signaled for the next right, and the car followed them through the turn. Samantha's knuckles turned white as she clutched the armrest, and her grip didn't loosen as Blake took a circuitous route through Midtown on their way back toward the donut shop in the West Bottoms.

They took an extra fifteen minutes to get back to Sam's car, but she was used to that. What she hadn't been expecting was Blake pulling into the empty parking spot next to her car and turning to her to ask, "What was that all about?"

She should have explained herself, probably as soon as they'd turned left and the Prius had kept driving straight, but she couldn't. She picked at her cuticles, something she'd only picked up since this whole thing with Mason had started. Before that, she hadn't done it since she'd left her parents' house.

"I didn't want to tell you yet, and I really hope it doesn't change your mind about bringing me onto your team for Garden and Gather, but I've kind of been dealing with a stalker for the last few months, and he drives a silver Prius."

Blake blinked at her as he assimilated the information. "It doesn't change anything, no. But I'd like to know as much as you're willing to tell me so that we can make sure we're doing everything we can to protect you."

Samantha told him everything, and not the short version, either. She hadn't meant to, but when she'd opened her mouth, the whole thing poured out like a pressure valve being released. She hadn't realized she'd been waiting to talk to someone other than Charlotte about what she'd been going through.

Not that Charlotte hadn't been supportive. But sometimes Samantha felt guilty for sharing everything with her friend. It was a burden Charlotte didn't deserve, yet one that Samantha often found too heavy to carry on her own.

Samantha wasn't sure when Blake had entwined his fingers in hers, but when she finished her story, she was clinging to his hand, her other clenched around her phone. The phone was still on silent from their time at the yarn store, but when Samantha tipped it toward her and saw it was ringing, she jolted to attention.

"Shit." Samantha leaned down, reaching into the footwell to disentangle her bag's strap from around her ankles.

"What's wrong?" The alarm in Blake's voice echoed her own as he too sat forward in his seat.

"I'm half an hour late for work."

He settled back into his seat with a sigh. "Oh, that's not a big deal."

Samantha raised an eyebrow at him despite her panic. "What do you mean 'it's not a big deal'?"

"I mean, it's your last day, right?"

"Yeah, and?"

"Is it really a problem if you don't show up?"

"I—" Samantha opened her mouth, but no more words came out.

"You hate it there, and it's not like your current employer will think badly of you for taking a well-deserved day off."

"But—"

"There's a place—a brewery—on the west side that's billed as being a friendly neighborhood joint, and I'm curious to see what that looks like. Why don't you come with me?"

"I . . . but—"

"If you're worried about the money, we can make it a work outing. You can tell me all the reasons their bar and setup are wrong, all the things you want to do differently, and all the ways I've already messed everything up."

She hid a smirk as she thought about it. It wasn't about the money, not really. Things would be close these next couple of weeks until she started getting her regular paychecks from Garden & Gather, but Blake was paying her a generous amount.

"I've never broken rules like that before," she said, her voice smaller than she would have liked.

"Ah, well, I never claimed I wasn't a bad influence." He flashed her one of his brilliant, shiny grins. "What do you say?"

Samantha made the mistake of meeting Blake's eyes, and the playful mischief glowing there was too much for her to resist. She couldn't even fight the smile forming on her lips.

"Alright. Let's go."

———————◦———————

"OKAY, BUT YOU SEE HOW that server right there had to wait to put in her order?" Samantha motioned with her Boulevardier toward where one server had basically jumped on the iPad the second another had walked away.

"What about it?" he asked. He'd also been sipping on a Boulevardier at Samantha's recommendation for a sophisticated whiskey drink, but he wasn't sure he was a fan of the bittersweet flavor.

"That tells me they don't have enough POS stations for how big they are. It's not even busy yet, and they're fighting over iPads? That means they're more willing to save a few dollars than to invest in good service, which would probably make them more money than they spent on it."

Blake nodded, watching the servers' expressions from where they sat at the bar, enjoying the way that Samantha had relaxed once she was comfortable in her environment. "How many POS stations do you think we'll need?"

"One more than you think you'll need."

"I have two."

"Behind the bar?"

"No, two in total. One for the bartender and one for the servers." Her eyes lifted to the ceiling as if she was calling for divine patience. "You'll want to have at least two for the servers. I would put one in the solarium since it's so far from the bar. That way, the servers can get orders back to the kitchen or the bar more quickly. But two behind the bar wouldn't hurt, either. Especially for peak times."

Blake pulled his phone out and added buying more iPads to his agenda, and he didn't miss the way Samantha smiled into her glass with ill-concealed satisfaction. He would pretend he hadn't felt that thrill of pride well in his chest. It was too similar to the way he'd felt when Kat had started to accidentally-on-purpose graze his arm with her nails or the way he'd delighted in successfully making Rachel roll her eyes and grin at the same time. Blake had learned not to trust that feeling. It only led to scandal and self-loathing.

"What do you think of their liquor selection?" he asked, and her attention focused in on the shelves behind the bar. They were stuffed with colorful bottles, many Blake was unfamiliar with, and more than he had expected since the place was primarily a brewery. Their selection of tap beer was enormous.

Samantha shrugged. "Way too many bottles. They probably only sell three or four of each type of liquor."

"Noted. I'll try to remind you of that when you have your first meeting with the reps."

Samantha spluttered and waved her hand. "I know most of those guys already. They can't play me."

Samantha looked so sweet and so young that he was certain most of them thought they could talk her into anything. Blake looked forward to watching her show them differently.

He imagined her flashing them a teasing smile, their superiority in working with a woman just rolling off her back. He imagined her telling them why their new recommendation was awful and why she wanted to stick with what she had. Or just tasting new wines and enjoying herself.

It might be too easy to admire her. Especially after he'd seen her vulnerability earlier. When she'd told him about her stalker, he'd wanted to protect her and possibly do bodily harm to him. Who in their right mind would try to harm someone so unassuming and sweet as Samantha?

Blake couldn't fathom it. He might not have always behaved like a gentleman, but at the very least, he respected a woman's boundaries.

He took another sip of his drink, and the bittersweet flavor of orange peel coated his tongue. "I'm not sure I like this," he said.

She swished the ice in her own drink, which was mostly empty. "Totally agree. Waaay too much Campari. When we get our liquor order, I'll make you one that's more balanced. You'll like it, I think."

The invitation to hit the liquor store and let her experiment with drinks over at his place was on the tip of his tongue. But no. That's what he would do if he were on a date. And this wasn't a date. This was a work outing. A bonding experience amongst coworkers. Nothing more.

Even if his body was responding to Samantha's proximity. To her smile. To the way that wisp of blonde hair escaped her ponytail and brushed across the pinkest part of her cheek.

Part of him was relieved he was finally able to be interested in a woman who wasn't Rachel, but the larger part of him berated himself for that woman being his employee.

Just another example of him always being interested in the wrong woman.

"I'd like that," Blake said instead, and he couldn't quite bury the feeling that he was making the wrong decision by not inviting her home.

Chapter Seven

Samantha readied herself for church in a daze on Sunday morning. She'd barely slept the night before, remembering the way Blake had stared at her lips for a solid ten seconds when he'd dropped her off. If she hadn't known better, Samantha would have said that Blake had been tempted to kiss her. But even though he hadn't touched her at all, Samantha couldn't stop fantasizing about what might have happened if he had.

Her mind still fogged with lustful dreams, Samantha donned her favorite flowy green dress that her mother would've never let her wear out of the house, let alone to church. The hemline hit above her knee. The neckline was a V that was almost deep enough to hint at cleavage. The gauzy sleeves were about the length of any respectable t-shirt, but they were split down the middle to allow for extra flounce. All her mother would have seen was more skin.

She would have told Samantha she was courting trouble in a dress like that, that others would only value her as much as she respected herself. That dressing provocatively only signaled that she had low self-esteem and needed the attention of men to feel valued. And she'd say it while insisting that all the value Samantha needed could be found in serving God.

But as Samantha rotated from side to side in the mirror, she thought she looked cute. Sure, her legs were showing, but though it was early fall, the weather had yet to turn cold.

When she'd staggered to the bathroom half an hour ago, Charlotte had called the green floral dress "sweet" and told Samantha she looked like a doll before she'd collapsed back into bed. She hadn't come home until about three in the morning, and though Samantha hadn't gotten the whole scoop yet, she was fairly certain her roommate had finally hooked up with the hot bartender she'd been gushing about for the last month.

Samantha was only slightly jealous. On one hand, she wasn't ready to be intimate with anyone after what had gone down with Mason. On the other . . . she would be lying if she said she hadn't maybe done a little bit of fantasizing about what last night could have been like. If instead of Blake driving her back to her car at the donut shop, he'd driven her back to his place, she'd made them a few cocktails, and, well . . .

In her mind, the orgasms she'd given herself had all occurred by his hand.

Samantha was aware of how problematic that desire was, but she was also honest enough with herself to understand that if he propositioned her, she might not be strong enough to say no. He was just so intensely beautiful that she couldn't help but want to sample a bit of that intensity for herself.

All night, her mind had conjured up scenarios of how delicious colliding physically with Blake would be, but . . . But. As relieved as she was that she could lust after another man given how badly Mason had scarred her, Samantha knew she would never cross that line with her boss. The job at Garden & Gather was too important to her healing journey.

This was a real, professional position, and she deserved this victory. She was not going to sabotage it.

Instead, Samantha was determined to focus on the opportunity she had in front of her to prove she was the best person for this job.

But first, she was going to that new church she'd seen when she'd been exploring the neighborhood around Garden & Gather. Samantha was actually a little excited about this one, and she hadn't been enthusiastic about any church she'd visited in years. Every time she sat in a pew in an unfamiliar building, made polite small talk with strangers, listened to a new preacher, and sang new songs, Samantha always felt like she didn't deserve to have a seat within those walls.

Even if everyone seemed welcoming. In fact, the friendliest churches made her feel the worst, like she was deceiving them.

Samantha wasn't sure she was a believer. She wasn't sure she ever had been. Growing up, she hadn't had a choice but to follow the set of rules her parents had laid out for her. Those rules left no room for deviation if she wanted to be able to sit for the next week.

But now? Samantha recognized that choosing a new church every week was akin to penance. She could almost hear her mother's voice in her ear telling her she was going to go to hell, so her regular attendance was holding the fear that hell was real at bay. But more importantly, her Sunday morning activities were her clinging onto the hope that just because she'd rejected the life her family wanted for her didn't mean she was a terrible person.

At her core, in the day to day, Samantha did not feel like she was a bad person. She felt like she was doing the best she could—that she deserved joy, and sometimes that joy came from the way gin smoothed over her tongue or whiskey sparked in her chest. Or the way a freshly uncorked bottle of wine smelled. But even though she didn't often drink past a pleasant buzz, Sam still felt guilty on some level that she'd made a career out of alcohol.

And maybe she went to church because some part of her held onto the hope that maybe she'd find a kind and supportive family to replace the one who didn't want her anymore.

Just thinking of the church she had chosen this week made her smile. It was nestled in a residential neighborhood not far from Garden & Gather's shopping center. The building wasn't large or imposing like the ones that looked more like a school than a church—it was one of those classic all-white churches with a bell tower and a tall steeple topped with an unassuming cross. It hadn't seemed large enough to house more than a sanctuary, but Samantha had learned by now that it was difficult to judge a church by the outside—even if the oranges and yellows and reds of the flower beds surrounding the front steps made it look cheerfully welcoming.

The church could have been in a painting, and Samantha was hoping she'd find an equally inviting congregation inside with a soft-spoken preacher proclaiming the divine beauty of creation rather than the brokenness of humanity.

As she pulled up to the church, hope fluttered through her chest. The same multi-colored mums she'd spotted earlier in the week bloomed around the church surrounded by cheerful ivy and other greenery Samantha couldn't identify. The parking lot was small but full, which suggested a loyal and likely intimate congregation.

A bashful anonymity clung to her as she walked through the doors, just like it did every week.

She accepted a bulletin from a casually dressed man who asked her if it was her first time visiting their church. When she answered in the affirmative, he escorted her into the modest sanctuary and motioned toward a pew on the right side of the aisle, three back from the front. She was just about to take a seat when a familiar voice called her name—and all the blood drained out of her head.

She teetered as she turned, the toe of her boot catching on her opposite ankle. A large warm hand gripped her elbow to steady her, and the shock of awareness that bolted down her spine at his touch was enough to make her stumble again.

"Whoa, there. You doing okay?" Blake asked, his hands on both her elbows now.

Samantha nodded and tried to say "yes," but no sound came out, so she swallowed and tried again. "I'm fine. I just didn't expect to see you here is all."

The visions of her fantasies were still too fresh in her mind—what his lips would feel like against hers, what he would look like with his shirt off and his hair mussed, the way his fingers would feel as they dug into her hips.

Her cheeks pinked as she realized she was standing in the middle of a church sanctuary thinking naughty thoughts about her boss.

"This is my dad's church," he said, "and I have a cousin—well, great-nephew—getting baptized today, so attendance was mandatory." He considered her for a moment, his sparkling eyes turning contemplative. "Did my mother invite you?"

Samantha raised her chin, trying not to let on that his suspicions had the power to offend her. She might have accepted an invitation to church from Yvette in a few weeks' time if she had asked. But even if Blake's mother's aim was to again force them to spend time together, that's not why Samantha would have accepted. "No. I drove past the other day and thought it looked cute."

Blake's eyes turned from contemplative to curious. "I didn't realize you still went to church." His gaze dropped to her lips, and tingles erupted in Samantha's belly. The heat from where his hands still grasped her elbows mixed with the tingles to cause a molten elixir that was going to turn her into a pile of sinful goo right here in the sanctuary.

"It's certainly picturesque," he said, and Samantha didn't have time to interpret his tone of voice because Yvette spotted them then and pulled her into an embrace, breaking Blake's hold on Sam's arms.

"Oh my goodness—how did you end up here, child? Did Blake bring you as a shield? I practically had to bribe him to get him to come today."

"It's just happenstance." Samantha clung to Yvette, so strangely thankful for the embrace that she felt tears prick at the back of her eyes. *Hold it together, will you? It's just a hug.*

"I'm going to call it divine intervention," Yvette said as she pulled away. "Come now. I have people I want you to meet, and then you're going to sit with us."

When Samantha opened her mouth to protest, Yvette raised a hand to stop her. "No arguments; it's already decided. And we're having a big lunch afterward to celebrate Elliot's baptism. You'll stay for that, too."

Samantha vaguely wondered if any excuse would have been good enough to garner her permission not to do as Yvette said, but since she didn't have any plans other than laundry and binge-watching Netflix shows, Samantha didn't even try.

She spent the next ten minutes being introduced to Yvette's friends and family members while Blake looked on with his hands in his pockets. His usual brightness seemed dimmed somewhat. His eyes were dull, his shoulders rounded. He was still gorgeous, but even the way he was dressed, with his white shirt and gray trousers, made him look like he was trying not to be seen. And Samantha couldn't figure out why that was.

He'd said he'd left the church, but he'd never clarified why. And only now did Samantha wonder if maybe his past was as traumatic as hers.

———◆———

OBJECTIVELY, THE SANCTUARY was a beautiful one. The walls were lined with tall, colorful, stained-glass windows. The woodwork was warm and cheery combined with the white walls and exposed rafters. But Blake had a hard time enjoying the beauty of the room when his own adolescent spiritual awakening had happened in this very hall.

At least that's how he'd thought of it at the time. The call to the front of the church near the end of one of his dad's first sermons. The prayer that was said. The baptism that followed. The call to the ministry. His ordination behind that pulpit. His first sermon.

But also within these walls, sitting in this exact pew, he had started to doubt himself for the first time. The day after his first rendezvous with Kat had been Christmas Eve. Blake had been equal parts elated and devastated as he imagined Kat going through the motions of Christmas with her kids and Nicolas. He'd desperately wanted to trade places with her husband that day. To have him somehow out of the equation entirely so Blake could drop into his role, despite Nicolas being his best friend. He'd wanted Nicolas to be the single one. The one on the outside looking in.

Blake had been that petty.

He recognized now that he'd been more in love with the idea of an instant family, of a shortcut to having what he'd always wanted, what Nicolas had seemed to cultivate so effortlessly. Blake had had the audacity to think that he could do better than his best friend at being a husband and father. He wouldn't have taken his family for granted the way he thought Nicolas had been doing.

Now he knew he'd been deluding himself. But that first day after, Blake had spent Christmas Eve vacillating between memories of his lustfully charged encounter with his best friend's wife and wondering what kind of man he was to give into that temptation—and if he'd even deserved to call himself a Man of God after that.

He'd deluded himself in so many ways during those months, made so many wrong choices. And sitting here in his father's church, watching his little cousin step into the baptistry, Blake couldn't help but think back to his own baptism. How, at sixteen, he'd been so proud to wade into the waters and allow his father to dunk him beneath the surface.

And only with twenty years' distance did Blake understand that he'd been proud of his father's smile. Of the way his father boasted that Blake was meant to follow him into the ministry. Of the way James told his testimony and always finished with how he was going to be an example so his own son didn't lose decades of his life to dissipation—how he was going to be a Man of God so his son would be able to enter adulthood with his head and his heart in the right place.

Blake had been so confident that had been true once upon a time, but now? He wasn't even sure who he was anymore.

And as he watched his ten-year-old cousin disappear beneath the surface of the pool, all he could think was that Elliot was probably doing what he thought he should do to gain approval from his parents and praise from the church. He likely didn't understand that a full-immersion baptism was meant to signify turning away from an old way of life and being reborn anew into the way of Christ. What vice was a ten-year-old who had been raised in the church turning away from?

Blake had to consciously unclench his jaw as those around him applauded. He couldn't even bring himself to pretend, even though his mother was grinning wide and clapping her palms together with enthusiasm.

A quick glance to his right showed him that Samantha was as quiet and stoic as he was. Her face was as pale as the white robe his cousin wore.

He raised his eyebrows at her in question, and her lips trembled as she gave an almost imperceptible shake of her head. Without thinking, Blake pulled her hand onto his leg and squeezed her fingers in comfort. Samantha squeezed back as he focused his gaze on the platform at the front of the room where his dad had started speaking.

He might have looked like he was listening, but his attention was completely on Samantha and the way she discreetly wiped away a tear with her free hand. When she squeezed his hand back despite her trembling fingers, he wondered exactly what trauma was in her past.

Protectiveness surged through him with a fierceness he had not expected. He would admit to lingering with her over drinks at the brewery the night before because of his nerves over coming here today. The distraction had been welcome, but he'd told himself the entire time it had just been a work thing, that witnessing how something as simple as a certain type of car triggered her panic just meant that he wasn't actually dead inside and he could care about other people in a normal way.

Blake had taken it as a sign that he wasn't fundamentally broken after all.

But now, as he noticed his thumb running tender circles over her palm? Was he supposed to convince himself that was a purely comforting gesture? Because Blake was finding it difficult to ignore how soft her skin was and how she smelled—sweet but grounded, like summer did after a rainstorm.

These were not things he should be noticing about his employee, especially not one he intended to work so closely with and rely on to make his business a success. Not when his track record with women and relationships was so dismal—because she'd have the power to tank his fledgling restaurant when he inevitably screwed up.

But at the same time, he couldn't make himself stop. Not even when he noticed his mother sneaking covert glances at his hand joined with Samantha's, their hands still resting on his thigh while her lips turned up in a smugly satisfied smile.

Chapter Eight

Samantha hadn't watched a baptism since she was in high school. She hadn't expected to have such an extreme reaction to watching a child that young go through the immersion, but all she could remember was her own baptism.

She'd been baptized at the same time her older sister had. Sarah had been eleven; Samantha had been nine. They hadn't been baptized in a church because her family had been attending a home church at the time with about four other families. The church had had no real pastor, but the man whose house they met at most often had become the de facto leader.

That man, Tim Jennings, had baptized Sarah and Sam in his backyard pool in front of the rest of the families and their children. Samantha remembered being proud that day. Because getting baptized demonstrated to her parents—and to others—that she was doing what she was supposed to do. That Samantha knew what was expected of her, and that she could follow through.

She remembered feeling a different type of triumphant the day she was allowed to follow in her sister's footsteps and get a job at Tim's little café in town. Between homeschool and helping to take care of her younger siblings, Samantha hadn't had much opportunity to experience life outside the confines of her family's home.

She'd found solace in sewing as a teenager. It was an approved activity that allowed her to express herself creatively, but her mom had complained about her requests for new fabric enough that her dad had agreed she could work for someone they knew and trusted. Samantha had jumped at the small opportunity for independence. And after making her family contribution, she could spend as much money on sewing supplies as she wanted.

She had felt so grown up and capable at first. Like she might be capable of true independence. Like if she didn't want it, she didn't have to choose the same lifestyle her parents had, even though that was the only choice that had ever been presented to her.

She'd even started to save a little bit of money. Samantha had had no real plans, but she'd known, on some level, that despite her family's claims of their unbreakable support structure, someday she might need to put herself first.

Her mistrust had grown after her father's ulterior motive for allowing Sarah and her to get jobs became apparent. As the months and years wore on and their parents continued to have more children, the percentage of their paychecks their father took as their "family portion" continued to grow.

Samantha had rebelled by sewing herself a skirt that hit above her knees and had had her access to the car keys taken away. That's why she'd walked to work that day.

The trek was five miles, and she'd left early so she could wash the summer heat from her face before her shift started—this was before she was allowed to wear makeup—and she walked into the back room at the café to find her sister bent over the back of Tim's desk. He stood behind Sarah with his hands on her hips.

Samantha froze in the doorway, needing a moment to understand what she was witnessing. And even then, her mind had tripped over how Tim Jennings was married to someone else. He had eight children, and Sarah wasn't his wife. Besides, Sarah was dating Tim's oldest son, Joseph. Their mothers were already planning their wedding.

But if that was true, why was this happening?

Samantha had muttered an apology and ducked out of the room. She was sobbing in the bathroom when Sarah found her a few minutes later, and Samantha couldn't explain why she was crying because she didn't know herself. Sarah had soothed her, telling her that it was okay, that it had been going on for a long time, and that Tim wasn't hurting her. That she'd admired him since she was a little girl and Tim had promised to always take care of her.

That had only made Samantha cry harder as she asked her sister, "Why?"

Sarah hadn't had any real answers, but she'd confided in Samantha after that. About her confusion. About how she wanted to please Tim and their father and be a good wife to Joseph when they got married. About how Tim had told her that since he was Joseph's father, she should be faithful to his wishes first.

Something didn't add up to Samantha, especially not after Tim had asked her to stay behind one day after her shift to make sure she knew it would be a sin to spread gossip and ill will about godly men. He'd implied—with a caress to her cheek and a too-thorough scan of her body—that he could take care of her, too.

Samantha had immediately enrolled in college and made plans to get out. She'd left the day after her sister's wedding. She'd walked around for the months in between feeling like she was going to puke at any moment—like there was no safe place to turn and nothing she could do for her sister.

Sarah didn't understand—or didn't want to understand—that she was being manipulated. Though, strangely, Sarah was the only person in her family Samantha still spoke to. Her parents had disowned her, her five younger siblings had been told to pretend she didn't exist, and only Sarah still called her. They shared their secrets with each other the way they always had, and Samantha guessed that Sarah was attempting to lure her back into their family's small, isolated, supposedly pious way of life the same way Samantha was hoping to lure her sister out of an unhealthy situation.

When Samantha had moved to the city, she'd extended an open invitation for Sarah and her children to join her if they ever needed a place to stay, for any reason at all. Her sister had yet to take her up on it, but Samantha offered it all the same.

She hadn't expected the simple act of watching a baptism to trigger her memories and force her to relive the horror of her sister's abuse. And despite Blake's father's chilly reception, she didn't automatically assume he was a man who abused his position, but as she watched Blake's cousin disappear beneath the water and emerge clean, she suddenly realized how early Tim's manipulation of Sarah had really started.

He'd started grooming her when she'd been a prepubescent child.

Samantha had squeezed Blake's hand as she'd focused on calming her roiling stomach. She hated Tim Jennings more than she hated Mason, and that was a lot.

The cadence of James Fairchild's voice finally soothed her. She liked the way he spoke with a vulnerable, fatherly authority. But as he preached, she noticed how often he had to pause to take deep breaths and how those breaths were almost more like a gasp. How he occasionally stopped to cough.

By the time the service had concluded, Samantha had successfully transferred her panic at her realization about her sister into worry over Blake's dad.

"Is your dad okay?" she asked as they stood for the final hymn.

Blake had dropped her hand then, as if he'd only just realized he'd still been holding it and now everyone could see.

Blake shrugged. "He says he's fine."

"He's not." But Samantha's words were drowned out by the piano.

The second the service was over, Yvette entwined her arm around Samantha's elbow and proceeded to introduce her as "Blake's new friend who is going to work at the restaurant" to basically all of her family.

Samantha thought it was curious that Yvette's family were members of the church and James's weren't. Samantha wanted to ask why that was but never found a good time to do so as she was shepherded through the crowd and escorted through the building to the parking lot and directly up to Blake's car.

A thrill trilled in Samantha's stomach when she spotted Blake unlocking his car door, sunglasses on, head down, lower lip captured between his teeth. He was so beautiful and so kind. She could still feel the warmth of his fingers entwined with hers. Remembering the sturdiness of his grip caused heat to bloom where the thrill had taken root. If she were somewhere else, not arm in arm with his mother, she might indulge in imagining what it would be like for him to touch her in other places.

"Oh, good—you haven't left yet," Yvette said as Blake paused in his open car door. "Samantha doesn't know the way to our house, and all the seats in my car are full of nieces. I thought you could give her a ride."

James had given a general invitation for the congregation to join the family for a celebratory potluck at the Fairchild's home, but Samantha hadn't presumed that invitation extended to her.

"Oh no. I don't want to impose." Samantha tried to pull away to extricate herself from Yvette's hold, but the older woman tightened her arm around Sam's.

"Nonsense. You're practically family already."

Samantha glanced at Blake for help, but between the sunglasses and the impassive set of his jaw, he wasn't offering much. She couldn't even tell if he was looking at her. "I-I . . ." Samantha wasn't sure what to say, but if she'd felt manipulated yesterday, this was just straight-up manhandling. She'd never met someone who wasn't related to her who presumed to meddle so much in her life before, especially on non-religious grounds. She wanted to protest, to say she needed to get home and do laundry or something, which she probably did, but Samantha also kind of wanted to go.

She hadn't been a part of a family gathering in so long. A sunny autumn backyard potluck sounded like the wholesome balm she'd been searching for on her church visits. A gathering in celebration. A warm and welcoming family. A place to belong and blend into and seek solace. Had that been what she'd been looking for all this time? A family?

The thought so astonished her that she almost missed Blake telling his mother to go, that he'd see to Samantha, but then Yvette let out a squeal of delight and darted away before either one of them could change their mind.

"You don't have to come." Blake shoved his hands in his pockets. Were his shoulders always hunched? Samantha didn't remember him standing that way, but it was possible she'd missed the slight slouch because she'd always been so dazzled by his eyes.

Samantha's eyes traveled up his body and focused on his mouth, trying to discern his mood. She had the distinct impression he was doing the same to her, trying to gauge her reaction to him after he'd held her hand throughout the entirety of the service.

"Is it alright if I'd like to come?" She took a tentative step closer to his passenger side door. "I meant what I said about imposing. If it's uncomfortable or inconvenient for you, I can go home."

"I'm fine with it, just as long as you're aware that we're playing right into my mom's hands. She'll have her entire family believing we're a couple by the end of the day."

Samantha popped open the passenger side door and stood inside it, leaning against the car's frame the way Blake was. "I guess it's good we know where we stand then," she said. Even though, in that moment, Samantha knew she was in danger of wanting more than she could have.

The ironic curve of his mouth as he said "I guess so" told her that maybe Blake wasn't as sure as he'd been before they'd shared a pew.

⎯⎯●⎯⎯

"THIS IS WHERE YOU GREW up?" Samantha asked as Blake pulled up to what he only now realized amounted to a small suburban mansion. Blake was actually embarrassed of how huge the house was now that Samantha was seeing it. Not that he had anything to be embarrassed about—he'd had nothing to do with the place.

"Nah. My parents bought this about ten years ago when the bakery was doing really well."

"It's so big." Samantha's cheeks flushed as her mouth dropped open.

"My mom likes to entertain, and I think she secretly always wanted a giant family, so even though all she got was me, she still has room for everyone." Blake felt the tips of his ears go pink. That was probably more information than he needed to share.

Samantha shut her mouth as she hooked her fingers through his. A shock of warmth shot up Blake's arm, reigniting the embers from the hearth fire that had been burning in his chest the entire church service.

"Did you know that I have six siblings?"

"Six?" Blake almost choked on his own tongue. He cleared his throat in an attempt to recover, even if the grin that curled her lips made his mouth go dry. "Wow. Six? I'm not sure my mom would have gone for that many. Maybe another one or two if she could have."

"Yeah, it was just me and my older sister at first, but when I was seven, my parents decided birth control was evil. That's when they left the church with a few other couples and joined a home church where having as many kids as possible was encouraged. My siblings just kept coming after that. I haven't even met the youngest one yet. He was born after I moved away." Samantha's fingers tightened around his, and he squeezed back as their conversation from the previous day made a little bit more sense.

Blake had met a few families like hers in the past. They'd been large, wary of others, dressed in simple clothes, and preferred to keep to themselves. They had never stayed more than a week or two at Grace Bible. Blake understood better the meekness he'd perceived in Samantha upon first seeing her. He also knew now that that behavior was more learned than inherent.

He admired her even more for having the courage to leave.

"I still can't believe your parents would disown you for doing what was best for you."

She shrugged, the motion causing his knuckles to brush against her thigh. "If you stray outside their definition of righteousness, you're too much of a risk. They treat you like a virus, like your intellect and independence might infect those around you."

Blake squeezed her fingers. "My family would rather keep you close so they could badger you back into the fold."

"Your family seems nice."

He couldn't help the grimace that flickered across his face.

"Or maybe not?"

"They're fine. Most of them are kind even. My parents are generous with what they have, and they've helped most of my family out at one point or another. And they're all going to ask a million questions about the restaurant."

"And you're not prepared for that?"

Blake sighed. "If that's all they would ask about, it would be fine. It's what they're digging for that I don't have the energy for today."

———⬥———

WHEN SAMANTHA ONLY stared at him, he let out a breath through his nose and said, "They're going to try to figure out what's going on with Rachel."

Samantha paused, furrowing her brow like she was dredging up the name from the depths of her memory even though she'd been so, so curious about who this Rachel woman had been to Blake. "The woman who needs a black baby blanket?"

A wry, sad smile twisted Blake's lips. "Yeah. We dated for a while, and now she's married to my ex-best friend."

"And she's pregnant?"

"Yeah."

"Oh." Samantha squeezed his hand. "I'm sorry. That sounds hard."

Blake nodded. "I just really don't want to talk about it today. Or at all, really."

Samantha raised their joined hands. "I could be your beard if you want. Give them something else to talk about for a while."

"You'd do that?"

Samantha shrugged like the idea of pretending to be his girlfriend for the afternoon didn't set a swarm of hopeful butterflies fluttering in her stomach. "It's not going to hurt anything, and I kind of miss being badgered by extended family, so you'd be doing me a favor, really."

Blake leaned over the console and cupped her cheek with his free hand. Samantha's heart skipped a beat when, for just a second, she thought he was going to lean over and kiss her. But he only traced a line over her cheek with his thumb, his eyes shining with gratefulness. "I do not deserve you."

Her cheeks burned with the blush that bloomed beneath her skin at his words, even as she fought the urge to ask him more about Rachel and how she ended up with Blake's friend. She couldn't figure out how in the world someone could not choose this beautiful, sensitive man.

She shrugged off the thought, reaching for the door handle. "Come on," she said. "It's time to make our grand entrance."

Chapter Nine

B lake stepped inside his parents' house with Samantha's hand still clasped in his own, but the euphoria at having an excuse to hold her hand whenever he wanted faded when he realized that he should have given this idea more thought.

The two of them had zero backstory, zero strategy for this fake relationship, and there were thirty people in this house waiting to descend on them. Those people would have questions and fawning exclamations about how good it was to see him at church and how they'd been waiting to see him *with* somebody. And they were going to make all sorts of assumptions about Samantha given her sweet green dress, endearing smile, and shining golden cross necklace.

He'd been dying to know why she wore it. Yearning to ask why she'd been at his dad's church. Wondering why she went to church at all if her background was traumatic enough for her to call it a cult.

If he was being honest with himself, he wanted to whisk Samantha away from the crowd of people who did indeed encircle them when they entered the backyard. He didn't know where they'd go, but back to his place for delivery and a detour to his bedroom sounded about right.

But he couldn't do that to her. Admitting that he wanted to keep her to himself was crossing a line. He could pretend for his family. He could paste one of his thousand-watt smiles on his face and pretend that his heart hadn't leapt at the excuse to keep holding Samantha's hand, but it wouldn't be fair to push for more than what she had offered. She had consented to an illusion. And she was his employee.

He suspected he wanted more than that from her, but he wouldn't allow himself to venture down that path for both their sakes. Not when he still felt a twinge in his chest when he thought of Rachel, and not when Sam was still dealing with that guy stalking her.

But that didn't mean he couldn't enjoy the little sips of her he was allowed. Blake distracted himself from thoughts of what could happen if he took her home by concentrating on the glow of warmth shining from where their skin met, hoping he could divert his own attention the same way he misdirected other people away from his true feelings with his practiced smiles. For a moment, he allowed himself to be present in a way he hadn't been in years.

Blake shouldn't have worried about their lack of a plan. Samantha was full of ready, simple answers. They met because of the restaurant. They were new and trying to take it slow, considering that they worked together. They couldn't wait for the restaurant to open. And OMG, his family would have to come try the salmon—that Blake knew Samantha hadn't even tried yet—because she had the best Sauvignon Blanc to pair with it.

Blake was only needed for the conversation to voice what his favorite dish on the new menu was. He felt a little sheepish admitting that his top choice was the pesto flatbread. But then again, pizza always had been his favorite, and his family knew that.

Halfway through a conversation with his aunt about the changes he'd made to the bakery's interior, his mother brought them each a glass of lemonade. She was doing nothing to disguise her self-satisfied smile, as if her maneuverings over the past week were solely responsible for the two of them holding hands in public.

Blake held his cup in his left hand so he didn't have to shift his grasp away from Samantha's fingers.

"Well, aren't you two adorable?" Yvette asked. "When did all this start?" She sounded like she had no idea, like she hadn't been pushing the two of them together at every opportunity.

Samantha's cheeks flushed, and Blake felt the tips of his ears go red. Samantha glanced at him in a conspiratorial way and said, "Oh, it just . . . happened."

His mother clapped her hands together with a squeal, and Blake was pretty sure he felt older than she did in that moment. He didn't like lying to his parents, especially his mom. The fact that he was definitely harboring a crush on his bar manager didn't make him feel any less deceptive, because he felt like he was lying to Samantha about his feelings for her, too.

He felt dishonest by making her think he only valued her as a friend and an employee when he was slowly admitting to himself that he wanted to kiss her. He'd had enough practice being honest with himself now that he could recognize the real reason he'd agreed to her idea: He hadn't wanted to let go of her hand.

Sure, he was exhausted with his family, and admitting that out loud to Samantha had felt good. But more than anything, Blake had been stalling leaving the car because the feel of her hand in his had somehow made him feel whole. Blake just wasn't sure if that was because she was the first woman he'd met who could distract him from his pining over Rachel or if he was genuinely interested in her.

Figuring out why was going to take some reflection on his part, but that could only happen when he didn't have the fresh scent of Samantha so close, distracting him. Despite the smell of the decaying leaves that crunched under their feet and the fire in the grill, all Blake could smell was the crisp linen, peaches, and lemons that he'd spent last night identifying as her laundry detergent and some combination of bath and body products. The smell had stuck in his nose all night long, and he'd half-dreamed that he was still sitting beside her at the restaurant. Only, in his dream, they'd been at Garden & Gather's bar, sharing a charcuterie board.

He'd woken up abruptly, not sure if the memory of leaning in to smell the pulse point at her neck as he'd tucked a stray strand of hair behind her ear was part of his dream or if he'd really done it. His first impulse upon seeing her at his dad's church had been to pull her into his arms and breathe her in. She smelled like absolution to him, as if she was so pure that she might be able to wash him clean of his sins by her sheer proximity.

He knew better. The attention of a good person couldn't fix the mistakes he'd made in the past. But maybe, if he took care with Samantha, if he was open and honest with her—and with himself—about how much he was tempted to kiss her and why, then maybe he could prove that he was worthy of her.

———●———

SAMANTHA DIDN'T THINK she would ever stop smiling.

She couldn't remember the last time she'd been to a family barbecue. It had possibly been back before her youngest siblings were born, when her parents had been members of a more conventional church.

Oh, they'd had gatherings growing up. And she'd even had a ton of fun playing with the other kids present at times. But as she'd gotten older, she'd mostly spent her time looking after the younger children and serving the men while the mothers cooked and cleaned.

There were still plenty of women in the kitchen at Blake's parents' house, but when Samantha had sneaked inside to use the bathroom, she'd found an abandoned sink full of dishes and a cluster of women circled around Yvette and her cupcakes laughing about how there weren't going to be any left for their husbands.

They pulled Samantha into their midst, and she spent the next thirty minutes telling them where she was from and, specifically, how she and Blake had met. The spilling-coffee-in-his-lap story had been a hit. One of the women even mentioned how it had been karma in motion and handed Samantha a chocolate cupcake as a reward.

Samantha knew she should probably ask what his aunt or great aunt or second cousin—Samantha had really lost track of who was who—what she meant about Blake somehow deserving to have coffee spilled in his lap, but she had been too distracted by the colloquial use of the word "karma." Even though it hadn't been used to describe what Karma was to Hinduism, even mentioning the concept around her family would have been enough to earn a lecture at best, punishment at worst.

Referencing other religions, acknowledging their influence, was forbidden. Even being aware of the word would have been proof of seeking outside influences, and being "in the world, not of the world" meant they were required to hold themselves separate—if not above—all things that did not have to do with the Bible, their immediate family, and the importance of spreading the message of God's Word.

Evangelism had been one of the reasons Samantha had been allowed to have the job at the café—so she could meet people and be an example of a godly woman in the world. No bother that she had been a child at the time and had barely been able to speak to strangers due to lack of practice. She'd trembled if she was asked anything other than "Are fries included with the burgers?"

Obviously, she'd gotten over all that, but there were still times when she forgot that pop culture references—most of which she didn't know—influenced even church people. But as she bit into the cupcake and sweet, rich dark chocolate melted over her tongue, Samantha reminded herself that one of the perks of leaving that life behind was allowing herself to enjoy this whole experience, what her father would have called "blasphemy."

Blake had wandered in eventually, and a smile so breathtaking spread over his lips and lit up his eyes when he spotted her that Samantha almost inhaled her third cupcake.

She washed it down with a sip of tea, mostly to buy herself a moment to decide how to react but also to hide just how much that smile affected her.

She'd wondered many times if he hid behind his dazzling exterior on purpose, but this was not one of those times. Blake appeared genuinely delighted to have found her. And Lord help her, she was in danger. No way was she going to be able to keep holding this man's hand and not fall for him completely.

Don't blush. Don't blush. Don't blush. But her internal reminder was useless. As her glass landed on the counter, Samantha's whole face burned from the full effect of his attention. His smile brightened to surface-of-the-sun levels, and Sam's mouth went dry.

Was he genuinely smiling at her like that? Or was it a show since his mother was here?

A pang of disappointment pricked in her heart as she remembered that this was a performance. They were pretending to be together because she'd been behaving like a teenager and hadn't wanted to let go of his hand.

Of course, Samantha had never held anyone's hand as a teenager. She'd been afraid to express any attraction at all for fear of being led into sin. But after witnessing what happened to Sarah? Samantha had dived headfirst into her first sexual experience not long after arriving at college. She'd experienced her first kiss and her first attempt at intercourse all in the same night. A boy had expressed interest in her, and Samantha had encouraged him more to prove to herself that she wasn't afraid to defy her parents—and by proxy, God—than as a way to enjoy intimacy.

Samantha had always assumed she'd missed out on that iconic teenage first love, the fluttery flush of a crush dissolving into something more. But judging by how her hand still tingled and how she'd begun fantasizing about drinking wine with Blake on a tablecloth on the floor of Garden & Gather with a charcuterie board between them, lit only in candlelight, she was guessing that maybe this feeling was recapturing a missed part of her adolescence.

She felt naïve and childlike even admitting that to herself. Especially given that he was not only her boss but literally thirteen years older than her. She'd learned from his mother yesterday that Blake had just turned thirty-eight. To Sam, that age gap was too big—her rational mind understood the vast difference in their experience. But that realization hadn't put a single dent in her crush so far.

Not even as Blake said "If you'll excuse me, ladies, we've got to get going" and wrapped an arm around Samantha's shoulders so he could escort her out of the house did his touch feel at all unnatural. She fought the urge to melt into him by reminding herself that he was just pretending.

When he dropped her off at her car, she thought he might have been contemplating leaning over the console and kissing her. Instead, he said, "You know, you'll be expected to show up at my cousin's wedding next month."

Did that mean they'd keep this charade up for an entire month? Samantha hadn't thought much beyond this afternoon.

"I'd be happy to go. Your family really is lovely."

"I'm glad you think so, at least." He did reach out and caress a strand of her hair, rubbing it between his thumb and forefinger, but she guessed it was mostly an unconscious contemplative gesture, as his expression told her he was processing something.

"Do you mind if I follow you home?" he asked, and Samantha might have forgotten to breathe for a second there.

Her surprise must have shown on her face because he pulled his hand back and gripped the steering wheel instead. "Just to make sure you get home safe. I don't like the idea of someone else following you home."

Oh, right. Mason. Samantha *had* forgotten about him, even if it was only for the second she'd been wondering if Blake was trying to invite himself over for coffee. Because the answer would have been yes. He could absolutely come inside and maybe drink some coffee—well, if Charlotte wasn't there to make things awkward. But how many times had Samantha made herself scarce for Charlotte?

But this? This was more practical.

And such a sweet gesture.

"That would be great, actually. I kind of hate driving anywhere by myself now."

Blake trailed her the whole way back to her apartment, never allowing another car to get between them. He parked behind her as she pulled into her assigned space then rolled down his window and asked her to let him know when she made it inside safely.

The words "Join me inside?" were on the tip of her tongue to request he ensure her safety for himself, but she only said "Sure, thanks" and turned to climb the stairs to the building's entrance without him.

Chapter Ten

The first thing that greeted Samantha when she entered Garden & Gather the next day was the aroma. The scent of garlic and steak wafted through the air, and her stomach rumbled. Blake had told her to come hungry so they could taste the new menu and possibly pair their offerings with some of the wine samples she'd asked a rep to bring them last week.

Samantha had to pinch herself—she still couldn't believe meetings like this were really her job now. She was getting paid to eat good food, pick out glassware, and sip wine while she worked.

Her excitement was almost enough to distract her from how her stomach tumbled when she thought about facing Blake again. At least his family wouldn't be around, so there wouldn't be any pretending with the chef. Well, she didn't think so.

They really should have laid down some ground rules. They hadn't taken the time to set any boundaries. Was this an all-the-time charade? Or did they only need to pretend when his family was around?

She nodded at the men who were staining her bar and sweeping the last of the sawdust and debris away. The construction was supposed to be finished in the next couple of days, and the decorator was due in at the end of the week. After meeting Emil and tasting the menu today, Samantha was going to have a full week of designing the drink menu, crafting specialty cocktails, interviewing bartenders and servers, figuring out her schedule, and starting to train everyone.

Basically, she didn't have time to worry about what her relationship with Blake was supposed to be. Not if she was going to make his restaurant happen.

So she really wasn't prepared for what happened when she entered the kitchen. As soon as he saw her, Blake wrapped an arm around her shoulders and led her to the prep table where the man who must have been Emil was plating the food.

A veritable feast was laid out before her: steak, pizza, pasta, sandwiches, appetizers, and house-fried kettle chips. Her senses were so overwhelmed with Blake's closeness and the giant array of all of her favorite foods that she almost missed her official introduction to Emil.

She was able to pull herself out of the fog and offer her hand to her coworker at exactly the right moment. But then she lifted her eyes to Emil's, and she couldn't help but notice the way his eyebrows were raised under his ball cap as he glanced back and forth between Samantha and Blake.

"It's nice to meet you, Samantha," he said. "Blake hasn't shut up about you. Now I guess I understand why." He pulled his hand back to motion between the two of them.

Samantha opened her mouth to protest, but Blake squeezed her closer and placed a kiss on the top of her head, short-circuiting her brain. She watched Emil's eyes crinkle as he smiled, and she decided that no matter what Blake was doing to her at the moment, she liked Emil. He looked kind.

"I'm so excited to try all of this. Tell me where you suggest we start, and I'll grab a couple of wine choices for us." She looked up at Blake, whose arm was still around her. "Er—where are you keeping the samples?"

She realized she'd spent entirely too little time in this building so far. She'd been doing a lot of her work from home over the past few weeks since the space was still under construction. She'd been brainstorming cocktails, making phone calls to beverage companies, placing help wanted ads, and getting Blake her basic supplies list—all while trying not to fantasize about what it felt like to have this man's hands on her.

"The whites are in the chef's cooler just here." He motioned behind her then peered over his shoulder to the other side of the kitchen. Then he sighed. "The red is on the floor next to the wine chiller. Fantastic."

"It's not going to hurt anything," she said, knowing that it wouldn't hurt the wine, at least. It could get them off on the wrong foot with the health department if the inspector showed up, however.

Samantha breathed in the scent of the food as Emil told her a little more about each dish. She chose four bottles of wine from the collection that had been delivered so far then handed the bottle of Cava to Blake. "Do you want to do the honors?"

Blake's brows furrowed for a moment, but he took the bottle as Emil clapped his hands together. "Beautiful. Starting the meal with a celebration. I like her already."

"I can't say no to that." Blake twisted the cage off the cork, offering them each one of his bright smiles. "We should celebrate getting this far, even if we have a lot of work ahead of us yet."

"That, and this is going to taste amazing with the cheese on the charcuterie board."

"Fuck yes, it will." Emil offered Samantha a fist, and she bumped it. She giggled a little as he grinned at her, and she could appreciate that Emil was good-looking, even with the silver at his temples.

He turned his smile on Blake. "I'm glad you brought somebody with taste into this place." He flashed Samantha a conspiratorial smirk. "This guy was living off boxed mac and cheese when I came along. He has the palate of an eight-year-old. Zero help planning the menu."

The cork popped free and shot across the room, bouncing off a stock pot hanging to dry by the dish rack. "Hey, I like everything on the menu."

"I'll be waiting for Samantha's opinion, thank you."

Sam's stomach growled as she swiped the bottle from Blake and poured three flutes of the sparkling white wine. "I'll have to remember to taste and not inhale. I'm starving."

"Same," Blake said as he took his glass. He grinned one of his more bashful smiles at her, and she did her best to tame her blush as she handed Emil his glass. The twinkle in his eye told her she'd been unsuccessful. At least he seemed to think she and Blake were cute together instead of condemning their situation as inappropriate.

"To Garden and Gather," she said as she raised her glass. The other two joined in the toast.

Samantha was the first to dig in after their wine, heading straight for the Manchego on the charcuterie board. She moaned as the flavor of the dry wine mingled with the sharpness of the cheese on her tongue. "I could eat this every day," she said before she felt two sets of eyes on her and realized she was the only one eating.

Her eyes darted back and forth between them. Emil appeared amused. Fond of her even, like she was an adorable child.

But Blake—Samantha had to pretend not to notice the way Blake's eyes had heated. The way he stood too close. It would be too easy to get lost in that heat, to stand there and stare at him, pretend that the feelings they'd been playacting the day before were genuine. Or that his were, at least.

Because she definitely had a crush. Maybe she was most of the way to smitten. Her mind would replay the way he'd draped his arm around her shoulder and pulled her in close for the rest of the day today. And probably tomorrow as well.

The original fantasy had lasted three days until he'd done it again, and then a few days later, he started adding squeezes and kisses on her cheek or the top of her head. Samantha cataloged every one, saving them up for when—if—they weren't pretending anymore.

Over the next two weeks, her days were full of good food and experimental cocktails. Of interviews and building her staff. Of holding Blake's hand whenever his mom was around, of sitting in their pew a second Sunday in a row. Of reminding herself that Blake's tender looks were all just for show.

On Friday, she spent most of the day putting her bar together. She arranged and rearranged the liquor bottles while Blake fought with installing the iPads so they'd be ready for the staff training that evening. Emil had taken the day off since he and his team would be in the next day to prep for their soft opening on Sunday afternoon.

She and Blake had just dismissed their front of house staff from their first meeting where they'd gone over the drink and cocktail menu. Tomorrow, the servers would be tasting the food and waiting on the kitchen staff once their work was finished for the day so they'd be ready to serve their friends and family on Sunday afternoon. Garden & Gather would be opening to the public on Monday, and every time Samantha thought of it, a wave that was equal parts excitement and equal parts anxiety rose in her stomach.

She had invited Charlotte to the friends-and-family lunch. She'd invited Sarah, too, but Samantha didn't expect her sister to come. She didn't expect much of a response outside of a *Congratulations!* text, but at least she'd tried.

Samantha picked at the crust of one of the leftover slices of pizza they'd ordered for the serving staff. She was exhausted, but it was a good kind of tired. The kind that came with satisfaction after a work week full of doing what she loved, and maybe after a full week of enjoying the weight of Blake's arm around her shoulder. A full week of the skin of his palm warming her skin when he hooked his fingers through hers, since her hands were always chilled from mixing drinks—that she didn't mind at all.

They'd decided that they should act like a couple all the time. Well, Blake had suggested that they should to keep anyone from being suspicious, but Samantha hadn't argued. She liked the excuse to touch him too much. She was a little afraid that her crush was too transparent, that he could see the way her heart sped and her stomach thrilled every time he reached for her, but he never said anything about it. So Samantha continued to act like she was only pretending to be enamored with him even though she felt herself falling just a little bit more every day.

When Blake reached around her to swipe a piece of the cold pizza out of the box and his front brushed against her back, Samantha corrected herself. She was falling for him a *lot* more each day. Definitely a lot more.

He didn't back away after he'd grabbed his food, and Samantha was so distracted by the shiver traveling up and down her spine when he spoke low and close to her ear that it took her a few seconds too long to understand what he'd said. "You never did make me a Boulevardier that wasn't too bitter."

"Oh. Would you like one?" Samantha's voice came out breathy and high, and her blood heated as Blake stepped even closer to her so his lips hovered just beside her ear.

"I think we both deserve a little break. Don't you?"

Samantha didn't trust herself to speak. Nodding alone took monumental effort.

"Teach me how to do it?" he asked. "So you don't always have to be the one that makes the drinks."

Was he implying that he'd like to make her drinks in the future? Her tongue felt like sandpaper as she eked out, "Okay."

Her feet were heavy, like cement had dried to the bottoms of her shoes as she rounded the bar. Blake kept close behind her, his fingers wrapped around the curve of her right hip. Samantha tried to remind herself that it was out of habit by now rather than because he couldn't stand not touching her.

She pulled a bottle of one of their better bourbons down from the shelf as she passed. Then Blake stopped next to her at the well as she plucked up the Campari and sweet vermouth. Blake's arm brushed against her shoulder as she explained the ratios she preferred for a more balanced drink then allowed him to chill and pour the cocktail. He chose to serve them in a rocks glass over the large cubes with an orange peel he took the time to cut into a fancy flower like he'd clearly been taught to do in bartending school.

"I feel like you know more than you let on," Samantha said as he handed her one of the glasses.

A twinkle shone in Blake's eye. Not his usual sparkle, something more sly than normal. "Would you believe it's a lack of confidence?"

Samantha barely held back her snort as she said, "Not even a little bit."

"I've never made anyone outside my instructors an actual alcoholic drink before." The twinkle drained away as his expression turned somber. Samantha wasn't sure what it meant, but she could sense a sort of deep wound that he couldn't conceal. Though maybe he wasn't trying as hard to hide around her anymore?

Samantha fought the urge to run her hand over his jaw. She yearned to feel the prickle of his short beard beneath her fingertips, to lean in close and see if his lips were as soft as they looked. She wanted to find out if he tasted like he smelled: clean and spicy with just a hint of mint and sugar.

But as intoxicating as she found his presence to be, Samantha just couldn't make herself vulnerable like that again. Instead, she raised her glass to his and clinked them together. "Then here's to your first drink," she said.

Blake tapped his glass against hers and watched her sip so intently that Samantha couldn't help but feel that her swallow was more of a sexual act than simply tasting his Boulevardier.

"What do you think?" he asked, even though he hadn't raised his own glass to his lips.

Samantha took another sip as much to wet her own lips as to assess the flavor. "It's good. Balanced."

Then Blake dipped his head and ran the tip of his nose across the bridge of hers. "I'm glad you like it," he said, just before he captured her lips in a kiss.

Chapter Eleven

B lake hadn't planned to kiss Samantha tonight. But over the last two weeks, not kissing her had become a battle he was finding increasingly more difficult to win.

Now that his lips were on hers, he couldn't remember why he'd thought this was a bad idea.

She was soft, and the sweetness of the vermouth lingered on her lips. Then she stepped up into him, and the relief that washed over him when she didn't shove him away was so consuming that Blake wrapped his hands around the dip of her waist and squeezed her into his chest. She was small—not as petite as Rachel had been but short enough he needed to duck his knees and support the back of her head with his hand to keep her from straining her neck.

Her skin was warm and smooth, her lips supple. Her tongue was sweet and seeking when she parted her lips for him like she wasn't used to kissing this way.

Blake's mind raced behind the kisses. She wasn't completely innocent. She'd admitted to sleeping with the guy who was stalking her, but that didn't mean she was experienced, either. Her upbringing had to have been sheltered if her parents were what he thought they were.

Had she even been allowed to date before she'd moved away?

The way she kissed him told him she hadn't spent a whole heck of a lot of time kissing. And that was a damn shame, because Blake thought he could stand here with her in this bar with his arms around her and his mouth on hers for eternity.

Was there a part of him that wanted to grasp her by the hips, hike her up onto the cocktail table, and peel the jeans down her legs? Absolutely, yes. But the more he slowed their kiss down—and she followed his lead—the more he decided that this woman deserved to be wooed. She needed someone to show her that what she wanted mattered, that her pleasure mattered. That she deserved to go at her own pace—and should ask for it—instead of pushing herself to meet her partner wherever they were at.

Samantha's head dropped back, and Blake kissed his way over her jaw and down her neck. Then, as a way to calm himself and abide by the decision he'd just made, he stood up straight and placed a kiss to the top of her head. He knew he should say something, reinforce the emotions he'd expressed in their kisses, but he was too busy trying to get his body under control as his heart slammed in his chest.

Samantha spoke first, her voice muffled from where she'd buried her face in his shirt. "Did you do that on purpose?"

A huff of air that was almost a laugh escaped from his chest. "Of course, I did. Why would you ask me that?"

"I thought we were pretending."

"Have you been pretending lately?"

He felt her stiffen, then Samantha shook her head so her nose dug into the spot where his heart still pounded.

"Me, either."

"Oh." There was a beat of silence, then Samantha asked, "So you wouldn't object to kissing me like that again?"

Blake indulged in a long inhale, cataloging the scent of Samantha's hair as the main source of her lemony scent. "I could waste away for want of kissing you," he said then wished he hadn't. That was a little too honest, even if he'd been trying not to feel exactly that as the time he'd spent by her side *not* kissing her had worn on.

"Ha!" Samantha's back shook with her half laugh like she thought he was being overdramatic, too, but she didn't let him go.

Her phone rang on the bar, a soft, musical tone, and Blake knew he was smitten when he found himself appreciating how even her ringtone was gentle and wholesome. Like the woman was built to be his own personal refuge.

Samantha broke away to answer it, and Blake missed the feel of her in his arms immediately. But then he looked around the restaurant, and he hoped he hadn't crossed an important boundary by kissing her. She was his employee, and they'd worked together so well so far—even their fake relationship had been met with seeming encouragement from everyone. The new staff basically treated them like they were married, like they'd started this place together, and Blake was buying into that fantasy—but was he buying into it too much?

She'd been into the kiss, but he needed to make sure it had happened because it was what she wanted.

Samantha placed her phone back on the table, her hand hovering over it. Blake stepped toward her to confirm that whatever was happening between them was okay but stopped when he noticed the tremors in her fingers. "What's wrong?"

Samantha's shoulders rose and fell as she inhaled deeply, then she exhaled a long breath through her mouth. "That was Charlotte."

Adrenaline surged as Blake's body readied to tackle whatever issue was troubling Charlotte so that Samantha wouldn't have to deal with it on her own. "Is she hurt?"

Samantha shook her head and swallowed, breathing heavily through her mouth like she was shoring herself up. Finally, just when Blake thought he was going to break from the tension, she said, "Mason tried to follow Charlotte home from the steakhouse tonight. She had to take a detour to her aunt's house in North Kansas City to lose him."

"But she *did* lose him?"

Samantha nodded. "She didn't see him on her way back to the apartments, but—"

"He was trying to figure out where you live now?"

Samantha nodded again.

"Do you feel comfortable going home?" he asked.

His mind raced with the possibilities as he waited for an answer. She could stay with him if she wanted, even though he only lived in a one-bedroom flat. His parents had plenty of room, and their house was nowhere near her apartment, but it was close to Garden & Gather, and he knew she feared Mason finding her here, too.

"Yeah, I need to be with Charlotte. She's shaken up." Samantha ran her fingers over her ponytail in a nervous gesture he'd never seen from her before. Her fingers were still trembling.

"Let me drive you."

"I—"

He knew she'd object to leaving her car here alone in the lot overnight—it might give too much away if Mason was anywhere in this area and happened to drive by. "Dad and I will come get your car after I drop you off. We can park it at my parents' house over the weekend. I'll pick you up in the morning."

"You're too busy for that," she said, a little of her usual tone coming back in her annoyance. He knew she was likely irritated at him for putting her before the restaurant. He *did* have to finish programming the menu into the point of sale program, and his office was still a mess, but he hadn't planned on sleeping much these next few weeks anyway.

"Your safety and peace of mind are more important."

Samantha shook her head. "Then you have to let me program the alcohol menu from home tonight. It's the least I can do."

Blake took her trembling hands in his and pulled her into his space. He couldn't resist her closeness anymore. Samantha crumpled into his chest like his touch was a relief, so Blake wrapped his arms around her in a solid embrace. "We agreed that the POS was my job."

"Please. It will keep me preoccupied tonight. And your mom will distract me in the morning."

The smile in her voice when she mentioned his mom only served to bury her deeper in his affections. His mother might try his nerves when she was matchmaking, but most of the time, Blake was grateful for her steady, optimistic presence.

"Heaven help Mason if he tries anything with my mother around. He's likely to get a steel-tipped stiletto to the temple."

Samantha gave a genuine giggle then, and warmth surged through Blake's chest, swift and heavy like a seventy-mile-per-hour wind on a one-hundred-degree day. He squeezed her closer and placed another kiss on top of her head.

"I kind of wish your mom was my mom." She craned her neck back so she could meet his eyes then cringed. "But in a not-creepy way where we can still hold hands and kiss."

"The kiss was okay?" he asked.

Samantha glowed when she smiled up at him. "The kiss was perfect."

When Blake was younger, before his father's conversion, he had practiced pretending to be fine in the mirror for hours on end. He knew how to tweak his expression in just the right way so that no one questioned if he was cowering or panicking or wallowing in self-pity. He knew every minute quirk his facial muscles could make, how to widen or squint his eyes, how to call up the illusion of an inner confidence that he'd rarely ever felt. That's why he knew exactly how to mimic the sunshine of the expression Samantha was giving him now, but he knew his mask had never shone as brightly as the genuine happiness she was broadcasting clearly over her features right now.

Blake placed a kiss to the tip of her nose. "Rain check on the Boulevardiers?"

She nodded. "I don't want to leave Charlotte alone too long."

"Then let's go."

———◉———

YVETTE PICKED SAMANTHA up Saturday morning for their third knitting class. Samantha hadn't made much progress on her blanket yet—only a couple of inches—but Yvette proudly pulled half of a small blanket out of her purse as Samantha buckled herself in.

"I finally figured it out!" Yvette scrunched the blanket, knitting needles and all, and Sam into a hug with a squeal then passed the blanket to the younger woman for her examination. Samantha did enjoy the way the color variation played out in the green yarn, and the wool fabric was soft and bouncy beneath her touch.

"It's gorgeous." Melancholy crept into Samantha's bones as she realized that if she ever wanted something as beautiful as this for herself, she was likely going to have to make it with her own two hands. Nobody would ever gift something like this to her the way Yvette would probably give this to her niece sometime in the next year or two.

But that was fine; she was used to making things happen for herself, and there was no rule saying that she couldn't keep this blanket for herself. Though in the back of her mind, she knew it was only a matter of time before her sister was pregnant with her third baby. Giving the blanket to her would be the practical thing to do. The nice thing to do.

Most of the time, Samantha would even feel good about giving her sister such a nice gift. But something about the way she and Charlotte had curled up together on the sofa watching Gilmore Girls and drinking wine the night before made Samantha want to keep the blanket for herself as a sort of comfort item—something tangible for her to hold on to since she didn't find as much solace in shows about idyllically flawed mother-daughter relationships the way Charlotte did.

Or maybe her first gratuitous purchase with her new paycheck would be enough yarn to make herself a full-size blanket and she would give this one to her sister, even if she wasn't sure when she was going to get any knitting done. She'd been too consumed with working at her new job, fantasizing about Blake, and worrying if Mason had found out where she lived yet to remember how to form a stitch on her needles.

Like the last two weeks, their first stop was the donut shop, and Samantha now found herself looking forward to the giant bear claws the girl at the counter set aside for them. Samantha could grow accustomed to the perks of being friends with someone as magnetic as Yvette, who people just did things for. But she had to continuously tamp down the part of herself that warned her not to get too comfortable, the part that reminded her all of this was temporary and she didn't deserve the respect and concern this family had shown her so far.

And even though she could feel the depression, the feeling that she was broken and bad and not worthy of anything from anyone, Samantha did her best to remind herself that all of that was learned. That was the way she'd been groomed to be obedient and faithful as a girl. She'd been told she was nothing if she did not keep God's will in mind or work at all times to serve Him, and she'd grown enough to recognize those lies as a method to prevent her from realizing she did, indeed, have power over her own life.

Maybe she'd never be as naturally effusive as Yvette or as awe-inspiringly beautiful as Blake, but she realized that if she put in the work to make friends with the woman who worked the front counter at the bakery, she would probably stash a bear claw for Samantha away after their knitting lessons were over. She stopped herself from adding: *once the knitting lessons were over and Yvette no longer wanted to be her friend now that she thought Blake and Samantha were together.*

Sure, Samantha's eyes still glazed over when she remembered the way he'd kissed her last night. And he'd said he wanted to do it again, but he hadn't, not even when he'd dropped her off at her apartment.

She would have liked him to, if for nothing else than to clear up the confusion about what the first kiss had meant. Had it been experimental? Did it happen because they'd been holding hands all the time and he needed to see if he really liked her or was just attracted to her because he was in a dry spell? Or did he actually want to be with her?

She wished she had an answer. But as she was contemplating Blake's words from the night before—that he "could waste away for want of kissing" her—and how the hope and desire that she didn't quite trust made her fingertips go a little numb, she bumped into someone. Coffee slopped through the lid of her to-go cup and onto a familiar black chef's coat.

"Whoa, there." Two hands landed on her shoulders and pushed her back a foot while also steadying her. "Late night, Sam?"

Samantha blinked up at Emil, feeling as displaced and confused as she probably looked. "Chef?"

"Morning." His grin was just as disarming as it always was, and Samantha knew that if she weren't so hung up on Blake, she would definitely have had a crush on Chef Emil, even if he was even older than Blake. His smile was so kind, and the way his hair was graying at the temples made him appear trustworthy somehow.

Emil had always looked safe to her, but today was the first time she'd seen him without his black toque, and his hair was both longer and darker than she expected. It might be silvering around his ears, but the hair that hung into his eyes was nearly black, and it had Samantha reevaluating his age.

"What are you doing here?" Her question came out sounding rude, and Samantha cringed as soon as she'd asked it. "Sorry. Obviously, you're here for donuts."

Emil only grinned down at her. "Sort of. The donuts aren't for me. I volunteer at a shelter sometimes, and the director brings in donuts and coffee for everyone on Saturday mornings. But his wife is pregnant and he's running behind this morning, so I'm picking them up for him on my way into the restaurant."

Yvette joined them then, a tray with their bear claws in one hand and her coffee in the other. "Oh, what a nice thing to do. How did you get started with that?"

Samantha did not miss the way Emil blushed at having Yvette's full attention on him, and she supposed no one was immune to the Fairchild effect.

"The last restaurant I worked at donated meals every so often. One of the reasons I left was because they stopped. I'm hoping that once Garden and Gather is up and running, we'll be able to start a program."

Yvette tilted her head to one side, and her eyes lit with mischief. Samantha could practically see the cogs turning in the other woman's brain even if she didn't understand why. "What shelter did you say this was?"

The name he gave meant nothing to Samantha; she'd never heard of it. But from the way Yvette's grin widened, she could tell Emil had given the name of the right shelter.

"Have you mentioned any of this to my son?"

"Only in abstracts, never in detail."

"Well, I think you should."

The girl who worked there, whose name Samantha should really learn, called for Emil as she heaved four big boxes onto the counter next to a big plastic coffee dispenser clearly made for travel.

"If you'll excuse me," Emil said, and Yvette waved him off with a smile.

Samantha glanced between the two of them, trying to decipher what Yvette was thinking as Emil hurried off. When she came up empty, Samantha asked, "Are you going to tell me what you're scheming?"

"You'll see. Now let's eat, or we'll be late for knitting."

Chapter Twelve

After the last two weeks of knitting classes, Samantha had expected to spend most of today with Yvette. So she wasn't surprised when they went out to an early lunch after their class or when Yvette suggested they grab another cup of coffee. Samantha was game.

She'd thought they would hit up the same drive-through they had the week before—the one on the way to Garden & Gather—so she did not expect to end up back at the donut shop, especially since the place closed in less than an hour.

Yvette parked in a spot near the back of the lot and scanned the cars as she drummed her beringed fingers on the steering wheel. "Now, let's see if I was right."

"Right about what?" Samantha also scanned the parking lot, trying to figure out what Yvette was looking for, but all Sam noticed was the lack of a silver Prius.

Then Yvette pointed near the front of the lot. "You see that big black SUV?"

There were a few, but only one was parked close to the donut shop. "Yes."

"Don't tell Blake, but I'm about to do some meddling." Yvette grabbed her purse and was out of the car before Samantha could pick her jaw up off the floor. What more meddling was there for her to do? She thought she'd already successfully shoved Blake and her together—surely that was enough, right?

Yvette was already halfway across the parking lot—the woman was surprisingly quick in her designer heels—when Samantha slung her bag over her shoulder and scrambled to keep up with her. "What—"

Samantha had been going to ask what they were doing, but Yvette was already waving to a man and woman who were on their way out of the donut shop. The couple stopped, and when Yvette met them on the sidewalk, she embraced the man, both of them all smiles as if they knew each other.

Unsure if she should interrupt whatever kind of reunion this was, Samantha slowed her step, trying to glean what she could by sight.

The man was broad and tall but not as tall as Blake. His t-shirt molded to his shoulders in a way that could definitely have been a distraction had he not motioned toward the petite woman by his side and said "This is my wife, Rachel. I don't think you've met" just as Samantha stepped into hearing range.

Rachel stepped forward, a curious look on her face as she extended her hand around her baby bump. "This is Yvette," her husband said then qualified, "Blake's mom."

A smile lit Rachel's face, and Samantha tripped up the curb as she realized who these people were. This was *Rachel* Rachel. Blake's pregnant ex-girlfriend who had married his ex-best-friend. Which meant that this man was . . . Samantha couldn't remember his name, but he'd been important to Blake at one point in time.

"It's so good to meet you." Nothing sounded forced or fake about Rachel's polite response as she shook Yvette's hand. And Yvette glowed—almost in triumph—as she glanced between the couple who, from what Samantha had pieced together about Blake's past, had broken his heart.

"I see congratulations are in order," Yvette said, nodding toward Rachel's stomach. Rachel and her husband shared a glance so full of pure joy that Samantha actually took a step back from the group. They radiated their love for each other. Their joy over their baby was palpable, and tears Samantha wasn't sure she understood welled in her eyes.

Rachel rested one hand on her bump while the other twined through her husband's fingers. "Thank you," she said, glancing at Nicolas again. "We didn't think it was going to happen this quickly, but we're excited."

"And what about the kids?"

The man laughed. "Ivy told me I was too old to have another baby this morning."

Rachel's grin brightened, and Samantha examined her partner more closely. He didn't look old to her. About Blake's age, perhaps? She did wonder how old Ivy, who must have been his daughter, was, though.

"And I'm pretty sure Oscar and Asher think they're getting a puppy instead of a younger sibling," Rachel said. Then she turned her attention to Samantha, curiosity in her eyes. "Is this one of your nieces? I remember Blake saying you came from a large family."

Yvette's laugh tinkled out of her as she linked her arm through Samantha's and pulled her forward. "Goodness, no. This is Samantha. She's Blake's girlfriend. Samantha, this is Nicolas Rivera and Rachel Ferrer. Nicolas and Blake have known each other forever."

Samantha nodded and shook both their hands with a "It's nice to meet you," though their smiles had visibly dimmed since finding out her relationship to Blake.

"We were just stopping by for a cup of coffee after our knitting class before heading into the restaurant to check on things. You know Blake's opening a restaurant, right? Opens this week."

"Naomi told us," Rachel said. "That's really great for him."

"We're having a friends and family day tomorrow as a sort of trial run. You should come!"

Yvette's offer was alarming for two reasons. One was that Samantha had spent half of her week putting together reservations, agonizing over seating charts, and figuring out which server would best cover which section, and there was no more room unless Samantha served them herself at the bar. The other was that the two of them were fidgeting like they were trying to figure out how to politely decline.

After an awkward pause full of reluctant glances between the two of them, Nicolas finally said, "We'll actually have all the kids tomorrow, but maybe we can come for an evening out sometime soon."

"Do," Yvette said, her smile never failing as Nicolas and Rachel passed more uncomfortable glances between them. "Blake would love to see you."

Rachel shifted between one foot and the other while Nicolas scratched behind his ear. "I'm really not sure about that. The last time we spoke . . . Well, it's probably best if we keep our distance."

His hand found Rachel's again, and they exchanged sad smiles as they stepped toward one another.

"I understand," Yvette said, her smile warm and welcoming. "But if you ever change your mind—and you should change your mind—I'm sure you can ask your friend, Emil, about reservations. He's the executive chef at Garden and Gather. I'm sure he and Samantha"—she bumped Sam with her hip as Nicolas's face fell into a frown—"can get you all set up. Samantha's the bar manager."

The two of them turned their attention back to her, and Sam was powerless to stop the blush rising to her cheeks. This was not how she wanted to meet Rachel. She didn't want to appear bashful and intimidated. She didn't want to be too terrified of her to speak.

Samantha wished she was standing behind the bar, throwing together an impressive drink and talking to them about their favorite cocktails, instead of this. The worried glance Rachel shot her, like she was concerned about her, made Samantha wonder what the other woman was thinking. Probably that Samantha was too young, too stupid, and too plain for someone like Blake to be interested in her.

She certainly couldn't hold a candle to the petite, fine-featured woman in front of her. Rachel was probably wondering what Blake saw in her. Which was okay—Samantha wondered the same thing most of the time. Did they really have anything in common, or was it just the restaurant? Had he really wanted to kiss her, or had he just gotten caught up in a couple of weeks' worth of touches?

"I used to be a bartender," Rachel said. Her voice was too quiet, like it was a secret, but Samantha understood what she was saying. Rachel had left Blake for Nicolas back when she had been a bartender. And they thought Blake was soothing his broken heart with someone younger and blonder and naiver who wouldn't realize he was just trying to replace the girlfriend he'd loved and lost.

Samantha was tempted to tell them not to worry, that she was entirely capable of taking care of herself, especially since she and Blake weren't really together. But she did understand a little bit more about why he would willingly participate in the deception. Nobody would have a hard time believing that she was a Rachel replacement until he was truly ready to move on.

"Did you work anywhere around here?" Samantha finally found her voice and was thankful the question she'd produced sounded somewhat normal.

Rachel shook her head. "No. Paradox in Topeka. It's a piano bar."

Samantha didn't know it. She'd never traveled further west than Lawrence. "That sounds fun. I've been in nightclubs, mostly. I'm looking forward to a quieter environment."

Rachel's lips spread into a tentative smile. "I can only imagine."

Nicolas's phone rang then, and they excused themselves to get home to their kids while Yvette steered Samantha into the donut shop.

Samantha held back her questions until they were in line for coffee. "How did you know they'd be here?"

Yvette shrugged one of her shoulders like none of that had been premeditated. "I didn't exactly, but I figured someone would have to return that big coffee urn Emil had earlier. I'm just so pleased I got the timing right."

Samantha didn't understand why Yvette appeared so satisfied with herself. As polite as they'd been, Rachel and Nicolas looked like they wanted nothing to do with Blake or Garden & Gather. And Samantha wasn't sure why Yvette was pushing for a reunion. Why in the world would Blake want to be friends with the people who had so clearly broken his heart?

"I know what you're thinking," Yvette said, "but it wasn't like that. Blake and Rachel had been broken up for a year before she and Nicolas got together. They didn't do anything to hurt Blake directly. They just found each other after a really hard time."

Samantha frowned, trying to puzzle it out while Yvette ordered their coffees. If Rachel hadn't left Blake for Nicolas, then why weren't Blake and Nicolas friends any longer? And why did everyone act like Blake was still pining over Rachel?

"I don't understand," she said once they were back in the car on their way to Garden & Gather.

Yvette flashed her a sad smile. "If Blake hasn't told you yet, I don't think I should say anything. It's his story to tell when he's ready."

Well, that didn't help. Now on top of her confusion, Samantha was dealing with the anxiety of imagining exactly what could have happened to end Blake and Rachel's relationship. And how bad it could have been. And if maybe Blake was the bad guy.

Chapter Thirteen

Blake kept wiping his hands on the towel he'd tucked into the waistline of his apron. He wore the same uniform as the servers: dark jeans, black button up, gray apron. He'd also donned a black tie since Samantha had said the day before that she planned to as well. He liked the idea of them matching, even if it felt a little cheesy.

But he hoped she saw the gesture for what it was—Blake wanted them to look like they were together, like they had planned this together. He wanted to show her that he could meet her where she was. Maybe it was a lot to ask a tie to do, but yesterday had been so strange, he would do just about anything to get Samantha back to that place where she sought him out with yearning in her eyes instead of the new wariness he now found in them instead.

His mother and Samantha had shown up in the early afternoon while Blake had been finishing the setup of the POS system and munching on the crusts of a flatbread. He'd been anticipating their arrival all day and relished the opportunity to pull Samantha into his arms and kiss her on the forehead. He longed to lean down and greet her with his lips on hers until they were kissing the way he'd done Friday night, but he was only willing to show so much affection in front of his mother. Especially since they still had to navigate what this latest development in their relationship meant.

Blake hadn't thought much of Samantha being a little stiffer in his arms than usual until his mother started speaking. "You'll never guess who we just ran into!" Then she recounted the whole of their encounter with Rachel and Nicolas in vivid detail.

Samantha quickly made herself scarce—presumably to go prepare for the evening's server training—while Blake had cursed and, as gently as he could, had asked his mother again not to meddle.

After Yvette had left, Samantha had avoided him as much as she could throughout the night and was mostly silent on the drive home. He hadn't dared reach for her, as he was beginning to suspect that his mother had told her about the affair that had caused the end of his relationship with Rachel. And he wasn't sure what to do about it, because he certainly did not have time to have a conversation with her about it today.

Samantha had insisted she was fine last night, just anxious about the next day and worried about Mason, but Blake had a feeling she was delaying telling him to never touch her again, that she was putting in her notice and didn't want to see him anymore. He figured she must just be waiting until after the event today to do it.

And then he remembered that Kat and Naomi were coming. Blake had asked Samantha to serve them specifically because he wanted to make sure they had the best experience, but he'd also been planning to introduce Samantha to them as his girlfriend because he wanted to gauge Kat's reaction.

If anybody would be honest about whether they thought Samantha was a good match for him, Kat would. He already knew she'd tell him that Samantha was too young for him, but he couldn't do anything about their age difference. He wanted Kat to see past that and approve of Samantha anyway. Of them together.

He wanted them to like Samantha.

And he wanted Samantha to get to know Kat and Naomi. They were two of his closest friends these days, even if they lived more than an hour away. Neither one of them judged him.

Kat couldn't exactly hold a grudge since she'd been the other half of the fatal affair. But Blake had expected Naomi to hex him or freeze him out after the affair had been discovered, but she'd been the first one to reach out to him, invite him over to her place for dinner so he and Kat could clear the air between them after all of their deceptions had come crashing down around their heads.

Maybe it was strange that the woman he'd once had an affair with and her girlfriend were some of the people he trusted most in the world, but it worked for them. Any residual feelings for Kat had flown out the window the second he'd seen the betrayal on Rachel's face. He just wished that he and Kat had realized they were better matched as friends before they'd started sleeping together.

He was trying not to dwell on that anymore.

Blake had been trying to convince himself that dating Samantha wouldn't be that big of a deal. That they could work together and kiss and maybe more after they left the restaurant at night, and everything would be fine. They could become partners. The restaurant would thrive, and his life would finally be different. Happy.

But he'd wanted them to spend a few more weeks getting to know each other before he told her his greatest shame. Maybe if he could charm her just a little bit more, show her he was just a man who had made some bad decisions and learned from them, maybe then he could tell her that he wasn't a faulty partner, just a broken and healing one, and she'd believe him, give him a chance.

But it was possible he'd missed that chance completely, and the idea had his nerves wringing in his chest and jangling down his arms. He was afraid his fingertips were going numb, which didn't bode well for his planned afternoon activities of delivering drinks and refilling water glasses as he greeted his guests.

He'd held it together well so far today by focusing on all the preparations. The friends and family dinner had been one of his favorite ideas his marketing person had suggested to him, but now serving people he knew felt like more pressure than serving strangers.

At least strangers wouldn't expect him to screw up.

No. Blake would not allow himself to go down that path today. Garden & Gather was about breaking out of his cycle of self-pity. The restaurant was supposed to be about inviting in new people, new opportunities, and new experiences.

His eyes sought out where Samantha was rearranging her cocktail table yet again. And for a brief moment, Blake allowed himself to feel the pining, the hunger of wanting a new relationship before he pasted one of his smiles on his face and prepared himself to give his team a pep talk before they opened their doors for the first time.

———•———

SAMANTHA SPENT THE first thirty minutes after the first round of guests arrived pouring wine and mixing cocktails. But as the initial rush tapered off, Samantha turned the bar over to the other two bartenders, checked in with the servers, then headed over to see Blake's parents.

Blake and Samantha had skipped church that morning to finish all the little last-minute details for the soft opening. Blake had fussed with the string lights in the greenhouse for an hour while Samantha had mixed a big batch of sangria and checked and double-checked their stock and ingredients more times than she needed to. She hadn't known what to say to him.

Yvette sipped at her tropical mocktail while James drank water and coffee as Sam approached their table. She couldn't help but notice the way James sometimes gulped for air after he spoke. It didn't seem right to her, but no one else demonstrated any concern for his well-being, so she didn't say anything. Especially not to Blake. How would that even go? "Hey, I know I've been pointedly avoiding you, but I'm fairly certain your dad needs to see a respiratory specialist."

Yeah. Samantha didn't think that would go over well.

She hated how intimidated she'd felt since meeting Rachel and Nicolas, like a child peeping around the banister at the top of the staircase after bedtime while the adults got to stay up late. Friday and her kiss with Blake seemed an age ago. Samantha would have liked the comfort of Blake's proximity as she worried about the possibility of Mason finding her again, but she felt that meeting Rachel had made their situation very clear—that the kissing had just been the result of their building sexual tension because of their charade. Nothing more.

Their second wave of reservations was scheduled to arrive at two o'clock. With it came the only table Samantha was serving directly today, two of Blake's friends. Two of his best friends, he'd said. Which meant that they were probably just as glamorous and beautiful as Blake and Nicolas and Rachel all were.

Samantha knew she was good at her job, but the idea of serving Blake's friends had her wishing her nerves had allowed her to eat something. Coffee on an empty stomach plus first-day jitters seriously had her shaking.

She snuck back into the kitchen to see if she could snag some fries just to get her through the afternoon. Once this was all over, she was going to camp out on the sofa in the lounge with a flatbread and a bottle of wine and hope Blake didn't ask any questions when she told him she needed her car back.

She couldn't keep up this charade—or her dignity—and still be dependent on him for rides everywhere. It was one thing to be lovesick over her boss, but it was a whole other thing to realize he was completely out of her league. To persist in indulging her feelings for him would only serve to prolong the agony. She would have to learn how to detach herself from the illusion.

"You all right, baby girl?" Emil asked from the other side of the line where he was plating a filet. "You look pale."

"Just nervous," she said, "and maybe a little hungry. Can I grab an order of fries?"

"You sure you just want fries?"

"I don't have time for anything else. My table's going to be here in about ten minutes."

Emil gave her a look that said he wasn't buying her nerves story and threw a small plate with a slightly charred filet in the window. "How about an overcooked steak? It's a travesty, I know, but better you eat it than me tossing it in the trash."

The steak was more well done than she generally preferred, but who was she to argue with free food? "Thanks."

Sam took the plate, grabbed some silverware from the dish pit, and snuck back to one of the prep tables that was out of view of the kitchen door. Still standing, she had shoved the second bite of her filet in her mouth when one of the younger cooks approached her, a glass of red wine in his hand. "Chef said to bring you this." The cook set the wine glass down next to her then scurried back to the line before she could thank him.

Samantha sniffed and swirled the wine before she sipped it. He'd sent her back the expensive cabernet she'd recommended to the servers the night before as a pairing with the filet. She took a deeper sip of the wine and sighed out her tension. This was all fine. Everything was going to be fine. She took another bite of the steak. The wine *did* help bring out the flavor in the beef that the overcooking had hidden.

Sam had almost started enjoying her meal until she heard Blake's voice from the front of the kitchen. "Hey, has anyone seen Sam?"

Samantha closed her eyes and crossed her fingers like that might help her disappear somehow, but damn Emil sold her out, directing Blake to where she hid.

Blake emerged around the corner a few seconds later, his face crumpled in a frown.

"Sorry," she said as she crossed the fork and knife on the plate and pushed the last few bites of the steak away. "I was hungry, and Chef had a steak he couldn't serve." Blake's eyes darted from hers to the plate to the half-drunk glass of red next to her on the table. "And he sent back the wine. I definitely would never have poured that for myself on the clock. I'll make sure I pay for it later."

Blake stepped closer to her. One hand closed around her elbow and pulled her against his body. "You're babbling," he whispered against her ear, wrapping his arms around her.

Samantha patted his back in slow, awkward taps to distract herself from the thrills that were running up and down her spine at his proximity. "Is everything okay?"

"I was going to ask you the same thing."

"I'm fine." She leaned back so she could look him in the eye. "Just needed a quick bite. I came in for fries, but I think Emil likes to spoil me."

Blake scowled at the glass of wine.

"I don't normally drink on the clock outside of a tasting," she said.

"I don't care about the damn wine. I care about my chef hedging in on my girl."

Two different notes resounded in Samantha's chest, and she wasn't sure which one to address first. The fact that she wasn't really his girlfriend, or the fact that even if she *was* his girlfriend, she wouldn't be comfortable with the possessive language. All it did was recall the memory of Mason shoving her into the lockers at the club and saying "You're mine, Samantha. You'll always be mine" even as his touch left bruises in its wake.

"It's not like that," Samantha said, not sure if she meant it wasn't like that between her and Emil or that it wasn't like that between her and Blake.

Blake's arms tightened around her. "Can we talk when the event is over? I feel like we've been off the last couple of days, and I don't like it."

Samantha didn't have any words, so she only nodded. She was definitely confused by what was happening right now. Did he think of her as his? Their kisses from Friday night replayed in her mind. The kissing, coupled with his annoyance at Emil, definitely pointed to that possibility.

Blake rested his forehead on hers and sighed in what sounded like relief. They stood like that for a minute, embracing, and Samantha let herself imagine what it would be like to be in a relationship for real. This comfort she was feeling, this safety—it would be so convenient to be able to reach for it whenever she needed, so reassuring to be able to trust in another's affection as completely as she wanted to believe in Blake.

He had just tilted his head down and captured her lips with his when the host said from behind him, "Um, Mr. Fairchild. Your guests are here."

Without dropping his arms from around Samantha's waist, Blake twisted to see the host. "Kat and Naomi are here?"

"Yes, sir."

"Please get them each some water and a glass of the cava, and let them know we'll be right with them." He turned back toward Samantha before he could see the host turn bright crimson and power walk out of the kitchen. Poor thing was only eighteen. She probably didn't know what to do with finding her direct supervisor kissing the restaurant owner in the kitchen.

Hell, Sam wasn't sure what she should do with it, either.

Samantha knew she should pull away from him so no one else would see, but when Blake ducked down to capture her lips again, she couldn't make herself. Maybe if she closed her eyes and wished, she could hang on to this self-deception for just a little while longer.

After too short a time, Blake pulled away and entwined his fingers in hers, tugging her toward the door. "Come on, let me introduce you to my friends."

Chapter Fourteen

Though Blake had told Samantha about Kat and Naomi, he had failed to mention that they were a couple, not just a couple of his friends. Samantha could tell they were together by the way they held hands across the table and gazed at one another with dazzled smiles.

As Blake and Samantha approached, the women both shot him proud, enthusiastic grins. The blonde one expounded on how gorgeous the restaurant was while the brunette mostly admired the blonde one.

Samantha was stuck on how gorgeous the women were, even though they looked nothing alike.

The blonde was tiny and thin with long, flowing hair and a flouncy white dress. She had a wreath of mums and wild sunflowers resting on her crown. The other was taller, and she wore a smart navy blazer over skinny jeans and a pair of men's brogues. Her hair was cut in a short, masculine fashion, but it only served to highlight her feminine features.

Samantha might not have approached the table had Blake not been by her side to propel her forward. She had very little direct experience with queer people. Not that she hadn't met any since she'd moved, but the friends she'd made at the club were all young and mostly single. Samantha had never really seen two women in a long-term relationship before. She was a little awed at their easy grace of loving one another in a world where expressing their love was considered an abomination—at least to the people Samantha had grown up around.

If Sam had been intimidated by the couple she'd met yesterday, that was nothing compared to the butterflies fluttering in her chest now. She was still struggling with being her normal straight self, and it took her a moment to realize that she wasn't just feeling nervous butterflies but jealous ones as well. She wanted to be able to exist as purely and freely as these two women, to exist without fear that she was disappointing someone or putting herself in danger of eternal damnation, but Samantha didn't think she'd ever outrun those demons.

The women both stood and embraced Blake with friendly, one-armed hugs when they reached their table, teasing him about how good he looked in his apron.

Then the blonde one pulled Samantha into a turn like they were on the dance floor. "And you and this beautiful creature matching is the cutest. Is this who you were telling us about?"

Blake caught Sam as she flowed out of the other woman's arms and crashed into his side. "Yeah, this is Samantha, my girlfriend. I am also lucky enough that she consented to be my bar manager."

He squeezed her into his side and buried his nose in her hair in an almost ostentatious show of affection before he said, "Samantha, this is Naomi Lewis." He nodded at the blonde before motioning toward the brunette with the short hair. "And this is Kat Rivera. They've been friends of mine for years, so take good care of them."

That name, Rivera, reverberated in Sam's mind as Blake left them, and Samantha asked "Wait—I met a Nicolas Rivera yesterday. Are you related to him?" before she had the cognizance to recognize that this woman was white and therefore unlikely to be Nicolas's little sister.

Kat and Naomi shared a knowing glance accompanied by sly smiles. "Nicolas is my ex-husband," Kat said, and there didn't seem to be any bitterness behind her words. "I'm surprised Blake introduced you. I didn't realize they were speaking."

"Oh, Blake's never said anything about him." Samantha's face burned as she realized her mistake. Had Kat left her husband for a woman?

Samantha knew that her red face and bulging eyes had ruined her chances of impressing these people. She wanted to slink away and hide but realized she now kind of owed them an explanation since she was the one who had walked into the awkward subject, even if unknowingly. "Blake's mom and I ran into him and"—she felt her face flush again, deeper this time—"his wife at a donut shop."

Naomi beamed at Samantha while Kat rolled her eyes.

"Isn't Rachel's little bump adorable? I can't wait for my new niece!" Naomi clapped her hands together, bouncing in her seat.

Samantha blinked. Were Rachel and Naomi related? They looked nothing alike aside from how tiny both of them were.

"You don't know that it's going to be a girl." Kat sounded grumpy, even as her eyes landed fondly on Naomi.

"Oh, but I do." Naomi tapped her temple. "I know her name and everything. Rachel is going to hate it."

"Rachel's not even going to listen to you," Kat said. "She doesn't believe in all your hocus-pocus."

"She absolutely does. She always has; she just pretends not to because she doesn't have the mental energy to acknowledge it."

"Now you sound like you're talking about me."

Naomi hummed and picked up her menu. "Well, you may hate it, but you and Rachel have a lot in common, actually." Then Naomi shifted her attention to Samantha and smiled in a way that signaled she knew Samantha was uncomfortable and looking for an escape. "I'll have a glass of the Chardonnay," she said, naming the most expensive glass on the menu.

Samantha shot her a thankful grin and turned to Kat, who ordered a refill on her cava. Then Samantha booked it back behind the safety of the bar and took a long, slow breath. These women were scary intimidating. Samantha would have thought so even without the added pressure of them being Blake's friends, but at least then she wouldn't have felt as much pressure for them to like her.

She'd totally screwed that up already.

"Hey." Blake's voice came from next to her ear as she snapped the cap onto the bottle of sparkling wine. "What do you think?"

Samantha could only muster a precipitous smile as she turned to face him. "They seem nice."

Blake's brow creased into a frown. "Did Kat say something rude to you already? She's really not that bad, but she can come off a little abrasive if you don't know her."

"No." Samantha shook her head. "They've been great. I'm the one who messed up."

Blake shifted so he could spy his friends around the fern at the end of the bar. Samantha snuck a look over her shoulder and the two women were chatting, totally absorbed in one another. "They look alright." He squeezed Samantha's elbow with one hand and brushed a stray hair out of her eyes with the other. "But how are you?"

Samantha shifted from one foot to the other. "I'm a little afraid to go back over there after what I said."

Blake grinned like what she said couldn't have been bad enough to be nervous about. "What did you say?"

Samantha almost didn't tell him. Not only was she embarrassed, but she had a hunch that the truth might upset Blake. She felt that bringing up anything to do with Rachel had the potential to bring him down, and she didn't want to do that, especially tonight. But she was so curious about the history behind it all and wondered if he would explain further if she brought it up again. He certainly hadn't said anything the day before when he'd first found out about his mother's meddling. "I recognized Kat's last name and said I'd met a Nicolas Rivera yesterday without realizing that he was Kat's ex-husband because he was with his new wife and Kat is here with a woman, and it didn't even occur to me that their relationship was a prior marriage, and now I feel like an idiot."

Blake had gone stiff beside her at the mention of Nicolas. His face had fallen into a deep frown when she'd mentioned Rachel, but his words didn't match his expression. "They aren't going to care about that."

"It was awkward."

"Only because you didn't know."

Samantha didn't see how that made it any better. "I don't know how not to feel awkward about it."

Blake looked to the ceiling, then when he glanced back down at her, one of his pretend smiles had made its way onto his lips. "Ask Naomi how her psychic training is going."

Samantha blinked. "Is that a serious suggestion, or are you making fun of me?"

"It's one-hundred-percent serious," Blake said, and Samantha supposed that made the conversation about Rachel's baby make more sense.

"Okay, but if they laugh at me, you're taking the table, and I'm hiding in the kitchen."

Blake kissed the top of her head and stepped back so Samantha could balance her drink tray on her palm. "They won't laugh, I promise."

And when Samantha set their drinks down and asked "Blake tells me you're doing some sort of psychic training?" to Naomi, they didn't laugh. Instead, Naomi's eyes lit up, and she bounced in her seat again. "Oh my gosh, yes! It's been the best thing. I used to think I was just intuitive, but a friend of mine is a medium, and he's been showing me that I can be more. The other day, I actually *heard* a message. I couldn't believe it."

Samantha wasn't sure *she* believed it. From the way Kat looked to the ceiling, Sam thought there was a chance she didn't put much stock in Naomi's abilities, either, but Naomi was alight with her excitement as she spoke about how she'd been meditating and using Tarot, her preferred tool, to gain more insight into her own abilities.

It all sounded equally unreal and terrifying to Samantha. Hearing voices she couldn't see and getting messages through cards? The idea of being surrounded by spirits and beings and not being able to sense them sent a shiver down her spine. She had a hard enough time dealing with the problems of people she *could* see—having to navigate a whole other realm of beings and their issues was not something Samantha ever saw herself being interested in.

Samantha tuned back into the conversation just in time to hear Naomi say to Kat, "But meditating has helped you so much."

"Your kind of meditating and my kind of meditating are vastly different."

Samantha resisted the urge to step back and simply watch these women like they were a television show. She sensed she could learn so much from them. Like, she hadn't known there were different ways to meditate. She thought it was all just sitting quietly with your eyes closed and trying not to let your thoughts overwhelm you. Was there a different way to do it? Maybe Samantha should try that method. She'd never been any good at meditating the few times she'd tried it.

"'There are more things on heaven and earth, Horatio, than are dreamt of in your philosophy.'"

Kat rolled her eyes at Naomi's recitation. At least Samantha knew enough to recognize the Shakespeare reference. "Stop wasting poor Samantha's time with your woo nonsense. Which appetizer do you want?"

Naomi glanced down at her menu like she hadn't even considered it yet. "Ooo! The charcuterie!"

"How did I know?" Kat raised her new glass of cava to her lips, and the sly grin there betrayed how much of her cranky demeanor was an act. The mischief in her eyes when she snared Samantha's gaze was conspiratorial, like they could be friends. "She still eats Lunchables most days for her midday meal."

"They are not Lunchables." Naomi's tone and accompanying gasp made sure the other women knew she was scandalized. "They are organic, grass-fed, pre-portioned, meat-and-cheese platters for convenience."

"Sorry." Kat's grin widened. "She eats *bougie* Lunchables every day. My mistake."

Samantha couldn't help but return Kat's contagious grin, then she pivoted toward Naomi and said, "I mean, I was never allowed to have Lunchables as a kid, so I totally buy them all the time now. They're so convenient."

"See!" Naomi stuck her tongue out at Kat, and Kat must have made some sexually suggestive gesture that Samantha missed, because Naomi's face flushed and her eyes turned from persecuted to heated. Feeling like she was half-intruding on an intimate moment and half-fleeing for fear of venturing too close to the sun, Samantha said, "I'll go get that order in for you" and retreated to the shelter of the kitchen.

———●———

BLAKE WAS SATISFIED with how the day was going. Impressed, even. There was a moment, when the majority of the orders were coming out, that he had to step into the kitchen to ensure the correct dishes made it to the correct table in a timely manner, but that was something he'd been prepared for based on his research. He'd been nervous that he wouldn't be able to read the tickets correctly, but he'd done all right.

Talking to the guests had been exhilarating. He'd gone around and spoken to just about every table in the restaurant to get feedback on the recipes, the service, the cocktails, the wine, and the atmosphere. Overall, complaints and criticism were low, but he had still taken a second—while drinking a glass of celebratory cava—to catalogue in his phone the things that still needed fine-tuning. Things like cleaning up the presentation of the pasta and burgers, bothering his supplier about delivering the wrong brand of olives for the bar, and asking Emil and Samantha if they could come up with some suggested wine pairings to help the servers get more familiar with both the wines and the dishes.

He was just tapping out a reminder to ask Samantha about doing a wine tasting with the front of house staff when he glanced up to see if she was still standing at Kat and Naomi's table. She'd been there, chatting with them as they ate, for the last ten minutes.

Theirs was the only table Blake hadn't talked to yet. Once he was finished with his wine, he would have to go over. So far, he'd been content watching Samantha interact with his friends. They all seemed to be enjoying themselves, but he'd also been waiting for Samantha to step away so he could find out if Kat and Naomi thought he was ridiculous for hoping he could have something real with Samantha.

Blake raised the champagne flute to his lips only to find that it was empty. And as the trembling in his stomach ramped up—the trembling he only now figured out he'd been attempting to cover with the alcohol—he realized he was a lot more nervous than he wanted to admit. Or perhaps he just didn't want to admit to himself exactly how hopeful he was. Because he knew there was a strong possibility that Samantha would want nothing to do with him after he told her the truth.

The truth was that he was the reason Kat and Nicolas's marriage had imploded. His betrayal was the reason his relationship with Rachel had crashed and burned. It was his fault that he and Nicolas were no longer friends. So he'd lived the last two years with the pain and regret of knowing that he'd hurt all of the people he'd loved most.

Maybe it had taken him this long to realize what everyone had been telling him for ages. His mom, Kat, Naomi—even Rachel the last time they'd talked—had encouraged him to forgive himself. To stop punishing himself for his past and allow himself to move on. Yes, he'd screwed up, but he hadn't been alone in his mistakes. They'd all been lying to themselves a little bit.

But Rachel and Nicolas, while they'd been tempted by their attraction, had never acted on it. And Kat had been so depressed and confused that Blake couldn't blame her for acting out of desperation. Only Blake had been the one with betrayal in his heart. He'd been so jealous of his best friend that he'd somehow transferred his longing for the kind of life Nicolas had to longing for Nicolas's actual family. Even his desire for Kat, desire that had been genuine on some level, had been based mostly in fantasy.

Even if the affair had been all-consuming in the moment.

But that night? Having Nicolas and Rachel walk in on him and Kat in bed together? That had been the single worst night of Blake's life, realizing that he had been living a fantasy when the real-life consequences of his actions were playing out directly in front of him.

All he'd been thinking about while he'd been sleeping with Kat was all he didn't have and all he stood to gain if he could somehow step into the life his best friend led. He hadn't seen everything he already had and what he stood to lose because of his own selfish shortsightedness.

Blake set the empty flute down and pushed off the counter. He didn't enjoy the cowardly feeling that had crept over him as he'd hidden behind the bar—he had no reason to be afraid of his friends' opinions. Or maybe he was just afraid Samantha would reject him in front of them?

Either way, he pocketed his phone and hid his trepidation behind a proud smile as he crossed the restaurant to join them.

Chapter Fifteen

"Holy hell, Blake—how did you make the vegetables taste so good?" Naomi asked with half a green bean sticking out between her lips as he approached the table. She covered her mouth with her hand and chewed, and Blake chuckled to himself.

He wrapped his arm around Sam's waist as he stopped at the edge of the table. She didn't pull away, so at least there was that. "That is all Emil, but if I had to guess, I'd say it was the monstrous amount of butter and garlic he adds to them."

Kat cackled, and Naomi slumped against the back of her chair and swallowed. "Nooooooo, don't say that. I'm supposed to be limiting my animal products and eating more fruits and vegetables."

"You're never gonna make it. I keep telling you," Kat said, carefully dabbing at the corner of her eyes so her mirth didn't smear her precise eyeliner.

"Your undying love and support means so much, babe." Naomi pretended to pout, but Blake caught the note of hurt in her eyes.

"Are you trying to go vegetarian?" Samantha asked. She was using her bartender voice, the one she used when she was talking with reps or on the phone. Blake considered it her "customer service voice."

But he wondered the same thing. The few times he'd had dinner at Naomi's house, the meals had always been well-rounded but centered around animal protein.

"No, she's trying to follow the psychic diet *Craig* put her on." Kat twirled her champagne flute on the table, and Blake recognized that tone. It was the same one she'd always used to guilt-trip Nicolas when she wasn't getting her way.

"What's a 'psychic diet'?" Samantha angled her head toward Naomi, genuine curiosity in her voice.

"My teacher, he swears that a vegan diet helps you stay lighter and more open to spirit. He thinks my fondness for"—she shot a pointed look at Kat—"bougie Lunchables and self-limiting beliefs are the reasons I've been having trouble opening my clairs."

Blake didn't know what clairs were, but he got the gist of what Naomi was saying. He'd grown used to only half understanding what she was talking about when she spoke about her woo-based work.

"So I've been working on trying to intentionally eat more plants and less meat—"

"Aside from the charcuterie boards," Kat interrupted.

"Hush, I had the veggie wrap for my entree."

Kat raised her hands in the air and slumped back in her chair, feigning surrender.

"Anyway." Naomi beamed up at Samantha. "Regardless of what my moody partner thinks, I've been trying to eat more plants that aren't soaked in butter or cheese or both, and it's a lot harder than I thought it was going to be."

Samantha nodded. "I'm not sure I could do that."

"She doesn't need to," Kat said. "She's got all the power she needs to do whatever she wants." Naomi shot Kat a dubious frown, but Kat only raised her eyebrows in challenge. "You're already psychic. But you know how I feel."

Naomi's frown softened into a grin, and the two joined hands across the table. Blake's heart squeezed at the sight. Their unabashed love was bittersweet. Not that he was jealous of them in any sense. Kat and he had been over for years, and Blake didn't want to go back. But he wanted something as secure and loving as the relationship they had.

Blake squeezed Samantha's hand in a gesture that mimicked Kat and Naomi's, maybe in a desperate hope that he *could* have something like that with her. That is, if he could navigate the issue of explaining his past with Kat without sinking the vessel that carried their budding relationship before it had even left the harbor.

Samantha engaged them in a conversation about their meal, then Kat asked Samantha if she'd ever read anything by Matt Zimmerman because she reminded her of the character in his latest mystery thriller. Blake nearly choked on his tongue at the question. Leave it to Kat to compare his girlfriend to what was no doubt a mousy murder victim.

Samantha's eyes had lit up at the question, though. "Oh my God, I know who you mean. I actually totally thought of my sister when I read that book. She's a natural blonde."

Blake frowned down at Samantha's head then, seeing the hint of roots for the first time. He'd never really noticed that they were darker than the rest of her blonde strands—how had he not realized before that she dyed her hair?

He stared as Kat and Samantha shared notes on the author's two books so far. She pulled her hand free of Blake's so she could gesture as she spoke, and Blake took note of this part of her he hadn't known anything about.

And when Samantha said she was sorry the next book in the series wasn't coming out until after Christmas, Naomi joined the conversation. "Maybe the next time Kat babysits his kids, she can try to steal an advanced copy. But you'll have to rely on Kat—I've tried sweet-talking my sister. No dice."

Samantha froze while Naomi grinned wide, and Kat cackled. Blake belatedly realized that the author they were talking about was Matthew. Blake only knew him as the quiet guy who trailed Naomi's little sister everywhere. But since Kat also worked for Naomi's sister, he was able to put all the pieces together.

"Oh, yeah. My sister, Jess—he's her forever person, and Kat watched their twins so they could go to a wedding a few weeks ago. You have to follow him on Instagram. He shares photos of himself with the babies. You have never seen anything so adorable."

Samantha opened and shut her mouth without words, but when Kat rolled her eyes again, she seemed to find them. "I didn't realize he was a local author."

Samantha smiled up at Blake, her eyes dancing with a mischief he hadn't seen in them before. "No wonder you were nervous to introduce me to your friends. They're all so much cooler than you."

The wine jumped in Blake's stomach, and the bubbles from the cava hit him all at once. Warm tingles cascaded down his shoulders, leaving what felt like a visible glow in their wake. If Blake had been able to pull his eyes away from Samantha's, he would have checked his forearms to make sure they weren't on fire.

Because Samantha was teasing him.

She'd never really teased him, and he hadn't realized until this moment that he craved that form of affection from her. A sign that she didn't view him as dangerous or just her boss but as someone worthy of her playful side.

Blake looped his arm over her shoulders, squeezing her into his side and placing a kiss on her temple. "Well, I couldn't have you realizing how lame I am by comparison right off the bat, now could I?"

To his surprise, Samantha popped up onto her toes and smacked a too-short kiss right on his lips. Blake had to fight the urge to pull her closer and deepen the kiss. He wanted to lay claim to her and broadcast this new relationship for everyone to see—Samantha was his, and he wanted to prove that he deserved her. But this unfortunately meant respecting her decision when she stepped away and turned back to the table to ask Kat and Naomi if they were up for carrot cake.

When she had bounced away to put in a slice of cake for Naomi and a coffee for Kat, Blake couldn't escape Kat's narrowed eyes.

"Did you hire her before or after you started sleeping with her?"

The tips of Blake's ears burned, and the back of his neck was hot when he intertwined his fingers behind his head and looked to the ceiling.

"Kat." Naomi flapped her napkin at her partner. "Hush. You're embarrassing him."

"It's an honest question." Kat ripped Naomi's napkin from her fingers, threw the linen back at her across the table, then poked Blake in the side. "So?"

"We, uh . . . We haven't slept together yet."

Naomi's eyes went wide, and Kat snorted. "I mean, she is of age, right? I'm assuming since she's your bar manager that she's at least twenty-one? Hopefully twenty-two?"

Blake stepped closer to the table as he glanced over his shoulder. Samantha could be back any moment with the dessert course, and he did not want her to overhear this conversation. His voice was low when he said, "She's twenty-five, and it just sort of happened, okay?"

Kat sniffed. "She seems very churchy, like there's a possibility she's still a virgin. You're really going there?"

"Kat." Naomi's voice held a warning.

"What?" Kat played with the corner of her own napkin, flipping the cloth between her fingers. "I'm not projecting. She's wearing a cross necklace beneath her tie."

"Just because you have trust issues with Christians doesn't mean everyone does." Naomi's tone was patient but sad.

Kat only harrumphed and said, "Well, they should."

Blake knew Kat had been working through a lot of issues over the past couple of years, but he only had a surface understanding of how angry she was about having to hide a huge piece of herself for so long. They'd had a couple of conversations about their backgrounds in the church—how purity culture enforced compulsory heterosexuality and how harmful that had been to her, specifically—but Blake had never experienced that for himself. He only knew that Kat was the happiest he'd ever seen her, and as grouchy as she could be sometimes, she was in a much better place now than she'd ever been since he'd known her. And he was happy for her.

"I think the necklace was a gift, but she's cut off from her family," Blake said, bringing the conversation back around to what he wanted to talk about.

"That's sad," Naomi said, a frown punctuating her words.

"She's made good friends with my mom." Blake's ears heated again. "I think she needs a family."

Kat nodded once. "As long as she's not using you to fulfill that need."

Blake glanced over his shoulder to see Samantha emerge from the kitchen. "Do you think that's possible?"

"I think the more important question is: Do you?" Kat shrugged. "I think she's cute. Young, but cute. And you haven't been with anyone at all since us, so it's probably good you're taking it slow."

"Hey, look at that! You can be nice to people who aren't me," Naomi teased, and Kat stuck her tongue out just as Samantha arrived back at the table.

"Looks like you all are having fun. What are you up to tonight?"

Kat and Naomi detailed their plans for doing some shopping while they were still in the city as Blake made his own plans for the evening in his head. And tried to push the confession he needed to make to the back of his mind so his nerves wouldn't overwhelm him.

———◉———

THE CLOSING DOWN OF the restaurant could have gone better. The servers had all wanted to leave the second their tables were gone, and debuting the binder with their side and closing duties had been met with grudging acceptance. Samantha had gritted her teeth through her smile and tamped down her frustration. Their attitudes might have possibly been her fault, though, because the last couple of times the servers had all been in the restaurant, she had been so anxious to spend time alone with Blake that she'd shooed them out prematurely. But the restaurant opened for real tomorrow, and surely they didn't think that she was going to stay and close the place down every single night.

Aside from that little hiccup, the afternoon had gone smoothly. The food seemed to have been well-received, and the drinks had been a hit. She'd noticed Blake making notes in his phone about presentation and sampling dishes for the thousandth time, but mostly he had been smiling. Really, truly, genuinely smiling without his mask like the event brought him the joy he'd been seeking.

That didn't make Samantha any less nervous about what was going to happen between them now that their staff was trickling out and they were going to be alone again.

Samantha was interrupted from her musings by one of her bartenders; the one who had the least experience behind the bar needed to change her schedule already. She'd known a slew of shift changes were coming—once the front of house staff got a feel for how much work even a little restaurant like theirs was going to be and how much money they could make per shift—but she'd hoped they'd at least be open before she'd have to rewrite the schedule.

Blake caught her eye as Ashley thanked her for being so accommodating. Samantha had the sneaking suspicion that Blake knew exactly what conversation they were having, and the amused sparkle in his eyes only annoyed Samantha more.

But her annoyance was accompanied by a flood of fondness, stronger and more palpable than she'd felt yet—except for maybe when she'd jumped up on her toes and kissed him in front of his friends earlier. She knew she'd gotten carried away with the charade and had been swept up by the teasing, but kissing him had felt so right in that moment.

Since their embrace in the kitchen, Samantha had almost been able to imagine that this whole thing between them was real. That she could forget about his past, forget about the people he had dated before. What she wanted was him, and if he wanted her, it wasn't illogical to assume that none of that mattered to him anymore, either.

After Ashley left, only the bump and crash of dishes in the kitchen told her that she and Blake weren't alone in the building. That didn't stop her from stepping close to his side when he approached, though.

"So what's the tradition after a big event like this? More shots?"

Samantha grinned. Blake hadn't been prepared for her to break out a bottle of Jameson and pour everyone over twenty-one a shot before they'd opened the doors. "I mean, we could. Or we could finish off this bottle of wine."

She nodded toward the half-open bottle in her hand, one Samantha normally would have stoppered and saved for tomorrow. Drinking it now was essentially a waste of product, and she knew she should be thinking of their liquor costs, but tonight she felt like celebrating. This whole restaurant thing was going to work out. And maybe, just maybe, she and Blake could make it work, too.

"I'm game," Blake said as Emil emerged through the swinging door of the kitchen. "How about it, Chef? A glass of bubbles to celebrate a successful soft open?"

Emil grabbed one of the clean glasses still sitting out to dry on the counter and held it out to Samantha. "It'll hold me over until I can get home and open my bottle of bourbon anyway."

"Was the kitchen stressful this afternoon?"

"My grill cook, who was supposed to have five years of experience in a steakhouse, only knows how to cook well-done steaks, so I had to leave the table and spend the whole time on the grill. That's how you got your lunch, by the way." He nodded at Sam as she handed him back a full glass of sparkling wine. "Hope it wasn't too awful."

"The wine you sent back helped."

Emil knocked back his glass, and Samantha held hers up toward Blake. He clinked his flute against hers despite the slight frown that had settled over his brow. "Are we going to be set for tomorrow?" Blake asked, and Samantha wondered if he was truly jealous of Emil like he'd implied earlier. She would have to tell him during their talk later that there was no reason for him to be.

"I'll have to hire someone else, but we have enough people to make it work this week."

Blake nodded and took another sip of his drink followed by a long, deep sigh through his nose. "Thank you both for all of your hard work. Our success today wouldn't have been possible without the both of you."

His eyes landed on Samantha's as he spoke, and gratefulness radiated off of him in almost melancholic waves as if he didn't believe he deserved the success that had come. And sure, maybe he was a novice restaurateur, but he had good instincts. Samantha tried to encourage him with her smile.

Emil only pushed his empty glass toward them on the counter and stretched. "The real work is only just getting started." He smacked Blake on the back and whipped off his toque. "You did great, Fairchild." Then he winked at Samantha. "Have a great night, you two. That bourbon's calling my name."

Samantha watched him retreat back through the swinging door into the kitchen, attempting to decipher what he'd meant by the wink until Blake upended the last of the bottle into her glass. "Is there anything you need to get done here before tomorrow?"

She shook her head and shifted away from him by an inch then flinched inwardly when his eyebrows creased into a deeper frown. Dammit. She wished she could explain why she was uncomfortable now that they were alone, but she didn't know how.

Except maybe she just didn't want to admit that she was anxious about what he wanted to talk about.

"Nothing that can't wait. You?"

"I'd just obsess over how much money we lost having a full staff on deck and selling everything for half price."

Samantha offered him her glass, feeling a little more guilty for not saving the wine even as her nerves evaporated. She doubted he would have even hinted at his worries with anybody else. Even with his friends earlier, he'd been guarded. He hadn't been at full shields the way he was at church or around his extended family, but he'd been cautious, even though she could tell he'd been pleased that Kat and Naomi had come.

"Will you take me to pick up my car?" she asked. His frown turned into an outright scowl. "Don't look at me like that; we're both going to be too busy this week for you to be my chauffeur."

"I don't mind." Blake took a sip of the sparkling wine and handed the glass back to Samantha.

She set it on the counter and took a strategic step closer to him. "I need to have my car back for my own sense of integrity. I don't like hiding."

"You have good reason to be afraid."

Samantha nodded. "But I can't live in fear."

Blake offered his hand to her, holding it up like he wasn't convinced she would want to take it. Given how standoffish she'd been over the last couple of days, she didn't blame him.

Samantha did one better and guided his hand around her waist until it rested on the small of her back. Then she reached her free hand up to cup his cheek. His fingers closed over the knot in her apron, and she could feel the flex of his jaw beneath her fingers.

"Will you follow me back to my place?" she asked.

"Of course."

"And maybe come in this time?"

Blake's fingers splayed over her lower back, and his jaw loosened even as he narrowed curious eyes at her.

"Charlotte won't be home for a few more hours. We'll have time to talk like you wanted."

Blake's head bent forward until his forehead rested against hers, and he sighed as he relaxed into her embrace. "That sounds perfect."

And because Samantha didn't want him to be nervous or hurt, she pushed up on her toes to leave an encouraging kiss on his lips. Only instead of the short kiss she'd had planned, the heat of his lips hit her at the same time as the bubbles from the sparkling wine, and she couldn't pull herself away from the intoxicating sensation. She wanted to lose herself in the decadence of him the way she'd done the first time she'd tried alcohol and misunderstood its potency. Before she'd suffered the agony of a hangover.

As his tongue slipped past her lips, Samantha wanted to give in to the flavor of him on her lips and forget about the pain that was possible later. She wanted to consume him, to wrap her legs around his waist and align the bulge in his jeans with the most sensitive part of her. She wanted to writhe over him and hear him curse.

Only.

She remembered the bank of windows behind them along the front wall, the greenhouse wall to their left. It was crowded with plants, but not enough to block the view. With the sun setting, they'd be in full view for any passersby.

Samantha pulled back, panting and fighting the urge to squeeze her legs together. "So my place?"

Blake nodded and kissed her forehead. He pulled her close, and she could hear his heart thudding in his chest. Her heart jumped to the same rhythm, pleased that he was just as affected by her as she was by him.

Chapter Sixteen

Pulling himself away from Samantha had been one of the most difficult things Blake had done in recent memory. His body had been ready to take her right there on the bar, and his mind had been telling him to make the most of the embrace. Because once they got to her house and he told her the truth, that might very well be the last time he got to hold her.

But Blake wouldn't do that to her. He couldn't sleep with her before he told her about his past, how he'd played the villain in that story. She deserved all the facts so she could make an informed decision about their relationship—whether or not she wanted to explore a deeper connection with him, specifically—before he pressed her for one physically.

His parents had already left for the Sunday evening church service when they arrived to retrieve her car. Blake had been hoping to procrastinate by talking with them for another half hour. He knew his mom would want updates on how the afternoon had gone, anyway.

Instead, he scribbled a note and left it on the kitchen table to let them know Sam had taken her car back—he didn't want them to think it had been stolen. Then he followed Samantha to her apartment.

She parked in her assigned spot under the awning and waited on the steps into the building as he found a space in the back. He could tell she was trying to be brave, but her eyes scanned the sea of cars and her fingers fiddled with her keys the entire time she waited for him to traverse the length of the parking lot. Even just standing on the threshold of her building for an extra couple of minutes left her visibly frightened.

Blake jogged the last few yards and wrapped his arm around her shoulder while she unlocked the outer door. Thank God the buildings were locked, at least. So many of the shitty apartment complexes Blake had lived in when he'd been Samantha's age hadn't even had locks.

Her apartment was on the second level at the end of the hallway. Grocery day was probably a bitch, but the second-floor location appeared relatively safe. It also had two deadbolts, and when they were inside, Samantha locked both of them, turned the lock on the knob, and slid the chain lock closed as well. He half expected her to cross herself as she sagged against the door, but when she closed her eyes and took three gulping breaths, Blake realized just how much fear she lived with.

"Are you alright?" he asked.

Samantha took another deep breath then rallied as she stood straight, shoulders back, chin high. "Coming home at night is the least favorite part of my day. I always feel exposed, like there's someone watching me, even though I know it's unlikely."

"I don't blame you." Blake wanted to enfold her in his arms, but he wasn't sure if that would be appropriate, given the circumstances. He hated that what he had to tell her might make her feel like he was untrustworthy, but her vulnerability only highlighted that he couldn't put off telling her any longer. Not if he wanted this to become a real relationship.

He settled for taking her hand and leading her toward the secondhand sofa on the far side of the room. "I won't let anyone harm you," he said and immediately felt like a liar. Blake very well could be the one hurting her in the next few minutes.

As he pulled her down, Samantha kicked off her shoes and tucked herself into his side. He held her as her breathing evened out and her body softened against his.

"What did you want to talk about?" she asked after a few minutes of silence.

"Us." Blake threw out the word so quickly, he knew he sounded defensive.

Samantha raised her head off his shoulder and peered up at him with apprehensive eyes. She rolled her bottom lip beneath her teeth then asked, "What about us?"

"We haven't had much time to talk about what's going on between us."

Samantha bit her lip again. Blake ran his thumb across the spot where her lip disappeared beneath her teeth, and her mouth opened. He knew he shouldn't kiss her before he started talking, not when they were alone in a private place where it would be so easy to lose himself in the sensation of her soft skin and summery scent. But he also wanted to reassure her that this connection was real.

She sighed into his mouth as he sucked that bottom lip between his teeth this time. He nibbled then swept over the small bite with his tongue. Samantha wrapped her arms around his neck then rose up on her knees and licked at the corner of his mouth.

Blake forgot that he was trying to take it slow with her and guided her leg over his lap so she was straddling him. She gripped his tie in one hand, and a finger on her other hand curled into the hair at the nape of his neck so that she was controlling the angle of their kiss.

"On Friday night, you said you weren't pretending anymore," she breathed out against his lips.

"I was never pretending."

Samantha's whole body relaxed, her weight dropping onto his lap so she was sitting on him, and her chest pressed against his with each heaving breath as she blinked up at him. "I don't understand."

Blake nuzzled his nose over hers and squeezed his fingers on the curve of her hips. She jerked against him in response, then her eyes went round as if she was surprised that her intimate proximity had aroused him.

He rolled up and into the crux of her thighs to emphasize her discovery. She whimpered, and Blake couldn't suppress his groan as her lips found his again. Then she picked up the rhythm, rocking into him through their clothes.

"I tried to deny how attracted to you I was at first," he forced out, trying to make sure she understood that he wanted a relationship with her before his body left his mind behind. "But, I—"

He paused as she spread her kisses down his jaw then nipped at his ear. He pressed her hips more firmly against his, and she whimpered again.

"Fuck—" Blake cursed, his fingers itching to search for the fly of her jeans so he could peel them off and resume their rocking without any barriers between them.

"But the more time I spend with you," he said instead, "the more I touch you . . ."

Samantha licked up the column of his neck, and Blake was pretty sure his vision had gone blank, not that his head had fallen back against the sofa as his eyes closed.

". . . God, the more I want," he continued. "With you, Samantha. With us. All the time."

He was aware that his thoughts were no longer making sense, but the rock and press of Sam's hips was driving him crazy. Her quiet whimpers were increasing in frequency as she followed her own rhythm against his lap, and he prayed she was close—because if she wasn't, he was in danger of coming in his pants.

Blake followed her lead, leaning into her rhythm, and within seconds, she was tensing on top of him, burying her mouth between his shoulder and the sofa to muffle her cries. He wanted to tell her not to stifle them, to let them out for the whole building to hear, that there was no shame in her pleasure. But then he might have been tempted to continue, and as much as he ached to find his own release, he still needed to tell her about Kat.

———◉———

SAMANTHA KNEW SHE SHOULD probably feel embarrassed about dry humping her boss on the sofa like they were teenagers, but right now, she was so boneless that she didn't think she could move. She had definitely lost all ability to feel. To think that after all these months of anxiety and worry, all she'd needed to relax was one really amazing orgasm.

Blake ran his hand up and down her spine in a soothing motion, and Samantha knew that if he kept it up, she could fall asleep like this. And while the thought was tempting, a part of her mind was aware that he had been trying to tell her something before their bodies had taken over.

She sat up abruptly, adrenaline surging through her calm as his earlier words finally registered. "Are you saying you were never pretending?"

He brushed a stray strand of hair out of her eyes. "I just wanted the excuse to be near you."

Samantha ran the tips of her fingers over his short beard, awed by his confession and wanting to offer her own. "I only suggested the fake relationship because I didn't want to let go of your hand."

A small smile spread over Blake's mouth, and he arched up off the sofa just enough to capture her lips with a kiss.

"If you don't think it will cause problems at work, I'd like to pursue a genuine relationship with you."

A thrill shot through Samantha. She'd fantasized about this moment in the last few weeks but had never let herself believe it could happen. "I'm less worried about work and more worried about fitting in with your friends."

Blake's smile collapsed into a frown. "Kat and Naomi loved you."

"I felt like a preschooler trying to play with the big kids."

Blake's hand cupped her jaw. "No one sees you that way."

Samantha knew she might regret bringing up Rachel, but she knew that if she let how intimidated she'd been by that woman fester, it wouldn't help any of the obstacles in her and Blake's brand new relationship. "When your mom introduced me to Rachel and Nicolas yesterday as your girlfriend, they couldn't stop looking at me like I was pitiful and naive."

Blake sighed as his head dropped back against the sofa cushions. He patted her thigh, and Samantha took that as a cue to slide off his lap. When she was settled, Blake said, "Just know that was more about their opinion of me than of you. And they have good reason to think badly of me."

Samantha's pulse beat in her ears. She'd known there was likely an unpleasant story lurking behind all of this. "Why is that?"

"You remember how you learned that Kat used to be married to Nicolas?" Blake picked his head up off the back of the sofa and met her gaze, sadness clouding the usual clear caramel color of his eyes.

Samantha nodded.

"Well, one of the main reasons Nicolas and Kat aren't married anymore is because Kat and I had an affair."

Someone might as well have punched Samantha in the chest for how well she was able to get her lungs to work. She'd thought that maybe Yvette had been wrong about Nicolas and Rachel waiting to start their relationship or, at the very least, the falling out between Nicolas and Blake had had to do with Rachel coming between them, but Blake and Kat? Samantha was still wrapping her mind around the fact that Kat had once been married to a man, because the way she presented herself was confidently queer.

Her thoughts were running through what she knew of these people so quickly that as soon as she was able to draw a breath, the only one of them she could voice was "While you were with Rachel?"

Blake grimaced. "Yes and no."

Samantha shook her head. "I don't understand."

To his credit, Blake did not look away as he explained how he'd always been jealous of Nicolas. How Nicolas and Kat had been having problems. How Blake had been there to listen to Kat when Nicolas hadn't been, and how it had just sort of happened. That for a few months, they'd had a clandestine affair until they agreed they couldn't deal with the guilt any longer. That Blake had started dating Rachel in an attempt to move on. How, even though he'd genuinely started to fall for Rachel, he'd still yearned for what Kat represented: a wife, kids, a home. How Kat had been one of the only people he could confide in with zero affectation, and he yearned for that connection with both Rachel and Nicolas, but he'd had too many secrets.

So one night Kat had called him because Nicolas had left after a bad fight, and she was panicked. Blake had helped calm her down, promised he would go look for Nicolas, but with just the two of them alone for the first time in months, they'd fallen into the comfort of their old physical relationship, despite agreeing that they wanted to try to make their actual relationships with other people work.

"We had agreed that it would be the last time. Then I would go out looking for Nicolas for her before I picked

Rachel up from work." He paused and ran his hands through his hair and sighed. "Only Rachel and Nicolas found us before we could find them. And then"—he gestured to the air around him—"my whole life fell apart. I had to move. I quit my job. Rachel wouldn't speak to me. Nicolas broke my nose."

Samantha gasped, and without thinking, her finger traced the bump on the bridge of his nose. She'd noticed the imperfection but thought it only added to his appeal. She'd never contemplated how he'd come by it.

Blake grasped her fingers and placed individual kisses on the tip of each one. "It's not something that I'm proud of, but it's an inescapable part of my past, and I wanted you to know about it because I don't want to keep any secrets from you. Keeping secrets and not trusting in myself or my friends is what caused all the trouble for me in the first place. And I don't want that to be us."

He grasped her hand between both of his, squeezing. She knew he was waiting for her to respond, but Samantha wasn't sure what to say. She felt like the whole scenario was too big for her to wrap her head around.

"You had an affair with Kat," she said.

"Yes." Blake nodded.

Okay. So he wasn't backing away from his original confession. "And Kat used to be married to Nicolas."

"Yes."

"And now Nicolas is married to Rachel, who you dated for . . . ?"

"Six months."

"And how long were Nicolas and Kat married?"

"Twelve years. They have two kids together. Ivy, who's almost thirteen, and Asher, who's ten."

Samantha remembered hearing those names outside the donut shop. Ivy had told Nicolas he was too old to have more kids, and Asher and . . . who was it? They had thought the new baby would be more like a puppy.

"And Rachel has a kid, too?"

Blake shifted but never let go of her hand. "Yeah, Oscar. He's the same age as Asher. Rachel's first husband died when he was a toddler. He—her husband—was actually one of Nicolas's best friends growing up."

"So they knew each other before?"

"More like they were aware of each other."

"And how did you meet Rachel?"

Blake swallowed and looked away as if he'd rather not answer, but Samantha was still trying to make it all make sense. She felt like she'd walked into one of the romantic dramas Charlotte liked to watch in the evening.

"She was the bartender at the restaurant we met at regularly."

"Paradox? The piano bar?"

Blake sat up. "Do you know it?"

Samantha shook her head. "Rachel mentioned it. She said she used to be a bartender, too." She took a breath. "And were things serious?"

Blake rolled his lips between his teeth, again appearing like he'd rather not answer, but he said, "I bought her a ring but never had the chance to actually propose."

"Because of the thing with Kat?"

"Yeah."

Samantha knew she was going to need a few days to digest all of this. She wasn't exactly thrilled with the news, but she also had so many questions about how everything had happened, so she didn't stop herself from asking them.

"How did Kat end up with Naomi?"

Blake snorted. "That's kind of a long story, too. But to shorten it, Naomi is Rachel's best friend. And since Rachel was hanging out with me all the time, Kat and Nicolas, being my best friends, were a part of the equation, regardless of the complications. So when everything happened, Naomi was one of the only people who was there for Kat. Naomi's always identified as pan, but Kat didn't come out as bi until she started dating Naomi. Her parents don't speak to her anymore because of it. But she'd secretly been struggling with her sexuality since she was a teenager. When she told me one of the reasons she slept with me was to prove to herself that she was still attracted to men? Well, that was a blow to the ego. But I guess I understand it, considering how much a part of evangelicalism compulsory heterosexuality is."

"Compulsory heterosexuality" wasn't a phrase Samantha had ever heard before, but it made complete sense to her. The way she'd grown up, she'd been expected to either marry a man and have as many children as possible or remain at home and help her parents raise the children they continued to have. What she wanted hadn't even figured into the conversation.

Especially not once she'd started talking about leaving. She'd been strictly forbidden to leave the family home and strike out on her own. And though she'd already been disowned, she could only imagine the horror and disgust that her parents would deflect back onto her should she admit feelings for anyone other than a straight white Christian man.

They would be livid. They would call her unnatural.

Samantha recalled the jealousy that she'd felt as she'd watched Kat and Naomi together earlier that day. She didn't think it was because of their sexuality so much as it was that they were living freely as themselves in full view of anyone who would be watching, and Samantha had never felt safe to do that herself.

And she desperately wanted to.

"That's really sad," Samantha said, finally realizing that Blake had been waiting all this time for an answer.

He nodded again and twined his fingers with hers. "It took us a minute, but Kat and I figured out that we were better off as friends. And I'm really happy for her. She has come into her own so much over the past couple of years. You have no idea."

Samantha curled her fingers into the hair at the nape of his neck. "And what about you?"

He closed his eyes and leaned back into her touch. "I'm working on it."

Sam exhaled. "Your mom made it sound like you haven't been in a relationship since Rachel."

Blake swiveled his head on the sofa to meet her eye. "I haven't."

"Not even a hookup?" she asked.

He shook his head. "I haven't even kissed anyone but you."

"Oh." Samantha wasn't sure why that struck her as odd for him. Perhaps it was because he was so perfect-looking that she couldn't imagine him being left alone for long enough to spend two years celibate.

He smoothed his fingers over her cheek. "You aren't running away?"

Samantha swallowed. "I mean, I'm not thrilled."

He huffed out a soft laugh. "I've been dreading telling you."

She nodded, taking another few moments of silence to absorb everything she'd learned. "It seems like you've grown from the situation, though?"

"You sound unsure."

"Ha!" Samantha hadn't meant to expel the sarcastic laugh. "I'm trying to be optimistic."

"But you want to run away?"

Physically, yes, Samantha's instinct was to hide, but her experience with him up until this moment had made her feel safe with him. And maybe she shouldn't, considering he had just confessed to adultery, but Samantha trusted that feeling.

"No. Just time to assimilate."

Blake exhaled through his nose, and his shoulders relaxed slightly. He had been afraid, she realized. Not just nervous about telling her but actually afraid that she was going to kick him out.

"This isn't a pattern for you?"

He shook his head. "I've never been very good at relationships, but that's the only time I've ever crossed those boundaries."

Samantha played with the collar of his shirt where the lapel rested against the knot of his tie. She wanted to pull on it, rid him of it so she could open the first few buttons of his shirt and see the divot of his collarbone. But instead, she asked, "What does that mean: You've never been good at relationships?"

One of Blake's hands rose to play with the end of her ponytail, his attention focused over her shoulder on where the strands of her hair met the tips of his fingers. "I've had a lot of different types of relationships. From fuck buddies I knew I didn't have a future with to women from the church I courted to save face. I always knew I wanted a family, but I'd been afraid of getting comfortable. It wasn't until Rachel that I truly gave a woman a fair chance at my heart."

Her wince was involuntary. Samantha couldn't help but imagine the tiny woman she'd met over the weekend standing arm in arm with Blake, the two of them flashing their dazzling smiles at one another. They would look gorgeous together. "Did you love her?"

"Yes." He opened his mouth then closed it as if he were finding the right words for what he wanted to say. "But I knew the life I had at the time would never have been compatible with her trauma. I knew we couldn't last, but I tried anyway."

Samantha wanted to ask so many more questions. She knew Blake had worked for the church, and she wondered what trauma he was referring to, but she didn't want to seem like she was just after the gossip. Instead, she asked, "Did you open the restaurant for her?"

Blake blinked at her, confusion marring his perfect face. "No. I opened the restaurant for me. I was tired of feeling like I didn't belong anywhere, so I made a space for myself."

Samantha allowed her fingers to ghost over the knot of his tie. She knew exactly what he meant. She hadn't felt at home anywhere in a long time, maybe ever.

And she should probably be running scared after his confession, but all she wanted was to make that lonely, lost look on his face go away.

Chapter Seventeen

Samantha tugged the knot on his tie free then set to work unbuttoning his shirt. "What are you doing?"

This was not the reaction he'd expected after his confession, but Blake wasn't about to argue. Though he wanted her attention, he also wanted to understand what she was thinking.

"I have been fantasizing about licking you right here." She traced the line of his collarbone with her finger then dipped her tongue into the hollow at the base of his throat. A jolt of pure want shot straight south.

"You're not freaked out?" His voice came out in a croak as her tongue lapped at his skin again.

"Not enough."

"Samantha?" He tilted her chin up so he could see what emotions were swimming in her eyes. He saw a mix of mischief and determination there, and he smiled at the sight.

"I've never felt like I've belonged anywhere either, but I don't feel that way when I'm with you."

Those might have been the sweetest words Blake had ever heard. He wanted to tell her that he thought she might be his missing piece. That he hadn't known he'd been looking for her, but he was so thankful the restaurant had brought her to him. That maybe she was the home he'd been missing all this time.

He chose to tell her through kisses and touches instead. Through the press of his mouth on hers, the tentative caress of his tongue over her teeth, his hands sliding up her sides to squeeze her breasts.

Samantha moaned and arched into his palms. She must have had the same thought—that there were too many clothes between them—because she yanked her own tie free and tossed it over her head. Blake helped her with the buttons down to where her shirt was tucked into her jeans then moved straight to her fly. The pink and cream bra she wore complimented the pale tones of her skin, and he was eager to see if her panties did as well.

Blake surged up to kiss his way down her neck while Sam wrestled with her shirt. She'd just shucked it to the floor when someone pounded on the door. "Sam!" The voice sounded frantic. Panicked. "God, Sam. Are you alright?" There was a jingling of keys and the sound of fumbling followed by a sob as Sam leapt from Blake's lap and punched her arms back through her shirt sleeves.

"Charlotte! It's okay. I'm fine!" Sam called back through the door as she rushed across the room to aid with the locks.

Blake stood and did up his own buttons. He knew he probably couldn't hide the rumpled way he looked or change the fact that Samantha's roommate would know immediately that they'd been fooling around on the sofa. Especially since Sam was still holding her shirt closed when her roommate collapsed through the door.

The color had leeched out of the other woman's cheeks, and her face was tearstained as she glanced between Sam and

Blake. Sam crashed to her knees beside her friend. "What's going on?"

"There's a note on your car. I didn't touch it, but I saw it when I pulled in. And it's nasty. Sam. Mason was here. Tonight. And he saw you two"—she flashed a look up at Blake—"come in together."

Blake saw the moment Samantha stopped breathing. Her face turned pale, and she went completely still as if her whole body had shut down.

Blake's own blood ran cold. He hadn't seen anyone when they'd come in, but his eyes had never left Samantha. He might have easily missed someone hiding in the parking lot.

He crouched down beside the two women, his hands squeezing Samantha's shoulders. "Are you okay?" he asked Charlotte.

She nodded and sniffed. "Did you, by chance, used to drive a black, sporty-looking car?"

He frowned. "I drive a quattro, yeah."

Charlotte raised her eyebrows at him like she didn't know what that meant. "Well, you might want to take a look at it before you use the present tense."

"What?" Sam snapped out of her shock. "What do you mean?"

"There's a black sports car near the back of the lot that's completely smashed up, like someone slammed into it and then bashed in the windows. I saw it when I came in, and then I saw the note, and . . ." Charlotte's lips trembled as she trailed off.

Samantha caught Blake's gaze. "I'm so sorry."

"Don't worry about it," he said, even as bile churned in his stomach. He'd understood why Samantha was afraid, but a part of him hadn't believed this guy would follow through on hurting her now that she had the restraining order. Clearly, he'd been wrong. "I'm just glad it was my car and not you."

"We have to call the police," Samantha said. "Now."

Blake's first instinct was to pack both women up and haul them over to his parents' house—and hire private security while he was at it—but Samantha was right. This was an attack and a violation of the restraining order. They had to file a report.

"I'll go call while you two get . . ." Charlotte scanned them up and down, a subdued mischief sparkling in her eyes. ". . . cleaned up."

"Thanks." Sam let out a breath that Blake took to mean she was girding herself for the ordeal that was to come.

Samantha's roommate pushed to her feet, sticking out her hand to Blake. "It's nice to meet you. I'm Charlotte."

He shook it. "Blake Fairchild."

"I know." The mischief gleamed brighter in her eyes. "Your—uh—buttons are done up wrong, and your tie is on the floor. In case you were wondering." She had disappeared out the door before Blake could look down and see that he'd matched his second button up with his third buttonhole, and the St. Christopher medallion his mother had given him was tangled in the fabric. He hastily fixed his clothes, his eyes on Samantha.

She had frozen in place on the living room floor.

"Hey." He ran his hand down her arm, pulling her to the couch and onto his lap. She fell into him pliant and limp, like fear had banished all of her fight. "It's gonna be okay."

Samantha only buried her nose in his shoulder and shivered. He held her until the sirens sounded and flashing lights reflected off the windows—and then he didn't even have to prompt her to get up. She untangled herself from his embrace, stood, tidied her clothes, set her shoulders back, lifted her nose into the air, and stalked out her front door like she was in charge of the investigation rather than the victim.

—————●—————

SAMANTHA DIDN'T WANT to talk to the police. She didn't want to admit that this was happening, that Mason had found her after all the precautions she'd taken. Or that he had damaged Blake's car.

Charlotte was already talking to a man in uniform when Samantha descended the stairs. "Is the note still on the car?" Samantha asked, interrupting Charlotte's explanation of what she found.

The officer raised an eyebrow. "Are you Samantha Reynolds?"

Charlotte looped an arm through hers in solidarity as Samantha answered in the affirmative. She was aware of Blake coming to stand behind them, and the officer's eyes flicked up to look at the new member of their party.

"And this is Blake Fairchild," Charlotte said. "I'm pretty sure it's his car that was smashed up."

"You haven't seen the damage yet?" the officer asked Blake.

"No. We were inside the whole time."

"And you didn't hear anything?"

Blake shook his head. The only thing he'd been able to hear was his blood rushing in his ears and Samantha's soft moans.

"I'll need you to come with me to confirm that the vehicle belongs to you."

Blake placed a kiss on the top of Samantha's head as he passed, whispering "I'll be right back" in her ear.

Samantha nodded then addressed the officer before they could walk away. "I want to see the note."

The officer called a second uniformed man over who supervised their perusal of the note tucked under her windshield. His near-constant scrutiny made Sam a little uncomfortable before she realized he was just making sure they didn't touch the paper napkin it had been written on. It read: *I saw you go inside with him just now. How could you do this to us? The way you look at him makes me want to smash his pretty boy face the way I smashed his car.*

Samantha's hand covered her mouth as the implications of all of this sunk in. She wasn't the only one at risk anymore. Charlotte had been followed, Blake was being threatened, and his car had been vandalized. Before, she'd been afraid that Mason might hurt her, but after this? He had implied that he would kill her for being with another man.

That wasn't what she wanted. Not for herself or for Blake.

Fifteen minutes ago, she was enjoying one of the most pleasurable sexual encounters of her life, and now she was paying the price. She heard the voice of Tim in her head, reminding her that evildoers who stray from the cradle of the Lord pay the price, both in this life and the next. Samantha loathed him and didn't believe the words, but she couldn't shake the superstition she'd been raised with. She knew all of that had only been said to manipulate her into complicity, but when she felt like she was being caged in by circumstance, she couldn't help but entertain the idea that she was being punished for straying from the fold.

A sob hiccuped through her chest and lodged in her throat. For a few seconds that felt like an eternity, she thought she wasn't going to be able to take a breath. Charlotte, whose arm was still linked with hers, pulled her closer as Samantha covered her mouth and the cry finally broke free. Hot tears coated her cheeks. Distantly, she knew she was probably hyperventilating as she cried, but she had zero control over her body in that moment.

At some point, Charlotte's hold on her was replaced by Blake's arms around her shoulders. She heard the officer asking questions, and the rumble in Blake's chest signaled that he'd responded, but Samantha was beyond hearing words. All she could think was that she would never escape. Mason would find her wherever she went, and she would never be free of him.

She'd already moved. Changed her job. Changed her hair. She'd upended her whole life just to get away from him. And maybe she wasn't sorry that she'd met Blake in the middle of it, but what person in their right mind would *choose* to be a part of this mess? Why would he stay now?

Slowly, awareness of the world outside of her panic crept back into her senses. She felt Blake's fingers tracing the tears across the curve of her cheek. His other hand splayed over the small of her back, securing her to his body. He swayed from side to side, rocking her with him as he whispered soothing words in her ears.

"Shhhh, Sunshine. It's gonna be okay."

The third time Blake repeated that as they swayed, Samantha sniffed. "How?"

"We'll do what we need to do to fix this. I'll press charges for the car. Get video footage from the apartment complex. That note on its own is pretty damning. It'll be alright. I promise."

Samantha bit back a retort about how he couldn't promise anything regarding someone else's actions, but then she felt something shift inside her. All this time, she'd been reacting to Mason's aggressions against her. Because she couldn't control how he was acting against her, but she could control her own actions. She was only responsible for her own actions, after all. And she didn't like how she'd been behaving since she'd started running.

Maybe she couldn't change that Mason was coming after her, but maybe she could do something other than hide. She wanted to show him that she wasn't a coward. She wanted to prove to herself that there was more to her life than this fear.

If Mason was going to keep messing with her, he was going to encounter someone stronger than he expected. He was going to find someone he couldn't touch anymore.

Samantha had no idea what that looked like yet, but she felt stronger, sturdier, as they finished their conversation with the police.

And though her limbs were shaking with exhaustion by the time the deputy suggested they find someplace else to spend the night, just in case, her physical reaction didn't lessen her newfound strength. It only meant that she was human—that she needed to find food and rest so she would be ready for the challenges tomorrow would bring.

Chapter Eighteen

Yvette met them at the kitchen door two hours later with cocoa and a plate of pumpkin scones set out on the kitchen table. A sad smile played on her lips until she pulled Samantha into an embrace that was far tighter and more forceful than she expected from such a willowy woman. "I am so sorry, Sam. This is all so horrendous, and you do not deserve it."

Samantha almost started crying all over again. Her own mother would never say anything like that to her. She could already hear her now, asking Samantha what she'd done to invite this sort of attention from a man. Because men didn't behave this way toward women who behaved themselves.

That voice played so often in her head that Samantha was pretty certain she didn't deserve a person like Yvette in her life. Someone giving comfort and compassion so freely felt off-kilter to her, like she was suddenly starring in someone else's life.

"Thank you for letting us stay here tonight."

Yvette only squeezed her tighter. "What are big houses for if I can't help out the people I care about?" Then Yvette turned her attention to Charlotte, who was still lingering in the doorway. "And is this your roommate?"

"Yvette, this is Charlotte. Charlotte, this is Blake's mom, Yvette."

"You're the one who used to own the bakery?" Charlotte peered around them toward the table. Samantha had lost her appetite, but she knew her roommate was prone to stress eating.

"I am." Yvette released Samantha from her hug and made room for Charlotte to enter. Blake, who had still been standing on the stoop, closed and locked the door behind them.

"Don't mind if I do." Charlotte crossed the room and scooped up a scone at the same time she sunk into a chair. She was already dunking her scone into a steaming mug of cocoa by the time Samantha took in the open-plan kitchen with its high ceilings and big windows.

Yvette had her hands on either side of Blake's jaw, examining him for all hints of emotion as she asked how he was doing. Sam had never felt so dejected. He'd been strong for her, but she could tell that he was upset about his car. She'd gleaned that he was proud of it—it had always been immaculate, both inside and out—but he also wasn't one of those guys who went on and on about how many horsepower his car had or anything.

She'd watched his jaw clench as the police had towed it away, and his shoulders had been taut the entire time they'd given their statements. They'd all had to pile into Charlotte's ancient Ford coupe to make it to Blake's parents' house, because the police had advised Samantha not to use her car or come home for a couple of days until they could pick Mason up for violating the order.

Samantha was just taking comfort in the fact that they planned to look for him at all.

And she was kicking herself for not checking her old email sooner. The detective she'd worked with to file the restraining order had asked if she'd received any communication from Mason, and at first she'd said no until the man asked her if she'd checked her old phone number and email. Samantha didn't even know how to check her old phone number for texts, but she could log into her old email account.

The messages she'd found inside were horrifying. He had been emailing her old account three times a day or more. Sometimes professing his love for her. Sometimes telling her where he'd seen her. Or how he'd followed her home. How he hated the new restaurant owner she worked for. How the rich pussy was too old for her and wouldn't be able to please her.

How had she not even considered checking for communication since she'd filed the order? It had been one of the things she'd been told to check once a week or so, just in case.

Samantha hadn't checked it once since she'd moved.

At first, she'd been afraid to do it. Then she'd gotten so busy with her new job at Garden & Gather that she'd just plain forgotten about it. And now Blake's car was destroyed.

And he'd spent most of the evening comforting *her*.

Samantha joined Charlotte at the table, wrapping her fingers around a hot mug of steaming cocoa. It smelled amazing. So did the scones, but at the thought of consuming something, Samantha's stomach clenched with nausea.

Maybe she didn't want to hide anymore, but that didn't make being bold any easier. She allowed Yvette to fuss over them for twenty minutes before a yawn stretched her jaw, and Samantha used the opportunity to ask about her room.

Yvette showed Samantha to a room on the second floor—Charlotte was right next door. Apparently, Blake's room was at the other end of the hall. Even though Samantha had known that Blake's parents wouldn't pair her with Blake under their own roof while they weren't married, it was still disappointing to know that she wasn't going to be able to cuddle with him overnight.

After another round of hugs from Yvette and Charlotte and a chaste kiss from Blake, Samantha shut herself into a cheery yellow room.

The walls were pale but warm. The bedspread was a sweet, buttery calico with tiny blue flowers topped with lush, lace-edged pillows in front of a white iron headboard. White wicker tables with cream-fringed lamps bookended the bed. She even saw a matching yellow-and-blue-flowered tissue box next to one of the lamps. The room was adorable, but Samantha was too exhausted to do anything but stand there and stare at it.

Today was supposed to have been good. A celebration. Yet already she was second-guessing her decision to be stronger, to be a challenge. Samantha wasn't certain she had the fortitude to maintain the necessary energy for that—at least not tonight. She could get some sleep and indulge in some of Yvette's baked goods, and maybe everything would seem easier by morning than it did in this moment.

Finally, she dropped her duffel bag on the chest at the end of the bed then collected her toiletries and arranged them on the counter in the en suite bathroom. She wasn't sure how long she could stay away from her apartment. Charlotte had brought up looking for a new place on the drive over, but what was the point if Mason was going to just keep following them?

Samantha washed her face and brushed her teeth, fumbling with the strange faucet and searching with squinted eyes for the towel holder—which was on the side of the vanity—because she'd taken her contacts out without locating it yet.

She contemplated showering but decided she was too tired. Instead, she changed into a pair of running shorts and an old t-shirt and crawled into the bed. It was big and soft, and she sank into it like it was a cloud. Everything smelled like lavender and lemon, and Samantha fought the urge to cry again. Blake had just lost what was likely a very expensive car because of her, and here she was imposing on his family and luxuriating in this beautiful room like she deserved to be here.

This was not the life Samantha was used to, and she couldn't help but feel like a fraud for the way that the Fairchilds were taking care of her.

She startled when a knock at her door broke the silence, but a moment later, Blake peeked inside. "Can I come in?"

"Sure." Samantha didn't like how small her voice sounded.

A shirtless Blake slipped inside her room and shut the door behind him.

"How are you doing?" he asked as he sat on the edge of the bed by her feet.

Samantha was aware she was staring, but she'd never seen a man that looked like him up close before. Not like this. He wasn't bulky, but his tall, lean build showed that he exercised. She'd had no idea he was hiding abs under his clothes. Should she have noticed that earlier when she'd been undoing his shirt? Had she been too focused on her own pleasure not to realize?

"Overwhelmed," she said when she remembered he'd asked her a question.

Blake nodded and motioned to the open space beside her. "May I?"

Samantha nodded and scooted to the left a little more to make room for him. She couldn't take her eyes off the way his muscles moved and flexed under his skin as he adjusted his position on the bed.

"Nicolas got me into fitness." The little grin on his face told her he'd caught her staring, and Samantha's cheeks burned. But Blake continued talking like he didn't notice how embarrassed she was. "We went to the gym together for years and years, basically until I started putting distance between us because of the thing with Kat."

"But you obviously kept it up," she said as Blake's arm wrapped around her shoulders and he pulled her into his side. Samantha allowed one finger to slide down the smooth, taut skin on his stomach, and his muscles jumped.

He gave a noncommittal grunt but captured her hand when she started to trace her way back up. "That tickles."

"Which only makes me want to touch you more."

Blake's grip on her hand tightened, and he brought her knuckles to her lips. "You can touch me as much as you'd like, but first, tell me exactly what's overwhelming you."

Samantha wanted to motion to the universe and say "everything," but then Blake kissed her hand again, and she realized, as tired as she was, she wanted to talk to him about specifics, not avoid the subject with generalities.

"I'm worried they won't find Mason or that the violation of the order won't be enough to hold him for long. I'm afraid that he'll come back to the apartment, that Charlotte will get tired of the hassle, that you'll decide I'm not worth the loss of your car."

"I don't give a damn about the car."

Samantha snorted. "Nobody drives a car like that and doesn't just not give a damn about it."

Blake's lips brushed over her cheek as he adjusted his position so he could pull her closer. "The car was an indulgence, and it can be replaced. I can't replace you."

Samantha's breath caught in her throat. He couldn't have meant that like it sounded—could he?

She wanted to tell herself not to read too much into his words, but at the same time, Samantha was desperate to take comfort in anything she could. And maybe, if that was the reason Blake had come into her room, she should allow his presence to soothe her instead of fighting him on it.

"I have always felt replaceable." The words she whispered shrouded her most well-guarded secret: That she wasn't special enough to be singular to anybody. That she was just there to be tolerated or enjoyed for a short amount of time and then discarded.

But even as she thought it, she realized the fear wasn't fair to Charlotte, who, though they'd only known each other a couple of years, had upended her life to help keep Samantha safe. And her sister. She might not have followed Samantha out, but she still made an effort to stay in touch, unlike the rest of their family.

So maybe she didn't have *nobody*. And maybe her circle was small. And maybe it wouldn't be a bad thing to let Blake in so he could be a part of it.

"Same."

Samantha almost missed his quiet assent. She kissed the warm skin on his shoulder and breathed in the cozy, spicy scent of him that reminded her of Garden & Gather, earthy and fresh and completely scrumptious.

"I suppose that goes hand in hand with not fitting in anywhere," she offered, even though she still had trouble believing sometimes that gorgeous, confident Blake Fairchild had trouble not owning whatever space he found himself in. But that was the illusion he projected. That confidence was a mask, and he let very few people see behind it. Samantha wasn't even sure that Blake knew she'd seen through it, or if part of their connection was because he recognized that she couldn't be fooled.

"You are safe with me." He replaced her hand on his stomach and swept a few strands of hair that had already fallen from her braid out of her eye. "I won't leave you to deal with this mess alone, especially not if my presence makes it worse."

Oh. So that's what this was. He was feeling guilty about his part in Mason's strike. "When I'm with you, I can forget about all the trouble."

Blake kissed the top of her head. "Good."

Samantha stifled a yawn, but Blake reached for the quilt at the end of the bed to cover her anyway. She accepted the blanket but snaked her arms around his body when he made to get out of the bed. "You should sleep. It's a big day tomorrow."

Sam clung more tightly to him. "Will you stay with me?"

Blake nodded, his eyes unfocused as he settled back against the pillows. Samantha knew she should rest her head on his shoulder and allow the exhaustion from the day to overtake her, but he was so comforting and so vulnerable that she couldn't help dropping her lips to his one last time.

His kiss was warm, sensual safety, and she needed physical reassurance from him right now more than she needed air. He broke them off before she was ready with a pleading, "Sleep, Sam."

She wanted to tell him she'd never be able to fall asleep with him in her bed, but even as she pulled the quilt up around her shoulders, she could feel the blissful darkness pulling her under.

———◉———

BLAKE HADN'T DRIFTED off until well after midnight. That, coupled with having to get up early and go to the police station to sign the official report before heading into the restaurant, should have had him yawning his way through his first official day as a restaurateur, but Blake couldn't stop smiling.

He knew he shouldn't be wishing away his first day. That he should be savoring every time the door opened and the host led new guests to a table. He knew he should be celebrating each time someone told him they lived in the neighborhood and had always wanted a restaurant like this nearby, or how excited people got when they realized his mom's cupcakes were on the menu. He'd already sold two sets of two dozen for the weekend, much to Emil's annoyance.

He'd grumbled "I'm going to have to hire a whole damn person just to keep up with the cupcakes" when Blake had passed along the second order. And Blake had only smiled at that, too. The idea of having that much business brought him almost as much joy as the memory of waking up next to Samantha did.

Because she was who he couldn't stop thinking about.

Not about how the car he'd spent so much time and money on was totaled, or how much he had to accomplish before he could go home, or how his apartment was kind of a wreck because he'd been spending so much time at work, but the way Samantha had woken him with curious fingers running over the skin on his chest. The cute little squeak she'd let out when he'd surprised her by wrapping his arm around her waist and pulling her in close. The way her lips had felt against his as he'd kissed her. The supple warmth of her body against his under the covers.

Blake hadn't realized how much he'd been dreading sharing a bed with someone again until Samantha had asked him to stay with her. Rachel had been the first woman he'd ever spent a full night with, rare as those had been with her. He hadn't realized how much he'd been afraid that nothing would ever live up to the comfort and satisfaction he'd felt sleeping next to Rachel. But as Samantha had rolled on top of him with mischief in her eyes, he'd recognized the wall Rachel had always kept up between them. He couldn't judge Rachel for that—it was just another one of the signs he should have noticed sooner. One of many signs that, as much as he had wanted to make things with Rachel work, told him they weren't right for each other.

But Samantha?

He'd expected her to still be in shock upon waking, the way she'd been the night before, but instead, she'd straddled his hips with her bare thighs and pressed her chest into his as a smile graced her lips.

"I can't stop thinking about where last night was headed," she whispered into his ear. All Blake could think about was how the only thing that was separating her breasts from his skin was the thin material of the old t-shirt she'd worn to sleep in and how quickly that shirt could be in a puddle on the floor.

He slipped his fingers under the hem to smooth over her silky soft skin at the same time she pulled his lower lip between her teeth. He hadn't expected Samantha to be a playful lover—not that they'd had much chance to consummate anything—but he'd prepared himself for her to be a little serious and a little shy. He'd been looking forward to coaxing what she liked out of her, but this surprising confidence was a heady delight.

She wiggled on top of him, grinding her hips against his in what he was sure was meant to be a flirty motion, but he had to swallow the moan from her mouth when he rocked up into the heat of her.

"You're teasing me," he said against her lips.

Samantha shook her head so that the tip of her nose brushed over his. "Never. I want you."

Blake was about to allow himself to forget that they were in his mother's house, birth control conversation and the fact that he didn't have any condoms be damned. He could have rolled her over and indulged his desire for her right then and there. And he'd been planning on it until his mom had knocked on Sam's door with a reminder that there were fresh waffles for breakfast and that she'd better hurry if she wanted any before Charlotte ate them all.

Mood killed, they'd disentangled themselves and descended the stairs for breakfast. But each time Blake had glimpsed Samantha today, they'd shared a secret smile. The kind that carried a promise. That they had each other, no matter the drama with her stalker. No matter that he was driving his mom's old wedding cake delivery van.

They would be there for one another. And he couldn't wait to start proving that to her tonight.

Chapter Nineteen

So if you don't marry that man, I think I will.

Samantha rolled her eyes and tucked her phone back in her apron. Charlotte had been texting her all day long about how delicious Yvette's cooking was and how she was going to find ways to eat with the Fairchilds more often.

Or you could see if Yvette would leave James and marry you instead.

Charlotte responded with the emoji tapping its finger against its chin like that was an idea worth considering. Samantha laughed then made herself put her phone away and step back out onto the floor. It had been a busy day. A really good day for the restaurant, but even so, Samantha knew she and Charlotte probably wouldn't be joking like this if Mason hadn't been arrested that morning.

Samantha had gotten the call just before the restaurant opened. Mason had been apprehended when he'd taken his car into a body shop to repair the damage done to it from ramming Blake's quattro. He'd told the mechanic he'd been involved in a hit and run, but the mechanic had thought the whole thing was fishy and had called in the plates, just in case.

Imagining the police swarming a garage and leading Mason away in cuffs was her new favorite fantasy. She could see the entire scene in her head as clearly as if she were watching a movie. Red and blue lights would catch on the floor-to-ceiling glass windows as the small garage was surrounded. Mason would be clueless and confused, the way he'd been in court, claiming his innocence despite the video evidence they had against him. He'd be making idle threats, telling the cops they'd regret doing their jobs like he was actually as important as he'd convinced himself he was in his head.

Samantha chuckled to herself every time she imagined him being shut into the back of a squad car.

Serves the motherfucker right, she mused.

Now she just hoped that he would stay in jail. But she would worry over all that later. Right now, Mason was not free to haunt her every step. She was free to live her life without fear or hindrance for possibly the first time ever.

Samantha felt like she could fly. Especially considering the way Blake's eyes burned when they caught each other's gazes across the restaurant. At every glance, confidence zipped through her body, leaving a pleasant, tingling zing on her skin.

That this man wanted her was surreal, but the memory of the night before, of his hands on her hips, his lips on her neck, the way his hardness had lined up just so with her perfect spot—the way he'd woken up with hungry intent in his eyes and need tensing the muscles she'd been resting on—had her swooning.

More than once today, she'd found herself frozen in the middle of making a cocktail as she remembered the release she'd had with their clothes still on and the implicit promise of how much better it could be once they were skin to skin. Then she'd shake herself back to reality and finish her drink.

Samantha was glad for the customers at the bar to distract her, thankful for finding all the little things she'd somehow missed programming into the register system or that for some reason none of the vodkas printed on the drink orders. She knew she'd be busy fixing all of that the next morning, but that was fine. All she had to do was make it through today. Because tonight?

Tonight was all for Blake.

They hadn't discussed it, but when Yvette had asked him if they'd be back for a second night, he'd told his mother that Samantha would be staying with him. Yvette had blinked then grinned and turned to assure Charlotte she was welcome for as long as was needed. Samantha wasn't entirely sure she was supposed to have overheard that conversation, but she had zero arguments with it. Blake lived alone. They were far less likely to be interrupted at his apartment than anywhere else.

And Samantha wasn't quite ready to go back to her apartment yet.

Even just considering that Mason had been watching her there sent shivers down her spine. She'd needed ten minutes to shake off the prickle of awareness that came with the feeling that someone was watching her, though her brain told her that Mason was locked away.

The evening rush kept her busy enough to forget about almost everything. They'd had enough walk-ins that there was a thirty-minute wait for unreserved tables, and the bar had been full since five o'clock. She knew every Monday wouldn't be like this, that the neighborhood was just excited that they were open, but Samantha allowed herself to revel in the rightness of how good she felt.

She'd been afraid that what she'd liked about her new job was the preparation, the building of something new, and that she'd get bored with being behind the bar like she'd been at the sports bar, and often, at the night club. And while the space was still new and shiny and the everyday problems had yet to kick in with full force, Samantha's heart glowed with contentment. Like she'd finally landed in the exact right place for her.

She couldn't keep the smile off her face as she worked, like that glow was begging to escape and shine its light on all of Garden & Gather's new patrons. And when she would catch Blake's eye as he chatted with guests at their tables or helped run drinks from the bar, anticipation would zip down her spine as she imagined their future. They would have tonight—the dark, sensual pleasure of their joining—but they would also have their partnership together. First here, building this restaurant, then maybe, if Samantha let herself hope just a little bit, *maybe* they could make something special that would last the rest of their lives.

She allowed herself five minutes while mixing cocktails of imagining what life would be like with him. What their little boy would look like running into Blake's arms when he came home from a long day of work. How they'd put their son to bed together then snuggle on the sofa and catch up on their days over wine before setting aside their empty glasses for activities that involved using both of their hands to disrobe one another.

Then she forced her attention back on her work and told herself to slow down. Just because he seemed interested in pursuing a relationship with her and had been planning to marry his last girlfriend did not mean that he was ready to jump straight into domesticity.

He was a thirty-eight-year-old bachelor. It was possible he'd changed his mind and wanted to stay that way. And as much as Samantha wanted to prove to the world that it was possible to raise a family in a healthy, secular way, she wasn't sure yet if that was something she actually wanted or if she just wanted to spite her parents.

She probably needed to figure that out before she got into an actual long-term relationship with anybody. But as Blake locked the doors after the last guest left and flashed her a heated look accompanied with a shy smile, Samantha didn't want to think about the future.

All she could think about was the now.

———◦———

THE DRIVE BACK TO HIS apartment took too long. Samantha hadn't stopped grazing her fingertips up and down his thigh as he drove, setting off fires throughout his entire nervous system and heating his blood. Blake burned for more of her touch, but he was running so hot by the time they reached his building and he showed her inside that he was afraid he would singe her clothes as he enclosed her in his arms.

Instead, when he steered her toward the sofa and pulled her down on top of him, she sighed into his kiss and melted into his embrace. Melting—that was a far better use for heat than burning. It was slower, subtler, more about joining than destruction.

Maybe that had always been his problem. He'd either burned too much or not enough. He'd never found that slow, steady flame that warmed and soothed and melted.

Samantha's body fused with his, every soft part of hers melding with the hard parts of him. Her velvet tongue dipped past his lips. She tasted vaguely of the wine he'd brought her when he'd forced her to sit down and eat something after the evening rush. The new-construction and herb-and-spice smell of the restaurant clung to her clothes, but he could make out her lemony scent as she closed one arm around his neck and scrunched the fingers on her other hand into his hair.

Her breasts smashed against his chest, and just the memory of the way she'd looked without her shirt the night before had his fingers searching out her buttons.

Samantha smiled against his lips as he pulled on the knot of her tie. They'd dressed alike again today. Blake was contemplating making the tie part of the uniform for management staff, but he wasn't thinking about that now. Figuring out how to get Samantha out of her clothes without separating her body from his was more important to him in this moment.

Kissing her was too vital to his survival to chance breaking contact for even a second. Samantha's thighs hugged his sides as she wrapped herself even tighter around him, and he gave up on the tie for a moment. He gave up on anything that wasn't soaking up as much of this woman as he could while he had her here where no one could disturb them.

"Do you have condoms?"

The question came between nips at his lower lip, and Blake had difficulty reeling himself in enough to use spoken language. His mode of communication had devolved to grunts and gropes, apparently.

"Blink twice for yes, once for no." Samantha gave a final nip to the tip of his nose and sat back with her gaze locked onto his eyes as if she were actually waiting for him to communicate through slow blinks.

"I have condoms." His voice was a hoarse, garbled version of his usual tone, but at least he'd managed to speak in English.

"Are they in your bedroom?" She rolled her hips on the last word, arching against the bulge in his jeans.

Blake took the opportunity to latch his teeth onto her left breast through her shirt. He didn't expect her to giggle and squirm on his lap like she was ticklish there.

Interesting.

"Do you want to see my bedroom?"

Samantha nodded and bit her lip as pink tinged her cheeks. "If that's okay?"

Blake bit the tip of her middle finger and held her hand over his heart. "I've had trouble thinking about anything else all day long."

Her fingers flexed on his chest. "Your heart is beating so quickly."

"I'm nervous," Blake admitted.

Her bottom lip disappeared behind her teeth again just as her brow furrowed, and Blake wanted to smooth his fingers over her eyebrows to make her frown disappear. "Why?"

"Because this feels like a big step for us."

Her cheeks flushed even darker as she ducked her head down. "I guess it is."

"Do you want to stop?"

Samantha shook her head.

Blake patted the side of her hip to signal to her that she should stand. "Then let's go."

His apartment only had one bedroom—it wasn't like she couldn't figure out where it was—but he liked that she waited for him to take the lead, like she wanted him to show her the way.

Somehow, he found the fortitude to guide her to her feet, but he couldn't keep his hands off her for long. He wrapped his arms around her shoulders from behind and guided her toward the bedroom while he laid kisses along the length of her neck. "This way, my love."

<hr />

SAMANTHA WAS SURROUNDED by Blake as he ushered her into his bedroom. His arms were locked over her shoulders, and his legs guided hers with each step as they shuffled into the room. When her knees hit the edge of his bed, he rotated her in his arms until he could lay her down on the bed. With a kiss, he straightened and started undoing the buttons on his shirt with one hand as he loosened his tie with the other.

And the realization finally hit Samantha: This was really going to happen.

She was going to have sex with Blake, her boss and the most beautiful man she had ever met. Because he wanted her as much as she wanted him. In spite of the cognitive dissonance that made it difficult for her to believe that someone as attractive as him was interested in someone as ordinary as her, Samantha didn't doubt for a second that he was in this for the right reasons.

They had chosen each other. Despite their problematic exes. Despite their past trauma. Despite everything, they were going to make this work between the two of them.

One by one, Samantha's garments fell away. First her tie, then her shirt. She kicked off her shoes as Blake fumbled with the button on her pants.

She was down to her bra and panties before she had the cognitive ability to remember that she wanted him naked as well. Samantha began tearing at his collar the same time he started kissing along the length of her collarbone. He pulled back and tore his shirt over his head, and suddenly he was bare-chested.

He pressed himself against her too quickly for Sam to run her hand down his chest, but his body pinned against hers on the bed was a more delicious experience than she had anticipated. Even with her bra between them, Samantha wanted to writhe against every inch of his exposed skin. Her spontaneous attempts to do so brought her back in contact with the bulge in his jeans without her meaning to.

Blake groaned, rocked into her core twice, and then tore himself away, shedding the rest of his clothes before Sam could even blink. He crashed down on her, his naked flesh heated against hers. She lifted her hips, and Blake peeled her panties down her legs. He shucked the rest of his clothes to the floor before he settled back over her, coaxing her to sit up just enough to rid her of her bra.

His lips landed on hers even as she felt him fumbling for a moment before she heard the rip of foil. Anticipation shot through her as he placed just enough space between them to roll the condom on, then he settled back between her legs.

Blake captured one of her nipples between his teeth and nipped at the same time he pressed his hips forward and slipped inside her with ease. Samantha's body filled with the weight and girth of him, but she welcomed the invasion.

He thrust once, then twice, his teeth still grazing over her nipple, and Samantha thought she might combust from the intensity of the depth of sensation pulsing through her. Each press of his hips against hers sent a shock of pure pleasure through her, and when she was finally able to guide his lips back to hers, Samantha wrapped her legs around Blake's waist and encouraged him to move on her faster. Harder.

She couldn't get enough of the feel of him inside her. The way he stretched her, reaching that dark recess in her body only her bedside vibrator had ever touched.

The more she moaned and thrashed against him, the more effort Blake put into trying to make her writhe. Between his kisses and the drive of his hips, Samantha wasn't sure she'd survive the experience.

Blake shifted over her, placing a hand at the small of her back and angling her hips up just enough that a moaning mewl erupted from Samantha's throat at the same moment Blake's mouth covered her pulse point and sucked.

Samantha's nerves exploded in sensation. She felt like her entire body had caught fire as her core ignited and her brain shuttered into darkness punctuated by pulses of pure pleasure. She was vaguely aware of Blake cursing from on top of her as his own movements became erratic then slowed.

He cursed again—a chorus of "holy shit"s and "fuck"s and "Jesus Christ"s peppered between kisses littered across her collarbone.

Samantha stroked a hand down his long, lean back. "I've never been worthy of blasphemy before." Amusement tinged her tone.

Blake pushed up on his elbows so his lips met hers in a slow, reverent kiss. "That wasn't blasphemy. That was worship."

Chapter Twenty

Samantha was obsessed with the sound of Blake's heartbeat. She'd ended up on his left side after they'd collapsed into heaps of mutually sated exhaustion the night before, and she was already planning to make this her permanent side of the bed.

She'd never had a side of the bed before.

Maybe it was the afterglow of the most extraordinary sexual experience Samantha had ever had, but the idea of being a person who had *a side of the bed* sent a shiver down her spine. Having her own side of the bed meant that there was someone to share the bed with. That there was someone who was choosing to sleep with her, who wanted to keep her close enough to be able to reach for her in the night. Someone who didn't mind if she accidentally drooled on them in her sleep.

Though Samantha still hoped Blake had slept through her wiping the small puddle off his chest with the corner of the sheet a few minutes ago.

His heart rate was still even beneath her ear. The steady *lub dub* coupled with his regular breaths all pointed to a deep, early morning sleep that she knew he needed. He'd barely left the restaurant these last few weeks unless he'd been hanging out with her, and while that had all been thrilling, Samantha found as much satisfaction in knowing he'd found comfort and repose with her as she had in the act of bringing him pleasure the night before.

Remembering the way he'd shuddered through his release, the string of curses he'd let loose when he'd gathered her closer into his arms as if there had been a way he could meld their bodies together further, caused her skin to heat again. She couldn't recall a sexual encounter before last night that hadn't been awkward or problematic in some way. Her previous lovers had often not taken her pleasure into account—nor had they been impressed with her inexperience.

But nothing about her encounter with Blake had been fumbling or embarrassing. Every part of their exchange had felt natural and right, as if they had always been meant to share those precious intimacies. She hoped they'd have multiple opportunities in the future to explore and learn more about each other in that way.

The last two nights had taught her that he slept on his back with his feet crossed at the ankle and one hand over his head. She imagined the other was usually sprawled out across his spare pillow, but since she'd been in bed with him, he'd kept it wrapped around her shoulders instead.

Her signal to his waking both mornings was not necessarily the change in his breathing or the rhythm of his heartbeat but in the way his hand smoothed down her side like it was doing at the moment. But the main difference between yesterday and what was happening now? Yesterday, Samantha had been clothed, and this morning, the only thing she wore was Blake's cozy down comforter.

And there was no one to interrupt them.

When Blake's traveling hand reached her breast, he squeezed then rolled, pulling her underneath him and entwining his legs with hers. The motion was so swift and unexpected from the man she'd thought was barely awake that Samantha shrieked out something halfway between a laugh and a yelp.

Though the sound was quickly cut off when Blake's lips crashed down on hers. His body pressed against her own just shy of crushing her, but the heavy weight was warm and soft, the perfect mixture of comforting and arousing.

"Good morning," she said when he broke off from her lips and nipped his way down her neck. She gasped when he sucked on her shoulder.

His lips curled against her skin before he returned the greeting. His voice was like gravel, still retaining the residue of sleep. That somehow made her less cranky about the fact that he'd likely just given her a hickey.

Blake continued nibbling down her body, moving over her chest until he'd captured her right nipple in his mouth. The bite stung just enough for her back to arch up off the bed. A half groan, half growl sounded from Blake's chest. And when he sucked hard on her breast, Samantha felt the pull and tug all the way down to her core.

Just as Samantha was feeling recovered enough to participate, Blake switched to her other breast. All she could do was cling to his shoulders as the shock of pleasure thrummed through her.

"Do you like it a little rough sometimes?" he asked.

Samantha didn't know what to say. She had no idea. She hadn't had enough sex to know what she did or didn't like.

All she knew was that she liked what he was doing to her now, so she said, "I like you."

That seemed to be the right thing to say, because Blake grinned, a hint of tenderness shining beneath the mischievous gleam in his eye. "I want you to like what I do to you."

Samantha curled her fingers in the hair at the back of his neck, pressing his head toward her breast at the same time she arched toward his mouth. "I have no complaints so far."

Blake's grin flared as he lowered his mouth back to her breast then sucked so hard she bucked underneath him. She felt the heat of him first then the weight of his shaft as it slipped over her folds in a dangerous caress that tempted her to open her legs and invite him in sans protection. The indulgent danger of it spurred her desire, and she tilted her hips just enough for the head of him to caress her clit.

Blake cursed and met her halfway on the next micro-thrust, pressing himself along her wet heat. They both moaned at the apex. Blake's lips melded against hers as he braced himself against the bed on his elbows, sliding through her folds with intention, deliberately pressing into her clit at the top of each thrust.

Samantha expected to burst with each press of his hips into hers, but the pressure only built inside her, winding her tighter and tighter in a way that made her never want to stop.

Blake broke their kiss and buried his face in her shoulder with another curse. His hot breath fanned over the skin on her neck as he panted, and sweat had begun to form between their bellies.

"I need you to tell me if I ever do something you don't like."

Samantha wasn't sure she had the words to assent, but she managed to force out an "Okay," before she coaxed his hips to roll against hers again.

"Sam, I'm serious."

"So am I." She bucked against him another time then found the shell of his ear with her lips and nipped the top. He cursed again, and Samantha loved how foul his mouth became in bed. She'd rarely heard him use four-letter words outside their couplings, and she felt like those words were reserved just for her and the effect she had on his body.

"I could stay here all day," he said as he placed small bites all the way up her neck.

"So could I, but we don't have all day, so we should probably get a condom."

Blake groaned in what sounded like mock disappointment then twisted to the side so he could reach for the cardboard box that still sat on top of his bedside table. He sat back just long enough to sheath himself then plunged inside her with one harsh push of his hips.

Sam cried out, recognizing the hint of roughness he'd mentioned earlier. And while the invasion into her sore body was a shock, she loved that he wanted her this badly, so she rocked back into his next thrust, meeting the force of his movement. He grasped her hips, tilting them up and causing her back to arch so he reached even deeper inside her.

Samantha hooked her heels around his thighs, inviting him to drive into her more completely. She'd never connected with another body like this, never felt someone else's need for her so desperately that she couldn't help but want more of him.

She could spend the rest of her life like this, giving and receiving. Panting. Moaning. Sweating. Wanting.

Her hands scrabbled for purchase on his skin as he wrapped one arm under her waist, pulling her closer. She didn't want to scratch him by digging her nails into his shoulders, but that was the only way she could find leverage. A cringe of apprehension echoed through her as she allowed her nails to sink into his skin, but instead of stopping and scolding her like the last time this had happened—the only other time she'd scratched a partner—Blake cursed on a satisfied growl and slammed his body into hers harder.

The slight shift in position he made to gain momentum was the exact amount of pressure she needed to ignite. Her whole body clenched around the point where she joined with Blake. Her existence centered around the electric pulse until she felt suspended in sensation that slowly spread to include the way Blake shuddered with her. And when he stilled, the first thing in the world she was aware of that wasn't centered around her orgasm was his lips on her neck.

"Jesus Christ, Sam," he breathed as he slowly rolled to the side. With a final kiss to the shell of her ear, he sat up and discarded the condom.

That was when Samantha noticed the welts on his shoulders from her fingernails. She traced over the longest one with the tip of her finger. Other than a muscle twitching in his shoulder, Blake didn't react to her touch. "Sorry if I got a little carried away with the scratching."

Blake shook his head as he rotated to face her on the bed, a grin on his beautiful face. His eyes sparkled, and he ran his fingers through his unruly hair as if to tame it, like he was self-conscious about how he looked, even now, here, alone with her. "Are you kidding me? That was perfect. And now every time I raise my arm today"—he demonstrated by reaching for his water glass on the bedside table and raising it to his lips with an exaggerated wince before holding it out to her—"I'll think of you, of us, in this bed."

Samantha took a sip from the glass, trying to contain the glow his words ignited inside her. She was afraid that if she smiled, the whole world would know she'd started sleeping with her boss, but she was having trouble caring. She was also pretty certain there would be no way she could conceal the fact that her brain short-circuited every time she looked at him.

"That wasn't . . ." He ran both hands through his hair this time. "I wasn't too intense for you?"

Samantha shook her head. She knew her eyes were wide and her hair was likely more of a mess than his, but she'd never had sex like that before. She'd never made a connection with another person that was soul-deep like that. "I loved it," she said then had to stop herself from saying "I love you." Because she wasn't certain if that was true or if she was just completely sex-addled. She'd definitely have to consider it once the glow dimmed a little bit and she could think about anything other than what he felt like between her thighs.

Even still, Samantha had a feeling she'd be riding that high for the rest of the week.

"Good. You'll tell me, though, if I do something you don't like?"

"Of course." Samantha had trouble conceptualizing that she might not be mesmerized by any touch from Blake, but she understood what he was asking. She appreciated the sentiment, since it showed he was being considerate of her pleasure and that he valued consent—and after how she'd grown up and what she'd been through herself, it actually meant a lot. But it was difficult to imagine him hurting her in any way when she was still reeling from her discovery that sex could be so much more than she'd ever realized.

On some level, she'd known that there had to be something more to it than awkward encounters and guys who cared more about their pleasure than hers, but comparing stories with Charlotte and other girlfriends, they'd decided that those encounters were likely rare. Samantha had had more orgasms in the last twelve hours than she'd had in all of her previous sexual encounters combined, and as she and Blake prepared for their day at the restaurant, she felt like it had made her a little bit dopey.

She couldn't keep her mind on any of the tasks in front of her. Images of Blake's body moving against hers would periodically steal into her mind, and she'd find herself zoning out at the cocktail table behind the bar as she remembered every touch, every sigh and moan, every spark zipping through her nervous system.

Then she would realize what she was doing and where she was, and her skin would flush crimson and she'd have to fan herself to bring her complexion back to normal.

More than one of her servers had asked if she was feeling okay, which had only made her blush more. One of those times had been when Emil had stepped out of the kitchen to grab some beer for one of his sauce recipes. He'd tossed out, "Nah, she's fine. She arrived with the bossman this morning. I'm sure he gave her a nice ride."

Sienna's eyes grew wide, and Samantha snapped her bar towel at Emil, catching him on the hip. He jumped like it actually hurt as she told him to mind his own business and get back to the kitchen. Then to Sienna, she said, "That was inappropriate, but Blake and I are together, in case there are any rumors flying around." They weren't hiding from the staff anyway. And if her upbringing had taught her nothing else it was that hiding from your feelings didn't work. They always had a way of getting out eventually.

Maybe if she hadn't hidden her misgivings about her parents and Tim Jennings, she could have convinced Sarah to come with her when she left instead of marrying Joseph.

Sienna nodded, her eyes still wide like she was scandalized. Great. Have the one server who'd had zero clue and her and Blake be the one who overheard Emil's lewd joke.

Samantha topped the mule Sienna had been waiting on with a lime and shoved the mug toward her, pretending business was the only thing on her mind, like it was no big deal the bar manager was sleeping with the owner. "Did you need anything else?"

Sienna shook her head and ran her drink to her table, which was, thankfully, in the greenhouse and out of sight of the bar. Samantha bit back her annoyance and was doubly thankful when Blake emerged from his office a moment later, greeted her with a kiss, and reminded her about the cocktail sampler flight she was supposed to have ready for the journalist who was coming in soon.

"I didn't forget. Did they say if they preferred a whiskey focus or a vodka-and-gin focus?"

"Can we do both? If not just for the photographs?"

"Ooo, I like that idea—just don't drink them all before you eat something."

"I'm bringing her out appetizers, too."

"Fancy," Samantha said even as jealousy sparked in her chest. As intimate as she'd been with him, the closest thing they'd had to a date had been their "work trip" to the brewery. And appetizers and drinks at a restaurant like Garden & Gather was exactly the kind of date she'd always wanted to go on. Even if logically she knew this was work for Blake, they'd still both been working so much. She wasn't sure if they'd ever get a chance to enjoy the atmosphere they'd been working nonstop to build.

But then Blake pulled her into his arms and kissed the top of her head. She heard him inhaling the scent of her hair before he asked, "Are you sure you're ready to go back to your place? We can stay at mine as long as you'd like."

She couldn't hide the unfurling warmth inside her chest at his question. "I'm out of clean clothes, and I need to check in with Charlotte. See how she's doing."

He pulled back, his hands skimming down her arms until he grasped her fingers and pulled her knuckles to his lips, kissing each hand in turn. "I understand."

"You're invited, you know."

His eyebrows raised as if he hadn't realized she'd meant she wanted *them* to stay at her apartment tonight when she mentioned needing to go there earlier.

"I was kind of hoping we could reprise last night. If you're interested."

The expression around his eyes changed from questioning to intrigued in less than a second. "I am definitely interested."

"Good." Samantha placed one last quick kiss on his lips before she shooed him out from behind the bar. As she heard the front door open again, she tried not to count the hours until close.

Chapter Twenty-One

The last people Blake expected to see sitting at his bar at eight thirty on a busy Wednesday night were his parents. They must have come straight from church. Which would have made complete sense if they were anybody else but, you know, his parents.

They usually went straight home after church. They didn't drink, they ate early, and his mom probably had a better chocolate cake than Emil could bake just sitting on the counter waiting for them to enjoy. He had no idea what they were doing there, and their presence was putting him on edge.

He'd been in his office since Emil had evicted him from the kitchen two hours ago. Over the last few days, Blake had taken up the habit of hovering around the expo station, helping to plate and organize trays to make sure the food got to tables quickly and efficiently. He also wanted to ensure the plate presentation was consistent from shift to shift and day to day since that was the first impression of the food a guest received.

Emil had had to remind Blake that all of that was technically the chef's job, so Blake had taken the hint and retreated. Lord knew he had no shortage of work to do in his office anyway.

His files were still in chaos. And on top of that, he had checks to write, phone calls to return, emails to read and respond to, events to start planning . . . Blake had barely given himself enough time to eat in the last few days let alone get caught up on, well, everything.

The fact that every time he sat down at his desk flashes of Samantha's bare skin immediately crowded his brain maybe didn't help. Nor did the recounting of the swell of her hip beneath his hand, the curve of where her shoulder met her neck, the back side of her knees as she opened her legs for him, or the way she tipped her chin up in ecstasy as he sucked her nipple between his teeth.

Blake had found himself shaking his head more than once to banish that particular image so he could double down and concentrate. And remembering it as he approached his parents wasn't going to do him any favors.

He'd expressed plainly that he'd stayed with Samantha overnight to ensure her safety. His mother was mature enough to recognize that adult relationships came with sleepovers, but he knew that the fact he was pushing forty wasn't doing him any favors with his dad.

Blake didn't really know what to tell him. He'd never exactly hidden the fact that he'd left the "saving himself for marriage" rhetoric behind in high school. He'd seen too many of his church friends get married just to have sex when they were eighteen or nineteen then watched those marriages devolve into misery and abuse—or just plain dissolve—within a couple of years to trust himself to make such an important decision based on lust. If only he'd been prepared not to make decisions based on loneliness, then maybe he'd have avoided the catastrophe with Kat.

But he wasn't entirely certain his dad wasn't going to scold him on the floor of his own restaurant for having sex with his girlfriend.

Girlfriend.

Even thinking the word filled his chest with warmth. Meeting her eye when she beamed at him from behind the bar as she set two steaming mugs down in front of his parents renewed his memory about the way her body felt pressed against his under the covers. Only two or three more hours and he could have her there again.

Blake plastered a smile onto his face that wasn't entirely false. He was always genuinely delighted to see his mother, and Samantha's grin tempted him into planning what he was going to do with her in three hours. But his father's strange cough coupled with the perpetual frown he'd worn since Blake had left his position at Grace Bible was enough for him to not get very far.

He almost felt as if his father could see the salacious blueprints for the rest of his night being rolled out, so Blake tucked them back inside his head where they were safe. Then he made sure he wore the fond smile he was fairly certain his mother couldn't see through to make up for how on edge he felt around his dad.

Blake missed those few blissful years when he'd had his father's respect, and he didn't think anything he did going forward would stop him from feeling like a perpetual disappointment.

Yvette spread her arms for a hug as he approached, but Blake did her one better by dropping a kiss on her cheek as she embraced him. "What are you two doing here?"

"Your mother was craving a decaf mocha," his dad said, extending a hand in greeting. Blake shook it, pretending that was the welcome he wanted from his father instead of something more intimate, even just a simple casual embrace. Blake didn't think his father offered those anymore.

"I needed a warm drink." Yvette cupped her mug and blew into the steam wafting over the top. "It's gotten so cold the last couple of days."

The temperature had finally dropped into weather more appropriate for the end of October, but Blake had barely noticed. He couldn't remember when he'd spent any amount of time outside. He'd even taken to running on the treadmill at his complex's gym just because it was faster than driving to his favorite running trail.

"Well, it's good to see you."

His mother squeezed his elbow. "So are you really going to leave this place long enough to attend your cousin's wedding this weekend?"

Blake nodded, even though he had completely forgotten about Faye's wedding.

"Don't worry—I'll make sure he gets there," Sam said from where she washed dishes a few feet down the bar.

"Oh, you're coming!" Yvette sounded ecstatic like Blake knew she would, but he didn't miss his father's scowl. And neither did Sam. Her expression fell into a flash of confusion before she rallied and plastered a smile back on for his mom.

"Blake invited me a few weeks ago." Her eyes shot to his then darted toward his father before she turned to smile at his mother. "If that's okay."

"Of course it's okay. It's fantastic."

James drummed his fingers on the counter, and Blake suspected his dad had figured out the reason for their visit to Garden & Gather at the same time Blake had: to make sure that Blake *and* Samantha were coming to the wedding.

Only Blake wasn't sure what his father disapproved of. Was it his relationship with Sam? Was it his new career? Or was it just everything about Blake's existence?

His mother had already started listing the relatives she wanted Samantha to meet, including the bride. Who, Blake agreed, Sam would probably get along with well. She and Faye were about the same age and worked in the same field.

Blake wondered belatedly if he should have involved his cousin in the building of Garden & Gather but shoved the idea aside. She could have said something, and she'd been busy planning her wedding. But maybe he should reach out once she was back from her honeymoon. Just because his dad wasn't happy with his decisions didn't mean he had to avoid the rest of his family.

To her credit, Sam seemed enthusiastic about the upcoming family gathering and even agreed to go dress shopping with his mother the next day just before shooting a glance at Blake. "That is, if you all think you can live without me over the lunch shift?"

It took Blake a second to pull himself out of the depths of her gorgeous eyes and hopeful smile and realize that she was asking him permission to take a break. "Of course, that's fine. Sienna and I can handle lunch."

"Or you could come with us." Sam raised her eyebrows as she bit her lower lip, looking so hopeful that Blake was tempted even if shopping with his mom was the last thing he wanted to do.

His father answered for him. "Blake needs to be here. If this is what he's chosen to do, this is where he needs to be."

Some of the old conviction Blake was used to from his sermons sounded in James's voice, but his last word was cut off by a wheezing cough that had his mother frowning at him over James's head. She reached out to rub her husband's back, and the cough ended as suddenly as it began. "That doesn't mean he doesn't deserve a day off."

"Or to eat food that's not on the menu here," Sam added.

"I like our food," Blake said. "Being able to eat it every day was kind of the point of starting the place." He was rewarded with Sam rolling her eyes at him and his mother huffing into her mocha. His father, Blake noticed, hadn't even touched his coffee. Blake wondered if he was afraid Sam had spiked it with whiskey and Irish cream instead of espresso and chocolate syrup.

"You are also allowed to take a day off," Sam said, and he focused his attention back on her. She was the one looking out for him in this situation. She was the one who made him feel good, feel wanted.

Blake wasn't responsible for the way his father reacted to his choices. If James didn't want to enjoy what Blake had created, that was his own issue.

"Sure." Blake stretched his arm around his mom, grabbed two empty wine glasses, and handed them to Samantha. "I will take a break, but not before the wedding. And eventually I'll settle into a regular day or two off a week."

Both his mother and Samantha furrowed their brows like they didn't quite believe him, and while Blake wasn't able to completely slough off the disappointment that he wasn't ever going to please his dad, he did take comfort in knowing that he had these two women on his side.

"Yeah, we'll have to work on that." Samantha smirked as she turned to pluck the new ticket off the printer and make the next drink.

She should talk. She wasn't delegating like she should—sending the bartenders home early and closing herself just to stay on the same schedule as he was, for example. But with Mason in jail, there was no reason she shouldn't be able to do things on her own. Go dress shopping, have a drink out with Charlotte, watch movies, go to bed early. Blake would have to set some boundaries for her work schedule in the next couple of weeks so she didn't burn herself out.

"You and your dad could go car shopping next weekend." Yvette nudged James on the elbow. James jumped then assented as if he'd only just heard what his wife had said.

"That's fine," James said to his mocha. "It's only a matter of time before that old delivery van gives up the ghost. Better get you something before you find yourself stranded on the side of the highway."

Car shopping wasn't necessarily the kind of quality time with his dad Blake was craving, but it was something. "That would be nice. Thanks, Dad."

James nodded, spinning the mug on the saucer.

———————●———————

BRINGING CHARLOTTE along on her dress shopping date with Yvette had sounded like a good idea at the time. Charlotte loved shopping, and she was always a pro at finding the good sales, but Samantha had also forgotten that the other thing Charlotte was really good at was finding clothes so scandalous Samantha could barely look at them, let alone wear them in public.

So far, she'd handed Samantha a red dress with such a low neckline that Sam was pretty sure her belly button would be visible if she tried it on. Then there was the short, black, sequined dress she wasn't convinced would cover her ass as well as a few others that were all a healthy combination of glitz and glamour. Samantha added a few more modest pieces to the collection for her to try on.

Yvette apparently already had her dress and was on the lookout for shoes. Sam had known that the Fairchilds were well-off based on the quality of the clothes they wore, how big their house was, and the kinds of cars they drove, but Samantha was not prepared for the sticker shock she felt when Yvette bought a seven-hundred-dollar pair of silver stilettos.

Samantha had gulped down her apprehension when Yvette steered them toward the designer department store. Charlotte had clapped her hands together in glee and told Samantha that even if she didn't find anything here, they'd at least know what they were looking for elsewhere.

Sam had claimed that she could just wear her green dress to the wedding, which she'd been planning to do all along, but Charlotte had pushed her through the door that Yvette held open for them and told her she couldn't wear a Target dress to a wedding at a boutique hotel.

"I didn't get it at Target," Samantha had said, but Charlotte had shushed her.

Charlotte had yet to pick one dress that Samantha thought she'd feel comfortable donning in public. Everything had bare shoulders or clung too tightly to her tummy or hit a few inches too far above the knee. Samantha wasn't prepared to show off that much of her body to anyone but Blake.

That didn't mean she didn't have a pile of dresses to try on. She just hadn't allowed herself to look at the price tags on any of them. She already knew she couldn't afford anything from this store, but she *could* do what Charlotte had suggested: find a cut that flattered her and look for something similar from a different store that was more within her budget.

Charlotte shoved her into a changing room and insisted she begin trying on the dresses and then modeling them because, quote, "If we leave you up to your own devices, you'll choose one of those pastel monstrosities." And Yvette's muffled giggle in the background suggested that she also did not believe in Samantha's ability to dress herself.

Just to spite her, Samantha chose the frothiest of the dresses, one that reminded her of pixies or fairies. It was a soft pink color, probably too light for her with her fair complexion and especially her new blonde hair.

When Samantha situated the dress on her body, she knew the color was way too light. And while she liked the cut of the dress with its fitted bodice, flowy sleeves, and fluffy skirt, she also knew that standing next to Blake in that dress would definitely make her feel like a kid.

She wasn't. She was a grown woman. Younger than Blake, for sure, but not indecently young, just on the lower end of appropriate. And everything had been going so well lately, Samantha didn't want to make his family—or him—think she was any younger than she actually was.

"Well?" Charlotte said from the other side of her changing room door. "Let's see your first choice."

Samantha twirled her hips back and forth so the skirt swirled around her legs. It was a fun dress, but totally not right for the occasion. Even she knew that. "You may be onto something with the pastel thing."

"I mean, I know I am, but show me where we're starting here."

Samantha peeked out from behind the door. "Okay, but don't laugh at me."

Charlotte motioned her forward, and Sam saw that Yvette had taken a seat in one of the armchairs near the three-way mirror. Both had too-wide grins on their faces that had to be their attempts at masking their desire to laugh.

"That dress looks great on you," Yvette said. "I love the skirt."

Charlotte took Samantha by the shoulders, revolving her on the spot like she was an earring display. "I mean, you look adorable. And if you were hosting a Disney Princess party for six-year-olds, I would tell you that you found it. This would be that dress."

"But for the wedding?" Samantha couldn't help adding a little hope to her question. Maybe it wasn't as bad as

Samantha thought. And sure, maybe this dress was a little extreme, but would there be anything she could wear that didn't make her look like a child?

"You'd look more like Blake's kid sister."

Samantha looked to Yvette, who only said, "I have a niece who's due for a princess party."

Blowing out a breath, Samantha turned back toward her changing room, a new fear springing forth that she'd either look like a teenager or like she was trying too hard no matter what she wore.

"Whoa, whoa, whoa." Charlotte's hand clamped down on Samantha's shoulder, rotating her around until her nose was practically buried in Samantha's neck . . . right where the fading hickey Blake had given her Tuesday morning was.

"Hold up, hold up, hold up," Charlotte said when Samantha tried to cover the mark with her hand. She'd been applying concealer and foundation to the mark since it had happened in an attempt to make it less obvious, but she hadn't done a good enough job for Charlotte's inspection, apparently.

"Did you see this?" Charlotte asked Yvette, who had pulled out her phone and seemed absorbed in texting someone. Samantha imagined she was texting her cousin or whoever the guardian was of the niece who needed that princess party. Yvette was probably offering to host and pay for the entire thing.

Yvette shrugged without looking up from her phone. "It's been there for days, but I thought it best not to say anything since I'm fairly certain my son put it there." Yvette set her phone aside. "I do have a trick for covering that up. I'll bring you my special concealer before the wedding."

Samantha nodded, trying not to think about why Yvette might be an expert at covering up bruises.

"Thanks," Sam said, suddenly too self-conscious to stand in front of these two people anymore. She knew Yvette was the one with abuse and trauma in her background, but that didn't keep Samantha from feeling exposed.

As she closed the changing room door behind her, Yvette called out, "Try on the gold and silver sparkle dress next!"

Chapter Twenty-Two

H*ow's the new gig treating you? And how's the blonde? You seal the deal with her yet? *eyebrow waggle**

Blake wondered if Kat somehow knew today was the first day he'd spent any time away from Samantha and chose now to text because of it.

I can't remember the last time I slept, if that tells you anything.

Not enough about whether it's the restaurant keeping you up or Bartender Barbie.

Blake's hackles raised at the unflattering nickname and set his phone down to make a round of the restaurant before replying. He wasn't any less pissed when the lunch hour seemed to be flowing smoothly and he could return to his office without feeling guilty about abandoning anyone.

The lunch crowd was smaller today than it had been all week. Blake was getting to know the employees well enough to recognize who was going to be dependable and who might need more support, but that didn't stop him from wanting to be out in the thick of it every time the restaurant started to fill up, even if it was slower than normal. He knew he needed to stand back and trust his team to do their jobs—to show his team that he trusted them—but he wasn't quite ready to let go just yet.

Garden & Gather was still so new that it felt as delicate to him as a newborn. His relationship with Sam was similarly precious and potentially precipitous. Sure, they were currently in the honeymoon stage and he didn't have any secrets left to tell her, but that didn't mean he felt confident in the longevity of their connection. It was difficult to be optimistic when he'd never had a relationship last longer than a few months.

His insecurity only made him all the more eager to call Kat out on her, well, cattiness.

Her name is Samantha.

I remember her name.

Then use it next time.

What, no please?

It wasn't a request.

Aaaaaaaaah. So you *have* slept with her. Next time, you could just say so, and I wouldn't have to needle you so hard.

It's none of your business.

Of course it's my business. She's going to come to me when you turn all broody and she doesn't understand why you only talk to her in grunts and fucks.

Blake started to type back that he did not do that then stopped himself. Because he *had* done that with Kat. Whenever he was frustrated or didn't know how to voice all the hard emotions churning inside him, he did tend toward trying to release the tension physically. Through exercise first, then, when that wasn't enough, through sex.

There had been multiple times when entire encounters with Kat had been nothing but how she'd just described it. Sometimes they'd barely uttered a word to one another.

What Blake really didn't want to examine was that he'd done the same with Rachel. He'd tried to prove to her that if he could fulfill her needs in the bedroom, the rest of their differences wouldn't matter. Even though he'd known that his career at the time had been an insurmountable obstacle between them, he'd tried to patch the gap with orgasms when he should have chosen her over his job.

That was the last way he wanted to approach his relationship with Samantha, even when he didn't have much practice in doing the opposite. Because sometimes confronting the things he was feeling inside evoked the pain and trauma from his childhood.

Times when food was scarce. When he was afraid of his father. Terrified that his dad might hurt his mother. When he'd pray under his covers at night that his dad just simply wouldn't come home. All of that was so long ago now that Blake liked to pretend that it didn't matter, but he knew it did.

He'd never gone to counseling, but he was self-aware enough now that he could recognize how so many of the things he did stemmed from having to pretend everything was fine. So much so that he'd eventually started doing it all the time, even when he was alone. He hadn't confided in anyone until Kat, which would have been fine if he'd not pinned all of his sexual frustration on her along with it.

With Rachel, he'd been too afraid of her rejection to give her much more than what she wanted to see in him. But he knew he wanted to give his all to Samantha. He just knew he'd have to take it slowly with her, both for his sake and for hers. But he definitely did not want Samantha learning about the nitty-gritty of his affair with Kat from her.

Why would you think she would come to you?

Blake was truly baffled by the thought. Sure, he'd introduced Kat to Samantha, but Sam had also been working at the time. It wasn't like they'd had time to become best buds or anything.

Because I gave her my number and told her to text me when you turn into a caveman.

Blake groaned. He wasn't exactly sure he liked not having control of that situation.

Did she take you seriously?

She laughed at the caveman bit, but she did take my phone number, so I'm expecting a text in approximately two weeks.

Blake blew out a breath so hard that it caught the lock of hair that always tried to flip in front of his eyes.

Your confidence in me is so reassuring.

Kat's response was an emoji blowing him a kiss, which was right on-brand for her. If they were in person, he might have been able to weasel out of her why she was so certain he'd screw up enough for Sam to want to confide in a stranger, but he knew he wouldn't get anything more out of Kat today.

The afternoon dragged without Samantha there to ply him with test cocktails or share a flatbread with. He was somewhat aware that he was more productive without the excuse to wander out into the front of the house to "check on things" when he only wanted to see her.

Blake knew on one hand that she was a distraction, but she was a distraction that he wanted, so it wasn't welcome when his father knocked on his door, let himself in, and said, "It's good to see you finally getting some work done instead of being out there panting after that girl."

"I've been managing to do both pretty well up to now." His annoyance gave him no room for denial. He really didn't care what anyone thought of the way he acted toward Sam other than Sam herself.

His father's jaw ticked as he moved a stack of files from one of the chairs in front of Blake's desk to the top of the teetering pile on the other chair and lowered himself into the cushions. Blake frowned at the heavy way his father's body seemed to melt into the soft chair like he didn't have the strength to hold himself at attention.

"I see you're all caught up." James nodded at the stack of files.

Blake motioned toward the blank space on the wall behind his desk. "My filing cabinet hasn't arrived yet, but that doesn't mean I'm not getting work done."

"You know you can't work eighteen-hour days forever, yes? It will catch up with you."

"I don't plan to, but I always knew these first few months were going to be grueling. Samantha helps with that."

His father harrumphed and muttered "She's a distraction you can't afford" at the stack of files.

"Pardon?" Blake pretended not to have heard. His father did not get to have opinions about how Blake did business when he'd already withheld his support for said business. And he really didn't get to have an opinion on Samantha, at least not until he could learn to call her by her name instead of "that girl."

His father shrugged. "Nothing you'll listen to anyway."

Blake chewed the inside corner of his lip to keep from saying something he'd regret. Even the words that did come out of his mouth were not nearly as respectful as they should have been. "Was there a reason for your visit outside of telling me, yet again, what I'm doing wrong?"

His father narrowed his eyes at him. "I didn't say you were doing anything wrong."

His derisive snort was entirely involuntary as Blake stood and leaned over his desk. "You haven't done anything but criticize me since I left Topeka."

"Since you left the church. Since you left God." His father's words were tired, and his head rested against the back of the chair like he didn't have the energy to lift it.

"I'm not having this argument again," Blake said as he came around the desk and leaned against the front of it. "I did what I needed to do for me. I was not in a good place back then, and if gaining distance from the church was what I needed to do, then so be it."

James shook his head against the cushion, but his eyes were closed, and Blake could plainly see the strain on his father's once-handsome face—not to mention the streaks of white that were beginning to mix with the steel gray of his hair, the dark shadows below his eyes, and the labored way his chest would rise and fall.

"Have you seen a doctor recently?" Blake asked, knowing it would only open another line of hostility between them.

"Recently enough."

"So, yesterday?"

James cracked an eye open and gave a huff through his nose. "I'm fine. I'm just old."

Blake did the math in his head. His mother was exactly twenty years older than him, and his dad was four years older than her, which meant he was only in his early sixties. "This is something else, and you know it."

"I'm fine."

"So fine that you're napping in one of my office chairs at four o'clock in the afternoon?"

"I've been up since five. Let an old man rest."

Blake crossed his arms, watching his father's chest rise and fall for a full minute before he spoke again. "You never said why you were here."

"Your mother wanted to meet here for an early dinner after she returned from shopping."

"Should I expect you two to check in on me daily?"

The hint of a smile tugged at the corner of James's mouth even as his eyes remained closed. "Probably. You know your mother."

Blake felt a mirroring grin tug at his own lips. He did know his mother. And it was basically a miracle that she hadn't been camped out at the bar since the moment the doors opened just to watch over him the way she used to do when he was a kid at the playground.

As if they'd summoned her, Yvette knocked on the open door then let herself in Blake's office. "There you are, darling. I thought you'd forgotten about me."

Yvette crossed straight to where James sat in his chair and smoothed back a lock of hair that had fallen into his father's eyes, the mirror image of the spot where Blake's hair never cooperated. And Blake mourned a little for the son he'd likely never have who might have had the same cowlick.

James captured Yvette's hand and brought it to his lips. "Never."

Blake averted his eyes from the rare display of intimacy between his parents, craning his neck to see if Samantha had lingered outside the office door, but there was no sign of her.

"How was your shopping trip? I assume the hunt for shoes was successful?"

"I bought two pairs. Though one was for Samantha."

Blake did not miss how his father's face fell into a frown as Yvette turned her satisfied smile onto Blake. "You won't believe the amazing dress we found for her—she *glows* in it. And the shoes were a bargain brand, don't worry. I knew she wouldn't let me buy her anything expensive, but that doesn't make them any less fabulous."

Knowing how little Samantha was used to having while recalling the general cost of his mother's shoes, Blake suspected that his mother's definition of "a bargain" and Samantha's were two very different things.

"Is she here?" He stood from where he'd been leaning on the desk. It was time to check on the restaurant anyway. The dinner crowd would be showing up at any time.

"She didn't make it past the bar without seeing something that needed her attention. Something about restocking."

The liquor order had arrived earlier, and the only reason Blake hadn't put it away was that he wanted Samantha to double-check that the order was correct. What had been delivered matched what was on the invoice, but Blake had already discovered that what was on the invoice didn't always match what had been ordered. He'd learned that the hard way with the crackers for the charcuterie boards. The stupid food company just sent whatever they had in stock whether it was what he and Emil wanted or not. He was about ready to just start buying them from the grocery store.

Blake forgot all his frustrations when he rounded the corner and was confronted with the site of Samantha bent over a box of whiskey, her ass in the air as she checked bottles off her list. His first impulse was to give her bottom a playful smack as he passed by, but he didn't want to startle her.

He settled for dropping to a crouch on the opposite side of the box she was inspecting. "Everything here?"

She looked up from beneath the hair that was falling in her face. "So far, but the liquors are all mixed together with the wine, which just makes zero sense. I think Phil must have been drunk when he packed this."

Blake snorted. He'd never talked to their liquor wholesaler when he hadn't seemed a little drunk. "Probably. Can I help?"

Samantha tapped a stack of boxes with the toe of her boot. "Bring these up to the bar?"

"Of course." She straightened at the same time he did, and as if they had shrugged off their roles as bar manager and restaurant owner and donned their roles as boyfriend and girlfriend, Blake started, "Mom said she bought you shoes."

Samantha scowled even as she stepped into his side. "She and Charlotte conspired against me and slipped the salesperson your mom's card while I was still trying shoes on. I never had a choice."

Blake wrapped his arms around her shoulders and tried to stifle his amusement. "Sounds like my mom."

"I should have guessed she'd do that and had mine out first."

He knew she wanted to prove that she could pay her own way, but Blake's possessive side liked that his family was taking care of her. "It just means she likes you. And that she likes us together."

"And now we're getting our hair and makeup done tomorrow. It feels a little like I am in for a makeover so I don't embarrass you all at the wedding."

Blake frowned. He hadn't even thought that was a possibility. How could Samantha embarrass him? "Nobody thinks that. Mom just has a habit of spoiling the people she cares about."

Samantha sniffed like she wanted to argue, but she didn't say anything except "She does do that."

"What's important is that you like the dress and the shoes. If not, return them, and wear something you already have. Skip the salon if that's what you want. I just want you to have a good time on Saturday." He kissed her forehead, and she finally tilted her head up to him, allowing him to place a kiss on her lips.

"I want to have a good time with you," she murmured against his mouth.

"Then that's what we'll do."

Chapter Twenty-Three

Samantha woke up in Blake's bed on Saturday morning. Muted sunlight filtered through the gap in the curtains as crisp autumn air bit at the tip of her nose. Blake had cracked the window before they'd fallen asleep last night, and her first thought was that it was going to be frigid outside of the covers.

He was already up for the day. From the last week of sleeping in the same bed with him, she'd discovered he was an early riser. He'd woken up to go for a run more days than he hadn't. And he'd even invited her to use his apartment complex's gym with him. Samantha had laughed. Her exercise was the evening rush, and sleep was too precious to cut it short.

She assumed that was where he was now, and Samantha buried her face in the pillow, pulling the decadently puffy down comforter over her head. This was the first morning in more than a week she hadn't had to drag herself out of bed first thing to be at the restaurant before it opened, and she was going to enjoy it.

Only . . . was that coffee? She stuck her nose out into the chilly air and sniffed. That *was* coffee. And bacon. "Oh, come on now, that's not fair."

"What's not fair?" Blake entered the room just then, already showered and dressed. How had he done that without waking her up? His bathroom was ten feet from her head.

"I was going to sleep past ten and drink coffee in bed while scrolling through Pinterest for cocktail ideas, and now you've made coffee and bacon and I have to get up."

The bed dipped as Blake sat on the edge next to her. He brushed the duvet and her stray hairs away from her face, and the only reason for him doing so that her sleepy mind could come up with was so she could better behold his magnificence. His eyes shone with genuine fondness and amusement as he gazed down at her.

"Well, you're in luck." He flipped his watch hand over and checked the time. "It's ten-oh-three, and I came in to see if you wanted to have breakfast with me before I head into Garden and Gather."

"Can we do breakfast in bed?" Samantha wasn't ready to emerge from her cozy cocoon just yet.

Blake's answer was to crack a grin and drop a kiss on her forehead. "Whatever you want."

Samantha grinned to herself as he rose, and she pulled the duvet more closely around her. "Can you—" was all she got out before she heard him close and latch the window. "Thank you."

He chuckled as he left, and Samantha rolled over and squealed into her pillow. She didn't know what she'd done to get so lucky as to have this man doting on her, but she never wanted it to change.

⸺⬤⸺

BLAKE HAD CHECKED HIS phone at every stoplight, which wasn't like him. He usually hooked his phone up to his console and never touched it while he was driving. But that had been before, when he'd had his own car with a touchscreen dash that allowed him to answer a phone call with the touch of a button. His mother's old delivery van had no such luxury. This thing was old enough to still have a cassette deck, so he felt obligated to hold his phone in his lap just in case something went wrong at Garden & Gather. It wasn't that he didn't trust his staff to do their jobs—he did. He just wasn't sure that he trusted the place to still exist without him there to safeguard it.

Blake imagined this was what new parents must feel like, that their children's new little lives were too precious to be trusted with anyone else. Leaving his brand-new restaurant while it was open meant it surely wouldn't exist by the time he returned.

He knew it wasn't rational, and it definitely wasn't sustainable. He'd have to back off eventually and let the place thrive. Maybe if Garden & Gather was successful, he'd open another restaurant. Maybe that's what he'd end up doing with his life. He could see himself finding contentment in building new communities across the city. It might even be fun to attempt different types of restaurants. A café. A burger joint. A cocktail lounge—or even better, a speakeasy.

So far, though, he just needed Garden & Gather to survive its first week, then its first month, then its first year. Then he could think about what came next.

His phone pinged again, but Blake knew it was Samantha. She'd been texting him all morning, sending him little updates of what she'd looked like getting her hair and makeup done with his mother.

His favorite had been a silly selfie of her with aluminum foil pieces all over her head making a fish face at the camera. He hadn't seen the final look yet or the dress she'd chosen, though she *had* sent a photo of the shoes on her feet. They were sparkly silver heels and flashier than he'd expected, but her caption *Do you think these will fit in your jacket pockets? I expect I'll only be able to tolerate them for about half the night* had also made him laugh.

Thinking of her still made him smile every time. And maybe their relationship was as new as his restaurant, but this was the first time he'd had complete confidence that a woman would stick around. Even with Rachel, he'd always half-expected each date to be their last—that she would tell him she couldn't do it, that she'd never be able to overcome his profession, that she was out.

He didn't have that fear when it came to Samantha. She was perfectly poised to be his partner in all things. And tonight was just another one of their happy firsts.

Only, when Blake pulled into his parents' driveway and he plucked his phone from the passenger seat, the text hadn't been from Sam, but from the police station. The officer he'd filed his report with had texted to say that Mason had been released on bail the night before. He wanted to let Blake know in case Mason sought retaliation against either himself or Sam.

Blake was grateful he had just arrived where Samantha was. That way, he didn't have to wonder for long if she'd received the same text—or better, a phone call and offer of support. Surely there was something the police could do to ensure Samantha's protection since Mason had shown he was capable of violence.

He asked the officer as much via return text but didn't expect a good answer. If there was anything they could do, they would have sent him more than a courtesy text of warning.

Blake let himself into his parents' house and followed the sound of Samantha's laughter toward the kitchen. Was it possible Samantha didn't know yet?

When Blake rounded the corner into the kitchen, he stopped short. Whatever dress he'd imagined Samantha had planned to pair with her sparkly silver pumps, the formfitting, dark-blue sequined piece she was wearing had not figured into his reckoning. The dress had a high neckline and long sleeves, but it hugged her curves all the way down to where it cut off well above her thigh, leaving miles and miles of her gorgeous creamy legs exposed. Everything about the dress was daring, more daring than he'd expected from Samantha, but the fit and the color suited her, bringing out the green in her hazel eyes. Her hair was pulled up in a sort of intentionally messy bun, and she'd had her roots touched up. Blake was aware of the light shimmering off her sequins, but he didn't think that was why she glowed. More like she'd somehow tapped into her inner radiance.

Blake wanted another moment to take her in before he had to shatter that loveliness by telling her the news about Mason.

It took him a moment to realize that the room had fallen silent.

Samantha was taking him in just as intently as he'd been staring at her. They'd inadvertently dressed alike with him in his navy suit and a silver-gray shirt. They probably appeared as though they were part of a bridal party. Either way, no one would mistake them for anything other than what they were: a matched set.

Blake's mother was looking back and forth between the two of them, glee written on her face as she watched them ogle each other. "I'm so glad you wore the blue suit," his mother said, as if he'd had any other options without looking too formal.

He cocked his head to the side as he considered his mother. She *did* know that this was the only appropriate suit he had and that he had zero time to have something else made. Had she steered Samantha toward this color?

He wouldn't be surprised. Even the dress she herself wore, a demure silver-blue piece with fitted lace sleeves and a layered skirt, complemented what he and Samantha were wearing.

"You both look lovely." He kissed his mother on the cheek before crossing to where Samantha stood in the corner. She still hadn't said anything, as if she were as stunned by his beauty as he was by hers. He thought he looked the same as he always did, but Samantha finally looked as though she wasn't hiding.

He'd always found her attractive, but it wasn't until he'd seen her just now that he understood she'd been dimming herself. Perhaps not on purpose, but in a way that made herself smaller so that she didn't take up space in other people's attention. And he wasn't sure whether that was a reaction to the way she'd been raised or if that was a response to Mason's actions. Either way, he wanted to know, and he wanted to work through it with her, because right now, Samantha was radiant, and the world deserved to see her shine.

That's when Blake decided that he *would* tell her about Mason, but he'd just wait until after the wedding. Tonight, when they were tucked safely back in his bed, he would let her know that Mason was free. He would give her these few hours of reprieve.

A few more hours wouldn't hurt anything.

Chapter Twenty-Four

S amantha had never been to a wedding in a hotel before. Every wedding she'd ever been to had been either in a home church or in Tim Jennings's backyard—which had basically been the same thing as church for most of her adolescence.

The only time she'd been to a boutique hotel had been when she and Charlotte had checked out that one with a nightclub in the basement in Lawrence because Charlotte had been interested in some guy who worked there. Samantha hadn't seen anything other than the basement, but she had a feeling that hotel wasn't nearly as fancy as this one.

Samantha knew she was staring, and she knew her neck was going to hurt before the end of the night, but everywhere they went inside this hotel, she had something to look at over her head. The lobby had housed a giant cascading chandelier. The hallways on the way to the ballroom had intricate molding, and the room where the ceremony was taking place had brilliant stained glass and shining wood columns that reminded her of a throne room—or at the very least, an old library.

She'd thought the Fairchilds' house was big, but this hotel boasted a level of opulence she was certain she'd never understand.

"It's pretty, isn't it?" Blake asked.

Right. Her backwoods Missouri upbringing was probably showing right now. She straightened her neck and pulled her shoulders back, attempting to find a dignified pose after her prolonged gaping. "I've never seen anything like this."

Blake pulled her knuckles to his lips, amusement sparking in his brown eyes as he kissed her hand. She'd almost forgotten he was holding it. Though it was probably a good thing he had been, otherwise she would have run into a chair or tripped over the short set of stairs that led into the ballroom because she was too busy staring at the decor.

"Faye works here; she's the restaurant manager. She's who told me I should go to bartending school."

Samantha blinked as they took their seats. "Wait. Your cousin is a restaurant manager, and she's not involved in *your* restaurant?"

Blake shrugged and motioned toward the soaring stained glass windows. "I can't pay her what this place pays her. And honestly, I didn't think that much about it. We've never been close."

"Why's that?"

The fact that Samantha hadn't already met Faye did seem odd. She felt like she'd met almost everyone else in Blake's extended family. And maybe he wasn't best friends with all of them, but he seemed involved enough.

He pressed his lips to her knuckles again before dropping her hand and readjusting himself in his seat so he could lean into her and whisper in her ear, "Faye is one of the few cousins who doesn't go to church. And since I used to work in one . . ."

Blake trailed off, and Samantha nodded. His job would have been an obstacle for someone who probably had good reasons not to be involved in church anymore. It had happened before. "I bet you'd have a lot to talk about now if you gave it a chance."

"You're right. Too bad she's going to be a little busy today. You'd probably get along with her really well, too." Blake placed a chaste kiss on her cheek. One quick press of his lips against her skin was all it took for her mind to flash back to last night and the way she'd straddled his hips and licked her way up his abs. She'd caught him staring at her breasts, mesmerized by them as she moved over him. The heat of that moment rolled down her back as she felt awe anew that he could look at her like she was something precious and desirable all at once.

The memory made her want to skip the wedding and pull him back to bed for the rest of the night, despite her proclamation that she was excited to meet his cousin. Faye who?

But then the music started, and Samantha remembered that they were surrounded by Blake's family. His parents were sitting just a few seats away, and the cousins and nieces and nephews who sat directly on either side of them could probably hear every word they'd been saying. It wouldn't do to announce her desires aloud, but when Samantha met Blake's gaze, the need for exactly what she wanted was written plainly across his face as well.

Samantha couldn't help herself; she leaned into him and returned the kiss on his cheek, just above his newly trimmed beard. She put as much sensual promise as she could muster in a momentary peck, but the smell of him—freshly showered mixed with his subtle cologne—sent a thrill trilling in her belly at the realization that this man was hers to love.

The second she thought the word, her whole body went numb. Love?

Had she really fallen in love with him so soon?

Samantha didn't know. She'd never fancied herself in love before, but what else could this be? She craved Blake. Preferred his company to anyone else. Found comfort and safety with him and constantly strove to be better for him. What was that if not love?

The idea was a thrill all on its own. She loved Blake. She was in love with him. And she got to spend the rest of the evening on his arm reveling in that love—the first night of the rest of a life lived in love with this man. She could hardly wait to begin.

<hr>

SAMANTHA HAD THOUGHT the hall where the ceremony took place was grand, but she had not been prepared for the simple beauty of the reception hall. There were floor-to-ceiling windows surrounding the entire room. The lights were turned low, and candles on the tables and small chandeliers hanging from the ceiling reminded Samantha of constellations. Which was appropriate, because they were so high up in the building that she felt like they were in the stars. The lights from the city below drowned out much of the starlight visible through the windows, but it was a clear night, and the moon was almost full. The effect was breathtaking.

She wondered if it would be possible for her and Blake to afford this room for their own wedding reception. But no, she was jumping ahead of herself. She'd only just realized that she loved him, and she hadn't even told him yet. Besides, he might not be ready to return the sentiment, not with all the upheaval he'd been through the last couple of years.

Samantha was patient enough to wait for him, but apparently not patient enough to keep her from planning their own wedding in her head. All throughout the ceremony, she'd imagined what their vows would be, what music she'd want played. What flowers they would decorate with. What color dress she would wear.

She'd been surprised when Faye had walked down the aisle in a powder-blue sleeveless mermaid dress. Samantha had never considered a wedding dress that wasn't white before then. She knew her own family would have been horrified at the idea, but her family was scandalized by everything she did, so what did it matter? She could get married in the navy-blue sparkly dress she was wearing now if she wanted.

But she wouldn't, as much as she liked how she felt in this dress. When Samantha got married, she wanted to wear a proper gown. One that made her feel like royalty.

And she wanted to see Blake all done up in a luxury tux. Even the idea of it made her salivate a little bit. She already couldn't take her eyes off how good he looked in his casual navy suit.

It shouldn't be legal for a human being to be as attractive as he was. Samantha had assumed she would have grown used to how gorgeous he was, but she still found herself taken aback by his beauty on a daily basis. Those expressive eyes, the jaw, the hair that even now looked like it wanted to evade the product he'd used to tame it. She knew by the end of the evening that stray lock would be hanging down in his eyes just as it always did when they closed the doors to Garden & Gather and headed home.

"Would it be gauche to be the first people to approach the bar?" she asked. They'd found their table a few minutes ago. They were seated with a couple who were friends of Faye's, one of Faye's new husband's college roommates, and another one of Blake's cousins that Samantha had met at the baptism reception a few weeks ago. So far, everyone was milling around the reception hall, taking in the decorations and stopping by the selfie table, but no one had approached the open bar on the far wall.

Blake craned his neck. "I figure it's probably about half-and-half drinkers versus teetotalers."

"So you're saying we need to lead by example?" Sam asked.

Blake pushed back his chair then pulled Samantha's out for her. "Absolutely."

"I will go with you," the college roommate said, joining them.

"What are we drinking tonight?" Blake asked as he kept a hand at the small of her back on their journey.

"French seventy-fives?"

"Champagne isn't enough on its own?"

Sam smiled. "Maybe later during the toasts or something. For now, I feel like celebrating."

"Again, champagne is perfect for that."

"Ah, but what's more festive than gin in champagne?"

Blake kissed the top of her head. "Just don't overdo it."

Samantha hopped up on her toes and placed a kiss on his lips. "Don't worry. I know my limits."

<hr>

Turned out, Samantha was a fun date to bring to a party. Blake had almost worried that she'd be shy and quiet and not want to mingle with anyone—or be just as obsessed with checking in on Garden & Gather as he was. But Samantha's phone had stayed in her purse, and she'd been doing her best to distract him.

He was ashamed to admit that he was having a little trouble keeping up with her. She'd pulled him onto the dance floor half an hour ago, and he'd just begged off to take a bathroom break, but really he needed a glass of water and a breather.

Samantha had stayed on the floor to dance with his cousin, Shannon, who had shyly asked Samantha to show her how to dance. Blake watched her from their table where he sipped his water. He forgot most days how much younger than him she was, but he supposed, as she moved to the music, that this was a blatant reminder of their age difference. Samantha could probably dance all night long.

The idea didn't bother him. He wanted her to have fun, and he would be content to join her only occasionally. Blake didn't think that fact made them any less suited to be partners. If anything, it gave him more insight into who she was. Tonight, he was getting a glimpse of the version of Samantha who had lived in the nightclub world for so long. He'd wondered how that had worked, how she hadn't been swallowed up by the pace and the culture, but clearly this was an environment she shined in.

He was beginning to believe she was capable of shining in any environment.

She was beautiful, and the more time he spent with her, the more he recognized that she glowed. And he'd seen that glow since that first day she'd showed up to her interview at the coffee shop. He just hadn't let himself see it at first, because if he had, he knew he would have never been able to walk away from her from the start.

And it was there, watching Samantha dance with his cousin, that Blake decided he was going to marry this woman. Then he would never have to walk away.

<hr />

SAMANTHA WAS WAITING for their next round of drinks, fanning herself with her hand, when the groom's college roommate joined her at the bar. "You look like you're having fun," he said as he leaned against the bar top next to her.

"I am. Faye and Rick put on a great party. How's your night going?"

The bartender set down the bottle of water she'd asked for, and Samantha cracked it open and took a deep gulp while she waited on her next French 75. Like she'd promised Blake, she'd been moderating her alcohol consumption while making sure she ate and drank plenty of water. She wasn't an idiot. She'd cut off enough intoxicated patrons to know how to tackle a long night.

"My night would be better if I could get your number."

Samantha choked on her newest gulp of water and had to wheeze through a few choking coughs before she could manage to squeak out a "Say that again?"

The roommate, Samantha couldn't remember his name—Brandon, or Brad, or was it Brady?—whatever his name was, he leaned in close to her at the bar, almost looming. "Look, I know you're here with Fairchild, and I respect that, but that doesn't mean we couldn't go out to dinner next week. You seem like a lot of fun, and you're hot as hell."

For the first time all day, Samantha felt nakedly on display. So far, she'd enjoyed being the dolled up version of herself. But right now, with what's-his-face grinning at her like she was an all-you-can-eat buffet, Samantha wished she'd brought her big winter cardigan with her so she could shrug into it and curl up with the ebook app on her phone on the sofa in the corner and become invisible.

"I'm sorry," she said, fighting the rising panic she felt as she realized she had nowhere to hide. "But I'm not just here with Blake. I'm *with* Blake."

The Roommate nodded but slid a step closer to her anyway. "I get that. But I was under the impression that all that was fairly new."

Samantha's heart thudded against her chest. She didn't know what to say or do to get out of this. The fact that she was here as another man's plus-one apparently meant nothing. She didn't know if she could find a safe harbor to take refuge in, so she went with the closest nugget of truth she could voice. "Just because it's new doesn't mean it's not serious."

The Roommate scooted another step closer to her so that the heat of his forearm radiated next to hers on the bar. "You don't have to settle for someone who's a decade older than you, you know. You can have whoever you want."

Before Samantha could say "Blake is who I want," a woman's voice from behind The Roommate's back said, "Hey, Brett. Rick is gathering all his friends up for shots. You should head thataway."

Samantha peered around Brett's shoulders just in time to see Faye motion over her shoulder with her thumb to where her new husband was indeed surrounded by a bunch of guys his age.

Brett tapped the top of the bar and said, "We'll talk later," like there was still a chance that Samantha was going to give him her phone number.

"Thanks for the save," Sam said to Faye as the bartender set two drinks down on the bar, Sam's French 75 and what looked like a regular glass of champagne for the bride. Faye thanked the bartender by name. Apparently, he was a Matt.

"Absolutely. No one deserves to be harangued by a desperate Brett. He's kind of an asshole, but Rick was in his wedding so we thought it would be rude not to at least invite him."

Samantha flinched. "He's married?"

Faye snorted. "God, no. That marriage only lasted six months before the bride came to her senses and got the hell out. But enough about him. I have been dying to meet you since I found out Uncle Blake was bringing a date."

"Uncle Blake?" Samantha'd thought they were cousins.

"Oh, that's what we all called him growing up since he was so much older than the rest of us. Anyway, when Aunt Yvette called to ask if we had room in the seating chart for Blake's new girlfriend, I had to stop myself from social-media stalking you—which I totally failed at, but in my defense, I was consumed by curiosity. Because Uncle Blake has never, not once, brought a woman to a family function."

Samantha had known this, but she hadn't realized *she* would be the object of curiosity. She wasn't sure what to say to this woman.

But Faye didn't give her a chance to respond before she continued. "Anyway, I love your cocktail posts. I totally stole the gin flip recipe for the winter cocktail menu in the restaurant. And if it ever gets awkward working with your boyfriend, just drop me a line. I am perpetually in need of good bartenders, and I can guarantee that with that face you'd be making bank in tips."

Oh, wow. Samantha had the distinct impression that Faye was adopting her in the same way Yvette had, and she now had a new friend whether she wanted one or not.

Samantha had zero objections. She liked Faye's energy, she just hadn't been able to get a word in, and the first sentence she managed was an embarrassed "Oh, I don't always look like this" accompanied by a flick of her hand toward her body.

"Nonsense. It's your face whether you're wearing professional makeup or not. And you're gorgeous."

"Um, thanks." Heat stole over Samantha's shoulders, spreading up her neck to her cheeks.

Faye took a sip of her champagne and examined Samantha. "I get the feeling that not enough people in your life have told you that, and that is a shame. Anyway, even if you don't want the job, I'd love to get to know you. I'm headed to the beach for the next two weeks, but I'll totally send you a friend request before I get on the plane."

"I look forward to it," Samantha said then added, "This place is kind of amazing. If I weren't so happy at Garden and Gather, I would be beyond tempted."

They spent the next few minutes talking about different aspects of the hotel and how stressful managing the restaurant was, and Samantha chimed in with her own anecdotes. There was definite friendship potential here, and if nothing else, Sam was glad to have another contact in the industry.

Samantha had just received a refill on her drink when Blake joined them, her purse dangling from his hand by the strap. He paused to kiss his cousin on the cheek and congratulate her again before handing the handbag to Sam.

"Your bag has been buzzing nonstop for the last ten minutes. I thought maybe you'd like to know."

"Is everything okay with the restaurant?"

Blake nodded. "I called to check in just in case. Everything's fine."

Samantha didn't know what else might be going on; her phone rarely blew up. But she'd left it in her purse all day for a reason. She didn't want to be interrupted by the world outside their little bubble while she had this first chance at a real date with Blake.

She took a deep sip of her drink, the bubbles starting to make her lightheaded with a pleasant buzz. "I'll check it in a second, but first, do you have any objections to some selfies for posterity?"

Blake raised one eyebrow at her but didn't object as she pulled her phone from her purse. One of Faye's bridesmaids arrived as she did, announcing that it was almost time to cut the cake and pulling Faye away.

"You two seem to be getting along," Blake said as he seated himself on the stool next to her so there was less disparity in their height.

"I think we could. We'll have to hang out sometime when she's not in the middle of getting married. Okay, smile."

Samantha ignored the notifications and snapped a few photos of them together. She wanted as many as possible—pictures with smiles, photos with silly faces, evidence of their kisses. This might be the only time she was made up enough to match his natural brilliance.

In the middle of a second round of goofy faces, a phone call interrupted the function of Sam's camera app. She blinked at the phone number she didn't recognize, but the area code was from the same part of Missouri where her parents lived.

Confused, Samantha swiped to answer.

"Oh my God, Sam. I didn't think you were ever going to answer."

"Sarah?" Samantha straightened, covering her other ear to block out the music from the party.

"Where are you?" Her sister's voice sounded weird. Higher than normal. Almost panicked.

"I'm at a wedding. Where are you?"

"I'm on my way to you."

"What? Why? Are you okay?"

Her sister let out a dry, unamused laugh. "I'm terrified and elated and I'm probably not going to sleep for fear that Tim and Joseph are going to break down our hotel room door any second, but I left."

Samantha stood, heading toward the ballroom door and away from the noise. She couldn't possibly have heard correctly. Blake followed her out into the hallway and paused beside her, looking concerned as Samantha listened to the story. Apparently, Sarah's husband had found out about her affair with his father and flown into a rage, both yelling at Sarah and manhandling their oldest, gripping her by the shoulders and examining her every feature as if trying to determine through sheer force of will if the child was his or his father's.

Sarah had waited for him to go to work, packed the kids up, and left.

"I have enough money for a hotel room for the kids for the night and gas to get to you," Sarah was saying. "I didn't know where else to go."

Sam was shaking her head, and she was pretty sure her whole body was trembling. "Of course you're coming to me. Do you think he'll follow you?"

"He doesn't get off work until eleven. I want to let the kids sleep, but I'll probably be on the road early. I don't like the idea of staying in one place too long."

"Absolutely. Get here as soon as you can."

She exchanged I love yous with her sister, then she hung up and sagged against the wall. The combination of alcohol and shock drained her of all her energy.

Blake pulled her into a hug and listened while she briefly explained what was going on. It felt so good to lean on him, to trust him to help her through this situation with her sister. She didn't know what she'd do with Sarah and her two kids in her tiny apartment, but she'd figure it out. And she wouldn't have to do it alone. Everything was going to be fine.

When she was feeling calmer, she stood tall under her own power, nervous but full of determination.

"While we're at it," Blake said, running a hand through his hair like he didn't want to say the words that were about to come out of his mouth. "I got a text earlier letting me know that Mason was released from jail last night. You probably have the same one."

At once, all of Sam's confidence pooled on the wooden floor under her feet. The color drained from her face along with every sensation until only dread and fear were all she had left.

Chapter Twenty-Five

B lake was still processing the switch that had flipped in Samantha the night before. He felt as if she'd overloaded after getting the news of her sister and Mason all at once and had launched straight into self-destructive mode.

After he'd told her about Mason, she'd said "You should have told me as soon as you knew" then marched back into the ballroom. Blake had stood in the hall, reviewing the night in his mind. He disagreed. He wouldn't have traded those past few hours of freedom for anything. Watching her uninhibited had been the highlight of his week, better even than seeing Garden & Gather full that first night.

But now that the truth about Mason was out, Blake needed to be there for her. He hadn't missed that flare of pure terror in her eyes before she'd covered it with her ire toward him. If she needed to be angry at him to get through this, Blake would take it.

He'd also make sure that no harm came to her, even if he had to hire a personal bodyguard for her himself. It would probably deplete the savings he'd set aside for Garden & Gather's first year, but wasn't that what investors were for?

Blake's thoughts drifted back to last night, replaying every detail.

The few moments he'd spent lingering in the hall had cost him. Samantha had marched straight up to the bar. By the time he joined her, two empty shot glasses sat in front of her on the bar, and one more was in her hands.

"Do you really think this is the solution?" he asked, his fingers reaching for the little cup of golden liquor.

"Let me know if you can think of anything better." She knocked back the whiskey shot like a seasoned pro, and Blake glared at the hovering bartender, who poured a glass of water then became scarce. He never should have served her.

Her words had already been slightly slurred in the hall. She'd been buzzed before this, but like she'd promised at the beginning of the night, she'd paced herself—until now. With the amount of champagne she'd already had, these shots were going to take her down fast.

"We should get things ready for your sister."

"I can't help my sister if I'm still dealing with Mason."

"Of course you can."

Samantha shook her head—and nearly shook herself off her barstool. "It's too much," she said as Blake heaved her back onto her seat. "It's all too much. I can't do it."

"You don't have to do it on your own." Blake did a quick scan of the room. They'd left their coats outside the room where the ceremony had taken place, but the hotel had moved the wheeled coatrack to the corner next to the door. "Come on, let's get you home so we can be ready for your sister in the morning."

Blake tugged her to standing by her elbow, but she dug in her sparkly heeled shoes. "I can't do it," she said again. When Blake pulled on her elbow, she repeated it, her voice rising in volume with each repetition.

Other guests were staring, and more turned their heads in their direction, as Samantha could be heard over the sound of the music, but thankfully she'd begun to cooperate with his attempts to corral her toward the door.

And of course he had to catch his father's eye on the way out. James's disapproving scowl told him enough about what his father thought of his girlfriend.

But that wasn't Blake's problem right now. Getting Samantha back to his place and taking care of her was his priority.

She was quiet on the drive home with only the occasional sniffle coming from the passenger seat. But once they'd stepped inside, Samantha had fallen apart. She was sobbing, mumbling blubbered words that vacillated between hatred for Mason, concern for her sister's family, and overwhelm from everything else.

He didn't think she'd remember him promising her the week off to help get her sister sorted come morning. He didn't think she'd remember most of the night, and as Blake tucked her into his bed after she'd cried herself to sleep, he thought maybe that was a good thing.

Blake had slept like crap and gave up tossing and turning before dawn. He'd spent an hour doing every bodyweight exercise he could think of in his living room. Running was how he usually worked through excess tension, but he didn't want to leave Samantha alone, not even to use the treadmills on the first floor.

He'd grown restless after seven, so he'd put on the coffee and decided to cook a big breakfast in the hopes Samantha would want something to help fight her hangover when she awoke. Even though he knew she could very well sleep until ten like she'd done the day before, he would have to wake her soon. Her sister would be arriving in town in the next few hours, and he knew Samantha would want to be awake and alert when she and the kids showed up.

Blake had just removed the pan of eggs from the heat when his doorbell rang. His first thought was that it was Samantha's sister, but as far as he understood it, Sarah and her kids were going to Sam's apartment—just another reason for him to get Sam out of bed.

The last person he expected to see at his front door on a Sunday morning was his father. He was always at the church before nine o'clock, and it was already almost eight.

"Hey, Dad." Blake opened the door all the way and stood back, allowing his father entrance.

"Good morning." James walked right past him and pulled out one of the chairs in the small dining area just off the living room.

Blake followed him, branching off toward the kitchen and pouring himself a cup of coffee. He held the coffeepot aloft so his dad could see it over the breakfast bar. "Would you like some?"

His dad waved him off like he knew he would. Unlike Yvette, James only drank one cup of coffee a day while he did his morning devotions at the kitchen table.

Blake took his time in the kitchen, checking that the burners were off and leaving the bacon to drain on a paper-towel-covered plate before joining his father at the table.

"What can I do for you?" Blake asked to get the conversation started even though he dreaded the answer.

James nodded toward the food. "I assume the fact that you're making breakfast means that your girlfriend is here."

"She's still in bed, but yes."

"Her display at the wedding last night was unacceptable."

Blake rolled his lips beneath his teeth to keep himself from saying everything that was in his mind. That he'd gotten Samantha out before she'd had a public breakdown. That she was entitled to getting a little overwhelmed because she'd had a lot going on. That she'd been doing pretty well, considering.

"There wasn't much of a display."

"There was enough of one."

"Is this really what you came here to talk about? Because I think Sam was justified in panicking a little after finding out that not only is her sister in the middle of escaping an abusive situation but also that her own stalker just got let out of jail."

His father rubbed his hand over his chin. "I'm more concerned with her coping mechanism."

Blake was barely able to keep himself from rolling his eyes. "She doesn't use alcohol as a coping mechanism."

"How certain are you about that?"

"Certain enough." Blake understood his father's unease, but there were times when he wasn't sure his father understood that not everybody had the same issues he did. Not everyone was an addict. Not everyone would spiral into alcoholism and abuse after one bad night out.

"She got bad news, and the first thing she did was turn to alcohol. Her entire career is based on drinking. She perpetuates substance abuse—"

"Stop it." Blake plunked his mug down on the table. "Just stop it. It's bad enough that you don't approve of me or anything that I do, but don't come for Sam. She is off-limits."

His father sat up straighter, the frown lines on either side of his mouth deep with disapproval.

"She is struggling in so many places right now, but this isn't one of them, and I don't understand why you constantly want to make it an issue."

James shook his head. "You're so much like your mother."

Blake didn't follow the leap in his thought process. "I take that as a compliment."

"As you should. Your mother has a great capacity for love, but it also makes her vulnerable to being taken advantage of."

"You think Samantha is taking advantage of me?"

"I just find it all a bit convenient that a woman who is down on her luck with no family, no money, a falling-apart car, and who has obviously led men on in the past starts working for you, and within two weeks, she has infiltrated every facet of your life so thoroughly that you're grateful to have her there manipulating you."

Blake stood, fury pulsing through his veins. "You need to leave."

James stood as Blake circled around the table but held his hands up like he was placating a wild animal. "I know it's not easy to hear, but you've been searching so hard for something meaningful that you're seeing what you want to see when it comes to that girl. You're not seeing the damage she could do to you and everything you've built."

Blake shook his head and took hold of his father's arm just above his elbow. The limb was thinner, bonier than Blake remembered, but right now, he did not have any sympathy for the state of his father's health. He was not going to allow a man who had only cared about Blake when he'd gone out of his way to please him walk into his home and insult the woman he loved.

"If you only knew how much she has given me—" Blake started, but his father's snort of derision cut him off.

"She's given you a distraction. And she's going to be your undoing."

Blake stopped at the door. "Then that is my problem to deal with."

His father placed a hand on Blake's shoulder. It took all of Blake's willpower not to shove his father's touch away.

"Just answer me this." James's fingers dug into Blake's shoulder as he squeezed. "If it came down to choosing between her and the restaurant you've worked so hard to open, what would you choose? Her? Or Garden and Gather?"

Blake swallowed. He wasn't sure he understood the question. Why would he have to choose? The only scenario he could see as a possibility was if Sam left him, but then, would there really be a choice? "I would choose Garden and Gather."

THE SOUND OF VOICES in the living room had finally coaxed Samantha from bed. She'd crept to where the bedroom door was ever so slightly ajar and opened it just enough to turn her ear toward the sound traveling down the short hallway. It took her a moment to recognize James's voice, another moment to realize that he and Blake were arguing—and that they were arguing about her. Then she heard Blake say her name amidst the jumble of other words.

The first full sentence she comprehended was: "What would you choose? Her? Or Garden and Gather?"

Sam's stomach clenched. She'd known James didn't quite trust her, but she didn't think he'd actually pressure his son like that. She held her breath, waiting for Blake's answer. She'd hoped her name would fall out of his mouth swiftly and with angry finality, but he was silent. And he was silent for too long.

Oh God.

He had to think about it. Last night, she'd been fantasizing about marrying him, and he had to assess whether he'd choose her over his restaurant?

Samantha shifted and realized she was wearing one of his t-shirts. She didn't remember changing, but most of the night after the wedding was fuzzy. She just knew she'd cried. And when she remembered why, she wanted to cry all over again.

She trembled, and her knees were weak. Dread and fear seized her lungs and made it difficult to catch her breath. Sam didn't have the tools to tackle all of this on her own. Or at all.

If she couldn't figure out how to take care of herself, how could her sister lean on her? They might not even have a safe place to live, not with Mason camping out at her apartment and smashing people's cars.

Panic welled, and Samantha struggled to breathe. She exhaled, but her throat closed up on the inhales. Her hand shot out to steady herself on the door frame.

And then she heard it, confirmation that she couldn't count on Blake. The words "I would choose Garden and Gather" fell from his mouth, and she swayed so hard she decided it would be safer if she were sitting on the floor.

Blake would choose his restaurant over her. Which meant that when push came to shove, his job would always be more important than whatever life they were able to build together.

Samantha saw it then, the loneliness of always coming second. The resourcefulness she'd developed since being disowned by her family would turn into bitter mistrust. She'd grow to resent him and the restaurant. She'd lash out in anger and isolate herself completely.

No, it was better to get out now before she came to truly rely on him only to be disappointed in the end.

Better to continue taking care of herself, taking care of her sister without letting the Fairchilds get too involved. Samantha could already picture Yvette swooping in with bags of designer kids' clothes, a car full of groceries, and an offer to let Sarah and the kids stay in their giant house. Yvette would be in heaven, and while Samantha would enjoy seeing Sarah and her kids well taken care of, there was also a large probability that Samantha would watch Yvette take care of everyone from the sidelines while becoming obsolete.

And for what? A man who wouldn't even choose her?

But why would he? She could only imagine what James was saying about her to his son. She knew he didn't approve of her, and she didn't know why exactly, but it didn't matter. He didn't like her, and he was out there convincing Blake that he didn't need her.

Well, Samantha didn't need him.

She could handle all of this on her own.

Samantha inhaled, gathering fortitude as her lungs finally expanded. She discarded Blake's shirt in favor of her party dress and pulled up her rideshare app. She hadn't used it since before Mason—she'd been too afraid to get into a car with a stranger. But even that was preferable to remaining in this building a moment longer.

The shield of safety she'd felt since meeting Blake had blinked out of existence. Now her skin crawled with a warning that felt like grime and self-delusion.

Nothing with Blake had been what it seemed.

She wasn't going to give her trust to someone who didn't value her. Not anymore. Not ever again.

Samantha splashed water over her face and dabbed away the traces of yesterday's mascara. She texted Charlotte just in case Sarah arrived before Samantha could get to the apartment. Then she took a deep breath, and with her head held high, she walked straight out of Blake's apartment.

Chapter Twenty-Six

"I think you need to let me decide my own priorities," Blake was saying when his bedroom door slammed.

Blake's breath caught in his throat, and he swallowed it down. By the time he'd found his voice again, Samantha had marched into the living room in her dress from last night, her shoes in her hand, and her nose in the air.

"What—?" He meant to ask her what was wrong, but he already knew she'd overheard his conversation with his father. He didn't blame her for leaving, for wanting to get out of a place where someone was so actively criticizing her.

But how much did she hear?

His question was answered as Samantha squeezed between himself and James without meeting either of their gazes and with a firm "Excuse me" to clear her way.

Stunned, Blake watched her tramp down the hall. She opened the door to the stairwell just as his mind caught up with what was happening. "I hope you're happy," he said to his father before dashing down the hall after her.

The carpet felt grimy beneath his bare feet, but he didn't have time to go back for shoes.

"Samantha!" he called after her, catching the whip of her hair as she rounded the curve of the flight below him. The slap of her own bare feet on the concrete steps sped up, and Blake put on a burst of speed to catch up with her.

"Samantha!" he called again as he closed in on her.

"Leave me alone!" she shouted over her shoulder.

He was only a few steps behind her now, and if he wanted to, he could reach out and close his fingers around her wrist, but he knew that would only piss her off more. "Talk to me. What's wrong?"

"Nothing's wrong." Samantha didn't look at him but kept marching down the stairs like he didn't matter. His apartment was on the fourth floor, but by now, the ground floor was just around the bend.

"I know that's not true. Talk to me. Is it Mason? Your sister?" He didn't ask "Is it me? Did you overhear what I said?" because he didn't want to know the answer.

Samantha whipped around at the bottom of the stairs, and Blake had to grip the railing to keep from stumbling into her.

"You know what? No. It's not any of those things. Because all of that is just what's been happening while I've been hiding, waiting for someone else to help me become brave. But all I keep doing is finding new ways to hide. And I'm done fucking hiding."

Blake descended the final step so the difference in their height wasn't so dramatic. "That's great; I can't wait to see that."

Samantha shook her head. "You're not invited." She was in the lobby and out the front door before Blake could even catch his breath.

Through the lobby's wide windows, he watched her duck inside a dark Honda he didn't recognize and disappear as he burst through the building's front door.

Then she was gone. Blake slid to the ground next to the door and reached for his phone to text her, but his pocket was empty. His phone was still next to the stove upstairs in his apartment.

Blake didn't know how long he sat there, but the cold was beginning to turn his toes numb when his dad shuffled through the apartment building's door and offered Blake his hand. There was a surprising amount of strength behind the arm that pulled Blake to his feet, and a part of Blake that had been worried about his dad for months loosened in his chest. Perhaps his father wasn't just being stubborn when he insisted he was fine.

"Is she gone?" James asked when Blake was back on his feet.

"Yeah." His voice sounded strained even to his own ears.

"I'm sorry, son." James patted Blake on the shoulder, but the younger man shrugged him off.

"Don't act like you care."

"I'm sorry if you're upset, but you'll move on."

Blake shook his head. This wasn't over between Sam and him. He wouldn't let it be. It was just a misunderstanding, that was all. If she would just talk to him, they would be able to work this all out.

He opened the building's door then locked his arm across the doorway, barring his father from entering. "You're not welcome here anymore."

Chapter Twenty-Seven

S amantha didn't allow herself to cry on the car ride back to her apartment.

She pulled up the notes app on her phone and did the same thing she'd done on her first bus ride out of Springfield: made a list of everything she needed to do—in this case, to help her sister. Depending on how much Sarah was able to get away with, they were going to need clothes, shoes, and a big trip to the grocery store for food. They were going to need air mattresses, sheets, pillows. Toothbrushes. To get the kids enrolled in the local school district. Samantha didn't even know what school district they were in. And Rebekah, at least, was school-age. Samantha couldn't remember if Faith was ready for preschool or kindergarten.

Sarah was going to have to find a job.

God. *Samantha* was going to have to find a job. A sob rose up in her chest, but she choked it back. No. She would not cry over him, not yet. Not over the job at Garden & Gather. She would figure something out. It wasn't like she didn't have other avenues open to her.

Listing those connections would help ground her.

She could call Emil. Ask him about the shelter that he worked with. See what resources were available for Sarah. Were they going to need a lawyer? Could she be accused of kidnapping? Of stealing the car?

Nothing would be in Sarah's name. The car would belong to her husband. She knew Sarah would have no credit, no work history, no bank account. She was starting her adult life from scratch the same way Samantha had done when she'd gone to school.

She didn't see the Jennings letting her sister go that easily. Not when she'd been theirs to manipulate and control for years.

Sarah would have to file a restraining order—first thing in the morning, as soon as the courthouse opened. Samantha at least knew how to do that.

She'd call Emil. Find out the name of the shelter. And she'd make her sister and her nieces breakfast. Make them feel safe and loved and supported through this transition the way nobody had done for her.

She could do this.

Samantha could make this happen for them, and if Mason showed up in the meantime, then heaven help him, because she had more serious things to worry about than a boy throwing a tantrum over not being allowed to be an abusive asshole.

Tears pinged at the backs of her eyes, but she wouldn't let herself cry over Blake, over the brief glimpse into the promise of the life she thought she'd been building with him. But that had been an illusion like the makeup that had made her look worthy of him last night.

Samantha wasn't pretty. She wasn't glamorous. Life didn't come easily for her the way it did for Blake.

And it was time she stopped pretending otherwise.

———⟨●⟩———

SAMANTHA DIDN'T COME to work on Sunday.

She no-showed on Monday as well.

Blake had expected as much when she wouldn't return his phone calls. Every text he'd sent had been left unread. He suspected she'd blocked his number.

She wasn't responding to his mother, either, though that didn't stop Yvette from updating him every time another one of her calls went ignored. At least she knew better than to talk to him about his father.

He would never forgive his father for hurting the woman he loved.

He couldn't forgive himself, either.

Blake lived in a state of constant tension for the next week, debating with himself the merits of showing up on Samantha's doorstep to make sure she was still alive but knowing it would just make everything worse.

She'd had enough people in her life not respect her boundaries that he couldn't make himself just show up, as desperate as he was to make sure she was alive.

It didn't hurt that with her absence, he was stuck doing her job. The thought of hiring someone to replace Sam made his stomach turn. The implication that she was replaceable repelled him. He didn't want to hire someone new—he wanted Samantha back. He wanted her back at Garden & Gather, and he wanted her back in his arms. He wanted her back infiltrating every aspect of his life the way she'd been doing before. He liked her in his life, and he'd thought she was comfortable there with him.

His mother had thought so, too. She'd shown up at Garden & Gather as soon as church let out on Sunday, plopping down in front of him at the bar like nothing was wrong. She'd tossed her hair over her shoulder and clasped her hands together on the bar top. "Now what can I do to help Samantha and her sister?"

Blake shook his head. "How do you even know about Samantha's sister?"

"I spoke to Charlotte after you left last night. I'm assuming she's going to need a place to stay. And do you know if she has two or three children? Charlotte wasn't certain."

Blake shook his head. He didn't know the answer to that question. "You'd have to ask Samantha."

His mother's bottom lip thrust out like she was a toddler. "I've tried calling her twice so far this morning, and she hasn't answered either time. So I thought you might have more information."

Pain pulsed at the back of his head, and Blake had to remind himself to unclench his jaw or he'd give himself a tension headache. And he didn't have time to deal with that. "Dad didn't tell you what happened this morning?"

His mother squared her shoulders. "He did not."

Blake took a deep breath, pried his teeth apart, and gave his mother a short explanation of his altercation with his father and the subsequent fallout with Samantha.

She stayed silent as she listened, but her face turned red and she fidgeted in her seat as if she needed to be working on a remedy to the situation right then and there.

She barely lasted thirty seconds after Blake finished his story. "I need to go have a few words with your father. Then we'll figure out a way to fix this." She gripped his hand over the bar and squeezed. "We will fix this, Blake. I promise." Then she'd been out the door, her heels clicking against the floor with righteous indignation.

But that had been almost a week ago, and neither Blake nor his mother had had any luck contacting Samantha. Even Charlotte had asked Yvette to give them some time, that they were busy with Sarah's family and Samantha would contact them when she was ready. That was the only reason Blake knew Samantha was still alive, but he couldn't help but think that Charlotte was trying to placate them. He didn't think Sam had any intention of contacting them ever again.

"Knock, knock," Emil said as he tapped on the doorframe of Blake's office. "Mind if I use the computer to start next week's order?"

Blake checked his watch. It was seven o'clock on a Friday night, so he frowned at his chef. From the amount of noise emanating from beyond his office, Blake had assumed the place was full. "They don't need you in the kitchen?"

Emil shrugged. "Giving my team a chance to prove themselves. They know where I am if they need something." He pulled his toque off as he stepped into the room and collapsed into one of the armchairs in front of Blake's desk. He yawned but still accepted the laptop when Blake handed it over.

"What are you still doing here, anyway?" Emil asked as he yawned again. He'd been putting in almost as many hours as Blake had lately.

"I'm hanging out in case they need help at the bar through dinner, since we're still down a bartender." That was his official excuse, anyway. Really, Blake had been staring at the wall wondering what was going on with Samantha. If she'd found another job. If she was coping with her sister's family invading her life well. If she was safe.

Emil tapped the lid of the laptop which rested, still closed, on his knee. "Have you talked to her?"

Blake shook his head as numbness suffused his limbs. There had been too much to do to confide in Emil about what happened with Samantha, and until now, Emil hadn't asked.

"You're both so stubborn." Emil ran his hand through his hair and opened the laptop.

Blake blinked at his chef. "Have *you* talked to her?"

"Couple times." Emil never took his eyes off the screen as he said, "I have a contact at a women's shelter who is helping Sarah with the legal stuff, making sure the kids have clothes, that sort of thing."

"Oh." Whenever Blake thought about shelters, he thought about Nicolas. Only Blake hadn't thought about Nicolas in weeks. Not really. He'd been so wrapped up in Samantha and the restaurant that he hadn't had a chance to notice how much he'd been missing his old friend lately.

"I used to have a friend who works at a shelter around here."

Emil's concentration appeared to be on the screen in front of him. "Nicolas Rivera. Nice guy. Cute wife. He's the one who told me you were looking for a chef when I put in my notice at the Bistro."

Was it possible to pause the universe for just a second? Because Blake felt as if his whole body stopped functioning. He lost all capability to think, breathe, or hear.

His heart missed a beat then thumped in his chest as he sucked in a breath. The sounds of the restaurant finally restarted, and his brain booted back up. "Nicolas is helping Samantha?"

"More Sarah than Sam, but yeah."

Blake shook his head as jealousy burned in his chest. How was it that Nicolas ended up with everything Blake wanted? He knew better than to think that his old friend would be romantically interested in Samantha. He was far too besotted with Rachel to stray. But he was allowed to see Samantha when Blake wasn't.

Nicolas was helping Samantha in the way Blake had planned to before he'd ruined everything.

Blake could blame James all he wanted—and he was still angry with his dad for his part in the breakup—but Blake had been the one to cause Samantha to lose faith in him. He was the one who hadn't found her to apologize or explain.

"How is she?" Blake asked.

Emil shrugged. "Devastated. Exhausted. About the same as you, I imagine."

Blake frowned. "It was a misunderstanding, what happened. She thinks I don't—" Blake's throat constricted. He couldn't even say the words out loud, couldn't give voice to the idea that he didn't love her. And yet, somehow, that was *exactly* what Samantha thought. That she came second to his business, to his job—just as Rachel had known she eventually would be when he'd worked for the church.

He scrubbed his hands through his hair as he breathed through his nose, trying to quell the panic and despair that rose up in him in equal measure at the thought of Samantha existing in the world thinking he didn't cherish everything about her.

"Don't tell me," Emil said. "You should tell her all that."

"I'm pretty sure she's blocked my number."

Emil snorted. "I wouldn't be surprised."

Blake shook his head. "I can't just show up at her door, not when she's been dealing with a stalker. I can't give her cause to worry about two men following her."

Emil sat forward, closing the laptop as he did, and he finally looked Blake directly in the eye. "When the alternative is losing her completely, I think it would be worth the risk."

The two of them stared at one another for a full minute, his chef practically daring him to go grovel at Samantha's feet. When Blake couldn't take it anymore, he asked, "How'd you get involved with the shelter?"

Emil sat back in his chair, cradling the back of his head in his hands, his elbows wide. "I've been meaning to talk to you about that."

Chapter Twenty-Eight

It took Blake another five days to drum up the guts to drop by Samantha's apartment. He half expected not to be let in when he buzzed, but the door clicked open without anyone asking him questions over the intercom.

Maybe she'd seen him drive up somehow? He didn't know how she would have recognized his new car. He'd used his insurance money from the totaled quattro to purchase a new Audi SUV. This model had more room for picking up supplies or helping with catering drops when they were established enough to offer that service. And maybe, in the back of Blake's mind, he'd been thinking about car seats and helping pick Sarah's kids up from school while Sam smiled at him from the passenger seat.

Today, there was only a bouquet of red roses in the passenger seat and an extra case of sparkling wine in the back seat for the last-minute bridal luncheon they'd booked for the next day. But perhaps his visit tonight would change that.

Blake barely dared to hope as his heartbeat echoed in his ears.

He knocked on Samantha's door, holding the bouquet up in front of him—possibly as more of a shield than anything else. He could hear the clamor of little feet followed by the muffled sound of a woman's voice before the chain clinked. Blake swallowed his anxiety as the deadbolts released. He took a deep breath and affected a smile he knew wouldn't hide his nerves from Samantha.

Only Samantha didn't answer the door. A pretty plump blonde woman with Samantha's hazel-green eyes stood blinking at him instead.

"Pwetty fwowers" came from an awed, high-pitched voice in the vicinity of his knees.

"Pretty man," he heard the woman who must have been Sarah say beneath her breath, but he ignored it as he crouched down in front of the little girl and offered her a genuine smile. She couldn't have been more than three or four and had strawberry-colored hair that curled out of two little pigtails on each side of her head. She wore footy pajamas with rainbows and unicorns on them, and Blake's heart panged with longing.

He missed kids. One of his favorite parts of his job at the church had been creating fun ways for the kids to be involved. The youth programs had always served as a sort of surrogate for not having kids of his own. And this wee little thing made him ache for a reality where the car seats he'd envisioned in the back of his SUV were for the children he and Samantha would have together. "I brought these for your Aunt Sam, but can you take care of them for me?"

Sarah's hand tightened on the child's shoulder as Blake held out the bouquet that was almost as big as the child was. "Pwetty," she said again as she took them in both chubby arms.

"Don't hug them too tight; those flowers have thorns. They'll poke you," Sarah said as the little girl looked up at her mother with wide eyes as if not comprehending that something so beautiful could hurt her.

"You must be Blake," Sarah said to him, and he straightened to standing, suddenly blushing. He should have expected that Samantha would talk to her sister about him—and that he would be the villain, as usual.

"Yeah, Blake Fairchild. You're Sarah?" He stuck his hand out.

Sarah bit her lip before accepting. "That's me." She barely touched him before withdrawing her hand. "This is Faith."

"It's nice to meet you, Faith." The little girl only stared up at him and hugged the flowers near the top of the bouquet, where, true, they wouldn't poke her, but she was also crushing the blossoms. "I'm guessing Samantha isn't here?"

"Sorry, she's at work. I'll tell her you stopped by, though."

He nodded. "I'm glad she found a job. Can you ask her to call me? Even a text, just to check in."

"I can. Whether she will is an entirely different story."

That was nothing less than Blake expected. He nodded again, starting to feel like a marionette. "I just wanted to say that I'm sorry and offer to help you all out in whatever way I can."

Sarah scanned him up and down, a frown tugging at her lips as she appraised him. "We're doing okay."

The air mattresses on the living room floor and abundance of clothes and dishes strewn about what he could see of the apartment told him maybe they weren't, but he just said, "If you do need anything."

"Mo-om, is that the pizza?" another voice singsonged from inside the apartment. Another little girl emerged from the hallway that led to the bedrooms.

"Nope, a flower delivery for Aunt Sam. Why don't you help Faith get the roses in water?" Sarah shifted Faith behind her, coaxing her back into the apartment. "I'll tell her you stopped by."

Then she shut the door, and Blake stood in the hallway alone.

———◉———

FIVE MORE STEPS. FOUR. Three. Two. One.

Samantha sighed in relief as she slammed her car door shut and flipped the switch to lock it. Just about the only thing she didn't like about her new job at the hotel was the walk to the parking garage at the end of the night. Everything else about it—the coworkers, the hours, the tips—was fantastic. Sure, she'd only been there a week, and Faye, who had gotten her said job, was only just back from her honeymoon, but somehow, she already felt like she fit in.

Sam had never felt that before, not even at Garden & Gather. She had loved it, yes, but she'd been so busy worrying about her staff respecting her despite her relationship with Blake that she hadn't had much time to just enjoy the job she was doing.

Maybe because being a bartender supervisor was relatively low pressure. She'd been making sure everyone wasn't over-pouring and had helped the bar manager figure out the missing ingredient to one of the winter cocktails, but she wasn't in charge of everything.

She felt supported, respected, and was making damn good money so far. But the restaurant closed at eleven, and by the time she walked out to her car after midnight, there weren't exactly many people left at the hotel to walk out with her to the parking garage around the corner.

It was a quick walk. Well-lit. And the hotel had security cameras. She even checked in with security to let them know she was leaving so they could watch her walk to her car on camera, but she still felt exposed. The walk to her car at night was just about the only time Samantha remembered she still had a stalker out there.

She hadn't seen or heard from Mason since he'd been released from jail. She'd found herself sending prayers out into the universe that his recent experience with incarceration for violating his restraining order was enough of a scare for him to keep his distance.

That didn't make the five minutes she was alone in the dark each night any less scary.

Sam started her car straightaway and waited until she was at the first stoplight to plug in her phone and turn on her music. It was one of Charlotte's old CDs, but Samantha sang along to the words anyway, trying and failing not to think about Blake and what he was doing now. How Garden & Gather was faring as they veered toward the holiday season. How Yvette had taken the news of the breakup. If Blake ever went home anymore. If he'd set up a cot in his office at the restaurant and just slept there so he didn't have to face any other aspect of his life.

Part of Sam knew that she was being unfair to him. Another part of her didn't care. Sure, maybe things hadn't gone his way over the last few years, and he did seem to want to bury his head in the sand and ignore the rest of the world sometimes, but he'd been making an effort with her until—well, until he'd decided not to.

And as much as Samantha missed him, she also recognized that she deserved better. A lot better.

Sam's cell phone pinged when she was a few blocks from their apartment complex, and with Blake on her mind, she half expected the text to be from him even though she knew that was impossible unless he'd changed his number. She'd blocked him so she could have room to think, and while she'd toyed with the idea of unblocking him after he'd dropped off flowers the week before, she hadn't been able to bring herself to do it. She was still too hurt.

And really, she was better off not relying on anyone else too much. As crowded as it was, she and Sarah and Charlotte had been making things work so far.

The text, it turned out, had been from Charlotte. *Just a heads up. Your sister has company in the living room, and the kids are passed out in your room. You can bunk with me tonight if you want.*

Samantha frowned at her phone. Who in the world?

Sarah didn't know anyone in Kansas City but her and the folks Nicolas and Emil had introduced them to at the shelter. Perhaps Sarah had made a friend there. But then why would Charlotte be making herself scarce? Charlotte loved entertaining.

Samantha was still frowning when she opened the door then stopped short.

The apartment had been a disaster since her sister had moved in. There simply wasn't enough room for all of them. But the whole situation was too new for them to even consider if they were going to look for a place for all of them to live or if Sarah was going to look for a place on her own at some point.

It was embarrassing enough to have kids' clothes and toys strewn about an already crowded space, but to see Emil sitting on her sofa in the middle of it all?

Talk about mortifying.

Samantha flushed as she stepped into the room—she had the distinct feeling that she'd interrupted something. Sarah was blinking up at her with feigned innocence in her eyes. The two of them were not exactly close to one another, but both leaned in toward each other, facing the center of the sofa where a takeout box sat. The kind of boxes they used at Garden & Gather.

An open bottle of wine sat on the coffee table in front of them.

Well, hell. Samantha hadn't expected that. Like at all.

She stared at Emil, trying to reconcile the fact that the flirty chef was actually in her home and apparently putting the moves on her very newly single sister.

After a moment of staring, she blinked herself out of her shock with a lame "Hey" then decided to just go about her business, hanging her keys on the hook by the door and dropping her bag and her coat over the back of one of the dining room chairs.

"Samantha! Exactly who I was here to see."

Emil hopped off the sofa and scooped up a box that had been hidden in the detritus on the coffee table. Samantha shot Sarah a look as he crossed the room—she very highly doubted that Emil was here to see her. Sarah shrugged and picked up her wine glass, taking the tiniest sip. It was possible tonight was the very first time Sarah had tried alcohol.

"I was thinking about what you said last week regarding your problem with leaving your new job, and I brought you something."

They'd gone to the Saturday morning social last week at the shelter. Partly because of the free donuts, and partly because a lawyer who sometimes took pro bono work for women had come by. Sam and Emil had caught up a little bit, but Samantha had missed the part where the chef and her sister had made a connection. She pursed her lips and looked down at the package. It was a small rectangular box wrapped in shiny blue paper.

"You wrapped it?"

He shrugged. "They offered at the store. Holidays and all that."

Holidays? It was only mid-November. Had Samantha stepped into an alternate dimension once she'd entered her apartment? Maybe if she left and came back in, the world would be slightly less off-kilter?

She didn't. She took the package from Emil instead. It was deceptively heavy.

"Open it," Sarah called from the sofa. A grin curled her lips like she already knew what it was.

Sam tore the paper and thought she must be reading the box incorrectly. "Is this really a stun gun?"

"Of course it's a stun gun. You think I just have spare stun gun boxes lying around?"

"I don't know. Nobody's ever given me a weapon before. Maybe you have a whole heaping pile of them."

Emil laughed. "Nope, sorry. Closest I can do are my knives."

She would bet he did have his knives in his car. He didn't leave them at the restaurant when he wasn't there, instead rolling them up in a case to take with him every night when he left.

Samantha opened the box, pulling out a little black handheld rectangle with two prongs at the end. "What am I supposed to do with this?"

Emil took the stun gun from her. "Make sure it's charged, hold it while you're walking out to your car, and if anyone gets too close—" He touched the prongs to her shoulder. "Zap."

Samantha looked down to where the metal connected with her black button-down. "Does it work through clothes?"

"Supposed to. I wouldn't recommend testing it, though."

Sam shook her head. Something like this had never occurred to her. But maybe it should have? It certainly made her less vulnerable. "Thanks."

"You think you'll use it?"

"Yes, of course. I'll just have to find a place to charge it where the kids won't find it."

Emil nodded, but Sarah appeared unconcerned when Samantha looked to her for permission. "What? Joe had guns. This does far less damage. And if I tell them not to touch it, they won't touch it."

Samantha nodded, trying not to think about how easily her sister's soon-to-be ex-husband could have used those guns on her. Or how he might show up with guns blazing, demanding to take her back with him.

The first few days Sarah had been in Kansas City, she'd been looking over her shoulder as if she suspected Joseph to appear at any moment. Samantha had imagined a handful of different scenarios where he and Mason both caused trouble, popping into their apartment and demanding what they thought was owed them, spewing the worst of some toxic, possessive bullshit and disregarding the sisters' desires.

Samantha had done her best to shove those fears deep down. Allowing the worry to take over would only keep her from doing what she needed to do to protect her sister. Like giving her sister the support to continue pursuing a divorce and making sure she couldn't be accused of kidnapping. Not to mention making sure the kids were in school and that they had enough money to pay all the bills.

Part of that necessitated walking to her car from the hotel after hours. And the stun gun would make her feel a lot less vulnerable while she did so without actually hurting anyone—well, too much.

"Thank you, Emil." Tears pricked at the corners of her eyes. She hadn't expected to cry, and she didn't want to acknowledge how starved she was for someone to care for her for once, especially after being teased with it from the Fairchilds. She hadn't expected the care to come from this direction, and she was grateful.

Samantha swallowed past the thickness in her throat and gave her friend a quick hug before awkwardly embracing her still-sitting sister. "I'm going to sleep in Charlotte's room tonight. Have fun."

.

Chapter Twenty-Nine

D onuts at the shelter had quickly become Samantha's favorite part of the week. She got the community of knitting class without the fear that paying for yarn and coffee and lunch every Saturday was going to break her budget. Instead, Sam and Sarah and the kids ate the complementary donuts and drank the free coffee and were able to socialize with other women and children who had been through what Sarah was experiencing. A woman called Star led a group therapy session afterward while Nicolas and, to Samantha's surprise, Emil made up games for the kids to play.

Samantha brought her knitting with her and was finally making actual progress on her baby blanket. She would finish it within the next few weeks. Her plan was to donate it to the shelter, start another one, and then donate that one when she finished it as well. It seemed like the least she could do with all the help they were receiving from the place.

"I never did learn how to do anything handy like that." Samantha jumped at the unfamiliar voice. Everyone had just split into their groups, and Samantha had planned to finish the row she was working on before sweeping through the room to collect the discarded coffee cups and consolidate the leftover donuts into fewer boxes. Cleanup had become her habit over the last couple of weeks.

When Sam looked up, Rachel was lowering herself into the chair next to her. Her skin had been prickling with awareness of Rachel's presence all day today. She didn't come with Nicolas every week, and so far Samantha had been able to avoid having a direct conversation with her. She still felt ungainly and bashful around the other woman, even though Samantha knew there was no reason to be intimidated. Sure, she'd been Blake's girlfriend first, but now Rachel was married to someone else—and Blake and Samantha weren't anything anymore. Her fears of not measuring up to the standard Rachel had set were moot.

But Samantha still feared that talking to Rachel might confirm her suspicion that she was lacking some special spark that would have caused Blake to choose her over his restaurant. That Rachel had been too good for him and little stunted Samantha wasn't nearly good enough.

She hated that even just a simple compliment from Rachel had made her blush. She shouldn't be bashful about her accomplishments; she should smile and say "thank you" and show off her work. Instead, Samantha ducked her head and muttered, "I've only just learned."

"It's really cool. And it looks so cozy. May I?" Her hand hovered near the length of blanket that pooled over Samantha's knee.

"Sure."

Rachel slipped her delicate fingertips over the rows of garter stitch, testing the texture of the fabric before pinching one of the folds between her thumb and forefinger. "It's so soft and springy."

Samantha didn't know what to say to that. All she could think about was Yvette's claim that Rachel would want a blanket made out of black yarn for her baby. Plus, it was the yarn that was springy—Samantha had had nothing to do with that.

But Rachel kept talking. "Nicolas's mom is like a legit seamstress. And she's teaching Ivy—that's my stepdaughter—how to sew. She tried to show me how to make a blanket for this little one . . ." Rachel patted her belly. "But I couldn't ever attach ribbon to a square of flannel, so I decided to stick to cooking."

Did that mean Rachel was a good cook? Samantha didn't really know anything about her outside her black wardrobe and recent dating history. "I have zero idea how to cook, even less now that my nieces are living with me. They've been refusing to eat anything but boxed mac and cheese and takeout."

Rachel nodded. "They're going through a lot. They'll get back to healthier foods eventually."

Samantha huffed out a disbelieving sigh, and Rachel answered with a tinkling laugh that implied she understood. "I just published a collection of recipes for a kid-friendly Thanksgiving." Rachel pushed herself out of her chair and crossed the room to her purse like her belly didn't weigh her down in the slightest. She returned a moment later, holding out a business card with her website on it. "Maybe it'll give you some ideas for a couple of dishes you can take to the Fairchilds' next week."

"We're not going anywhere for Thanksgiving."

Rachel blinked at Samantha's abrupt tone. "Oh, I'm sorry. I thought Yvette would—"

"She probably would have if Blake and I were still together." Samantha hadn't been able to let Rachel keep talking, not when she was clearly going to bring up everything Samantha was trying to forget she'd lost.

"I'm so sorry. I didn't realize."

Samantha shrugged. "It is what it is."

Rachel squeezed her elbow just as a cacophony erupted from the recreation room where Nicolas and Emil had corralled the children. Rachel winced. "I'd better go check on them. Do you want to come?"

Samantha held up her knitting. "I think I'm going to keep working on this. But thanks for the link—I'll check out the website. I know Sarah's really frustrated."

Rachel offered a kind smile before sweeping through the door and down the hall.

Samantha allowed the stillness of the quiet room to sink into her bones. Quiet was not something she'd had much of in the past few weeks, and she'd forgotten how much she sometimes needed just a few moments of solitude to rest and recharge.

That was what she would focus on, not how disappointed she was that they wouldn't be attending Thanksgiving at a warm and inviting home like Yvette's. She could make their apartment cozy and fill it with delicious food then slip into her bedroom in the afternoon and curl up with her quilt when she needed a moment to mourn what she'd lost.

WHY AM I JUST NOW FINDING out that you no longer have a girlfriend?

Blake almost turned off his phone to avoid having this conversation. He hadn't told Kat because he hadn't had the brainpower or the self-assurance to deal with her particular brand of sympathy. She tended to listen with one part sincerity and three parts taunting superiority. His awareness that her passive-aggressive—sometimes aggressive-aggressive—responses were her defense mechanisms at work didn't soften her jabs any.

How did you even find out? he typed back, because he knew if he didn't, she would bombard his phone until she annoyed him into responding.

*Bartender Barbie knows Rachel somehow. *eye roll* Rachel told Naomi. Naomi told me.*

Don't call her that. Blake gritted his teeth. He wanted to ask how Rachel knew Samantha, but this was just confirmation of what he already knew: They'd seen each other at the shelter. He didn't necessarily need to be reminded that Nicclas once again was taking on the role Blake wanted for himself. Stepping up when Blake couldn't.

The fact that Emil had been willing to give her the stun gun on his behalf was of little comfort. Did he feel better knowing she had some form of defense against Mason should he appear? Yes. Yes, he did. But he didn't like that she needed it.

He liked Kat's derogatory nickname for her even less.

What? She dumped you. I can call her whatever I want. And that was me keeping your delicate feelings in mind.

How considerate. *My feelings are not delicate.*

Puh-lease. How many times have you puked over her?

More times than he wanted to admit. The first day she'd walked out, he'd been too numb, but the next morning? When he'd woken up without her next to him and the memory of watching her climb into that car and drive away from him replayed in his mind's eye? Yeah, he'd had to make a mad dash to the bathroom. And every morning after that until recently.

That hadn't happened to him since Rachel. And he didn't want to talk about it. Before that, he'd only been consistently sick with emotion before his father's conversion. The anticipation of James coming home from a business trip intoxicated and moody from travel had never done Blake's stomach any favors, and he didn't like being reminded of it or the feeling of helplessness he associated with it.

He tucked his phone away and got back to work going over the reports for the accountant.

He wouldn't be able to know for sure until the accountant interpreted the data for him, but the numbers were looking good. He knew the first month or two would be busier and there'd likely be a drop-off in the new year, but the sales they were seeing were more than he'd expected for his brand-new restaurant.

At least something in his life was going well.

And he enjoyed the work. He left each day with sore feet and exhaustion weighing down his shoulders, but at least he fell into bed with little time to dwell on how Garden & Gather was the only thing that was going right.

Blake hadn't spoken to his father since that morning. His mother was walking on eggshells around him, attempting to garner peace between her husband and son while respecting that Blake had every right to be upset. He hated how much she was being hurt by the feud. The way her eyes had filled with tears when Blake told her that he was going to spend Thanksgiving volunteering at the shelter rather than deal with James had gutted him. Hurting her was inevitable, though, as long as she insisted on trying to convince Blake to forgive his father.

Breaking Samantha's heart was an unforgivable offense as far as Blake was concerned, and James's motives had been entirely selfish. Maybe Blake could have behaved better, done more, but he'd been paying his penance. It was just unfortunate that his mother had to be caught in the middle.

Blake had invited her to help out at the shelter with him. She would have been the perfect buffer between him and Nicolas, possibly even more so between him and Rachel—whom Blake wasn't exactly ready to see. But he'd rather deal with his past than look his father in the eye and pretend he wasn't still livid with him.

And maybe it was time to offer an olive branch to his former friend. Nicolas had wanted to try to be friends again once upon a time, but Blake had shut that down. Maybe he shouldn't have.

When Blake rose to go help close down the bar an hour later, he opened the notification from Kat waiting on his phone.

Hey, look. There's nothing wrong with being sensitive. That you're hyperaware of how those around you are feeling has always been one of your most attractive traits. You are considerate and caring, and you deserve someone who recognizes that without exploiting it the way I did. And if

Bartender Barbie can't see how amazing you are, then she doesn't deserve you, either.

Blake responded with a heart emoji, because that was about as honest and mushy as Kat was capable of being. And he was grateful, at least, that there was still one person capable of seeing him, despite everything they'd put each other through.

Chapter Thirty

"I've been meaning to tell you all night: I love the new hair."

Samantha ran her fingers through the ends of her ponytail. Despite having been a brunette most of her life, she still wasn't used to having dark hair again. She kept catching the chestnut ends out of the corner of her eye and startling before reminding herself it was her own hair and not something looming over her shoulder. "Thanks, Sarah did it for me yesterday. I was ready to go back to my original color, you know?"

Faye shrugged as she polished a glass. "I mean, you made a totally hot blonde, but I get it. The upkeep is obnoxious."

Samantha shrugged. She'd only been blonde for a few months—and she hadn't paid that much attention to her roots—but there had been a sort of relief in returning to being a brunette. Like she wasn't hiding anymore.

She'd gone blonde to make herself less immediately recognizable, but that hadn't mattered; Mason had found her anyway. So staying blonde had seemed pointless. An impulsive decision made in a moment of panic had felt like self-protection, but it had really been self-deception.

An inkling of unwanted clarity zinged through a part of her conscious brain that she had been trying to ignore. The part of herself that suspected that self-deception might be exactly what she'd done with Blake. The part that Samantha was definitely not ready to listen to.

"Yeah, it wasn't worth it in the long run," Samantha said as she wiped down beer taps. "We did Sarah's, too. It's the first time she's dyed her hair. Turns out, she's always wanted to be a redhead."

Faye carefully hung the row of wine glasses she'd just polished on the glassware rack, nodding. "Totally makes sense. She can finally let loose a little. Speaking of, is she still letting loose with that hot chef?" Faye's exquisitely filled eyebrows only exaggerated the comedy of their suggestive wiggling.

Samantha snorted, nearly dropping the rocks glass she'd been stowing in the cooler. "I don't really know. They're keeping it pretty low-key if they are. Or she might just be hiding it from me because I *may* have expressed the teeniest amount of concern that maybe jumping into a new relationship when her soon-to-be ex-husband is still refusing to sign the divorce papers might needlessly complicate her life."

Faye's eyebrows nearly reached her hairline. "Did she not take that well?"

"She basically told me to mind my own business, but she finally has a job, and I don't want her to glom onto the next guy that shows interest just because she's always been supported by a dude, you know?"

"Mm-hmm, mm-hmm, mm-hmm. So get that." Faye picked up a bottle of Irish whiskey, poured two shots, and handed one to Samantha. "Or . . . hear me out. Maybe you need to give her space to make her own mistakes."

Reluctantly, Samantha clinked her glass against Faye's and tossed back the shot. "Yeah, but the last time I did that, she ended up being abused by two men and fleeing her home in the middle of the night."

Faye held her hand out for Samantha's empty shot glass and dropped them in the dirty side of the dishwasher before grabbing a champagne flute from the clean side to polish. "I totally understand the hesitancy, but part of learning to be independent is allowing her to learn from her past and her mistakes at her own pace. And honestly, the guy bought you a stun gun. How bad can he be?"

"Fair." Samantha really couldn't find an argument against Emil. She'd liked him from the first day they'd met.

But her sister had only been on her own for a month. She'd *just* started her housekeeping job at the hotel. She'd never relied on herself before. Samantha wanted Sarah to know how empowering it was to be independent, but she also understood that Sarah had to want that, too.

Both Sam and Charlotte had been attempting to bring up solutions to their cramped living situation with Sarah for the past couple of weeks. The kids couldn't keep sleeping on air mattresses in the living room forever. And sooner or later, the craving for real privacy was going to turn desperate. The fact that Sarah waved off all conversations of getting her own apartment or all of them going in together to rent a house made Sam wary that she was waiting for Emil to invite her and the kids to move in with him. She was both skeptical that he would—at least, not so quickly—and determined to make her disapproval known should the proposal come up.

Faye dropped her bar towel in the hamper and clapped her hands together. "And done."

Samantha turned in a quick circle to make sure the servers hadn't missed any glasses then tossed her towel on top of Faye's.

"Why don't you grab the lights and clock out while I grab my coat from my office, and we'll take out the trash on our way out."

Shoot. Samantha had forgotten about the trash, but she appreciated Faye's economy of motion since it was past midnight, the hotel was enormous, and the soles of her feet were starting to ache. Also, her suggestion meant that Faye and Samantha could walk to the parking garage together, so bonus.

Sam always appreciated company when walking out. It was still her least favorite time of day, but she had been coaching herself that it wasn't that big of a deal. That the system the hotel used had served them for years, and everyone had been just fine that whole time.

By the time Faye waved goodbye as she split off to her reserved spot on the third level and Sam trudged up the stairs to her spot on the top floor, Samantha was grinning. Her mind was on the upcoming holiday party she was going to bartend, mentally calculating the tips she was going to receive and how much of that she could conceivably put toward Christmas gifts for the girls, when she heard a car door slam a few feet behind her.

Urgency quickened her steps while alarm bells sounded in her brain. She had never, not once, run into another person in the parking garage after midnight. She hadn't even worried about it. It was the walk on the exposed sidewalk in the city center that unnerved her. The comforting cocoon of the parking garage had always made her feel safe. Sheltered. Still, she'd made it a habit to carry her stun gun in her hand on her way to her car every evening, and she was sending all of her mental gratitude to Emil as the hairs on the back of her neck rose.

Footsteps scraped along the grimy pavement behind her, and Samantha wished that the unlock feature on her key fob hadn't stopped working two years ago. She would have to waste precious seconds unlocking her car door before she could escape inside and jam the automatic locks to encapsulate her in relative safety.

It was fine—it was probably just the houseman on the way to his car. Scott usually got off about this time, and Andy would be coming in for the overnight shift. Only hotel employees parked on this level, and Samantha had never once felt threatened by any of the people she worked with, even if they weren't in her department and she didn't know them very well yet.

The fall of boots against pavement grew heavier and more harried as Samantha lost all doubt that this person was following her. Then the pursuant called her name, and Samantha's feet faltered.

Fingers wrapped around her right bicep, bruising and cruel even through her winter coat. "I've always liked you better as a brunette. You look like my Samantha again." Mason's voice was as icy as the December air surrounding them as he whipped her around and slammed her into the side of her car.

"I look like myself again." Her voice shook, but she did not back down. Reclaiming her chocolate-brown hair had been an act of defiance. A statement that she would not live in fear. She had promised herself she was not going to cower at the idea of Mason any longer.

Samantha twisted, breaking his hold on her arm, then she jabbed her stun gun into his chest and pressed the trigger before making a run for it. Distantly, she was aware of Mason falling to the ground behind her as she sought the safety of the heavy iron door behind the stairwell and dialed 911. Her heart thudded so hard, it was impossible for her to draw breath even as nausea roiled in her stomach.

Mason had found her.

And not just found her, but he'd stalked her enough to know where she parked and when she would be leaving work. And he had waited for her.

He'd attacked her, and she'd defended herself.

When the dispatcher answered, she had to ask if anyone was there and if she was alright three times while Samantha hyperventilated into the phone. She was finally able to force out "I have a stalker, and I just used my stun gun on him" between heaving pants.

The dispatcher stayed on the phone with her as the nearest police cruiser made its way to her, but Samantha never left the stairwell. She couldn't see all of him from the narrow window in the door, just his feet protruding from between her car and the red SUV parked next to it.

She concentrated on the toes of his Chuck Taylors, waiting for the white tip to twitch in the dim light, but he never moved. Samantha didn't know how long Mason would take to revive, but she feared his wrath at her defensive move despite being proud of herself for actually taking action.

If he recovered before someone could get to her, she didn't know if she'd have the chance to stun him again.

She teetered on the edge of terror the entire wait. Her mind spun with imagined retaliations at the same time she realized this event was a turning point. She had hurt him. She had proved to him that she wasn't easily manipulated. She had stood up for herself, and she had shown that she was not defenseless.

The rational part of her understood that even without the consequences of violating the restraining order for a second time, he would no longer view her as an easy target. She had proved herself stronger than he'd anticipated. But the part of her that had lived in terror of his reemergence for the last six months couldn't evaporate just because she'd defended herself at long last. It would take time for her fear to dissipate. For her to trust a man again.

The squad car arrived within a few minutes, though it felt more like hours. Samantha had remained on the phone with the dispatcher the entire time, watching through the narrow window on the stairwell door for any movement in the garage beyond. She could still see Mason's green Chuck Taylors sticking up from behind her car, but she had no way of knowing if he was conscious from her hiding place.

But the process of the police arriving, the way they'd roused Mason, handcuffed him, and escorted him into the back of the squad car all while shepherding her, was calming and comforting in a way that Samantha hadn't expected. Perhaps it was the reassurance that she'd done the right thing or the way that Mason wouldn't even glance in her direction, but Samantha felt stronger, steadier than she had in months. Years. Possibly ever.

They called Charlotte to come pick her up, assuring Sam that she would receive no fines for leaving her car in the garage overnight.

Even when she was locked into Charlotte's car with her friend squeezing her arms around her neck and murmuring her thanks to Samantha's friends for the foresight of a stun gun, Samantha could only think about how much she wished she'd been able to stand up for herself sooner.

Chapter Thirty-One

B lake popped the top off the Christmas-themed garment box his mother had just handed him, careful not to knock over his toddy or her mulled cider as he did so.

"Now, I know a Christmas sweater is generally considered a cringy gift." Yvette fidgeted in her chair as Blake parted the tissue paper. "But you've always looked so good in green, and this isn't really a Christmas sweater. The shop girl called it a 'Norwegian-style ski sweater.' And it looked so warm, and it's been so cold the past couple of winters."

True to what Blake would expect from his mother, the sweater was tasteful. The wool was a dark hunter green with a white colorwork band of snowflakes across the chest and a thick, squishy collar with a half zipper. Blake pulled the sweater from the box to gauge its size, even though Yvette had never purchased him an ill-fitting garment. She had a knack for knowing what would flatter her friends and family.

"What do you think?" she asked. "Will you wear it?"

"Of course, I'll wear it. If I put a sport coat over it, I can even wear it at the restaurant."

Yvette's shoulders relaxed as her lips spread in a wide, satisfied smile. "My thoughts exactly."

Blake folded the sweater and tucked it back into the box then slipped it underneath the gift bag on the spare chair at their table. For the first time since October, Blake sat at a table in a restaurant that wasn't his own. For the first time in two months, he'd eaten food that wasn't on Garden & Gather's menu, and he had to admit that, as distracted as he was, it was nice to sit down and eat a salad and a steak instead of inhaling another flatbread at his desk between rushes.

Meeting for dinner the night before Christmas Eve had been his mother's idea, since Blake still refused to see James, and James, in turn, had decided he didn't care to see his son until he came to his senses. Yvette had refused to relay any messages between the two but had also refused to choose between the two of them. Which Blake could forgive. She had a marriage to think about, and while part of Blake would never understand why she'd stayed with James after everything he'd put her through, he'd recognized long ago that their relationship was none of his business. If only his father could give him the same courtesy, then maybe Blake would have been the one Samantha called last week instead of Emil.

Blake still couldn't wrap his mind around it. The memory of Emil calling him at two in the morning and opening with, "Holy shit, man. She used the zapper. On her fucking stalker. Just zapped the hell out of him in a parking garage."

It had taken Blake twenty minutes to get the full story out of his chef, both because Emil kept veering off on tangents about how much foresight Blake had had in purchasing the self-defense weapon for Samantha and because Emil's call had woken Blake from a dream where Samantha had been safe in his arms, not in danger and alone in the middle of a freezing night. He'd had trouble wrapping his mind around the dissonance at first, but he'd woken up quickly when the words "the police found restraints in Mason's car" came through the phone.

Restraints.

That part kept tripping Blake up. Mason hadn't just been attempting to attack and traumatize her, but he'd intended to kidnap her. To take her someplace Blake might never be able to find her.

The what-ifs hadn't stopped playing in his mind. What if he hadn't thought of the stun gun? What if he hadn't been able to convince Emil to give it to her? What if she'd refused to use it? What if she'd forgotten to charge it or hadn't had it on her that night?

He'd spent more than an hour lost in anxious speculating over the last few days. Even now, in a warm, candlelit restaurant, his mind was trapped in a grungy parking garage imagining how frightened Samantha had been. How alone. How freaking brave she'd been to even put up with the hotel's ridiculous policy to just let people leave on their own late at night.

"Is this gift for your father?" The image of the parking garage dissipated in his mind's eye as the rustle of his mother's hand caressing the tissue paper poking out of the gift bag ripped him back to his reality. The chill of the parking garage lingered in his bones and settled across his shoulders despite the warmth of the dining room he now sat in.

Blake forced his lips into a soft smile, one he hoped his mother would take at face value. Because no, he *hadn't* purchased his father a present. So he deflected instead. "No. That one's for you, too."

Yvette blinked away the disappointment in her eyes, using a smile that mirrored Blake's but wasn't fooling him at all. She couldn't hide how much she'd been hoping the mysterious gift bag would be an avenue for reconciliation between her son and her husband. "But you already got me the perfume."

Blake lifted the bag by the handles and held it out toward his mother. "And I saw this and thought you would like it, too, so I got it for you."

Yvette's arm dragged to the floor as soon as she picked it up, clearly unprepared for the weight of the bag. "Oh my word. What in the world?" She settled the gift on the floor by her feet and pulled the tissue paper from the top in that careful way she had, somehow not wadding it. "Is this what it looks like?"

A genuine grin crossed Blake's lips at the undisguised glee in his mother's voice. "I thought you might have more luck with this than you've had with those little pots in the windowsill."

For as long as he could remember, his mother had been trying to grow herbs in her kitchen window. She liked to use fresh herbs in her cooking and baking but ended up replacing the plants every couple of months because she never had been able to keep the plants alive for long. The little hydroponic countertop garden with a grow light should take care of most of his mother's indoor gardening problems.

Yvette squealed and clapped her hands, exclaiming how excited she was to plant a new set of herbs in the wintertime.

Blake attempted to listen, but his mind was already wandering to his apprehensions about tomorrow. He'd let Emil not only talk him into providing food for the Christmas Eve party at the shelter, but he'd also cajoled Blake into volunteering to work the event. On some level, he knew that Emil was aware of Blake's history with Nicolas, and Blake wasn't necessarily ready to come face-to-face with Nicolas again.

Only a year before, Blake had told him that they didn't have to try to be friends anymore as a way to let Nicolas off the hook. Blake didn't want his friend to feel guilty because he was falling in love with his ex-girlfriend. Even then, jealous as he was, Blake hadn't wanted to stand in the way of their happiness.

He had possibly still been punishing himself for his sins of the past few years. For lusting after what Nicolas had. For coveting his best friend's wife, his family life. For despising his friend instead of supporting him the way he should have done.

For days, he'd been going over in his head all the awkward directions the night could take. Nicolas could ignore him. He could call him out in front of everyone for being the man who'd caused the end of his first marriage. Rachel could be there, and the women would all give him that knowing look, laced with accusation. He was one of the bad ones. One of the ones who would break your heart and betray your trust.

When Blake pulled up to the back door of the shelter behind Emil, his heart was hammering in his chest. The fabric of his winter coat pulled too tightly across his chest as he fought to take a full breath. A panic attack hadn't snuck up on him in years, but he'd had them often enough in his adolescence to know that he just needed to breathe through it. Though it would be better if he didn't have to breathe through it while carrying heavy insulated boxes full of food into an unfamiliar place.

Emil had already rung the bell on the back door by the time Blake joined him there and set the boxes down to wait. He shoved his hands in his pockets more to make himself take up less space than because he was cold. He'd wished Emil had grabbed some food instead of waiting for the door to open so he could have followed that lead. Blake would have felt as though he had more of a purpose than just showing up like a stray at a former friend's workplace on the verge of hyperventilating.

Nicolas propped the heavy door open a moment later. He wore a broad smile and the same navy sweater he'd had on the last time Blake had seen him. That had also been a few days before Christmas, a full year ago now. A year since Nicolas had offered to renew their friendship and Blake had declined.

"Right on time, as usual." Nicolas held his hand out to Emil for a shake but pulled him in for the same kind of one-armed hug that Nicolas and Blake used to share. "I hope you brought extra. We've got a lot of hungry people here tonight."

"Always." Emil motioned to Blake. "You know Blake Fairchild."

"Of course." Nicolas offered Blake his hand the same way he had done to Emil. It was muscle memory that allowed him to settle into Nicolas's embrace, because Blake's conscious mind had shut down, not quite comprehending this remnant of their former friendship.

"It's good to see you, Blake." Nicolas's voice was soft and sincere, and a wave of gratitude swept over Blake, one so powerful that his nose tingled with the possibility of tears.

And then his mouth formed words without his permission. "You, too. How's the wife?" Blake cringed inwardly. His inquiry could have been construed as passive-aggressive, but Nicolas's grin didn't falter as he stepped back and ran his hand through his shaggy hair. "Good. She took the kids to her mom's for Christmas Eve dinner and saved all the presents for me to wrap when I get home. She says it's because of the belly, but I have a suspicion it's her way of punishing me for missing dinner."

Nicolas's smile never faltered as he spoke. Amusement sparked in his eyes at his new wife's behavior, and Blake saw confirmation of what he'd known last year when he'd sold Nicolas the engagement ring. Those two understood one another and loved each other in a way that Blake wasn't sure he'd ever find.

He could imagine the same scenario happening back when Nicolas had been married to Kat, only the present wrapping wouldn't have been a playful joke between the two of them; it would have bred bitterness and resentment. Kat would have accused Nicolas of planning time away from the family, and Nicolas would have come back with how lucky she was that he hadn't volunteered for the Christmas Day shift instead. It would have been a weeks-long fight, and

Nicolas would have started out his greeting with a scowl and a lamentation about how pissed Kat was going to be at him.

It was basically a miracle that both of them were in better places now. Blake was just sorry he'd been the reason they'd realized they were better off apart. The apology almost slipped past his lips, but Nicolas had already stepped back and asked Emil what he could help carry.

And then Blake was following them inside the new building and into a kitchen that paled in comparison to the one he'd built at Garden & Gather. The stove was small. The ovens had clearly been purchased used. Stainless steel refrigerators lined the walls instead of a walk-in. But what they did have was a gorgeous buffet.

Now Blake understood why Emil had chuckled and said "um, no" when Blake had asked him if they needed to load up the chafing dishes. The center had built-in hot pans. The water inside them was already steaming, so the pans were ready to warm the meat and tortillas for the taco bar they had brought. The other slots were refrigerated and ready for the salsa and toppings.

Blake had wanted to cater a full turkey dinner for the shelter, but Emil had steered him away from it. Partially to give them an easier time with the prep, and partially because the tacos would be self-serve. Less formal. More like a party. And everybody liked tacos.

The surge of the women and children milling about in the dining area just outside the kitchen toward the buffet line certainly reinforced that point. And the exclamations over the taste and texture of the food filled Blake with pride even though he'd mostly watched as Emil and his staff had done all the work. He had helped with the tortilla press, though, and had officially been converted to fresh tortillas only.

Apparently, they were using Emil's mother's family recipe, and Blake had learned more about his head chef than he'd expected. With the last name Laurent, Blake had always assumed he was of French descent, but his mother was Guatemalan.

Blake had the impression that his mother's history was a point of pride for Emil, despite the fact that he could pass for someone of European descent. As they'd cooked earlier, Blake had learned of the hardships his mother had faced. Of the Mexican restaurant Emil had grown up in because that was the way his mother's family had survived in the Midwest. Of the way his mother's family had taken them in when his father had fucked off to the East Coast for a prestigious chef position and never came back.

Blake had reciprocated by expounding upon just how much he admired his own mother and how confused he was sometimes that his parents had stayed together after everything their father had put them through. He had not expected to say any of that out loud considering how content Yvette was to stay by James's side over the years. But especially after witnessing how good divorcing had been for Kat and Nicolas, there were times when Blake wondered if he and Yvette would have been better off leaving James behind after his multiple betrayals.

There were also times Blake wondered if he would be in a healthier place had he not had the weight of his father's expectations weighing on him as he'd gone through his formative teenage years. Perhaps he would have been able to find a partner before he was pushing forty. Perhaps he would have trusted himself to not break a woman's heart the way he'd watched James do to Yvette. Perhaps he would have trusted himself to build a family without the possibility of building trauma into their DNA.

Maybe the whole reason he'd let Samantha walk away from him was because he was certain that, when push came to shove, his father's weaknesses would manifest in his own behavior. And he would absolutely never willingly subject another human being to that sort of humiliation and pain.

Did that stop Blake's heart from stuttering when Samantha entered the dining room? Not in the slightest.

Especially because she was wearing the same exact sweater he was, just with a more feminine cut.

Holy hell.

Somehow, his mother had purchased them matching sweaters. Samantha's whole family wore new sweaters, in the same style as his, only theirs were a different color. Where his and Samantha's was green, Sarah's and her daughter's sweaters were a deep crimson. If someone were to group them all together for a holiday photo, they would make a merry bunch. But seeing as Samantha was doing her best to pretend he wasn't there, Blake knew that no family photo would be forthcoming.

No matter how desperately he wanted to corner her and kiss her and tell her how much he liked her dark hair and then demand she tell him why she'd consented to see his mother if she was refusing all contact with him.

But Samantha somehow avoided interacting with him for the entire evening. Every time Blake had sought her out, she'd been three steps ahead of him, maneuvering through the other women gathered as if she were a mirage.

And by the time he and Emil were loading their carriers back into their cars, Blake hadn't managed to say a single word to her, despite how much he'd wanted to secret her into one of the storerooms and tell her how sorry he was for that day back in October.

Chapter Thirty-Two

His phone rang too early.

Without even opening his eyes, Blake knew that he had had too little sleep. It was his own fault for staying up too late the night before.

When they'd left Garden & Gather after the evening rush, he'd accompanied Emil to dinner. He'd thought the plan had just been to go out for pizza and beer, but Blake hadn't realized that it had been a ruse to force him into Nicolas's proximity. And from the way Nicolas's eyebrows creased upon spotting them, Blake was certain that Nicolas hadn't expected them either.

Emil, it seemed, had been playing matchmaker.

The first beer had been a little awkward. They'd defaulted to talking about their jobs because they both had those in common with Emil. But when the pizza arrived with their second round, Emil pushed his chair back on two legs, raised his beer to his lips, and asked Nicolas, "So how's the wife feeling? Must be pretty good still to let you out of the house."

Nicolas's eyes sparked, and his mouth widened in an electric grin even as his gaze darted over to gauge Blake's reaction, just for a second. "Rachel is out on a date with another man, so I don't think she can give me too much trouble."

Blake, who had been attempting to take a nonchalant sip of his beer, nearly choked on his swallow. Emil clapped him on the back as he coughed then said, "That might be more than I needed to know about your relationship."

Nicolas laughed. "Not like that, you perv. Dex is like her little brother. She's been teaching him how to cook, and tonight he's making her dinner."

For a second, Blake had to search his memory for who that could be. When he'd known Rachel, she hadn't been close to anyone but him and Naomi. But then the memory of the work friend she'd talked about most clicked. "The bartender with the funny speech patterns?"

"Yeah. I think he was making her pasta from scratch tonight. Noodles and everything. She was so excited."

"Do you know the type of sauce?" Emil asked, and Blake found himself leaning forward with interest. Funny how he'd followed Rachel's career since they'd broken up. He knew her writing career had been born out of her cooking blog, but in the weeks since he'd found out Emil and Nicolas were friends, he'd never thought about the many common interests Rachel and Emil might share. Nor how much opportunity he and Rachel had to bond in new, purely platonic ways now that Blake had inserted himself into the food and service industry.

Was that the point Emil was trying to make by throwing them together like this? That he and Nicolas—and possibly he and Rachel—had a base to start a friendship on? How much did Emil know of their pasts? Blake had never revealed the details, but the chef must have had some idea.

"They have some frozen tomatoes leftover from the gardens this year. I think the plan was to make an arrabbiata sauce. The baby loves spicy food."

As the conversation transitioned away from food and to talk of Nicolas's burgeoning family, Blake found himself jealous again, but not in the way he'd thought he would be. Looking at the sonogram picture of Nicolas and Rachel's baby on Nicolas's phone stoked that familiar envy to a smoldering burn in his chest. The difference was that this time Blake didn't find himself wishing that Rachel was having his baby instead, but rather he longed for the opportunity to one day show off similar pictures of the child he'd created with Samantha.

The disappointment of not being able to connect with her on Christmas Eve still stung. Over the last few days, he'd just been replaying how much greener her eyes looked paired with her dark hair and hunter-green sweater. How her cheeks had flushed when she'd seen him. How he'd been desperate to fold her into his arms and tell her how worried he'd been about her.

He wanted to tell her how he would give everything else up if only it meant that he would be the one she turned to.

The yearning, yawning emptiness that had been the center of his chest since Samantha had run away from him filled with hope. Maybe she would still reject him, but he would hate himself forever if he never set the record straight and told her how much he loved her.

Buoyed by the decision, Blake stopped holding himself back. Stopped worrying that Nicolas was going to decide that this evening was a joke and that Blake didn't deserve his friendship. Instead, Blake finally let himself relax and enjoy the present moment for the first time in his recent memory.

Possibly the first time in his adult life.

And when he'd finally fallen into bed last night, tipsy and optimistic, he'd planned on mimicking Samantha's sleeping habits and not crawling out from beneath the covers until ten am at the earliest.

So this pre-dawn phone call was already putting a damper on his plans. He needed adequate sleep to sketch out his grand gesture to win Samantha back.

"Hello?" His voice croaked into the phone, but considering he hadn't even opened his eyes yet, Blake was proud of himself for not rolling over in bed and ignoring the call altogether.

"Blake?"

His mother's wavering voice wicked all of his sleepiness away in an instant. He sat up in bed, shoulders tense, mind alert. "What's wrong?"

A sniffing sob met his ear from the other end of the line. "It's your father."

⟶ ◉ ⟵

SAMANTHA WAS ON HER hands and knees in her disaster of a living room, mopping up the coffee spill from where Faith had been dancing like the cartoon on TV and kicked over Samantha's new Christmas mug when her phone rang. The mug itself had survived. Samantha wasn't as optimistic about the prognosis of their cream-colored carpet. She could see their five-hundred-dollar deposit slipping through her fingers like she was trying to capture the snowflakes that were falling outside.

She searched for her phone underneath the sofa cushions—which were also on the living room floor—as the jaunty ringtone taunted her. She had to unbury the device from the chaos that had been having the girls home from school during winter break.

"Only one more week; just one more week" had become Sam's mantra over the last couple of days. She and Sarah had been working opposite shifts—Sarah's housekeeping job was during the day, while Samantha worked the evening shift with an hour of overlap in the early afternoons before Sam had to be into work. She was counting down the hours until she was free from the chaos of two children going through epic changes.

Finally, Samantha found her phone under a blanket, beside the couch, sticking out of a snow boot, and she hurried to answer Faye's call before it went to voicemail.

Faye graciously waited for Faith to stop her sprint across the living room while cackling like a Batman villain before she said, "Now this is going to sound weird, but hear me out. I need you to not come in for your shift tonight."

Samantha blinked at the nest of blankets and pillows on her living room floor, confused. "It's a Friday night."

"I know, and it means I'm going to have to stay, which I totally don't want to do. And I can't actually tell you not to come in—I am just recommending that I cover for you, because once you hear the news, I have a feeling you might like to be elsewhere."

Samantha's heart stuttered, her thoughts immediately turning to Mason. But he was still locked up, so there was no way he could be infiltrating the hotel somehow.

"What's going on?"

Faye sighed into the phone. "I'm not even sure I should be telling you this, but I think you're a good person, and even though you're younger than me by two months and I get a little creeped out when I think about that, I also think you're really good for Uncle Blake, and he's been a solemn, solitary bore since you two split, and Uncle James is in the hospital, and I think Blake needs you right now."

Samantha's brain had trouble parsing the words at first. Blake's solemnity she could believe; he'd worn his usual veneer at the Christmas Eve party a few days ago. Despite her attempts to pretend he wasn't there—and possibly once or twice avoid him outright—Samantha's gaze had been drawn toward him. She'd had an acute awareness of where he'd been in the room at all times, and she hadn't been able to resist the urge to ogle him.

Even after all the hurt she'd endured, he was still the most beautiful man she'd ever seen.

He'd caught her watching him once or twice. His eyes had burned, his expression turning from shiny to stony like he couldn't hide how difficult it was for him to see her, and Samantha had made herself flee.

She hadn't been hiding from him, exactly, but from her desire to go to him and smooth his brow with the pads of her thumbs then trace the contours of his beard while he wrapped his arms around her waist.

She yearned to be folded into those arms. The compulsion to bury her nose in his shoulder, smell his subtle woodsy scent, and relish in the way he made her feel tiny was so overwhelming that Samantha almost forgot how small he'd made her feel in an emotional sense. How she'd almost convinced herself to accept less than she deserved. And no amount of puppy dog eyes on his part were going to make her forget that she deserved dignity.

The rational part of Samantha's mind caught up with her as the gravity of what Faye said kicked in. This wasn't all about Blake, even if Faye was suggesting that Samantha should be there for him. "Is James going to be alright?"

There was a pause, then: "I don't really know that much. I know he was taken to the hospital this morning and that he's been in surgery and Aunt Yvette and Uncle Blake are there waiting for more information. But Aunt Yvette also said that Uncle Blake has been beating himself up because everything could be very serious and he hasn't spoken to his dad since the morning you two broke up, and I don't know." There was another pause as Faye sighed heavily. "I just thought that maybe you could help."

Samantha didn't know what to say, so she just allowed the silence to stretch between them on the line.

Finally, Faye broke the awkwardness of the quiet. "You know, because Uncle Blake hasn't talked to his dad because of the things he said that made you leave. I'm not expecting you to absolve his guilt over everything that happened, but like"—Faye took another deep breath—"but I think he really loves you and he was punishing his dad for how things ended with you. And now he doesn't know if Uncle James is going to make it, and he's kind of sad about the last couple of months, and I don't know, I thought maybe if you showed up, it would just . . . help."

Samantha's jaw worked, and she knew Faye didn't know she wasn't sure how to respond. Sam was doing her best to conjure words, but her mind couldn't decide where to start first—her first instinct was to ask "what hospital?" and just go, but she wasn't sure what help she would actually be.

There was a certain amount of moral support that could be offered through physical proximity—she knew that—but she didn't want to send Blake mixed messages. Yes, a part of her would care about him and his family forever; it was the reason she'd accepted the gifts from Yvette. But she didn't want him to think that everything was magically fixed between them just because she showed up.

At the same time, though, the thought of not going to him was unfathomable. He was in pain. Likely confused. And Samantha wanted to comfort him on a visceral level.

In spite of everything, Blake's pain was her pain. Even if it made her hate herself just a little bit.

"He hasn't spoken to his father in two months? Because of me?"

"Because of the way James spoke to you and about you. Everybody knows it started a rift between them. I thought you knew that, too."

"I had no idea."

"Well, they haven't spoken since the day after my wedding, because Blake has been adamant that his father apologize to you, and James wouldn't, so that was that. Until this morning."

Until this morning. When Blake would have realized his father's life was in danger and the guilt of leaving their relationship estranged would have driven him to the hospital. He would be desperate for reconciliation, or at least understanding and acceptance. And he would be hurting, sitting in a waiting room broken and helpless, trying to be strong for his mother when he was breaking himself.

Faye was right. Samantha would prefer not to go into work tonight.

"What hospital did you say they were at?"

Two hours later—and with a lie to the nurse at the information desk about being James Fairchild's daughter-in-law looking for her husband—Samantha wound her way back into the waiting room at the far end of the ICU. This one was more comfortable than a normal waiting room, furnished with armchairs and sofas and dining tables. It was a quiet space made for long, anxious waits and solemn news.

And there he was on a blue sofa at the back of the room. Her feet stopped as her heart jumped in her chest. He was wearing the same green sweater he'd been wearing on Christmas Eve. She looked down at her own chest and spied the snowflake pattern visible from beneath her coat. They matched again today. Perhaps sporting the twin to Blake's sweater had helped sell the lie of being his wife. Perhaps the nurse was just bad at her job.

It didn't matter, because the way Blake's body appeared to be collapsed in on itself as he leaned over his knees and cradled his forehead in his hands made it clear that he was suffering. His hair stood at all angles, and she imagined him thinking of all the ways he and his father had been at odds while running his hands through his chocolate mane in frustration.

He must have felt her presence then, because his head raised, eyes blinking as if he didn't trust them to show him the truth. His skin was paler than normal, and there were deep purple circles under his eyes. Then Samantha watched a new wave of sadness wash over him, watering down his usually vibrant eyes as he stood with slumped shoulders.

Samantha broke then, shedding her bag and coat onto random chairs as her feet carried her toward him. She threw her arms around his waist while his banded around her shoulders in a hard yet trembling embrace. His nose nestled next to her ear, and he inhaled a deep, shaky breath. "You're here."

Samantha nodded, allowing the heat of his body and the smell of his soap to crash into her with the comfort of a warm blanket on a cool night. She had missed that woodsy scent so much, it almost didn't feel real to have access to it again.

"I'm here."

Chapter Thirty-Three

B lake had arrived at the hospital after a rinse in the shower and a hastily reheated cup of yesterday's coffee tossed in a travel mug to find his mother crumpled into an armchair, still wearing her house shoes.

Her hair was still piled on top of her head in the messy bun he associated with the kind of deep cleans that preluded the holidays when he was a kid. Bags were visible under her eyes that were smudged with yesterday's mascara.

Blake couldn't remember the last time he'd seen his mother without a full face of makeup. When he was growing up, she almost never left her bedroom without it. Even when things had been bad. Maybe especially when things had been bad.

She hadn't told him what was wrong when she'd talked to him on the phone. Only that when his father had returned from his morning walk, he had knelt down to pick the newspaper up from the driveway and collapsed. She'd just been descending the stairs to start her yoga—which explained her pink tights—when she'd seen James fall through the window.

The paramedics couldn't diagnose him and hadn't been able to revive him right away, but she'd thought it was possible that James had had a heart attack or a small stroke.

Blake had been hoping his mother would have more answers when he arrived, but she wasn't up to speaking. She only collapsed against him with silent tears running down her cheeks and clung to his waist until Blake felt the arms he'd draped around her shoulders start to go numb from inaction.

Finally, he cleared his throat enough to ask, "Do you know anything?"

Yvette sniffed and shook her head. "They're supposed to be letting me know what they found any time now."

Blake eased his mother back into her seat and took the one beside her so he could continue holding her hand. "Can I get you anything? Coffee? Something to eat?"

Yvette shook her head. "I can't. Not until I know he's going to be okay."

Blake nodded and sipped his own tepid coffee. Maybe the coffee hadn't cooled, though—maybe his body was just so numb that he'd lost all awareness of temperature and taste. His senses were wrapped in a fog of dread and also a strange sort of misunderstanding about the turmoil boiling inside him.

Because now that he was here with his mother, knowing he could take care of her, most of his panic had subsided. Yvette was worried about her husband, but she was safe. Blake could help remind her to take care of herself, and that calmed his nerves considerably.

The numbness was what confused him. He didn't think it was caused by the shock of his father being in mortal peril—he felt more adrift than anything, like he was lost in a field.

He didn't know how he felt about his father, and he wasn't sure how to find his way back to honest affection.

Everything was just gray, a combination of love and resentment. Wanting to make James proud and being forever disappointed in him. The memory of the way he didn't trust Blake. The way he made Blake question things he knew were right for him. The way he hadn't even given Samantha a chance because he was too afraid to face his own trauma.

Blake shook his head at himself. There had been times in his life that Blake had wished his father would simply disappear. That James would be crossing the street one day and be hit by a bus so he and Yvette would be free of him forever. There had been years, decades maybe, where Blake had derided himself, stricken with guilt for ever wishing such a thing. During the times when he'd been more or less what James had wanted him to be, everything had been good.

But in his father's philosophy of life, there was no room for growth—or at least, there was no room for growth outside of the way James had grown.

Blake had found himself wanting to tell his father that there was more than one path. That it didn't take becoming a Christian to be a good person. That Blake didn't begrudge his father his beliefs, but that they'd begun to feel like more of a trap to Blake than the salvation they were supposed to be.

But Blake didn't even know where to begin on that front. He never had, so he'd put it off. Part of him thought that having an open and honest conversation with his dad might be painful, but he often wondered if such a conversation might be the key to building a more equitable relationship with him.

He'd only find out if his dad pulled through.

The doctors came out a few minutes later. Blake held his mother as they explained that his father had had a slow-moving pulmonary embolism, the cause of his symptoms over the last few months, and it had caused a blockage that would take surgery to remove before it actually *did* cause a heart attack or a stroke. The doctors were optimistic about the surgery's rate of success, but they emphasized that the recovery would take some time so Yvette would be prepared. According to them, the process wasn't without risks, but they did mention that Yvette's quick response to James's collapse had likely saved his life.

Yvette calmed after that and let Blake lead her down to the cafeteria. But all he could find was a sad-looking croissant to have with her yogurt and some bitter-smelling coffee. He got himself the same.

She nibbled and sipped between wringing her hands together. Her wedding ring flashed as she twisted it on her finger, and the words were out of Blake's mouth before he could stop himself. "Why did you stay with him?"

Yvette blinked and set down her Styrofoam coffee cup, then she sat up straight as her nerves seemed to disappear. "I've been waiting for you to ask me that question since you were sixteen."

Blake's brow furrowed. "It made sense then; he'd changed so much for the better over what he was."

"But it doesn't make sense now?"

"I'm just beginning to wonder if he's ever actually supported you, or if his affections were withheld until you complied with what he wanted, the way he is with me."

His mother stilled completely. Blake wasn't even sure she was breathing until she released a long sigh through her nose. She tapped her nails on the tabletop in sharp clicks as he waited for her to find her words. "Your father is my best friend. He was before you came along, and even when he was drinking, there were times when he was wonderful."

The snort he emitted was entirely involuntary, but his mother shook her head. "I know it's probably difficult for you to remember. You were so young, but it was only really bad those last couple of years before his conversion. And deciding to leave him was the scariest thing I'd ever done—until he asked me to stay."

Blake let that thought roll around in his mind a little bit as he sipped his own too-bitter coffee. "He had to convince you to stay?"

"He had to convince me to let him move back in."

Blake had to push himself back from the table at that revelation. "I don't remember him moving out."

Yvette scooped up a spoonful of yogurt then let it slop back into her bowl. "I'm sure to you it just seemed like he was gone on business since he was here during the day on weekends and had dinner with us a few nights a week, but he slept on his brother's sofa for six months while he proved to me he had changed."

"I didn't realize."

Yvette nodded then snagged his limp fingers with her own and pulled her hand into his. "I did my best to keep everything normal for you while we figured ourselves out."

Blake spun his coffee stirrer between the fingers of his free hand, twisting it into oblivion while he processed everything his mother was saying.

He'd had no idea James hadn't always lived with them. The way he remembered it, his father's miraculous conversion had occurred, and his life had instantly altered for the better.

"Why did you decide to let him move back in?"

His mother's lips turned up in the corner but remained firmly pressed together in the middle, her eyes glassed over in her melancholy. "I told him he could move back as long as he stayed sober and agreed to allow me to live a life that didn't revolve around him. I wanted a chance to live my dreams, too. To do something for me. I told him I wanted to start the bakery, and if he couldn't support that, help me around the house, and be a father to you all while going to seminary, then he needed to find somewhere else to live and someone else to be his wife. He agreed."

Blake squeezed Yvette's hand. "I never knew that." He also hadn't given his mother enough credit over the years. She was much stronger than he'd realized.

Yvette squeezed his hand then sat back in her chair. "Of course, you didn't. I made sure you didn't know at the time, but I can see now how not having this conversation with you when you were twenty could have influenced how you interact with your father now. But you were so enthusiastic about what you wanted then. I had no idea you were seeking your father's approval with your choice of career."

Blake shifted in his seat. "I'm not sure I was aware that was what I was doing, but it makes sense looking back."

"I'm proud of you for standing up for yourself, but you should understand that your father knows he made a mistake. He wants a relationship with you, even if he's not very good at communicating that."

Blake nodded and gripped his Styrofoam cup again, not sure what words were needed in this situation. Eventually, he took another swallow of the bitter coffee, already going cold. "But he's held up his end of the bargain with you?"

The corner of Yvette's mouth twitched like she wanted to smile but couldn't. "I wouldn't be here otherwise."

———◆———

BLAKE WAS PRETTY CERTAIN Samantha had fallen asleep in his arms. She'd been in the waiting room with him for three hours now, and they hadn't said a single word to one another outside of their greeting. They'd just held each other.

He knew they couldn't avoid having a conversation about why she was here. About how she'd even known. But that would come later. For now, Blake was content to hold her.

From what he'd seen of her apartment when he'd tried to bring her flowers, he had a feeling she hadn't relaxed since her sister had come to town. This was likely the first bit of real quiet she'd had in two months, so Blake was happy to act as her pillow for the moment. Happy to have a connection while he waited.

His mother had gone home to shower—and likely bake cupcakes for the nursing staff—after they'd gotten word that his father had made it through surgery with zero complications. He was resting, and they'd be allowed in to see him sometime that afternoon.

But when the afternoon waned with no word, Blake started worrying again. Had something gone wrong in the intervening hours? Blake's heart rate hadn't been normal all day, but the idea that his father was in a room somewhere, possibly dying all alone, didn't do anything to lower his blood pressure.

If it weren't for Samantha, he was pretty sure he'd be pacing the room, going out of his mind. But because she was here in his arms, he was replaying the story his mother had told him and the words Samantha had said to him over and over again until they started to meld.

I wouldn't be here otherwise and *I'm here* became *If I didn't love you, I wouldn't be here for you otherwise.*

Even though Samantha had never expressed that particular emotion toward him, he couldn't help but hope. Just a little bit.

He didn't have a chance to puzzle it out, though, because the nurse peeked through the waiting room door then. Samantha stretched as she sat up then stifled a yawn. The nurse gave them a polite smile that implied she'd witnessed this very scene before. "Mr. and Mrs. Fairchild, you can go in now. He's awake but groggy."

Samantha stayed put as Blake attempted to tug her forward by the hand. "Are you coming?"

She bit her lip. "Your dad doesn't like me."

Since Samantha wouldn't stand with him, Blake pivoted in his seat so that he could wrap her in an embrace. One hand closed around her waist while the other rose so he could stroke his thumb over her cheek. "I don't really give a damn what he thinks. All I care about is that you're here by my side, Mrs. Fairchild."

Samantha's cheeks turned red. "I had to tell them I was your wife for them to let me up."

"Do you see me arguing?"

"Bla-ake!"

"Mr. Fairchild?" the nurse asked from the doorway.

"We're coming." Blake's eyes never left Samantha's as he lowered his head so the tip of his nose swept against hers. Then he whispered, "Stay with me?"

Sam's fingers tightened around the hair at the nape of his neck—hair that was getting too long—as she nodded, her forehead still pressed against his. "Always."

Chapter Thirty-Four

"Your stomach is growling." Samantha ran her hand over his jaw, tilting his head toward hers.

They'd been sitting together by his father's bedside for the last two hours, and he hadn't eaten anything besides half a soggy croissant all day.

Yvette had come and gone. She'd stayed in the room for thirty minutes, gripping Blake's hand half of the time and hugging Samantha the other half. Then she'd made excuses that she needed to go update the family on James's condition and had been gone for the last hour. Blake suspected that seeing James hooked up to tubes and monitors in a hospital bed was too much for her. He couldn't blame her.

He looked vulnerable. Fragile. Yet Blake found he felt the opposite of his mother. He couldn't tear his eyes away from where James's chest rose and fell in a slow but steady rhythm. Almost as if Blake looked away, his father would stop breathing altogether.

James had yet to wake completely. He was still dozing in and out of drugged sleep, which the doc said was normal. James would be sleepy and groggy for the next few days because of the medication, but he should be more wakeful toward the evening.

"I don't want to leave in case he wakes up."

Samantha smoothed her thumb over his upper lip, teasing like she might kiss him there. He wanted her to kiss him. Part of him wanted to take her to a quiet place and express how much he'd missed her, but he felt bound to his father's bedside. As angry as Blake had been with him, he didn't want him to wake up alone.

"I can go get you something to eat. Whatever you want."

All Blake could think about was the vegetarian flatbread from Garden & Gather, but he didn't want to do that to Samantha just yet. This new budding of their relationship probably couldn't withstand the memory of the place that had broken them up so soon.

"Do you not have an appetite? Should I just pick something?" Samantha asked when he gave her no response. She was already pulling her jacket off the back of her chair, preparing to go.

"No, I know what I want to eat. I just don't want to ask you to get it." Just the thought of the flatbread made his stomach growl audibly.

"Clearly, you're starving." Samantha's arms punched through her jacket sleeves. "And I want to go get you food. I'm getting a little hungry myself."

"Even if it's to Garden and Gather?"

"I said I would get you food, and if you're craving one of those flatbreads, that's what I'll go get."

"How did you know—?"

Samantha cut him off with narrowed eyes. "We haven't been apart that long. Which one is your favorite this week?"

"The veggie."

With a soft grin, she ducked down to grab her purse and glanced a quick kiss off his lips. It was too short—not nearly long enough to express his gratitude for her presence.

She entwined his fingers with his. "I'll be back soon."

Blake pulled her back toward him before she could step out of his reach. 'I look forward to it." He guided her lips toward his with a hand at the back of her neck.

And, finally, he kissed her properly. Not as thoroughly as he would like, but enough to get lost in the soft feel of her lips. To taste the sugary lip gloss she always wore. To remember the feel of her body against his.

He pulled away before he could get lost. "And maybe we can talk later?"

Pink had risen in Samantha's cheeks, her eyes were wide, and her lips were still swollen and parted as she caught her breath. She looked so inviting that if they were anywhere else, Blake would have pulled her onto his lap.

Instead, he let his hand fall away from hers as she backed up a step, nodding. "I think we should, yeah."

As soon as the door closed behind her, James made a noise from the bed like he was trying to shift himself.

Blake was on his feet next to him in the span of a heartbeat. "You shouldn't try to move. You just had a pretty major surgery."

James raised the hand that was closest to the door. "Was that Samantha who just left?"

His voice was scratchy and hoarse, like his throat was completely dry. Blake didn't know if his dad could have water yet. He should probably have called the nurse in since his father was awake enough to talk—it was the first time all day.

But he should probably answer his dad's question before he did. "Yes, she's going out to get us something to eat."

His father made a sort of wheezing noise. Blake couldn't determine if it was meant to be a snort or a grunt of approval or just him gathering the strength to speak again.

"Good. Maybe you'll finally stop being angry with me."

Blake rolled his eyes and pushed the call button for the nurse. "I think it's wise we don't discuss all of that right now."

———⬥———

THEORETICALLY, SAMANTHA had zero problems going into Garden & Gather. The only reason she'd been avoiding it had been because Blake Fairchild had broken her heart. She had fallen in love with him there, and it was difficult not to associate the restaurant with the man himself. There was so much of *him* in it—from the copper café tables under the awning to the rosewood host stand to the Edison bulbs staggered over the bar.

As foreign as it felt to enter through the front door, Samantha felt the last of her anger fall away for what Blake had said that morning so many weeks ago. This restaurant truly had been a labor of love for him. Though she knew they still needed to talk about that day—what had been said and how and why they had broken—walking into Garden & Gather felt exactly the same as walking into his embrace.

And she'd been in his arms recently enough to say that with authority.

She grinned and hugged herself as she turned in a circle. Nothing about the place had changed. The warm lighting, the plants hanging in the greenhouse, the clink of silverware, and the muted conversation just audible over the jazz in the background welcomed her soul.

"Can I help you?"

Samantha jumped, remembering that she was here on a mission. Turning toward the voice, Samantha found she didn't recognize the woman at the host station, which meant she wouldn't know who Samantha was or who Samantha once was—or at least who she had been to Blake.

"Oh, I was just going to order some food to go from the bar."

"I can take care of that for you." The woman's smile was bright and helpful.

Samantha brushed off the offer by saying she was going to order a drink while she waited, but really, she wasn't after alcohol. She just wanted to be the rest of the way in the restaurant instead of on the threshold. She was so taken with the feel of the restaurant that she didn't notice who she'd sat down next to until after she'd placed her order.

Rachel's voice almost startled the wine straight out of Samantha's hand.

"Oh, hey!" Samantha left her glass of Vernaccia in favor of embracing Rachel and offering Nicolas a smile. "What are you two doing here?" She knew they lived on the west side of Lawrence, so any time they came into Kansas City, it was a commute.

"Naomi, the meddler, got us a gift card, so since the kids are with her and Kat for the week . . ."

They exchanged some niceties and short anecdotes about the holidays, and Samantha tried not to get too distracted by the way Nicolas's hand never left Rachel's thigh, even as his eyes scanned the crowded restaurant.

Rachel, it seemed, was also aware of his restlessness. "I know it's a slim chance on a Friday night during the holidays, but we were kind of hoping to see Blake."

Samantha's smile fell away. "Oh, he'd be so happy you were here. I'll make sure to tell him when I bring back the food, but he's at the hospital right now." She gave them a quick rundown of the day's events so far, explaining that she was at Garden & Gather specifically to grab Blake his preferred comfort food.

"Ah, man. I should call him." Nicolas spun his beer on his coaster, and Samantha didn't miss how quickly Rachel's hand landed on his knee with a reassuring squeeze.

Nicolas was truly afflicted by the fact that his former friend was in distress, and Rachel's pinched brows showed that she felt the same. Samantha was more relieved than she wanted to admit that Rachel had shown support for her husband and his emotion rather than offering an immediate inquiry into what she could do for Blake. It was still difficult for Samantha to wrap her head around sometimes, because Rachel seemed so settled in her life now, but she also could not forget that at one time this woman had been Blake's lover.

Samantha really tried not to dwell on that, so she offered them a melancholy sort of smile. "He'd probably really appreciate that, but maybe wait until tomorrow? He's been at the hospital all day today, and I'm hoping to coax him home to rest after he eats."

Nicolas nodded, spinning his glass again. "That makes sense."

"But you should keep us updated," Rachel said. "We can organize a care package or something at least."

"I'm sure I'll see Yvette again tonight. I'll see what I can arrange for their needs."

"Text me tomorrow." Rachel's sympathetic smile almost made Samantha feel like she was a friend she could trust. Almost.

"I will."

The bartender, Will, someone Sam had trained back when she'd still been the bar manager, set a brown paper bag full of food down in front of her and turned as if he was going to just leave her debit card sitting on the bar. "What do I owe you?" she asked before he was out of earshot.

He turned to face her, shifting from one foot to the other. "The boss man called. He said not to take your money."

Samantha chewed her lip, torn between arguing with him and being grateful that her already tight budget wasn't being stretched to breaking by G&G's prices.

"Really." Will put his hands up like she'd aimed a pistol at him at high noon instead of an eyebrow raise. "He said to comp the food since it was all for him and to not let you pay for it."

"What about the wine?" It was technically against the law to discount alcohol.

Will shrugged this time. "I'm not to take your money. I assume he's going to cover it."

Samantha huffed a breath through her nose. She'd have to argue with him about this later. "I'm only not fighting this because he needs to eat."

Will just raised his hands higher above his head and backed away, absolving himself of any blame.

"I should head out." Samantha gathered the bag into her hand as she stood. Rachel and Nicolas nodded, offering their assistance a final time as she searched her coat pockets for her keys.

Despite the uncertainty with Blake's dad, Sam actually felt good about the way this day was going.

<hr>

"YOU'RE SPOILING HER." James's voice wheezed out of him as Blake hung up the phone. He'd just called Garden & Gather to make sure they didn't charge Sam for his food.

"I never pay for my food. I'm not going to make Samantha pay for it, either."

His father shifted in his bed like he was trying to sit up and failed, so he altered the height of the bed instead so he could more easily look at Blake. "You're mistaking that for a criticism." He paused to pull in a breath and then sighed it out. "If she's who you want, you should never stop spoiling her."

Blake raised his eyebrows and took a step closer to the bed. He had so many questions on his tongue, so many things he wanted to ask about. Why James would suddenly be giving him advice on keeping Samantha. Why he had been so adamantly opposed to her in the first place. Why he would sabotage Blake's relationship with her and then suddenly change his mind.

"There were too many years where I put an undue burden on your mother. Where I put my own pleasure before hers. But she's the reason I wanted to become a better man. And if this Samantha makes you a better man, who am I to judge?"

James laid his head back and closed his eyes, clearly exhausted by his speech.

Blake still had questions. Still yearned to ask why nothing he did would ever be good enough for James. Still sought to understand why his father's approval was so elusive. But as much as he wanted to demand that of his father, Blake found himself lacking the motivation to actually voice his concerns. Possibly because James lay broken and struggling himself.

Or possibly because as much as Blake wanted that validation, he'd learned just today, while holding a sleeping Samantha in his arms, that he didn't *need* it.

Those few brief years when he'd had his father's open approval had been nice, but Blake had been lying to himself. He'd mistaken paternal acceptance and the appearance of piety as contentment, when truly the whole time he'd been in the ministry, he'd bucked and roiled against the constraints and didn't understand his own restlessness.

And he'd made mistakes because of that.

In the last six months, that restlessness had fallen away. His life made sense in a way he'd never expected it to. Garden & Gather provided satisfaction in his day-to-day life, but the last two months without Samantha by his side had been painful and lonely, and if he had the choice, he would absolutely keep her. Though he recognized that was a choice she had to make for herself.

"James!" Yvette appeared in the doorway then, and Blake understood why she'd been gone so long. She'd transformed herself from the messy bun and leggings to the kind of stunning she'd been for Faye's wedding, just in a white pantsuit instead of a gown. Her long blonde hair shone, and her skin appeared to glow. She looked like an angel, and Blake could only imagine what his father was seeing as a sleepy grin spread over his lips and he reached his hand out toward his wife.

"My love," he said, and Yvette's heels clacking against the floor was the only indication that she was walking rather than gliding as she crossed the room to his side. She clasped his hand, mindful of the needle taped to the back of it and brought his fingers to her cheek as her tears brimmed over.

Blake turned away at the tenderness in his father's voice as he told Yvette not to cry over him, that he was going to be fine. He might not always understand their relationship, but the love they felt for one another in that moment was palpable. He tiptoed from the room, giving them their privacy.

And he decided that as soon as Samantha returned, he would offer himself to her and hope there was enough left between them to start again.

Chapter Thirty-Five

All it took to get buzzed into the ICU this time was holding up a bag of food, presenting a bashful smile, and murmuring a quick "Bringing food to my husband." The nurse even smiled back at her, like this was a common occurrence in this ward. Sam supposed people who were worried their family member might not survive the day probably had a tendency to forget to take care of themselves while they sat in anticipation of bad news.

When Samantha found Blake pacing in the waiting room, dread iced through her veins. Had something happened while she'd been gone? Had James made a turn for the worse in the hour she'd been away?

His gaze lifted to hers at the sound of the brown paper bag settling onto the table beside him. The way his eyes burned when he looked at her took her breath away. Samantha had previously considered herself an expert on reading the expression in Blake's eyes, but she'd never seen this one before—they looked like they'd been lit by a fire from the inside.

Blake didn't break eye contact as he strode across the room and pulled her against his chest. The arm at her shoulders swept up, cupping the back of her head and angling her chin so that his eyes could burn into hers.

"Is everything alright?" She knew this wasn't about his dad. He would be burning in a different way if something had gone wrong. This was one-hundred-percent about her. About them.

"It's just dawned on me how much time we wasted apart due to a misunderstanding—and that I owe you a thousand apologies for making you feel less than worthy of my love. Because you are so much more than I deserve. And if you want me, I am yours. Forever."

Samantha didn't need to think. The embers of her attraction to him had smoldered inside her all day, waiting for the crisis to be over to act on how much she wanted to hold him, but he'd sparked her body into life with his sheer intensity, and all she wanted in the whole world was to devour him. She surged up on her toes, her lips meeting his in a hot kiss.

Blake sighed into her mouth and banded his arms around her waist, pulling her so tightly against him that she could feel every inch of his hard body against hers. The growing bulge that pressed against her belly tempted her to forget about where they were. The sofa to her left invited her to give in to the flames and allow Blake to consume her right there in the hospital waiting room.

His hand slipped below the hem of her sweater, skimming along the skin over her hip then dipping into the waistband of her jeans. A surge of warmth flooded her chest knowing that he, too, was contemplating how to accomplish their physical reunion without getting kicked out of the hospital.

The idea of stripping his clothes off and pressing all of her skin against his—of having permission to be intimate with him again—had her lips parting in a smile.

"What?" Blake was still trying to kiss her despite not being able to fight his own grin.

"Nothing. I just missed you is all."

Blake's arm tightened around her back, and the hand in her waistband flexed. "You have no idea how much I missed you."

The gentle lap of his tongue against her lower lip and the way his fingers swept just a hint lower were promises she intended to make him keep.

Excitement blossomed in Samantha's middle. The day she'd met him, she'd been so flustered that she'd spilled coffee in his lap, but now here they were, about to get inappropriate in a secluded hospital waiting room.

"Oh!" A chair bumped into a coffee table behind Samantha, and Blake stiffened as he pulled her closer into him as if he could protect her from the innocent bystander. "Sorry, my loves. I didn't mean to interrupt the reunion."

Yvette's voice was soft and sweet, and Samantha was almost as excited to have access to this woman again as she was to be back in Blake's arms.

"It's fine, Mom." The way Blake clung to her and spoke through clenched teeth made it clear that it was not fine. That he was just as frustrated as she was. But then his stomach growled, and Samantha remembered the bag of food on the table behind her.

Samantha patted Blake on the stomach and turned, attempting to ignore the desire still pulsing in her core as she turned back to the table. "I brought flatbreads for us to split and that cranberry salad you like. I know I haven't had enough produce today."

Yvette's feigned smile crinkled her eyes but didn't brighten them as she slipped into one of the chairs at the table while Samantha unloaded the food. She gave Blake his own flatbread and set the family-sized salad in the middle of the table, stabbing three plastic forks into the greens before centering a second flatbread between herself and Yvette.

"Is James still awake?" Samantha stabbed at the salad with her fork when neither of her companions made a move to eat. She wasn't sure how Yvette was feeling, but she knew Blake was likely reluctant to eat despite the fact that his stomach had been growling for more than an hour.

She was not prepared for how much the flavor of the food was going to impact her. That first bite transported her directly back to October and the hope and community she'd felt when she'd first tasted the menu. When she'd been falling in love with Blake and teasing Emil. When she'd been realizing that she was capable of so much more than she'd thought.

The food from Garden & Gather still tasted like potential. Like possibility, like family and the future. Indulging in these flavors again felt like coming home after the relative chaos of the last few months. Samantha was proud to be her sister's shepherd in adapting to life outside her family's isolated existence, but she would be lying if she said she didn't miss the support of these people in particular.

Everyone she lived with was feeling the strain of having so many people in such a small space. Charlotte barely came out of her room. Sarah spent over an hour in the bathroom every day. Samantha had been finding things to do at work after the restaurant closed just to avoid going home.

But right now, all she needed was a martini, and she'd have the makings of a proper night out—well, if she weren't currently sitting in a hospital.

"He dozed off." Yvette's fork dangled from her fingers. "It's really hard for me to watch him like that. And at the same time, I don't want him to be alone when he wakes up."

Samantha squeezed Yvette's fork-free hand.

"We can go sit with him when we're finished eating." Despite his reluctance to start, Blake had devoured more than half of his flatbread already.

"No." Yvette shook her head as she punched her fork back into the salad. "You've been here all day. I'll stay with him tonight. You two should go. I imagine you have a lot to talk about."

A brief sly smile flitted across her face, but sadness and stress quickly shuttered the short-lived hint of mischief.

"You shouldn't stay alone." Blake only had two squares of his flatbread left. Samantha had only just bit into her first.

"Susanna is coming as soon as her grandchildren are in bed, and your father is in the next room. I won't be alone."

The frown on Blake's face indicated he did not want to leave his mother, but at the same time, his knuckles grazed over Sam's knee under the table. That was all the signal Samantha needed to coax him back to his apartment where they would have more privacy.

———— ◉ ————

THE DRIVE BACK TO BLAKE'S apartment was silent and would have been charged had she not been lulled into sleepiness by the decadence of his heated seats and her full belly.

Samantha hadn't realized how starved for comfort she'd been since she'd blocked Blake from her life, and she'd forgotten the luxury that followed in his wake like he was the human embodiment of a god of plenty.

She knew that was her perception of him based on her struggles, but Blake did have a knack for draping a sense of well-being across her shoulders like he might with a blanket on a cold night. He made it look so effortless that she found herself powerless to shrug it off.

Her body and all her instincts told her that he was safe to trust. That it was so easy for him to give her what she needed not because it was truly as simple as he made it look but because he paid attention. He'd seen her for who she was almost immediately. He hadn't let her hide behind her insecurities anymore, and he'd given her the opportunity to blossom in both her relationship with him and the strength it took to leave him.

But perhaps there was a different type of strength in admitting when something—someone—made her feel safe.

BLAKE HADN'T BEEN SURE what to expect once they arrived back at his apartment. Had he wanted to resume what they'd started in the waiting room? Absolutely. But then the drive back to his place took almost thirty minutes, and he was fairly certain Samantha had fallen asleep during the ride.

He was fine with helping her into bed and waking up with her warm, soft body pressed against his. He knew he'd barely sleep with her sunshine-and-lemon scent playing in his nose, but he was no stranger to sleep deprivation. He'd forgo sleep for a lifetime if it meant he got to have this woman in his bed.

What he didn't expect when he opened the passenger side door was for a giggling Samantha to launch herself into his arms. When he'd seen her like this before, there had been wine involved, but he knew she'd only had water from the vending machine bottles with dinner.

An involuntary grin split his lips. "What's so funny?"

She gripped the lapels on his coat as she pulled herself back on her heels. "I am having trouble believing this is real, and also, I really, *really* want to take your pants off."

That was all Blake needed to hear. He hooked an arm beneath her knees and carried her to the corridor that connected the resident parking garage with his building then into the elevator up to his floor. She teased his ear with her tongue the whole way—she knew that was the way to make him blaze.

He didn't bother stopping in the living room to divest them of their coats and shoes. Blake carried Samantha straight to his bedroom and dropped her in the middle of his bed. With a shriek, she bounced then caught him by the collar, pulling him into her laughing lips.

Blake allowed himself to get lost in the pleasure of the feel of her body underneath his. Of her fingers raking through his hair. Of her legs wrapping around his waist and squeezing her center right against the bulge in his jeans. His tongue traced down the column of her neck.

She was more delicious than any food, than any wine he'd tasted since he'd started this new leg of his life.

"Samantha?" He didn't mean for it to come out as a question. But he couldn't help it.

"Yeah?" Her word was a sound between heavy breaths.

He rocked his hips up and into the apex of her thighs. "Is this what you want?"

The hands in his hair trailed down until she cupped his jaw. One of her thumbs smoothed down the hairs over his top lip. "You mean, do I want you?"

She rocked into him this time, and Blake cursed. They still hadn't even taken off their coats. But as much as he wanted to relish the feeling of her skin on his, the fear that this was temporary won out.

"I mean, do you want what this means? I can't make love to you and just go back to not having you in my life tomorrow."

Samantha loosened her legs around his waist. "I came to you tonight because I wanted to. Because I couldn't stand the thought of you alone and hurting. I'll never be able to handle that. I want to be with you. I want to support you. I want to love you and make you feel safe in the same way you make me feel protected and cherished."

Warmth blossomed in his chest at her words, and he couldn't hold himself back from searching out her skin. He traced his hands up underneath her sweater to squeeze her tits over her lacy bra then swept down over her hips and across her shapely thighs until he met the tops of her boots just beneath the crease of her knee.

He couldn't remember ever hearing anything quite as erotic as the sound of her sigh when he unzipped her boots and discarded them. The rest of her clothes joined the boots on his bedroom floor piece by piece until she was bare before him. He still hadn't shed one stitch of his own clothing.

Blake had to swallow to keep himself from drooling straight onto her chest. He allowed himself the indulgence of running his hands all the way down her body from collarbone to toes before he pushed himself to standing and disrobed.

Samantha's eyes only left his for quick glances south, once over his abs, then again when he pushed his boxer briefs to the floor to reveal his straining erection. Blake hadn't been this painfully hard since the first time they'd been together, when it had been literally years since he'd been with anyone.

Right now, all he wanted was to sink between Samantha's thighs and watch her sigh with pleasure. He pulled a condom from the bedside drawer, and as soon as he was sheathed, Sam's legs fell open. She trailed a hand from her center up to her stomach to her breast and over until she reached her shoulder and trailed off.

Oh, hell. If that wasn't an invitation, he didn't know what was. Blake hovered over the top of her, his lips capturing hers seconds before he lined himself up with her pulsing core. She arched up into him as he pushed inside her. His mind blacked out with pleasure at the heat of her surrounding him before that sigh he'd been waiting for fell from her lips and urgency descended on him.

Blake pumped into her, and Samantha's heels dug into his backside. Her nails bit into his shoulders as the pace amped up until his headboard was slapping against the wall. It crossed his mind that he was perhaps too voracious for her, but Samantha continued to arch into him, meeting him thrust for thrust.

"I need to be on top," she gasped after a few minutes, and who was Blake to argue? He would give her whatever she wanted.

He rolled them so that she emerged on top, her knees straddling his hips. Samantha barely missed a beat as she kept up the rhythm he'd started, her hands braced on his shoulders and her breasts bouncing in his face.

Blake captured one of her nipples in his mouth and sucked in as one hand came to the small of her back to hold her against him. Sam adjusted her rhythm accordingly, grinding more than bouncing, and Blake saw stars as he hit a spot inside her he didn't think he'd ever felt before. She moaned and adjusted the angle of her hips so he would hit that spot again and again.

Not able to help himself, Blake clasped onto the curve of her hips and thrust up into her as her lips came down on his. She moaned louder, bordering on a scream as she ground against him every time her hips descended. Then she stiffened over him, and wetness gushed over his hips as Samantha made a sound he'd never heard before.

Jesus. She'd never come so hard that she'd gushed—at least, not with him—and the knowledge made it impossible for him to hold back. As the evidence of her orgasm coated his skin and soaked into his comforter over his hips, he couldn't stop his orgasm from ripping through him. His mind soaked in the intensity of their reactions to one another, and he wondered how he could recreate that same reaction from Sam in the future.

For now, he was powerless to do anything but catch his breath as Sam collapsed on top of him, kissing his neck.

After a trip to the bathroom for each of them and the exchange of his wet comforter for a spare quilt, the two of them were drifting off in each other's arms, spent and satiated.

Blake did not wake until the sun peeked through his window the next morning. Samantha was still in his bed, but when he tightened his arm around his waist and nuzzled her ear, he realized that she was already awake, here in his bed, checking her messages on her phone.

"Is everything okay?"

"It's fine," she said, nestling her perfect ass further into the cradle of his hips. "I just never let Charlotte or Sarah know I wasn't coming home, so I'm letting them know where I am."

"Do you need to get home?"

Samantha shook her head against the pillow. "Thankfully, it's Charlotte's day off, so she can stay with the kids while Sarah goes to work. Doesn't make me feel like any less of an asshole, though."

Blake's arms tightened around Samantha's middle. "Why do you feel like an asshole?"

"Because they depend on me."

"And you're not allowed to have a personal life?"

"We have a schedule, and I was supposed to bring the kids to therapy this morning."

"What time is their appointment?"

"In an hour."

The last thing Blake wanted to do was let Samantha out of his bed, but he said, "We can go drop them off and grab breakfast while they're in session if you want."

"Can we get them donuts on the way?"

Blake huffed out a laugh. "Only if we get up now."

"I have to work tonight, but I can make it up to you after I get off—if you want."

Blake captured her lower lip between his. "Oh, I totally want."

"I look forward to it." Samantha twined her fingers through his hair, guaranteeing everyone would know what they'd been up to when she showed up to help her family with their day, but Blake couldn't seem to make himself care what anybody else thought about his relationship. What was going on between him and Samantha was between him and Sam, and him and Sam alone. Nobody could change that.

"I love you," he said when she moved away to pull on her clothes from yesterday.

Her green eyes shone as she shoved her legs into her jeans. "I love you, Blake. So much."

Epilogue

November 2020

Samantha handed her twentieth curbside customer of the evening their date night picnic package. And yes, she'd been counting. Since she and Blake had gotten married last year, she'd known she hadn't exactly needed to worry about money. A few weeks before they'd tied the knot, he'd confided in her about the fortune his mother had made through her bakery when it was open and how much money she'd made by licensing her cupcake recipe to other restaurants and bakeries around the KC Metro area. And when they'd gotten married, Samantha had become privy to how Yvette had set up a fund to take care of her son should anything happen to her.

Looking at the figures, Samantha appreciated how much of the Fairchilds' wealth had actually been due to Yvette's efforts. And Yvette's willingness to fill cupcake orders for special occasions had been a big part of why Garden & Gather had been able to keep their doors open since the pandemic had started. It hadn't been enough to keep them operating at full capacity, but after nearly a year, they'd started to find a new normal.

Unfortunately, they'd had to lay off most of their staff, which Samantha hated, but they'd had zero other options.

She'd been laid off from the hotel in March, and there'd been no word of when they might open again. Thankfully, between herself, Blake, Emil, Sarah, and the sous chef, they were able to fill most of the curbside to-go orders the restaurant received. But that also meant that Sam and Blake had been working sixty-hour weeks the last few months just to make sure the restaurant didn't fold before a vaccine was developed.

They did have heaters on the patio, and most evenings, the five tables next to the greenhouse were booked enough to keep them hustling. It was a delicate balance, having enough food in stock to serve everyone and making sure they were selling enough not to dip into the red. Emil's idea of date night picnic packages that included a starter, a main course, a dessert, and a bottle of wine for two had become their signature and would probably be a permanent fixture of their menu when they opened back up to the public.

Samantha had spent several months making sure that Blake wasn't panicking that he'd lose the restaurant he'd fought so hard to save that she was almost too nervous to tell him the news that might unravel everything.

Because sure, when they'd married last year, they had decided they wanted kids. Blake had just turned forty, after all—but that was before the restaurant industry had taken the worst hit in a century. Daily, he voiced his worry that they'd have to give up his apartment and move in with his parents the way Sarah and the kids had just so they had a few extra dollars each month to throw Garden & Gather's way.

Now Samantha worried that he would completely freak out when he learned that she was expecting. She wondered more and more if she shouldn't have picked up the part-time call-center work Charlotte was doing from home just so they had some income that wasn't the restaurant.

But that was her old self thinking, the Samantha that had been perpetually broke and didn't have anyone to rely on or back her up besides an equally broke Charlotte.

Samantha wasn't in that place anymore. And even if it was kind of a scary time to be pregnant, Samantha had kept the news to herself for two weeks now. With the nausea she'd been fighting all day, she knew she wouldn't be able to keep the secret much longer. Especially with the way the blue paper mask she wore when talking to guests smelled like chemicals and a book that had been dunked in a toilet.

She hadn't been hiding her pregnancy per se; it had just been such a special surprise that she wanted to hold it close and treasure the news before she shared it. And maybe she was a little bit afraid to acknowledge the pregnancy out loud, considering how long it had taken to happen. Guilt had been eating at her lately, though, because Blake deserved the opportunity to celebrate the good news, too.

The ticket printer whirred, and another online order popped up at the same time Blake emerged from the kitchen. His eyebrows pinched as he looked at her and course corrected to join her at the bar POS. His arms wrapped around her from behind as his chin came to rest on her shoulder. His lips brushed against her neck as he said, "Why don't you go lie down on the sofa in the office and let me get this one. You're looking a little green."

Her heart rate ticked up, then she chided herself for feeling nervous. Blake would be ecstatic. He'd wanted kids his entire adult life. But that didn't stop the butterflies in her stomach. She swallowed back the swell of nausea that rose with them. "I'm afraid if I set that precedent, then I'll spend the next nine months on the sofa instead of helping out here."

"Nine months?"

Samantha could feel his confusion in the way his body tightened and his head tilted to the side. She guided his right hand to rest just below her belly button. "Give or take."

She covered his hand with hers, and her husband's whole body stilled. He even stopped breathing. "You're joking."

"Sure not."

"But it's been a year, and nothing."

"Well, now we've got something."

Blake rotated her in his arms so that he could look into her eyes. His expression was wide with awe, joy lighting his dark-brown eyes. "We should celebrate. Is it too soon to celebrate?"

Samantha shook her head. "I don't think so. It's worth celebrating."

A grin broke out across his face the same time Emil emerged from the kitchen. "Hey, I need that wine for the—"

Samantha giggled. Apparently, Blake had been supposed to grab the wine Emil needed to make one of their sauces, and he'd gotten distracted. It was a common problem when Samantha was around.

"Emil, grab that bottle of champagne from the liquor cabinet." Then Blake named the most expensive bottle they had in the restaurant, and Samantha gasped. Blake's grin only grew. "We're celebrating."

Emil's flat stare conveyed that he was not amused. He'd been in a foul mood for most of the last few weeks. Samantha had to pretend that it had absolutely nothing to do with her sister, but she knew the two of them hadn't spoken since Halloween. "What are we celebrating exactly?"

Oh, yeah. He was annoyed.

Blake beamed down at Samantha as he said, "We're going to have a baby."

"Well, shit. Okay, I guess we *should* celebrate." Emil's words sounded more grudging than exuberant as he disappeared back into the kitchen, presumably to retrieve the champagne.

Samantha grinned back up at her husband, allowing all her worries to fall away as Blake wrapped her in his arms. The feeling of safety and contentment was always there when she needed it.

"I think we have some sparkling cider in the back, too."

Sam shook her head. "If I have anything right now, I'll probably puke. But thank you."

Blake's eyebrows scrunched like he'd forgotten that there were side effects to this whole "growing a person" thing. "Maybe you should go lie down."

"I'm fine right now. Really."

Blake's narrowed eyes said that he was not convinced.

"I'm serious. I will lie down if I need to." Samantha rested her head on his chest, and his arms banded around her back. "Right now, I have everything I need."

There was a pop from the kitchen followed by the clang of something hitting one of Emil's hanging pots. Then a loud "Fucking mother fucker!"

Neither of them could hold back their laughter. "Maybe you should have opened the bottle."

Blake nodded then kissed the top of her head before he pulled from her embrace. "You're probably right. With the mood he's in, I'm surprised he didn't break the bottle over my head."

Samantha rolled her eyes. Blake was the only person Emil was even pretending he liked at the moment. Maybe the shared bottle of pricey sparkling wine would be a good way for them to let off some steam.

Because when it came down to it, Samantha wouldn't change a thing about her life, grumpy chef and all.

THANK YOU FOR READING!

I HOPE YOU ENJOYED reading *Regret and Everything After*. It's always important to me to write my characters with nuance and compassion, even when they aren't very compassionate with themselves. If you've read *Lightning Crashes*, it might be easy to cast Blake as a villain rather than someone who was struggling and making mistakes. The title of *Regret and Everything After* comes from the idea of Blake struggling to reconcile his actions and his intentions, and then live with guilt. The title also works for Samantha though, who underestimates herself throughout the story because she was undervalued throughout her upbringing. According to her family, Sam doesn't deserve happiness, but we're in the business of Happily Ever Afters. Everyone deserves their HEA.

Want to Connect with Me?

I am @marlaholtauthor[1] on Instagram. I'd love to see your bookstagram posts or just chat about the book. I can't wait to meet you!

Finally, leaving reviews is one of the best ways you can support the Indie Authors you love. I'd be forever in your debt if you took the time to review *Regret and Everything After.*

⸺●⸺

---

1. http://instagram.com/marlaholtauthor

Also By Marla Holt

When Abe Met Lane: The Prequel Novella to The Other
Lane

The Other Lane: A Modern Fairy Tale

The Try Again Series:

Ethan & Juliet: An Opposites Attract Second Chance
Romance

Sparkle & Shine: A Second Chance Romance

Read & Wright: A Second Chance Romance

The Incident Series:

Love, Van B: An Incident Series Novella

The Van Birch Incident: A Forbidden Rock Star Romance

The Deception Incident: A Secret Baby Romance

The Betrayal Incident: An Age Gap Romance

The Lightning Crashes Universe

The Curse Breaker: A Short, Spooky Romance

Haunted Attraction: A Haunted House Romance

Lightning Crashes: An Exvangelical Romance

Page of 335